DEATH BESIDE THE SEASIDE

ALSO BY T E KINSEY

A Quiet Life in the Country

In the Market for Murder

Death Around the Bend

Christmas at the Grange

A Picture of Murder

The Burning Issue of the Day

DEATH BESIDE THE SEASIDE

A Lady Hardcastle Mystery

T E KINSEY

THOMAS & MERCER

Text copyright © 2019 by T E Kinsey
All rights reserved.

Published by Thomas & Mercer, Seattle

www.apub.com

Amazon, the Amazon logo, and Thomas & Mercer are trademarks of Amazon.com, Inc., or its affiliates.

ISBN-13: 9781542016056
ISBN-10: 1542016053

Cover design and illustration by Lisa Horton

Printed in the United States of America

DEATH BESIDE THE SEASIDE

Chapter One

When you're packing for a holiday, even Sunday can be a source of joy. I've never been overly fond of Sundays and I usually try to put off getting up to face the day until the last possible moment. But this Sunday we were preparing for a week away, and I was up and doing long before my usual hour. The local birds were still mid-chorus by the time I had the range lit and the kettle on. We were going to the seaside and I wanted everything to be ready.

Notwithstanding our comparative nearness to the coast, and in spite of my repeated requests, we had spent a little over two years at Littleton Cotterell without once having been to the seaside. At least twice a month I suggested that we should jump into the motor car and see the sea. With the same frequency, Lady Hardcastle agreed and then promptly did nothing about it. When challenged about this inaction in the winter, she would say, 'I know I said we should, but don't you think it's just a little too cold?' In the summer she would say, 'Of course we shall – I promised, didn't I?' But some other project or obligation invariably got in the way.

By the end of June 1910, I had begun to despair of ever visiting the seaside again. It came as an extremely pleasant surprise, then, when one day, entirely out of the blue, Lady Hardcastle announced over breakfast that she had booked us into the Steep Holm View Hotel in Weston-super-Mare.

'I know it's only Weston, and we should probably be going to somewhere scenic in Devon or Dorset, but the hotel itself comes highly recommended.'

'By whom?' I said.

'Gertie Farley-Stroud,' she said. 'I asked her if she knew anywhere fun to stay in Weston and she came up with a few places. Then she called me back later in the day and said that we absolutely had to stay at the Steep Holm View. It seems someone had just recommended it to her. Less imposing than the Grand Atlantic, but a little more elegant and refined, they said. "Cosy" was the word she used, I believe.'

'I see,' I said. 'Will there be toffee apples? Cockles? Sticks of rock with "Weston-super-Mare" written all the way through?'

She laughed. 'There might well be. Although I think sticks of rock are more of a northern thing, aren't they? Blackpool and the like. There will almost certainly be brass bands, though, as well as at least one orchestra, and probably a Pierrot show. Punch and Judy, too, I shouldn't wonder.'

'There's a pier, isn't there?'

'The "Grand Pier", so the literature assures me.'

'And donkey rides?'

'Famously, donkey rides are offered on the beach at Weston, yes.'

'Then put me on the list of attendees,' I said. 'When do we leave?'

'Monday morning,' she said.

It was Friday.

'As a matter of interest,' I said. 'When did you make the booking?'

'What, dear?' she said absently, having already picked up the morning post and moved on to other things. 'The booking? A couple of weeks ago, I think. I thought it would be a nice surprise.'

For my part, I thought it would have been nice to have more than a weekend's notice of the trip, but I decided it would be churlish to say so.

And so it was that Sunday 3 July 1910 was spent in a familiar frenzy of packing. Evening dresses were selected, along with afternoon dresses, morning dresses and a selection of outdoor clothes. The summer weather had been grey and unseasonably cool thus far, and the newspapers glumly predicted that this would continue for the foreseeable future. That the future foreseen by the weather forecasters at the Met Office seldom stretched beyond the coming twenty-four hours didn't stop the newspapers bemoaning another lost summer. I packed mackintoshes, just in case it rained, but I decided against heavy boots and coats – it was a seaside holiday, after all, and I'd definitely be speaking up against any day-trip proposals that entailed trekking in the wilderness.

As usual, I was also instructed to pack watercolours and a portable easel – 'just in case I get the urge to paint'. Lady Hardcastle was an accomplished artist, but most of her artistic energies were devoted to the making of 'animated' moving pictures, usually involving tiny hand-made puppets. Nevertheless, she felt herself to be under-packed and unprepared if she set out on a journey to somewhere scenic without her paints.

Field glasses, it was suggested, might be needed for the observation of birds, and for looking out to sea at passing ships on their way to and from the docks at Bristol. I never objected to the packing of field glasses, having retained the childlike glee of seeing distant objects brought within touching distance by the mystical magic of precision-made German lenses.

'No need to bring the golf clubs,' said Lady Hardcastle. 'The links are lovely, I'm told, but I can't imagine being invited to play. Do you think we'll need tennis rackets?'

'We have room in the motor car,' I said. 'It would be no trouble.'

'No, let's save room for souvenirs. You never know what delights we might find.'

Earlier that year, we had taken delivery of a brand-new motor car, designed and built by Lady Hardcastle's friend, Lord Riddlethorpe – known to his friends as 'Fishy'. He owned a motor-racing team and had been toying with the idea of building road-going versions of his racing motor cars. The idea was to provide enthusiasts with the thrill of owning a powerful racer in a machine that could also be used to potter down to the country for the weekend loaded with a wife and her impedimenta.

A prototype had been designed and Lady Hardcastle had been given the job of testing it out, being someone who was both keen on driving and who also had extensive knowledge – by virtue of actually being one – of what the modern lady required from a motor car.

It was a lengthy beast, powered by a racing engine of Lord Riddlethorpe's own design. It had only two seats, but unlike almost all other vehicles of the day, both the driver and passenger sat together in an enclosed compartment, protected from the elements. Having travelled many miles in our old Rover 6, shiveringly exposed to whatever horrors the English weather had chosen to throw at us, I considered this innovation to be worth most of the price of admission on its own.

Its capacious boot, too, was about to prove its worth. There would be space enough within to carry all our baggage and still leave room, as Lady Hardcastle said, for souvenirs. I couldn't for the life of me imagine what manner of souvenirs we might bring back from Weston-super-Mare, but it was pleasing to know that there would be space for them if we found them.

It was around forty miles from Littleton Cotterell to Weston and even in the new motor car – with its terrifying top speed of nearly sixty miles per hour – the journey would take more than two hours once we had weaved our way through the traffic in Bristol. Accordingly, we had agreed to set off as early as we could to maximize our time beside the sea.

Miss Jones, Lady Hardcastle's cook, and Edna – whose official title was housemaid, though she also carried out many of the duties of a housekeeper – had been given the week off, so it was up to me to organize breakfast before our early start. The range was lit, the bacon sizzling, and I took Lady Hardcastle a tray of morning coffee and a round of buttered toast to get her started.

'Good morning, my lady,' I said brightly to the human-sized lump under the covers.

An indistinct croak emanated from somewhere near the pillows – ever since I had known her it had been Lady

Hardcastle's habit to sleep entirely under the bedcovers. A hand appeared, tentatively pulling down the sheet and exposing blinkingly unready eyes to the muted daylight.

'It's a lovely day,' I said. 'Well, when I say "lovely", obviously you have to put that into the context of our otherwise disappointing summer. It's not raining, at least.'

'I smell coffee,' she said. 'And toast.'

'Your elegantly ladylike conk serves you well,' I said. 'I thought you could get a head start on breakfast while I put the finishing touches to the main event downstairs. It'll be on the table in ten minutes, with or without you.'

I would have preferred to set the tray on her lap, but she was still some minutes from being able to sit upright and I was conscious that the bacon would be burning soon, so I left the tray on the floor beside the bed and slipped out. A hoarse, 'Thank you, dear,' followed me down the stairs.

It took another twelve minutes for me to get breakfast to the morning-room table, and fifteen for Lady Hardcastle to appear in her dressing gown, still yawning and rubbing sleep from her eyes.

'Whose idea was it to get up this early?' she said as she sat down.

'Yours,' I said. 'You insisted that we be on the road by nine so as to enjoy as much time as possible "eating ice cream and paddling in the sea".'

'I dimly recall saying something of the sort. Why didn't you stop me?'

'I tried. You said, "Pish and fiddlesticks, Florence Armstrong. We shall have our fun and plenty of it. We can be in Weston in time for lunch if we get our skates on." You insisted that you would have no trouble rising in time for breakfast and a nine o'clock start. My protestations were thereafter in vain.'

'That sounds familiar, too. I should pay you more heed.'

'I try to tell you that often,' I said. 'But you pay me no heed.'

'Must try harder. Are we all packed?'

'Just a few last-minute bits and bobs,' I said. 'And I'll need a hand heaving the trunk into the boot – it's a two-man job, I'm afraid.'

'We'll manage. I say, that bacon looks good.'

We ate our breakfast and made speculative plans to do sea-sidey things.

'I, for one, want to stroll along the prom,' I said. 'And if there's no brass band playing tiddley-om-pom-pom I want my money back.'

'I'm sure we can manage that,' she said. 'Oh. Wait. Is the car fully fuelled?'

'I topped it up yesterday while you were fiddle-faddling about in the orangery.'

'I like to think of it as "making moving-picture history",' she said. 'But fiddle-faddling is as good a description as any. What about the oil?'

'Oil and water checked. Battery checked. Windscreen cleaned. We really are very ready.'

'Then all that remains is for me to dress more appropriately for polite society and we shall away.'

Less than an hour later, she was dressed in her travelling clothes and we had hoisted the trunk into the car.

Among the many new and exciting features added to the motor car by Lord Riddlethorpe and his engineers was one that had been especially designed to save me from exhausting effort and to remove the risk of barked shins and broken wrists. Once running, an internal combustion engine is a modern marvel that turns petroleum spirit into work. I was convinced that it would change the world, but only once it was running. Until then, it was a recalcitrant lump of iron that had to be coaxed into operation by the vigorous cranking of a heavy handle. When the engine had thus been brought to life, it was possible for the starting handle to spin wildly, whereupon it assumed the most famous of a swan's many attributes: it could break a man's (or woman's) arm. Lord Riddlethorpe's technical magicians had added a small electric motor that was able to undertake this perilous cranking operation at the press of a button, saving me from exertion and injury.

Once we were settled in the comfortable cabin, Lady Hardcastle pressed the button. The engine started first time. We were on our way to Weston.

The new motor car was officially named the Riddlethorpe Shinatobe, after the Japanese goddess of the four winds. Lady Hardcastle's report on the vehicle began with her firm assertion that no one would know how to pronounce the name, nor would they know who or what Shinatobe was even if they managed to say it correctly.

She had no better suggestions, though, and had named the motor car 'Phyllis' for reasons I couldn't fathom. Whatever her name, she loped easily along the Gloucester Road towards Bristol. She was a noisy creation but the roaring of her over-sized engine did, at least, warn other road users of our approach. Horses were particularly discomfited by the sound, and we found that incidences of fist-shaking and shouted admonishments from their owners had increased dramatically. Few had been pleased to see the old Rover, it's true, but there was something about Phyllis that seemed to annoy almost everyone.

We passed through the centre of the city without incident and were soon out into the countryside on our way towards the Mendips and the sea.

'Do you know what I find strange about Phyllis?' said Lady Hardcastle as she changed gear to climb another hill. 'Not having to get togged up to drive her. Part of me misses all the palaver of hats, goggles, and gauntlets.'

'Perhaps,' I said. 'But a larger part of me doesn't miss the wind, the rain, and the biting cold. This is much more civilized.'

'You're right, of course. Oh I say, look. The cows are lying down. And you know what that means.'

'I do,' I said. 'It means they're tired.'

She laughed. 'We've known each other far too long,' she said. 'But it still might rain.'

'It might. But I packed umbrellas and mackintoshes. We'll be fine.'

The countryside wound by in a seemingly endless procession of hedgerows, fields and cattle. It was oddly mesmerizing and I found myself being lulled into a comfortable doze. It seemed as though barely any time had passed before we saw a signpost telling us that we were less than five miles from Weston-super-Mare.

The town, when we arrived, seemed very fresh and new. As a child, I'd visited seaside towns all over the country – there were few places the circus hadn't been to. But my memories were of old fisherman's cottages, markets selling the day's catch, and huge sheds for drying nets. Weston gave the appearance of having been built overnight at the end of the last century by the same builders who had shaped the outer suburbs of Bristol – sturdy houses fronted with undressed stone with decorative sandstone at the corners and around the windows.

I made a mental note to find out the correct architectural terms for these features, but my train of thought was derailed by a sudden, 'Whoops! Oh dear. I do hope he's all right,' from Lady Hardcastle.

'Who?' I asked, turning to look out through the small back window.

'Nothing, dear,' she said breezily. 'Chap on a bicycle. I'm sure he'll be fine.'

I returned to my contemplation of Weston-super-Mare. There were older buildings here and there, but it had the appearance of a young, bustling town. It looked like a town with confidence, a place of pleasure and possibility. As we wove our way through the residential streets, past busy little shops and into the crowded centre, there were people everywhere. Traffic was heavy, too, with carts and wagons of all shapes and sizes carrying essential supplies to and fro, and even the horses looked young and energetic. There were a few motor cars, as well, but nothing as outlandish as Phyllis.

It wasn't long before we found ourselves on the seafront, heading towards the pier. To our left were small stretches of grass. Beyond them, the promenade, bounded by the sea wall. Beyond the sea wall was a smooth, sandy beach. And beyond that . . . mud. Endless miles of mud.

'Where's the sea?' I asked plaintively.

'Out,' said Lady Hardcastle.

'What, "out" as in "gone to visit some friends in Ireland, back next week" out?'

'It's the Bristol Channel, dear,' she said. 'When the tide goes out, it really, really goes out.'

'Does it ever come in?'

'Twice a day, just like everywhere else. Some high tides used to flood the town.'

'I can't say I'm not slightly dismayed,' I said. 'We can only paddle at high tide?'

'Were you really intending to paddle?'

'Well, no,' I confessed. 'But it would have been nice to have the option.'

She laughed. 'There's the Grand Atlantic on our right,' she said. 'It is rather grand, isn't it? That's the pier on our left, do you see?'

'I do see,' I said. 'A walkway on stilts. Is it to keep people's feet out of the mud?'

She laughed. 'It strides bravely out into the sea when it's in.'

'I look forward to seeing it,' I said.

'Oh, and here's the Royal,' she said. 'So that means . . . Ah, yes, look – there's Steep Holm View.'

The hotel was a good deal less grand than the Grand Atlantic, and somewhat smaller than the Royal Hotel but it was, nevertheless, an impressively imposing Victorian structure. Broad stone steps led up from the pavement to a pair of shiny doors, propped open in the mild – but still decidedly grey – July weather.

There was a blue motor car, rather more ordinary than our own, parked directly in front of the steps. I could just about make out a figure hunched over in front of the vehicle and then saw the familiar movements that accompanied the cranking of a starting handle. I turned to Lady Hardcastle.

'If you slow down a bit, you can have that spot right outside the doors,' I said. 'That chap's just about to leave.'

'You read my mind as always,' she said. 'I say, remind me to tell Harry he has a West Country doppelgänger.'

I looked at the man as he clambered into the driving seat of his motor car, but I couldn't see much of a resemblance to Lady Hardcastle's brother at this distance.

'Really?' I said. 'I'm not convinced, but I'm sure he'll be amused.'

The blue motor car pulled away and Lady Hardcastle parked Phyllis in the space recently vacated by the mundane machine.

'Here we are, then,' she said. 'Delivered directly to the door, safe and sound.'

The motor car – which I was certain was quite the most unusual vehicle ever to have driven along the seafront – was attracting a good deal of attention from passers-by. One small boy gestured so forcefully at us that his toffee apple flew off its stick and rolled into the gutter. He had to be restrained by his mother from retrieving and eating it. As we alighted, her irritation at our having distracted her son with our infernal machine turned to indignant disapproval. She looked at Lady Hardcastle. She looked at me. She said, 'Well!' in a tone that signified that we were everything that was wrong with the world, grasped her now crying son firmly by the hand and dragged him away.

We mounted the steps to the hotel and the inner door swept open as we approached. The unseen hand that had opened it was revealed to belong to a liveried porter who bowed as we entered and bade us welcome before returning to his chair by the door. The welcome was echoed by the clerk who stood behind the elegantly decorated front desk.

'Good morning, madam,' he said. 'Welcome to Steep Holm View. How may I assist you this morning?'

'Good morning,' said Lady Hardcastle, accompanying the words with her broadest smile. 'I'm Lady Hardcastle. You have a couple of rooms for me, I believe.'

The clerk beamed back. 'Of course, my lady,' he said. 'Adjoining rooms with a sea view for you and your maid.' He picked up the hotel register and swept it across to her with a practised flourish. 'If you would be kind enough to fill in the relevant details . . .'

She took the proffered pen and began to write.

The hotel foyer was of modest size, but had been decorated in the modern style and appeared much more spacious than it actually was. The floor was tiled in pale marble set with an intricate mosaic of swirling whiplash curves, like the fronds of some giant ivy. The curves were repeated on the lower part of the wall, and on the bannister of the broad staircase that swept up from the far corner behind us.

'I heard a motor car arriving, did I not?' said the clerk. 'Will my lady's driver be bringing in your luggage? I can send the porter to help.'

'I drove myself,' she said. 'The luggage is in the boot.'

'Very good, my lady.' He summoned the porter with a wave. 'Lady Hardcastle will be in rooms four and five. Her luggage is in the boot of the motor car parked outside.'

The porter took the room keys and asked us to follow him. He led us up the stairs and along the mezzanine landing that looked down into the foyer. A short passage led past two doors to another staircase. From the summit, another passage led us to rooms four and five, at the front of the hotel.

He opened the door to number four and stood aside to allow us to enter.

'The facilities are at the end of the corridor,' he said, pointing the way. 'I shall bring your luggage up presently.'

'Thank you . . . ?'

'Brine, m'lady. Billy Brine.'

'Thank you, Brine,' said Lady Hardcastle, pressing a few coins into his gloved hand.

'There's a bell pull by the door if you should need anything,' he said. 'The dining room will be serving dinner from seven o'clock. Breakfast is served between half past six and ten o'clock in the morning, but we'll be happy to bring a tray to your room if you prefer.'

'Thank you,' she said. 'We haven't made plans yet.'

'Very good, my lady. Will there be anything else?'

'No thank you, dear. Just the bags.'

'At once, my lady.' He bowed smartly and left us to explore our rooms.

'This looks very cosy,' said Lady Hardcastle. She approached the large bay window and looked out. 'And there's the promised sea view. I can see the pier. And the . . . the whatever that building on the end of the promontory is.'

'Looks like a theatre of some sort,' I said as I joined her. 'If we unpack your field glasses we might also be able to see the sea.'

'Give it six hours,' she said. 'It'll be here. Look, you can see the high water mark on the sand. Those little rowing boats will all be afloat by teatime.'

I turned away to examine the room. There was a brass bedstead decorated with the same swirling ivy motif that had adorned the foyer. A nightstand stood beside the bed, holding a candle and matches, though there was no evidence of either being used – the hotel was fully electrified. Against one wall was a washstand with an ornately decorated bowl and ewer. The wardrobe and chest of drawers were of matching inlaid wood. The rug was a luxuriant Axminster in blue and gold. This was certainly no cheap dosshouse.

'What's your room like, I wonder,' said Lady Hardcastle as she picked up the keys and headed towards what we presumed was the connecting door. It unlocked easily and opened to reveal another door, this time with no keyhole or handle.

'I'll go next door and open it,' I said.

I took the keys from her and went out into the corridor. The door to number five opened on to an almost identical room, complete with the same rug and furniture. The washbowl, the ewer, and the candlestick were identical. Even the glass shade on the electric light on the wall was set at the same wonky angle.

I crossed to the connecting door and opened it.

'Yes?' said Lady Hardcastle. 'Can I help you?'

'Please, missus,' I said. 'Can we 'ave our ball back?'

'What's your room like?' she asked.

'Exactly the same as yours,' I said.

'Splendid. I think we shall be very comfortable here.'

There was a knock at her door.

'I'd better get that,' she said.

It was the porter with his first load. He hefted the trunk from his wooden hand truck and placed it in the middle of the room near the wardrobe.

'Just a few more things,' he wheezed. 'I'll be back in a jiffy.' He set off once more.

'We'll be here all afternoon waiting for him to bring all our gubbins up,' said Lady Hardcastle. 'What say we leave the unpacking for later and go for a stroll?'

'I thought you'd never ask,' I said.

Lady Hardcastle stopped at the reception desk to enquire about the tide times and was shown a typewritten sheet. She asked about the weather, too, but was told by the still-smiling clerk that, 'We just look out of the window, I'm afraid, my lady.'

'It's probably the best way,' she said. 'Oh, and what's on the promontory that we can see from our windows? Miss Armstrong thinks it might be a theatre.'

'Miss Armstrong is correct,' he said with a small bow in my direction. 'The Knightstone Pavilion and Opera House. And beyond that, at the very end, are the Knightstone Baths.'

'Well done, Armstrong,' she said. 'Dinner is served from seven, I understand.'

'It is, my lady. With afternoon tea at four.'

'Splendid. I think we shall dine here this evening. Do we need to book?'

'No, my lady, there's no need. We are able to cater for everyone's needs, and have ample room.'

'Wonderful,' she said. 'Thank you for your help.'

'My pleasure, my lady.'

The porter held the door for us as we stepped out into the fresh sea air.

Phyllis was still attracting attention but we left her where she stood and turned left towards the promenade and the pier.

The promenade was a wide, paved thoroughfare with a low wall of local stone on one side to discourage unwary pedestrians from falling the three or four yards to the sandy beach below. To the other side were a pair of parallel roads, with elegant formal gardens between. This meant that the main hotels and guest houses had an uninterrupted view of the beach, but were still a good seventy yards from it. It gave the seafront a spacious, almost luxurious feeling.

The entrance to the Grand Pier was whitewashed and turreted, making it look like a miniaturized castle guarding the delights beyond. I doubted that those delights were anything to write home about, but the addition of turnstiles and a small admission fee made the whole enterprise seem far more exotic and enticing than it probably deserved. Posters advertised daily Pierrot shows and nightly music hall entertainment 'from some of the biggest names in the country'.

The weather was on the cooler side of mild, and we still hadn't seen the sunshine, but there were plenty of people strolling along the seafront nevertheless. Hats were occasionally clutched as the breeze coming in from the Bristol Channel threatened to dislodge them.

'It's a little bracing,' said Lady Hardcastle. 'I wonder if we mightn't have been better off in Nice or Cannes.'

'Nonsense,' I said. 'You can't beat the good old English seaside. Where else would you see a stall selling cockles, mussels and whelks? Or that eager little girl down on the beach with her little bucket and spade, so serious and determined as she makes her sandcastles? And listen . . .' I paused to allow us to make out the sounds of a brass band playing on the end of the Grand Pier. 'Where else can we stroll along the prom—'

'Prom, prom,' she interrupted.

'Listening to an actual brass band?'

'Playing "tiddly-om-pom-pom",' she said. 'Just as you wanted them to. You're quite right, of course. It's thoroughly charming. I'd just rather it were a tad warmer. And perhaps sunny.' She sniffed the air. 'But you've forgotten the most important thing,' she said.

I caught the smell, too. 'Fish and chips?' I said.

'What more could two sophisticated ladies want for lunch?'

'Can we sit inside, though, please?'

'Oh.' She seemed crestfallen.

'You've been complaining about the weather since we stepped outside,' I said.

'Yes . . . but . . . fish and chips . . . in newspaper . . . on the prom . . .'

'Go on, then,' I said. 'Just this once.'

She bounced off towards the source of the delicious frying smell and I followed.

After a lengthy conversation with the shopkeeper – during which we learned that his wife was a martyr to her lumbago and that his eldest boy had just enlisted with the Somerset Light Infantry – we took our paper packages to one of the public benches along the promenade. There we ate our cod and chips, liberally seasoned with salt and vinegar, and accompanied – at Lady Hardcastle's insistence – by pickled onions.

'This is the life, eh, Flo?' she said as we chomped away.

'I'm sure you said the same when we were eating *moules frites* at a pavement café in Bruges. And again while we were eating bratwurst and sauerkraut at a pavement café in Munich. Oh, and while we were eating *fusilli alla Genovese* at a . . . let's see if I can remember . . . ah, yes, a pavement café in Venice. You just like eating outdoors.'

'That must be it. I think the fresh air makes the food taste better.'

I couldn't help but agree with her, though I could easily have forgone the pickled onion.

With the food eaten, the grease wiped from our lips, and the wrappers carefully deposited in a nearby bin, we set off to continue our stroll. A little beyond the pier, we passed a Punch and Judy man packing up his tent.

'Are you here every day?' asked Lady Hardcastle.

'Every mornin' from ten o'clock, ma'am,' said the little man.

'Then we shall make every effort to catch you before you leave.'

'Much obliged, ma'am,' he said. 'It's been a bit quiet this year, what with the gloomy weather an' all – a few more customers is always welcome.'

We wished him good day and carried on. We decided not to visit the shellfish stall, though Lady Hardcastle insisted that a pint of cockles would be just the thing when we were watching the Punch and Judy show on another day.

The ice cream stall, on the other hand, drew us both. There was a small queue, and we waited with some excitement for our cornets.

'We live in an age of wonders,' said Lady Hardcastle once we had been served. 'From the "penny lick" in a frighteningly unhygienic glass to these new edible cups in just a few short years. Who knows what we'll get next?'

'Indoor dining tables?' I suggested.

'Oh, pish and fiddlesticks, you curmudgeonly maid,' she said. 'Come on, let's see what else we can find.'

We got as far as the man with a barrel organ and a capering monkey performing for a small group of children opposite the Grand Atlantic Hotel, before we decided that we'd seen most of what the promenade had to offer, and turned back. We checked the playbill at the entrance to the pier which seemed to indicate that the 'Summer Extravaganza' was a variety show featuring an impressive bill of well-known music hall artists.

The Knightstone Pavilion was hosting a German season covering everyone from Bach to Wagner.

'We'll not want for entertainment,' said Lady Hardcastle as we made our way back to our hotel. 'I have no idea what the quality will be like, but one can't fault their ambition. Let's get ourselves unpacked and we can plan our adventures over a nice pot of tea.'

Chapter Two

There was a spacious salon on the ground floor at the rear of the hotel. It was filled with comfortable armchairs and sofas in the same fashionable style as the rest of the establishment and looked extremely comfortable and welcoming. There was a baby grand piano in the far corner.

At six o'clock, we were surprised to find ourselves the only ones there. We had expected to meet at least one retired colonel, sipping his chota peg and regaling anyone who sat still for long enough with tales of the time when 'Old Johnny Blenkinsop woke up to find a cobra on the verandah outside his bedroom window' or some such far-fetched nonsense. Instead, we were quite alone.

We chose a pair of chairs in the corner nearest the door, from where we could observe the comings and goings of our fellow residents. Sadly, our plan fell at the first fence. So deep were we in conversation about the relative merits of laces and buttons for the fastening of boots that we entirely failed to notice the arrival of a grey-haired waiter. He coughed politely.

'Would the ladies like a drink before dinner?' he said softly.

'I say, what a splendid notion,' said Lady Hardcastle, for all the world as though the idea simply hadn't crossed her mind until that instant. 'What do you think, dear? Gin slings all round?'

'Why not?' I said. 'We're on holiday after all.'

'We most definitely are. Two gin slings, please.'

'Very good, my lady,' said the waiter with a small bow. 'You're in room four, I believe?'

'I am indeed,' said Lady Hardcastle.

With another bow, he slipped away as silently as he had arrived.

'So much for our fabled espionage skills,' I said. 'We'd be dead and stuffed in the kitchen bins by now if we were on a job.'

'You would, perhaps. I see myself as being the sort of girl to be bundled up in an exquisite Persian rug and dumped in the Caspian Sea at dead of night.'

'There's a class struggle even in death,' I said. 'But that doesn't disguise the fact that we allowed an old geezer in a white tunic to sneak up on us after we'd deliberately positioned ourselves in view of the door so we could see what was going on.'

'You said it yourself, dear,' she said brightly as the waiter returned with our drinks on a silver tray. 'We're on holiday.'

'So I understand, my lady,' said the waiter. 'Will there be anything else?'

'These will keep us going for the time being,' she said. 'Thank you.'

I saw her signing the chit for the drinks, but by the time I'd taken my first sip, the waiter had evaporated again.

I held up my glass. 'If I'd already had one of these,' I said, 'I'd swear it had gone to my head and that I'd blacked out and missed the departure of our waiter friend. But I'm boringly sober, so I can only assume that he is possessed of demonic powers.'

'It's part of their training, dear. While you were learning how to mend clothes, clean jewellery, and mock your mistress, hotel waiters were being taught how to transport themselves from room to room by the power of the mind alone.'

'Fair enough,' I said. 'I must say that my maidly skills have proved a great deal more useful while working for you than flitting unseen could ever have been.'

'Do you ever regret coming to work for me?'

I gave her a puzzled frown. 'It's a bit early in the evening to be getting maudlin. You've not even touched your gin.'

'I'm sorry. It was joking about being bundled into the kitchen bins, I think. It suddenly hit me that I've exposed you to some horrible dangers over the years. It wasn't at all what you agreed to when I tempted you away from Jane Tetherington's household with an offer of an early promotion to lady's maid.'

'You silly old biddy,' I said. 'I wouldn't have missed it for the world. I've seen things – done things – that the seventeen-year-old me had never dreamed of. And she'd grown up in a circus and had read every book she could get her hands on, so she had some pretty wild dreams. So shut up and drink your gin.'

'Right you are, dear. And thank you. Shall we eat early and see if we can get in to see *Orpheus in the Underworld* at the Knightstone?'

'Aren't they doing Germans?' I said. 'I thought Offenbach was French.'

'Prussian by birth, dear. What on earth did they teach you at that Welsh village school?'

'I stand corrected,' I said. 'But I'd love to. It doesn't look like there'll be much competition for tables at dinner.'

◆ ◆ ◆

We took our time over our drinks as our conversation took us on a journey from boots to motor cars to international politics, calling at popular music, theoretical physics, and the cultivation of apples for cider. It was a quarter past seven by the time we put down our glasses and set off in search of the dining room.

It turned out to be next door. It was slightly smaller than the salon, though just as tastefully decorated. There were six tables, each set with the same modern tableware with matching candlesticks. In the centre of each was a long-necked posy vase holding a single oxeye daisy. The most remarkable thing about the tables, though, was that five of them were already occupied.

Four of them – any of which could comfortably have seated four diners – were occupied by lone men, all in well-cut evening wear. Three were Europeans by the look of them, each with a neatly trimmed beard that made him almost indistinguishable from the others. One wore pince-nez spectacles that gave him a Germanic appearance for some reason. Another wore a jewel-encrusted lapel pin so ornate that it looked more like a brooch, but nothing else about his appearance gave him away.

The third was unremarkable apart from the scowl he wore as he regarded his soup – probably a Frenchman. The fourth man wore tiny spectacles and was easy to tell apart from the others.

Not only was he clean-shaven, but his facial features were very obviously from the Far East. The Western formality of his dinner suit prompted me to plump for Japan.

The fifth table had been taken by two ladies, one of middle age and the other very young, possibly not even twenty years old. I could make no guesses about their origins, but their clothes were of an unfamiliar style.

I was trying to decide whether they might be Americans, when my thoughts were interrupted by a voice so unexpected that it actually made me jump.

'Table for two, my lady?' said a waiter who had managed to appear with the same unearthly stealth as his older colleague.

'Yes, please,' said Lady Hardcastle. She indicted the solitary empty table. 'We'll take that one, I think. Do you agree, Armstrong?'

'It seems perfect for our needs,' I said.

The waiter bowed. 'Excellent choice, ladies,' he said.

He conducted us to the table and held our chairs for us. A moment later he returned with menus.

'Chef's soup today is cucumber, pea and lettuce,' he said. 'I shall bring you some water in just a moment.'

With that, he vanished.

'No, really,' I said. 'How do they do that?'

'It is a little unnerving, isn't it. It's almost as if . . .'

Her voice trailed off as her attention was grabbed by something going on behind me. I turned to look and saw a forlorn, timid-looking, bespectacled man in a rumpled dinner suit, engaged in a conversation with the waiter.

'No, honestly, it doesn't matter,' said the man. 'Truly. I can come back later. Really. Don't go to any trouble on my account.'

Such scenes are played out every day in hotels and restaurants all over the land. Ordinarily I would have turned back to perusing my menu with little more than, 'He'll be fine – there'll be a table free in less than an hour,' passing briefly across my mind, if not my lips. But there was something about his tone of voice, a weary resignation, as though this were but the latest cruel twist to be visited upon him by an uncaring and capricious fate. I turned back to Lady Hardcastle and raised my eyebrows questioningly. She nodded her agreement – she'd heard the same thing as I. I turned back to face the door once more.

'I say, waiter,' she said.

The waiter looked at us.

'There's room at our table if Mr . . .'

'Doctor,' said the rumpled man. 'Doctor Goddard. Percival. Percival Goddard.'

'If Dr Goddard would care to join us, we'd be delighted to have his company.'

The waiter smiled and gestured towards one of the empty chairs at our table.

Once the business of seating him, setting another place, and providing him with a menu (complete with the news that Chef's soup was exceedingly green), Lady Hardcastle took care of the introductions.

'It's a pleasure to make your acquaintance, Dr Goddard. I am Emily, Lady Hardcastle, and this is my maid, confidante and all round right-hand woman, Miss Florence Armstrong.'

'How do you do?' said Dr Goddard diffidently, looking up only long enough to briefly meet our gaze before returning to his scrutiny of the menu. 'It really is most awfully generous of you to allow me to . . . I mean to say, thank you. One can always wait, of course, but I was hoping to get to the Knightstone. To the Knightstone Pavilion, yes. To see the, ah, the—'

'The Offenbach?' suggested Lady Hardcastle.

'Yes, the Offenbach. It's a German season, and people think he was French. But he was born in Cologne, you see. Not many people are aware. Where the perfume comes from. Yes, the perfume.'

'We were thinking of going, too. It's an interesting piece, isn't it?' said Lady Hardcastle. 'Do you remember they played the "Infernal Galop" when they danced the can-can at the Moulin Rouge, Armstrong?'

'Oh,' said the doctor. His face flushed. 'I'm sure I've never been to the Moulin Rouge. No, indeed.'

'Oh, you should,' said Lady Hardcastle with a grin. 'It really is the most tremendous fun.'

I raised an eyebrow in an attempt to convey the idea that it wasn't at all nice to tease the poor man. She relented.

'So what brings you to Weston-super-Mare, Dr Goddard? A lovely summer break?' she said.

'Work, I'm afraid. I work for the government, you see. A scientist. For the government. There's a big meeting in, ah, actually I can't say where. This is by way of being a staging post. Yes, a staging post. A chance to be nearby while I make my final preparations, but far enough away so as not to draw attention to the venue. We've all been sent to different locations so we're not all travelling together, you see. I rather feel I won first prize. It's a lovely little town. It has a charming museum, you know. Lots of fascinating archaeological specimens.'

'We shall add it to our itinerary,' she said. 'Where do you usually live?'

'I'm afraid I can't say that, either. I'm so sorry. I'm really not terribly good at all this. What about . . . what about you? Have you come far?'

'Not far at all,' she said. 'We live in a little village just north of Bristol. We've lived there for a little over two years and it suddenly dawned on us that we'd never visited the region's most famous seaside town.'

This was overstating it more than a tad. It had dawned on me during the summer of 1908, just after we moved in, but I decided not to say anything.

As we ordered our meals and ate, Lady Hardcastle worked hard to make the nervous doctor relax. I tried to stay out of it as much as possible – I wasn't certain how well he'd cope with two of us badgering him. By the time we had finished our blackberry and apple crumble, he seemed almost to be enjoying himself.

'Do you have a ticket for the operetta?' asked Lady Hardcastle as our bowls were taken away.

'I do, yes,' said Dr Goddard.

'Have you been before? Is it busy? Are we likely to be able to get tickets at the door?'

'Oh, I should think so,' he said. 'Yes, I should think so. It's popular, but there seemed to be people buying tickets last evening. Yes, last evening there were. Definitely.'

'Then we might bump into each other later on,' she said. 'Thank you so much for being such a charming dinner companion.'

She stood to leave, and in his own haste to stand, the poor doctor knocked his chair over backwards. It bumped into the table behind him, and one of the diners, the middle-aged woman, tutted loudly. 'Well, of all the . . .' she said. Her accent was American. Dr Goddard, flustered and reddening, righted the chair while mumbling apologies.

'Happy fourth of July, madam,' said Lady Hardcastle. 'You're well shot of us. Look how clumsy we are.'

We left together.

When we set off down the corridor to our room, Dr Goddard continued up another flight of stairs, with our good-byes and hopes for further meetings following him up to the second floor.

The performance at the Knightstone Pavilion wasn't quite up to the standard one might expect in a major city, but it was competent and enthusiastic and far exceeded my expectations for a seaside orchestra and chorus. As we moved out of the little theatre and along the short causeway with the rest of the throng, Lady Hardcastle expressed slightly more enthusiasm.

'It's not an easy piece for provincial orchestras,' she said, 'especially when they have a long and varied season to prepare for, but that was simply marvellous. I feel quite invigorated. And look, I don't even need to open my umbrella to see us safely home.'

'It was certainly fun,' I said. 'Morally questionable, but quite entertaining.'

'I've never been sure how I should feel about Eurydice, what with the affair and all, but everyone dances a galop at the end so who cares?'

'True. Although after seeing the show at the Moulin Rouge I did rather expect them all to show their bloomers at the end.'

'Disappointed, then?'

'Of course – who doesn't like bloomers?'

'When you put it like that . . .' she said. 'Oh, I say, there's Dr Goddard. He appears a little lost.'

I looked in the direction indicated and finally caught sight of Dr Goddard. He did, indeed, appear to be a little bewildered, until I noticed that he was reading his programme as he walked along. His fellow concertgoers swarmed round him like a river parting to pass a boulder lying in its path, and by some sort of animal intuition he seemed to be able to avoid those few who were moving even more slowly than he.

Everyone was dressed for an evening out. If it hadn't been for the smell of the sea brought in by the stiff breeze whistling up the Bristol Channel, we could be at any popular entertainment venue anywhere in the world.

As I watched Dr Goddard's precarious passage along the short causeway, I noticed other clues to the unusualness of our location. There were one or two coils of rope along the narrow parapet, alongside enormous iron mooring rings. There was a broken lobster pot awaiting repair. And leaning carelessly against a lamp post next to a bench stood a man in sea boots, a pea jacket and a sailor's cap. He was too far away for me to see his face clearly, but I imagined him smiling as he smoked his clay pipe and watched the world go by.

'I wonder what that fisherman is doing here at this time of night,' I said, nodding towards him.

'I noticed him, too,' said Lady Hardcastle. 'Perhaps he's just waiting for us all to get out of his way so he can get his boat ready for tomorrow. Or pick up that lobster pot so he can take it home and mend it.'

It was good to know that she was still as observant as ever.

A sudden commotion drew our attention away from the salty sea dog.

'Get out of the bleedin' way, you old fool,' said a man who was walking along arm in arm with a pretty young woman.

With that he barged into Dr Goddard, knocking him to the ground.

'I did warn you,' said the young man while his girlfriend giggled coquettishly and looked up adoringly at her beau.

By the time we reached the stricken scientist he was sitting up, fending off both solicitous offers of help and irritated tuts for being in the way.

'Dr Goddard,' said Lady Hardcastle. 'Are you all right? You seem to have taken quite a tumble.'

I offered him my hand and helped him to his feet. He seemed slightly taken aback at the ease with which I pulled him up.

'That's the thing about maids,' I said. 'We do a lot of fetching and carrying. Builds up the strength.'

'Much obliged, I'm sure,' he said, dusting himself off.

'You look a little out of sorts,' said Lady Hardcastle. 'Why don't you come with us back to the hotel and we'll buy you a drink in the salon to settle your nerves. I always find that brandy works wonders in these situations.'

'Well . . . I . . . ah . . . well . . . you see . . .' he mumbled.

'Splendid,' she said breezily. 'That's settled, then. Come along.'

She marched briskly along the causeway with the doctor and me trailing in her wake.

A few moments later, she caught up with the loutish young man and his besotted girlfriend. As she passed him, she somehow contrived to tangle his legs with her umbrella and sent him sprawling head-first to the ground. A small cheer came up from a few of the concertgoers who had seen him knock the doctor down.

'Oh, I say,' said Lady Hardcastle. 'I really am most dreadfully sorry. It seems to be quite the evening for people falling over. I do hope you're all right.'

The young man snarled a handful of colourful obscenities, which prompted an elderly lady to strike him on the head with her own umbrella.

'There's no need for language like that, young man,' she said, eliciting more cheers and laughter from the passing crowd.

As we caught up, I saw the doctor draw his foot back to give the lad a kick, but he thought better of it and we passed him without further incident.

Once out on to Knightstone Road, the crowd thinned rapidly and we were able to take a leisurely stroll back to Steep Holm View.

'Did you enjoy the performance?' asked Lady Hardcastle.

'Very much,' said Dr Goddard enthusiastically. 'One of the second violinists lost his way in the second act, and both the timpani were the tiniest bit flat, but otherwise an excellent performance. I've always enjoyed the story. I particularly like the way that the gods ignore Public Opinion.'

'It seems we all had a very pleasant evening, then,' said Lady Hardcastle. 'Let's get inside and sample the hotel's brandy.'

The salon was empty and we chose the corner furthest from the door, where three comfortable-looking armchairs were arranged around a small table. We settled ourselves into the chairs and I was about to make a joke about the waiters not being possessed of magical powers after all when one of them materialized. From nowhere. The space he occupied had been empty just moments before and there was nothing to indicate how that same space had come to be entirely filled with waiter.

'Would the ladies and gentleman care for a nightcap?' he said.

'You have hit upon the very reason for our being here,' said Lady Hardcastle. 'Brandies all round, I think.'

Before Dr Goddard had time to demur, the waiter had once more vanished into the ether.

'How do they do that?' I asked for the second time that evening.

'Do what?' asked Dr Goddard.

'That appearing and disappearing thing that waiters do,' I said. 'You never see them arrive, and yet there they are. You never see them leave, and yet there they are, gone. It's witchcraft.'

'I would have suggested that they have perfected a way of moving too fast for the eye to see,' he said, 'were it not that Dr

Einstein has shown that if you accelerate a hotel waiter to those kinds of speeds, his mass would increase to the point where a wooden floor like this one couldn't hold him. We'd all be drinking our brandy in the cellar.'

The waiter, meanwhile, had reappeared with three drinks on a tray. 'I'm sure we could make room in the cellar if sir would be more comfortable down there,' he said.

'No, no,' said Dr Goddard hurriedly. 'I didn't mean . . . I was just saying that as a waiter approaches the speed of light, his mass tends towards infinity . . . and . . .'

'Very good, sir,' said the waiter. 'Will that be all?'

'For now, yes,' said Lady Hardcastle. 'Thank you.'

'Oh, but just one more thing,' I said. 'How do you . . . ?' But he was gone.

'You're a physicist, then, Dr Goddard,' said Lady Hardcastle. 'What a fascinating area to be studying now. We're learning so much.'

'Well, I dabble, you know,' he said, taking a large glug of his brandy. 'Part of my brief is to keep up to date with new developments in all areas of science, engineering, and medicine.'

'How wonderful,' she said. 'I try to keep up, but there's always something that stops me from leafing through the journals.'

'You have an interest in science?' he said, with a tone of surprise.

'I read natural sciences at Girton in the eighties,' she said.

'Well, I never,' he said, his surprised tone now drifting towards outright incomprehension. 'I had no idea that women . . . that is to say, ladies . . . that they . . . you . . . We had a ladies' department at my university but I never really . . .'

'Don't worry, Dr Goddard, it still takes a lot of people by surprise. Where did you study?'

'King's College, London,' he said. 'Medicine. Though I've never actually practised as a physician. I sort of got distracted by—'

He stopped talking abruptly. I turned to see a hotel guest poking his head through the door. It was the diner with the pince-nez spectacles.

Seeing that there were others in the room, he tutted and withdrew.

'He's an odd fish,' said Dr Goddard.

Lady Hardcastle turned to see who he was talking about, but the man was long gone.

'Who is?' she asked.

'Kusnetsov,' he said. 'Sergei Kusnetsov. He's a Russian count or some such.'

Bad show, Florence, I thought to myself. You guessed he was German.

'Good heavens. For such a small hotel it seems to have attracted a very international clientele. First that American lady who tutted at us at dinner, and now a Russian count. We are in exotic company.'

'You don't know the half of it,' he said. 'The American lady is Adelia Wilson. She seems to be here as part of some sort of tour to educate her young niece, Eleanora – though what the poor girl will learn about the world in a seaside hotel in Weston-super-Mare is anyone's guess. But those are just the tip of the iceberg. I think we three are the only English people here.'

'Oh, how delightful,' said Lady Hardcastle. 'Who else is there?'

'Let's see,' said Dr Goddard. The cognac was working its magic and he had become visibly more relaxed. 'Did you see the dandy with the jewelled pin on his jacket at dinner?'

'Yes,' said Lady Hardcastle. 'I saw him.' She would have noticed everyone, of course – old habits die hard.

'Ernst Schneider of Vienna, here to take the sea air after conducting some manner of important business at Bristol. The Japanese gentleman?'

'Sitting to the Austrian chap's right,' she said. 'Primly dressed. Spectacles. Very upright posture. Carried himself like a military man.'

'Good lord, you are observant. That's Kaito Takahashi. Or Takahashi Kaito, one ought to say – they put the family name first, you know.'

'It's common in East Asia,' she said, but offered no explanation as to how she knew. There might be time later for tales of our journey across China.

'So I understand,' he said. 'He's taking the air and investigating English provincial life. He works at the embassy or consulate or whatever it is in London. Again, I can't quite fathom why Weston has attracted his interest in particular, but there you go.'

'And the big man scowling at his soup in the corner?' asked Lady Hardcastle. 'Who was he?'

'That's Jean Martin, a marine engineer from Nantes.'

'What a thoroughly cosmopolitan bunch,' she said. 'I wonder what drew them all here.'

'It's probably the extraordinary skills of the waiting staff,' I said. 'News of their efficiency must have spread around the world.'

'The lady is too kind,' said the waiter. 'Would the ladies and gentleman care for another drink?'

I looked down at the table and saw that our glasses were empty. I added an ability to see through walls to the list of the waiter's talents.

'More brandy?' suggested Lady Hardcastle.

We nodded our assent and the waiter vanished.

'Seriously, though,' said Lady Hardcastle. 'It is a little odd. In an earlier life I might even have characterized it as "suspicious".'

'A previous life?' asked Dr Goddard. 'As a scientist?'

She laughed. 'No. Like you I never managed to practise my mystic arts. My late husband was a diplomat. We saw many of the world's capitals together, and many of the world's professional rogues. If he and I had been holidaying together and this many foreign nationals had cropped up unexpectedly, we would immediately have assumed that something was up.'

'You've lived a much more interesting life than I,' said Dr Goddard. 'A student of natural sciences, a diplomat's wife. It makes my plodding efforts seem decidedly humdrum. I've only travelled as far afield as Edinburgh, and that was only because I fell asleep on the train and failed to get off at Carlisle. I've certainly never been in a position where I might imagine a gaggle of foreigners to be suspicious.'

'You're still not in such a position,' she said. 'I was merely astonished by the vast range of nationalities represented in this bijou hotel. But enough of that, I want to hear your opinions on Dr Einstein's work. I read the paper but I confess that some of the mathematics left me behind. Do you agree with him? Is the speed of light an absolute limit?'

'Well . . .' he began, but I confess my mind began to wander and I heard little more of their conversation, although I'm sure that at one point they were talking about shining lanterns at each other from a train moving at the speed of light.

The next thing I was properly conscious of was the magic waiter coughing politely and asking if we wouldn't mind calling it a night. I, for one, agreed.

We said our goodnights at the top of the stairs on the first floor, and left Dr Goddard to stumble upward to his own room.

'What a charming little chap,' said Lady Hardcastle as she let us into our rooms. 'There's something rather endearing about those nervous scientific types.'

'He was interesting company,' I agreed. 'Do we have any plans for tomorrow?'

'Beyond trying to make it downstairs before all the eggs have gone hard and the kedgeree has run out, no,' she said. 'I thought another walk on the prom to fill our lungs with sea air, and then perhaps a drive? There are plenty of places to explore.'

'Sounds like an excellent plan to me,' I said. 'Goodnight. I'll wake you if it looks like you'll oversleep.'

'What would I do without you?' she asked.

'I have no idea. Oversleep?'

'Almost certainly. Goodnight, tiny servant. Sleep well.'

Chapter Three

We made it to breakfast by nine and all the kedgeree had gone. A dearth of curried rice and egg notwithstanding, we managed to scrape together a more than adequate breakfast from whatever the other guests had left behind.

As we ate, we refined our plans for the day's activities. Despite all our excitement – or all my excitement, at least – we hadn't really thought much beyond getting to Weston and settling into our hotel. What we would actually do with ourselves once we were there had never really come up. Today's planning meeting was only a little more productive, but at least there was food and drink.

I was partway through my third cup of coffee, and Lady Hardcastle her second sausage sandwich, when the sound of anxious voices in the corridor outside interrupted our deliberations.

Lady Hardcastle stopped mid-sentence and looked towards the dining room door.

'Your hearing is much better than mine,' she said. 'Can you make out what they're saying?'

I turned away and listened intently but I couldn't make a great deal of sense of it. 'Something, something, disarray,' I said. 'Clothes everywhere. Something about broken lock. Oh.' I turned back to face her. 'Lady Hardcastle.'

'Yes?' she said.

'No, I mean that's what I heard them say.'

'Well, you know what Oscar Wilde had to say on the subject of being talked about.'

'I rather think that when the rest of the conversation involves disarray, broken locks and the strewing of clothes, "not being talked about" is actually the preferred option.'

'You may be right,' she said. 'I wonder what's going on.' She returned to her sandwich with a nonchalance that suggested she wasn't wondering particularly hard.

'Well, they've gone now,' I said. 'So perhaps we'll never know.'

'Oh, I'm sure that we shall, sooner or later, but "sufficient unto the day" and all that. Do you think we should take a drive today, perhaps? Where should we go?'

'Did you know that there's an abandoned fort at Brean Down?'

'I did not. Iron Age? Medieval? Norman?'

'Palmerston,' I said. 'Middle of last century.'

'Ah, yes, dear old Lord Palmerston and his fantasies of a French invasion. It makes one wonder, doesn't it? They have a beautiful, richly fertile country, with villages full of farmers and cities full of artists, playwrights, philosophers, and musicians. Their culture and sophistication is the envy of the world. And so, of course, the first thing they'll think of doing when they have a spare five minutes is to sail up the Bristol Channel and invade poor old Weston-super-Mare.'

'We had been at war with them less than fifty years earlier,' I said.

'With Napoleon. But once they'd got their brief flirtation with world domination out of their system they went straight back to painting on the banks of the Seine and being condescending about everyone else's cooking.'

'Well, whatever use the fort may or may not have been, it blew up while you and I were still in India and now it's derelict. I thought it might be interesting to go and have a look round.'

'It would certainly make a nice change from all those crumbling medieval ruins. Is it easy to get to?'

'Not really. You can see it from the prom, but to get to it by road you need to drive all the way down to Bleadon to cross the River Axe and then come back up again on the other side.'

'Well, it's that or a donkey ride on the beach,' she said.

'We should definitely ride on a donkey before we go home,' I said. 'But I've rather talked myself into exploring the fort now. It'll be fun. We can imagine ourselves as the last defenders of the Weston pier. None shall pass while Hardcastle and Armstrong are manning the guns.'

'Avast there, ye scurvy dogs,' she said.

'Something like that. Although it would be more humane to lob oranges at them rather than cannonballs if they were afflicted with scurvy. I favour a more caring approach to defending the empire.'

'Load the guns with grape?' she suggested.

'Very droll. We'll need coats – I imagine it can get a bit breezy up there.'

'Then let us away and change,' she said. 'We can be back in time for tea and donkeys.'

◆ ◆ ◆

On our way to the stairs, we saw a well-dressed man behind the reception desk, talking to the uniformed clerk. Also hovering there were the salon waiter from the night before and a young chambermaid.

At the sound of our boot heels on the marble floor, the well-dressed man looked round. He bustled out from behind the counter to greet us.

'My lady,' he said. 'I'm so sorry to interrupt your day, but I wonder if I might have a brief word with you.'

'Of course, Mr . . . ?' said Lady Hardcastle.

'I do beg your pardon,' he said. 'I am Valentine Hillier. I am the manager of the Steep Holm View Hotel.' He swept his arm to indicate the extent and magnificence of his domain. He looked very pleased with himself, and not entirely without justification. It was a lovely hotel.

'How do you do, Mr Hillier?'

'How do you do?' he said with a bow.

'And what might we do to help you?'

'It's a rather delicate matter,' he said, lowering his voice as we approached and looking round for eavesdroppers. 'We have suffered a slight embarrassment. One of our other guests, you see . . . we're rather concerned about him. He seems to be missing.'

'Oh dear,' she said, without troubling to lower her own voice even a little. 'Who?'

He flinched slightly and looked round again. 'Dr Goddard. I gather from one of my staff – he indicated the waiter from the salon – 'that you were the last people to see Dr Goddard last night.'

'We met him on the way back from the Knightstone and went to the salon for a nightcap.'

'Just so. Just so. And then . . . ?'

'We were turfed out at around half past one. We said goodnight to him at the landing and he went upstairs, presumably to his room.'

'And you didn't see him . . . again?'

Lady Hardcastle raised her eyebrows. 'No,' she said.

'I didn't mean . . . I say, I really am most dreadfully sorry . . . I never meant to imply . . . But you see, the thing is, we have absolutely no idea where he is. Young Myra here, one of our finest chambermaids, has just been to see to his room. He's not there.'

'Were you expecting him to be there?'

'Well, no. It has been his habit in the few days he's spent with us to rise early and take a morning constitutional along the promenade. He returns for breakfast at nine, and in the meantime the maid takes care of his room so that he can return to his work after breakfast. This morning he hasn't been seen at all. He usually drops his key at the reception desk but Mr Nightengale, our reception clerk, says he hasn't passed through reception.

None of this would have been of any concern, but when Myra went to his room she found the lock broken. The room itself was in a state of some disorder.'

'Disorder?' said Lady Hardcastle, addressing herself to the chambermaid.

'Yes, m'lady,' said the maid. 'A right mess. The chest of drawers was emptied on the floor, clothes was flung from the wardrobe.'

'Was anything missing?' asked Lady Hardcastle. 'Watch? Cufflinks? Cash?'

'He kept all his valuables in a little leather case on the writing desk,' said Myra. 'It was still there . . . but . . .'

'But?'

'Well, I don't think I was supposed to know about it, but I couldn't miss it. I swept under the bed every mornin' and there it was. I wasn't pryin' nor nothin'.'

'What was under the bed?'

'A big strongbox. Heavy, it was. Metal. It were made of metal.'

'And what about this strongbox?' asked Lady Hardcastle. 'Is it gone?'

'Yes, m'lady,' said Myra. 'There weren't no sign of it. I looked real careful, like.'

'It doesn't sound good.' Lady Hardcastle turned back to Mr Hillier. 'Have you called the police?'

'Ah,' said the hotel manager. 'That's just it, you see. Here at Steep Holm View we pride ourselves on our discretion. We find that many of our guests prefer to avoid the attention of the press and we are always at pains to maintain an atmosphere in which they feel that their privacy is safe.'

'But you have a man and his strongbox missing from a room that appears to have been comprehensively ransacked,' she said. 'Surely that warrants a call to the police?'

'We have no incontrovertible proof that anything untoward has happened,' he said. 'There might be a perfectly innocent explanation. As soon as we involve the police, we expose ourselves to the prying eyes of the press and that would be very bad for business. What I was wondering . . . what the hotel's owners and I were wondering . . . given your reputation . . .'

Lady Hardcastle raised an eyebrow. 'My reputation?' she said.

'Your name has appeared in the newspapers more than once. You solved the Bristol arson case. Not to mention the Littleton Cotterell Witch.'

She frowned slightly but said nothing further.

'I've followed your exploits with interest,' he continued. 'And as soon as I mentioned to the owners that you were staying here, they . . . Well . . . You see, you've had such a great deal of success with similarly delicate cases . . . and we were wondering if you wouldn't mind looking into this one for us. Strictly on the QT. The service would attract a fee, naturally, and we would be more than willing to cover your expenses. And, of course, there would be no question of your being charged for your rooms.'

Lady Hardcastle regarded him silently for a moment before saying, 'The decision is not mine alone to take. If you will excuse us, I need to confer with Miss Armstrong. We shall be back presently with our answer.'

With that, she turned on her heel and we walked smartly up the stairs to our rooms.

◆　◆　◆

'What do you think?' asked Lady Hardcastle once we were back in her room. 'Shall we help?'

I looked out of the window. I could see the Knightstone causeway. Beyond that the pier and the beach. There were donkeys but no sea – it was still at least a couple of hours to low tide but the sea was already out of sight across the mud. I'd been lobbying for a seaside holiday for a couple of years. I was also the one most likely to complain that our lives were always complicated by murders and mysteries. I longed for the chance just to stop and rest, and allow ourselves to be entertained by Punch and Judy, and Pierrot shows.

But there was an excited glint in her eye at the thought of another adventure. For all that she had been the one who had suggested our retirement to the country, I knew that she missed the thrill of being in the thick of things. It was hard to say no when I knew how much she was longing to get stuck in again. And, if truth be told, I knew I would enjoy myself, too.

'I think it's an utterly idiotic idea,' I said. 'At the very least it will entail considerable amounts of faffing about, not to mention once more irritating the forces of law and order. At worst we could be subjecting ourselves to recklessly foolhardy levels of danger. We have no idea who Dr Goddard is, nor who might have meant him harm.'

She looked crestfallen.

'That being said,' I continued, 'I think we ought to lend our prodigious talents to finding out as much as we can. I liked Dr Goddard. He was bumbling, shy and awkward, but in a thoroughly endearing way. Of course we shall help find him.'

She beamed.

'But on one condition,' I said.

'Oh?'

'Yes,' I said. 'The one thing we know about Dr Goddard is that he claimed to be a scientist working for the government. If you contact Harry and let him know what's going on, I'll follow you into the flames.'

Lady Hardcastle's brother, Harry, worked at the Foreign Office. It was an open secret between us all that his work was more about the gathering of intelligence than the scrutiny of international trade agreements.

'I shall wire him at once,' she said, now grinning madly. 'We'll not regret it. It'll be fun.'

'Riding donkeys and eating toffee apples is fun,' I said.

'Yes, but that will make us fat and lazy. This is the sort of fun which gives life an edge.'

'It's the sort of fun which can bring life to a sudden, horrifying, and extremely messy end,' I said. 'But I've said I'll help, and help I shall.'

'Splendid. Shall we still change for outdoors?'

'Later, perhaps. I rather think our first move should be to cast our expert eyes around the good doctor's room. At the very least we should be able to tell very quickly whether it has been searched by an amateur or a professional. It'll give us somewhere to start.'

'You see?' she said. 'You're champing at the bit just as much as I am. You already have a plan.'

'It's more a case of being compelled by a nun,' I said.

'Force of habit?'

'Exactly that.'

She grinned again. 'Come then, tiny assistant. Let us return to Mr Valentine Hillier and offer him our services.'

We returned to reception to find that the manager, Mr Hillier, Myra the chambermaid, and Mr Nightengale the reception clerk, were all still there, waiting for our response. The waiter who had shopped us as the last people to have seen Dr Goddard had, predictably, vanished.

Mr Hillier looked up expectantly as we descended the last few stairs.

'My lady?' he said. 'Miss Armstrong? Do please tell me that you have good news.'

'If the news that we are prepared to offer our limited expertise in order to solve the mystery of the missing scientist can be characterized as "good", then yes. We shall help you,' said Lady Hardcastle.

'I confess myself to be extremely relieved,' he said. 'Thank you so very much.'

'We only spoke to Dr Goddard for a short while last evening but I, for one, found him to be very pleasant company. I should hate to think that something awful has happened to him and if there's anything we can do to help find him, we certainly shall.'

'He has been a most agreeable guest.'

'Quite,' she said. 'I need to send an urgent confidential telegram first, and then we shall begin.'

Mr Hillier appeared slightly apprehensive. 'A telegram, my lady?' he said. 'It really is rather important to the hotel's owners that news of these events is kept strictly between ourselves. Discretion is to be our watchword.'

'I understand that,' said Lady Hardcastle. 'And "discretion" would be my middle name had not my parents chosen Charlotte and Ariadne instead. But I really must insist on the sending of this – and I emphasize this next word most strongly – *confidential* telegram as a condition of our involvement.'

'Well . . . I . . . You see, it's the hotel's owners who are insisting. I . . . If it were up to me . . .'

'We can wait if you need to contact them,' she said equably. 'We were planning an excursion today and we can just as easily set off in the motor car if we're not required here.'

Mr Hillier paused a moment longer until resolution seized him. He produced a telegram form from one of the shelves on the desk and passed it across the counter with a pencil and an envelope.

'I shall have the porter take your telegram to the post office as a matter of urgency,' he said.

'Thank you,' said Lady Hardcastle. She wrote her message to her brother Harry on the form and sealed it in the envelope. Mr Hillier called the porter over and sent him on his way.

'First things first, then,' said Lady Hardcastle. 'We should like to examine Dr Goddard's room for ourselves.'

'Of course,' said Mr Hillier. 'Myra will show you.'

Myra stood in the doorway of Dr Goddard's room as we entered, but wouldn't come in.

'I doesn't want to touch nothin' as I shouldn't,' she said.

'Quite right, dear,' said Lady Hardcastle. 'But don't fret about it too much. Is this exactly as you found it this morning?'

'More or less,' said Myra. 'I might have nudged a few things while I was checkin' for the box, but I didn't move nothin' very far.'

'Splendid.'

The room had been thoroughly and systematically searched. Items of clothing and underwear had been dropped on the floor. Every drawer in the wardrobe and chest of drawers had been removed and placed on the floor upside down. The doctor's sponge bag was inside out and its contents in the washbowl. Jars and bottles were open and emptied. The bed had been stripped and its mattress upended. It was apparent from scratch marks on the floor that the large items of furniture had been moved. As Myra had already said, Dr Goddard's cufflinks, and his watch and chain had been tipped out on the writing table next to the leather case in which he kept them. There was a five-pound note as well as nineteen shillings and fourpence in change spread out on the table beside them.

'Thoughts, Flo?' said Lady Hardcastle.

'They knew what they were doing,' I said. 'The only things we'd have done any differently would have been to pick the lock instead of bursting it open, and to tidy up after ourselves. No one would have known we'd been here.'

'I agree,' she said. 'Breaking the lock is suggestive of haste. And of not being overly concerned about someone hearing and raising the alarm. I'm not sure how that squares with the thoroughness of the search, mind you – that would have taken quite some time. But I'm definitely not convinced it was a common-or-garden burglary.'

'No,' I said. 'Even if you ignore the fact that a thief wouldn't have left a watch and chain behind – not to mention ignoring the best part of six quid – it's not a thief's search. A burglar might have been almost as thorough, but not to the extent of looking to see if there was anything stuck to the bottoms of the drawers. I don't think he would have moved the furniture, either. It's a spy's search. A male spy, at that.'

'How so?'

'He kicked the door open when it would have taken him less than a minute to pick the lock. That's masculine problem-solving.'

'Quite,' she said. She turned towards the doorway to speak to Myra. 'You sweep the floor every day?'

'Yes, m'lady,' said Myra. 'Dust and sweep, and make the bed. Fresh water in the ewer.'

Lady Hardcastle looked down. 'How often is the floor polished?'

'Once a week on a Saturday. We gets a lot of people leavin' on Saturdays, so we gets a chance to do it while the rooms is empty.'

'What have you seen?' I asked.

'There, down the side of the bed,' said Lady Hardcastle, pointing. 'Scuff marks on the floorboards.'

I took a closer look. 'Shoes?' I suggested. 'As though someone were dragged out? Dead or unconscious.'

Myra gave a little gasp.

'That was my thinking,' said Lady Hardcastle. 'Though I'm still not convinced.'

'Someone took Dr Goddard and the strongbox, then?' I said. I turned towards Myra. 'This strongbox,' I began. 'You said it was big. Did you try to lift it? Was it heavy?'

She hesitated for a moment before saying, 'I did give it a little try, yes. It was difficult to pick up. I didn't want to move it – I was worried about it scratchin' the floor.'

'Where are you going with this one?' asked Lady Hardcastle.

'There's no sign of damage on the floor under the bed,' I said. 'I think Myra is right – if anyone had simply dragged a heavy box out from under there, it would probably have scratched the floorboards. But there's no sign of that sort of damage. A few light scuffs, but nothing major. I'd say the box was removed carefully.'

'And why be careful to leave no sign of moving the box, if you've already turned the whole place upside down?' she said. 'Or, put it round the other way: why carefully take the box and then make a frightful mess everywhere else?'

'To make it look like a burglary?' I said. 'Divert attention from the real target? But then . . . why leave the obvious valuables behind?'

'If only we knew what was in the box,' said Lady Hardcastle.

'What if it were something fragile?' I suggested. 'Something the thief thought might break if handled too roughly. That might make him take more care over it.'

'True,' she said. 'But that would imply that the thief knew what it was. If he knew that what he was after was something fragile in a heavy box, why would he be looking for documents taped under drawers?'

We stood a while, looking around at the wreckage, each lost in our own whirling thoughts. Our silent contemplation was interrupted by a shy little cough from Myra in the doorway.

'Do you think Dr Goddard is . . . ? Do you think he's . . . ? Do you think he's dead?' she asked quietly.

'Well now,' said Lady Hardcastle. 'That's quite the question. It's possible that these marks on the floor were indeed made by Dr Goddard's shoes. If that's the case then it's also reasonable to assume that he was dragged across the room at some point. To my way of thinking, if a chap is happy to leave this sort of chaos behind him, he'd not be too bothered about leaving a corpse as a final flourish, so if he was taken, he was most likely taken alive. But that's all a bit melodramatic at this stage. It's more likely that he went out for a walk in the middle of the night and has no idea what's been going on in his absence. From the little we know of him, he does seem like the sort of chap who would wander about without a thought for what people might think. The scuff marks are probably just the result of his own clumsiness.'

'I can't say I disagree,' I said. 'Why take the doctor and the box? The heavy box is almost certainly the prize, so why burden oneself further with an unconscious scientist? Much more likely that he's taken off of his own accord.'

'Quite so, my dear Flo. When was Dr Goddard due to check out?'

'I don't know, m'lady,' said Myra. 'Not for a few days, though – I gots no special instructions for his room.'

'In that case, please leave it as it is. There's nothing further to be learned from the broken lock, so have your carpenter fit a new one and keep the place locked up. We need to talk to your Mr Hillier next, so if you need to get about your work, please do. You've been most helpful.'

'Yes, m'lady. Thank you, m'lady.' Myra gave a little curtsey and vanished.

◆ ◆ ◆

Mr Hillier was not at the reception desk when we returned downstairs. Mr Nightengale, the clerk, told us that he had returned to his office.

'Thank you,' said Lady Hardcastle. 'And where's that?'

'Oh, I'm most terribly sorry, my lady,' he said. 'Of course you don't know. Why would you? Out into the corridor, first door on the left.'

She thanked him and we set off in the direction indicated.

We knew straight away that we had found the right place – the door was marked 'Manager's Office' in an elegant gold script. Lady Hardcastle knocked smartly and reached for the handle. Before she could take hold, it was snatched from her reach as Mr Hillier opened the door from the inside. He looked extremely anxious.

'Ah, Lady Hardcastle. Thank goodness you're here. Please come in,' he said.

He showed us to two chairs facing his desk and we sat down.

'Can I offer you any tea? Coffee?' He indicated a fully laden tray on a small table by the window.

'Thank you, that would be most welcome,' said Lady Hardcastle. 'Coffee for me, please.'

'And for me, please,' I said.

He bustled about in a most efficient manner, preparing two cups of coffee. I guessed that he had worked his way up through the hotel ranks to manager – he had the air of someone who had been well trained in the waiter's mystic arts. I smiled as I wondered if he, too, could dematerialize at will.

He brought the cups over. 'Biscuits?' he asked. 'Our chef makes the most delicious ginger nuts.' He fetched a plateful from the table and held them out.

'I seldom say no to a biscuit,' said Lady Hardcastle and helped herself to three. Having nowhere else to put them and a shortage of hands in which to hold them, she balanced them on the edge of her saucer. I did the same, but I took only two.

Mr Hillier resumed his seat. 'Now that you've had a chance to look around Dr Goddard's room,' he began, 'what do you think?'

Succinctly but thoroughly, Lady Hardcastle described our observations and recounted our thoughts on the disappearance of the strongbox and its owner. By the time she was finished, Mr Hillier's look of anxiety had been replaced by the faintest glimmer of hopefulness.

'My word,' he said, his eyes wide. 'You don't think . . . ? You don't think he's dead, do you?'

'Obviously we can't be at all sure at this early stage but things don't look quite that bleak yet,' said Lady Hardcastle. 'I expect he'll turn up in a few hours, tired and hungry, and bemused by all the fuss. And if he didn't disappear of his own volition, then someone is holding him somewhere. Being kidnapped by person or persons unknown isn't the way most people would choose to spend their holidays, but it's still better than being dead.'

'Yes,' he said doubtfully. 'Of course. Where there's life there's hope.'

'If he's still alive we'll do all that we can to ensure he stays that way. Even if—'

'I know what you're going to say,' he interrupted. 'But I really cannot countenance the involvement of the authorities at this stage. I must insist, for the sake of the business, that informing the police must be our absolute last resort.'

'Very well,' said Lady Hardcastle. 'We shall do all we can to make sure it doesn't come to that.'

'Thank you.'

'What do your staff know?' I asked.

'Only that Dr Goddard's room has been ransacked and the man himself hasn't been seen since he left the salon last night.'

'They'll know a lot more before the hour is up,' I said. 'Myra was present while Lady Hardcastle and I discussed our search. Are you happy for us to proceed as though they all know what's going on?'

'Well, yes,' he said. 'I suppose we have no choice. But why?'

'We shall need to speak to them,' said Lady Hardcastle. 'They may have seen or heard things in the night. Do we have your permission to question them?'

'Oh, I see. Yes, by all means. But please try not to alarm them too much. Some of the younger ones can be a bit skittish.'

'Thank you,' she said. 'And do we have the run of the hotel?'

He thought for a moment, seemingly trying to make up his mind whether to give us that much trust. Eventually he came to a decision.

'Yes, actually, why not?' he said. He took a small key from his pocket and unlocked one of his desk drawers. He produced a key attached to a heavy, plain brass fob. 'This,' he said, holding it up, 'is a master key. It will open almost any lock in the hotel which is why it bears no identifying marks. Please take the utmost care of it.'

Lady Hardcastle passed the key to me and I put it in my pocket. I briefly wondered what it didn't open if it could open 'almost any' of the hotel's locks. It made no difference, though – the picklocks concealed in my brooch would take care of anything which remained closed to us. I wondered if I would ever find out.

'If any of your other guests see us snooping about and ask what we're up to,' said Lady Hardcastle, 'we shall tell them that we're writing an article about the hotel trade for the *Bristol News*. We have a contact there who will confirm any such claim without question if it comes to it, but I'll warn her in advance just to make certain.'

'You seem to have thought of everything,' said Mr Hillier.

'We do try to,' she said. 'Now, if you'll excuse us, we'd better begin. The sooner we start, the sooner we can have Dr Goddard back safe and sound.'

Chapter Four

We retreated to the sanctity of what we were now describing as our 'suite' while we contemplated our next steps. Lady Hardcastle had headed a new page in her journal, 'The Case of the Missing Scientist . . . and his Mysterious Strongbox'.

'Not the catchiest of titles,' I said as I read over her shoulder. 'But helpfully descriptive, nonetheless.'

'I'm not hoping to sell it as a penny dreadful,' she said. 'In years to come, when I'm dead and gone, you'll be glad of my clumsily literal headings. When you come to write my biography, you won't have to spend hours trying to fathom why I chose to head the section "Of Pelicans, Aspidistra, and Blancmange" and then spent four pages detailing my musings on possible future developments in the world of steam engines. If I write about steam engines, my contemplations will be headed "Steam Engines" and there shall be no doubt about my intentions.'

'I think it's sweet that you imagine I shall spend my declining years writing your biography,' I said.

'I expect it to be frank but flattering,' she said. 'And if it's not, I shall haunt you.'

'Meanwhile . . .' I said.

'Yes, quite. Meanwhile, we have a missing scientist and a mysterious strongbox.'

'Just like it says in the title.'

'Just so. The lock was forced. The room was tipped upside down. The box was taken. The scientist was dragged out, probably unconscious, but possibly dead.'

'That's a lot of things to be happening in such a small, ordinary room,' I said.

'Ordinary . . .' she said slowly. 'I know it's vulgar to talk about money, but these rooms aren't cheap. If we were trying to spot the odd man out at dinner last night, I'd have put a guinea on Dr Goddard. Actually, it would have been of more benefit to give the guinea directly to Dr Goddard. Everyone else looked as though they were worth a few bob, but our dining companion in the rumpled dinner suit didn't really appear to be the sort of chap who could afford to stay at Steep Holm View.'

'Appearances can be deceptive,' I said. 'Government scientists are usually portrayed as a bit scatterbrained. He might be an eccentric millionaire, so wrapped up in his work that he forgets to buy new clothes.'

'Possible, but unlikely.'

'Perhaps his department is paying,' I suggested.

'Perhaps. It's not quite the behaviour of the civil service we know and love, though, is it? Old Mother Harridan's Boarding House a mile from the seafront is more their level.'

'Add it to the list, then,' I said.

She finished her sketch of the missing scientist and wrote a short list of our discoveries on the next page.

'What do we do next?' I asked.

'Interview the witnesses,' she said. 'Well, that would be the next step in a detective novel. The trouble is that we don't appear to have any witnesses. No one has come forward and said, "I don't want to cause an unnecessary fuss, but I saw a chap cosh that scientist fellow and drag him out of the hotel last night. I didn't think anything of it until I heard you all talking about how he'd gone missing." As far as we know, no one saw anything.'

'As far as we know,' I said. 'And as far as they know. But I'd put that guinea you were waving about just now on someone having seen something, even if they don't know that they did. We need to find out which staff were on duty last night and try to build up a complete picture of the comings and goings. It wouldn't hurt to talk to the other guests, too.'

'It's a start,' she said. 'I tell you what, why don't you get yourself below stairs and see who keeps the duty roster while I talk to Mr Nightengale on the front desk to get the guests' room numbers. We can meet back here in . . . what? Half an hour? Will that be long enough?'

'It should be plenty.'

◆ ◆ ◆

We went back downstairs together and caught a glimpse of Mr Hillier's retreating back as he returned to his office. We approached the reception desk where Mr Nightengale was already smiling a welcome.

'I am at your service, ladies,' he said. 'Mr Hillier has asked that all the staff offer you every assistance, and I shall be pleased to do whatever I may to clear up this terrible business.'

'Thank you,' said Lady Hardcastle. 'We'll try not to cause too much disruption. We don't want our "help" to turn into an imposition.'

'Nothing is too much trouble, I assure you,' he said.

'You're very kind. Our first order of business is to find out a little more about your other guests and to speak to whichever of your staff was on duty last night. Might I see the register, please?'

'And may I see the duty roster?' I added.

'The hotel register is right here,' he said, lifting it from the lower part of the desk and placing it in front of Lady Hardcastle. 'I keep the duty roster in a ledger. If you give me a minute I can fetch it for you.'

'No need,' I said. 'Presumably you post a copy in the staff area for them to refer to?'

'Why yes,' he said. 'As a matter of fact I do. I had a notice-board put on the wall for that very purpose. We also use it for other reminders – guests' special requirements and the like. Go along the corridor and—'

But I was already on my way. 'Don't worry,' I said over my shoulder. 'I'll find it. Thank you.'

The staff door was easy to spot – indeed I'd spotted it on our first visit to the salon. A corridor led down the side of the reception and where it turned right to take guests to the dining room and salon, there was a door. It had a keyhole, but no handle

– instead there was a slightly worn, but still brightly polished, brass push plate etched with the same whiplash curve motif that decorated the rest of the hotel. This was very obviously the staff door to the kitchens and beyond.

I pushed the door. It opened easily against the slight resistance of the sprung hinge that closed it behind me as I passed through. Once on the other side, things were markedly less glamorous. The walls were painted a pale blue instead of being hung with expensive wallpaper. The floor was of linoleum-covered stone rather than polished wood. And the lighting, though still pleasingly electric, was provided by bare bulbs while the lights in the residential part of the hotel were covered with decorative glass lampshades. We were in the realm of the staff.

The short corridor led me past a doorless room in which there was a large table and an open dresser containing stacks of the hotel's crockery. I presumed the room was used as a staging post or marshalling area when service was busy. A wide stone staircase just beyond the doorway led downwards.

There was a familiar clatter of dishes being stacked, and the banging of some foodstuff being sternly shown who was boss on a chopping board. The smells were the familiar mix of bacon, sausage, and curry powder that accompanied the preparation of breakfast in English hotels and big houses.

At the bottom of the stairs was a noticeboard covered in green baize. Pinned to it with brass drawing pins was a selection of notices. There was an announcement that this week's skittles match had been postponed because of illness among members of the Grand Atlantic team. Staff were encouraged to remind their friends that Reverend Barnard from St Philip's Church was offering reading classes at the vicarage. Miss Wilson in room ten breakfasted early, but returned to her room and should only be disturbed before eleven o'clock in the morning in the event of fire, flood, or the coming of the Apocalypse – 'Her own words', the sign noted.

Finally, I lit upon the duty roster. One male and one female member of staff were scheduled to work between eight each night and six the following morning, presumably to cater to guests' whims at any hour. Last night it had been the turn of Vincent Fear and Marian Higdon. By some quirk of scheduling – or possibly the mean-spiritedness of Mr Nightengale – they were both rostered to be back at work for a half shift at one o'clock that afternoon.

I toyed briefly with the idea of exploring the staff area more fully, but the ticking of the clock on the wall behind me reminded me that my half hour was probably passing faster than I imagined. I looked at it and saw that I still had time for poking about but, on balance, I thought it would be better to get back to the suite and tell Lady Hardcastle what I had found out. It wouldn't have taken her long to get the list of hotel guests, and the sooner I was back, the sooner we could get cracking.

Lady Hardcastle was already in her room, sitting at the writing desk by the window.

'Successful trip?' she asked as I came in.

'I have the names we want, and they're coming on duty now.'

She looked at her wristwatch. 'One o'clock? After a night shift? That's rather harsh.'

'That's what it says on the rota,' I confirmed. 'It's tough being a servant.'

'So it would appear.'

'How about you?' I asked. 'Do you have the guest list?'

'Names and rooms,' she said. 'And it turns out that our friendly and helpful hotel clerk, Mr Sidney Nightengale, is something of a gossip. As well as room numbers, I have been given one or two titbits. Nothing salacious – more's the pity – but I still know that the Russian chap—'

'Kusnetsov,' I said.

'Even he. Dear Dr Goddard described him as an "odd fish", but I rather think that everyone probably seems an odd fish to a chap like him. Our indiscreet hotel clerk reports only that he makes his own Macassar oil with Russian bear oil, that he keeps a copy of *Pride and Prejudice* in the drawer of his writing desk, and that he has been seen closely questioning the Punch and Judy man. This struck Mr Nightengale as odd, but I have to say that if I'd grown up anywhere but England, I should have a great many questions about Punch and Judy.'

'I have a ton of questions about it,' I said, 'and I did partly grow up in England.'

'Exactly. So that's him. Then there was Miss Wilson senior, who is, apparently, rather prone to a certain bluntness in her dealings with others. She has issued strict instructions that she not be disturbed before eleven except in the event of fire, flood—'

'—or the coming of the Apocalypse,' I said. 'It's on the staff noticeboard downstairs.'

'It's the American way. Charmingly polite people for the most part, but they do seem to value forthrightness and plain speaking.'

'From the way her instructions were so obviously written verbatim on the noticeboard, I don't think it's quite so highly valued by the English staff,' I said.

'All part of their cultural education, I'm sure,' she said. 'There was lots more, but it shall have to suffice for the moment to know that I have been vouchsafed pages of tittle-tattle should we ever need to refer to it.' She waved her notebook.

'There's always room in the world for more tittle-tattle. Do we have an agenda?'

'We do. First item is to knock on the doors nearest Dr Goddard's room and see if they heard anything.'

'And who will we find behind those doors?'

She consulted her notes. 'The Misses Wilson have adjoining rooms to one side. Our odd Russian fish is round the corner at the other end of the corridor, so he might have seen or heard something, too. Martin, the Frenchman, is on the same floor, but he's right in the far corner. There's method in my madness, you know – I wasn't briefing you on Kusnetsov and Wilson just for a lark.'

'It all becomes clear,' I said.

'I think we ought to introduce you to the rest of the guests as my associate. The snobbish looks you get do rather bother me, even if you can shrug them off, and I think we might get more out of people if they don't dismiss you as a "mere" servant.'

'That's all right by me,' I said. I was in mufti anyway, so it would make everything easier to explain. 'And then the night shift when we've done that?'

'As soon as we can, I think, so we don't interrupt their day too much.'

She picked up her notebook and pencil and we set off in search of interviewees.

The Wilsons' rooms were, I judged, directly above our own. I was having trouble working out the layout of the place which somehow managed to have rooms and corridors where I thought there should be none, and blank walls where surely there should surely be more hotel.

Lady Hardcastle rapped smartly on the door, which was opened a crack a few moments later.

'Yes?' said a young woman. I couldn't see her clearly through the tiny opening but I assumed her to be Eleanora, the niece.

'Good morning, Miss Wilson, I'm Emily, Lady Hardcastle.' She held a calling card towards the door. 'May we come in and speak to you and your aunt?'

The girl opened the door a little wider and took the card. She shut the door.

Lady Hardcastle and I shrugged at one another.

A few more moments passed and the door opened again, wider this time. The girl stood aside to allow us to enter.

'Lady Hardcastle,' said a woman sitting at the writing desk by the window. 'Come in.' She appeared to be about Lady

Hardcastle's age – early forties – and was dressed in brand-new country tweeds. Notwithstanding her obvious American accent, there was something about her appearance that indicated she wasn't from round here. I wondered if it was her hairstyle.

She finished whatever she was writing and turned her chair to face us. 'I am Miss Adelia Wilson of Annapolis, Maryland. This young lady is my niece, Eleanora Wilson – my brother's daughter, God rest his soul.'

Now I was able to get a proper look at her, Miss Wilson junior appeared even younger than I had first imagined. I put her somewhere around sixteen or seventeen years old. She was dark-haired, like her aunt, and when she looked up from her inspection of her boots, her brown eyes twinkled. From her shy demeanour I had expected a plain, dowdy girl, but there was an unexpected spark of beauty about her. Hearts, I confidently predicted, would be broken as soon as this young woman stepped out of the shadow of her overbearing aunt.

'How do you do?' said Lady Hardcastle. 'This is my associate, Florence Armstrong.'

'How do you do?' said Miss Wilson senior.

Her niece nodded shyly.

'What can I do for you?' asked the older lady.

'Have you heard about the goings-on in your neighbour's room during the night?' asked Lady Hardcastle.

Both women nodded.

'The hotel management has asked us to look into it for them.'

'Have they? Have they indeed?' Adelia seemed amused by the notion. 'And why did they do that?'

'Who can fathom the minds of hoteliers and restaurateurs?' said Lady Hardcastle blithely. 'Theirs is another world. I merely answered the call.'

'Yes, but . . . Oh, never mind. I'm afraid I wear wax earplugs when I sleep so I hear nothing. I'm a light sleeper, you see, so I find that the slightest sound will waken me. And I do so hate to be disturbed. Eleanora might have heard something – the doctor's room is adjacent to hers. Did you, dear? Did you hear anything?'

It appeared for a moment as though the younger woman's fascination with her boots would win against any entreaties for information, but slowly she looked up and blinked at Lady Hardcastle.

'I retired early, to read, ma'am,' she said quietly. 'My aunt has always impressed upon me the importance of a good night's sleep and I find reading a few chapters of my book helps me. I suppose it was a little after ten o'clock when I became aware of the sound of someone in the corridor. He was trying the doctor's door.'

'Can you be sure it was the doctor's door?' asked Lady Hardcastle gently.

'Absolutely sure, ma'am. I have heard Dr Goddard come and go quite often – he rises early and goes for a walk along the shore, you know. I watch him from my window. I know the sound of his door.'

'What happened then?'

'There was some scratching, as though someone was trying to fit a key in the lock. It went on for a little while and I wondered if I ought to ring for a porter to come and help him. There was a loud snapping sound and a man's voice said, "Back later."'

'How odd,' said Lady Hardcastle.

'Is it?' asked Eleanora.

'Well, we know it wasn't Dr Goddard – he was in the salon with us not long after ten, and he'd been at the Knightstone Pavilion all evening listening to the Offenbach. So who was trying to get in? And if he managed it, why say he was going to be back later? And to whom did he say it? Most peculiar.'

'I suppose it is when you put it like that. The walls are too thick to hear what happened next, but a few minutes later I heard the door open and close again. The scratching came again, but not for so long this time. Then nothing. I'm afraid I drifted off to sleep then.'

'I see. You didn't think it odd that someone was trying to break into Dr Goddard's room?'

'It didn't cross my mind to think that it wasn't Dr Goddard himself. Or some member of staff. Why would it?'

'No, of course. What about later?'

'Later?'

'When Dr Goddard disappeared. He retired at about half past one. By nine o'clock this morning he was gone. His door was kicked in and the room thoroughly ransacked.'

'Oh my,' said Eleanora. 'Kicked in?'

'As far as we can make out,' I said.

'I heard nothing. They could have come in here? Oh my.'

'But you heard nothing,' said Lady Hardcastle.

'Nothing at all,' said Eleanora. 'Unlike my aunt, I sleep deeply. The next thing I knew about it was after breakfast when there was a commotion in the corridor. That was when the maid found his room in turmoil.'

'Ah, I see. Did she speak to you, then?' asked Lady Hardcastle.

Adelia interrupted on her niece's behalf. 'I told Eleanora to look next door to find out what all the fuss was about,' she said. 'I can't bear fuss. I was going to fetch that Nightengale fellow up here and give him a piece of my mind. That's when we learned that the room had been ransacked.'

'But you definitely heard nothing of the ransacking itself?' said Lady Hardcastle.

'We should have been far less surprised and alarmed by the condition of Dr Goddard's room if we had,' said Adelia. 'We may be ignorant hicks from the New World in your eyes, but we can put two and two together as easily as any European. If we'd heard a ruckus in the middle of the night, we might have expected to find the room rifled for goodness knows what.'

'Quite so,' said Lady Hardcastle with a smile. She looked thoughtful for a moment, as though trying to make up her mind whether to ask her next question. 'I don't suppose you know anything about Dr Goddard's strongbox?' she said eventually.

'We are aware of it,' said Adelia. 'I believe everyone is. It seemed to be the first thing he told people about himself.'

'Really?'

'He would introduce himself, then say, "I'm a . . . I'm a government radio engineer, you know. Yes, a radio engineer.

On my way to a conference, d'you see. Important whatnots in a strongbox and all that. You know the drill. Very important." I'm surprised he didn't mention it to you.'

Her impersonation was uncannily accurate and made me laugh in spite of myself. She glanced at me sharply, but seemed pleased with herself rather than disapproving of me.

'He didn't say a word to us. But he told everyone else?'

'Everyone. You've seen the dining room in this place – tiny. We maintain the fantasy that our conversations are private by pretending we can't hear each other, but nothing anyone says in there is private. Everyone knew he had a strongbox.'

'Did he tell anyone what was in it?'

'Not that I heard,' said Adelia. 'Come to think of it, I don't think I ever heard him tell anyone anything in any detail in there – he told me about being a radio engineer one evening when we were the only ones in the salon. But that strongbox sure wasn't a secret.'

'How very careless of him,' mused Lady Hardcastle.

'Trying to make himself seem more important than he really was, if you ask me,' said Adelia. 'A nickel will get you a dollar it was full of shirt collars and hair oil. Men do like to puff themselves up.'

'No doubt,' said Lady Hardcastle. 'Well, ladies, thank you for your time. Perhaps we might dine together one evening? It's been a while since I was last in your country – I should very much like to get to know you a little better if you can bear our company for an evening.'

'I'm sure that would be just . . . swell,' said Adelia with another smile. I wondered if it was a word she actually used in conversation or whether she was teasing us with her folksy Americanisms.

We said our goodbyes and checked the time. We still had a few minutes before the staff were due on duty so we set off along the corridor to visit Dr Goddard's other near neighbour, the odd fish Sergei Kusnetsov.

He was not at home.

'Well,' said Lady Hardcastle as we stood in the corridor. 'That's frightfully inconsiderate. One would think that with everything that's been going on, the least he could do would be to wait in in case we needed to talk to him.'

'The sheer effrontery of the man,' I said. 'I shall write a stiff letter to the Russian embassy.'

'If you would, dear, that would be splendid. I suppose there's nothing for it but to interview the staff. Let's have a word with Nightengale and see if he can be persuaded to free them from their labours for a few minutes to talk to us in the salon.'

'We could just go below stairs and talk to them there,' I suggested.

'We could, but my presence in the "underworld" always causes consternation – everyone looks at me as though I'm about to accuse them of stealing my handkerchief. And after last night's musical entertainment I'm doubly wary of visiting the underworld lest I'm imprisoned there.'

'As I understood the opera, Eurydice had fallen in love with Pluto while he was disguised as a shepherd. Have you been dallying with shepherds?'

'Chance would be a fine thing. But come, tiny associate, let us tarry no more. We shall speak to Nightengale again, interview last night's staff, and then have a late luncheon somewhere. Perhaps here to save us venturing too far.'

Nightengale was delighted to be able to help. The porter was dispatched to the underworld (as Lady Hardcastle had insisted on describing it, much to Nightengale's bewilderment) to summon Fear and Higdon, the staff who had been on duty the night before. While that was going on, Nightengale himself had installed us in the salon, offering us complimentary drinks and promising that Chef would be happy to prepare anything we should wish for lunch. For this, too, there would be no charge.

'This is turning into quite a cheap holiday,' said Lady Hardcastle when he had gone.

'It's turning into a busman's holiday, if you ask me,' I said. 'I thought we'd come to the seaside to get away from this sort of carry-on.'

'Pish and fiddlesticks. You'd be bored silly if we weren't mired in mystery and mayhem. There are only so many times one can ride a donkey up and down the beach before one begins to hanker for something more adventurous.'

'I haven't ridden on a donkey even once,' I said. 'And you still owe me a toffee apple and half a pint of winkles.'

'I can send out for some winkles if madam would like me to,' said the waiter, who had arrived with our drinks.

We waved him away with our thanks and settled to await our interviewees.

'What do you make of all this strongbox stuff?' I asked between sips of my drink.

'It's all rather odd, isn't it?' Lady Hardcastle replied. 'I think Adelia Wilson might have the measure of the chap, though – it sounds like a bored, lonely man trying to make himself and his job seem more interesting. I mean, think about it. If it really contained top secret material of any kind, he'd be terrified that someone would sneak into his room while he's out and pinch it. Or worse, sneak into his room while he's in, bonk him on the head, and then pinch it.'

'Or sneak into his room, bonk him on the head, and take both him and the strongbox.'

'Well, quite. It makes little sense. Although it definitely seems to be gone. As does he.'

'I have every faith in you.'

'You do? That's most gratifying. Thank you. Oh, here we are – I think these must be our night-time flunkeys.'

'You're not at all the social reformer you make yourself out to be, are you?' I said.

She ignored me in favour of greeting our visitors.

'Miss Higdon?' she said.

'Mrs,' said Marian Higdon.

'I do beg your pardon,' said Lady Hardcastle. 'And Mr Fear?'

'That's right,' said Vincent Fear.

They were wearing the same bronze-coloured livery as the rest of the staff, freshly laundered, crisply pressed, and perfectly complementing the hotel's décor. Marian Higdon was a short, plump, extremely pretty girl in her early twenties, with fair hair gathered up into her cap, and grey eyes that scanned the room with a jittery nervousness.

Vincent Fear was of a similar age, but taller, and skinny as a whippet. His face was angular, but there was something about it that suggested he might well turn out to be pleasingly handsome once he had grown into it.

'Please, take a seat,' said Lady Hardcastle, waving them into the two comfortable chairs that had been set opposite us. 'We shan't take up too much of your time,' she continued. 'I know how busy you must be. Can we offer you some of this cordial? We can order some tea or coffee if you'd prefer.'

'No, thank you, ma'am,' they said in unison. This synchronized response seemed to discomfit them even more than the invitation to sit with hotel guests and answer questions. They both blushed, but Lady Hardcastle ignored it as she fished in her handbag for her notebook and pencil.

'I understand you were both on duty last night,' she continued, now poised to take notes. 'I presume you've both heard about Dr Goddard and the state his room was found in this morning.'

They both nodded solemnly and mumbled that they had.

'We've been asked to see if we can't find out what happened,' she said, 'so we're trying to gain an understanding of the events of last night, from dinner time onwards. To put you in the picture, Dr Goddard came to the dining room at around half past seven and sat at our table. We ate together, and we didn't see him again until after the performance at the Knightstone. We had a nightcap in here in the salon and then we all retired at half past one or thereabouts. What we're interested in is what happened in Dr Goddard's room between when he went out to the theatre and when Myra went to clean his room first thing this morning. Did either of you see or hear anything unusual?'

They both looked pensive for a while.

Marian Higdon was the first to speak. 'Nothin' especially unusual,' she said. 'I took Miss Wilson a cup of cocoa at about nine o'clock – she rung down for it. But there weren't nothin' goin' on then.'

'Nothing at all?'

'Nothin' odd,' said Marian. 'Mr Schneider was in the corridor, but he weren't doin' nothin'. He must have been on his way back to his room.'

'Is his room on that landing?' asked Lady Hardcastle. 'I thought it was just the Wilsons and Dr Goddard, with Martin and Kusnetsov on the other side of the building.'

Marian thought for a moment. 'You're right,' she said. 'I beg your pardon. His room is round the back on your floor, next to Mr Taka . . . Takawhatnot.'

'Takahashi,' I said.

'That's him. Like you say, the back rooms on the Wilsons' floor are Mr Martin and Mr Kus . . .' This time she just tailed off and didn't even try to say the Russian's name.

I smiled at her. 'Kusnetsov,' I said kindly.

'Was it unusual to see Herr Schneider on the second floor?' asked Lady Hardcastle.

'I never seen him there afore, come to think of it,' said Marian. 'But I never thought nothin' of it. He might have been to see one o' t'others.'

'Monsieur Martin or Mr Kusnetsov,' said Lady Hardcastle as she continued making her notes. She looked up. 'But you saw nothing else? Were you called back to the Wilsons' for anything?'

'No, ma'am.'

'I see. And what about you, Vincent?' said Lady Hardcastle. 'Did you see anything on the second-floor landing?'

'Nothin' as I didn't expect to see,' he said. 'I was called to see Monsieur Martin near ten.' Unlike Marian, he pronounced it closer to the French way, as 'Mar-*tan*'. 'But I wasn't called back again, either. It was a quiet night.'

'And you saw no one up there?'

'Mr Kusnetsov came out of his room as I passed by on my way back down, but no one else.'

'Did he come downstairs?' I asked.

'No,' he said. He hesitated. 'I assumed he went to . . . to the . . .'

Lady Hardcastle smiled. 'My nanny always referred to it as "visiting Mrs Jones",' she said. 'The bathroom and toilet are in the same place as on our floor?'

'They are,' he said. 'At the end of the landin'.'

'You saw nothing else?'

'Nothin' upstairs, no.'

'But something downstairs?'

'Well, sort of,' he said. 'It wasn't anythin' we're not used to. Just some drunken fisherman stumblin' about in the alley up by the kitchen door.'

'You get a lot of that?' I asked.

'One of the 'azards of livin' at the seaside, miss,' he said. 'People comes stumblin' out of the pub and they goes down any convenient alley to . . .'

'To see if Mrs Jones is at home?' I said with a smile.

He blushed. 'We tries to chase 'em off if we sees 'em, like, but it only takes a bucket of water to clean up after 'em, so it's not worth puttin' in too much effort to get rid of 'em.'

'Was he one of your regular visitors?' asked Lady Hardcastle.

'It was three in the mornin' – I didn't get a good look. Just another fisherman, you know? Big boots, dark coat, cap. They's ten a penny round here.'

'I'm sure they are,' she said. 'And that was the night shift done?'

'We has plenty of regular duties, gettin' things ready for the mornin',' said Marian defensively. 'It weren't like we was sittin' with our feet up.'

'Of course,' said Lady Hardcastle. 'But you saw and heard nothing else out of the ordinary?'

'Not a thing,' they said in unison. They glared at each other, and then at me. I tried not to laugh.

'Well,' said Lady Hardcastle. 'You've helped us enormously. Thank you so much for your time.'

'Is it all right to go?' asked Vincent. 'Only we . . .'

'Of course, of course. Off you trot. If we have any further questions we'll send word via Mr Nightengale.'

They mumbled their thanks and goodbyes and all but scampered out of the room in their haste to be free of us.

'Have they?' I asked once they were gone.

'Have they what, dear?' said Lady Hardcastle as she leafed back through her notes.

'Have they helped us enormously?'

'I have no idea,' she said. 'They seem to have painted a picture of the everyday comings and goings on the second floor.'

'With Herr Schneider on the wrong landing,' I said.

'He could have been visiting one of the others,' she said. 'Who knows who knows whom?'

'Who indeed? What about the fisherman?'

'What about him? A fisherman piddling in an alley isn't really a clue, is it?'

'We saw a fisherman matching his description on the Knightstone Causeway,' I said.

'All fishermen match his description, dear,' she said. 'That's how one knows they're fishermen. You heard young Vincent: "They's ten a penny round 'ere."'

'Then I'm none the wiser,' I said.

'No more am I,' she said. 'What say we take up the hotel's generous offer of a free lunch and then go for an afternoon stroll. The sea air might clear our heads.'

'And a donkey ride?' I suggested.

'While eating toffee apples if you insist,' she said.

Now that was my idea of an afternoon at the seaside.

Chapter Five

The weather outside was as grey as ever, and the wind whipping up the Bristol Channel and across the bay was as biting as ever.

'This is still very bracing,' said Lady Hardcastle, hanging on to her hat to stop it blowing away.

'Perhaps it would be less blustery if we walked into town,' I said. I had to raise my voice to be heard above the sound of the wind.

'Nonsense. Where's your much-vaunted bravery in the face of danger?'

'I'm always brave in the face of danger,' I said. 'But I'm much less resilient in the teeth of a gale.'

'We should seek the shelter of a crowd. Look there – the Punch and Judy man has attracted a small knot of warm bodies. Let's insinuate ourselves among them and use them as a living windbreak.'

A few yards along the prom, not far from the entrance to the pier, stood the little red-and-white striped tent of the Punch and Judy show. Children had pressed their way to the front of the small group of onlookers and were laughing with spiteful glee as Punch battered his way through the bewildering mish-mash of characters, whacking them with his slapstick and proclaiming, 'That's the way to do it.'

We joined the crowd on the leeward side and for once I was grateful for my diminished height. I could no longer see the 'stage' upon which the peculiar puppet drama was unfolding, but I was completely shielded from the wind.

'Do you understand any of this?' I asked. 'We had a Punch and Judy man for a while as a sideshow at the circus when I was tiny, but I never knew what was going on. I just liked the silly voices.'

'I think that's the main appeal,' said Lady Hardcastle. 'That and clumping everyone over the head with a big stick. Doesn't he drop the baby, or some such? Then there's some sort of argument with his wife. And a policeman. I'm sure I've seen sausages at some point. And I think that once I saw him hanged. Or was he eaten by a crocodile?'

'In ours he just whacked the crocodile with the stick. It was mostly about hitting things.'

'The children love it, though,' she said. 'Listen to them.'

'Everyone loves a series of violent crimes,' I said. 'One murder after another. People find it entertaining.'

'Well, you know what they say: "There's nowt so queer as folk."'

The man in front of us turned round. 'Would you please be quiet,' he said with a slight German accent. 'It is hard enough for me to understand what he is saying with that device in his mouth, but I cannot hear him at all with this witless babble going on behind me.'

He was of average height – that is to say an inch or two shorter than Lady Hardcastle – and wearing a straw boater with a red-and-gold band. His eyes – one of which wore a monocle – were blue and his moustache and beard were fussily trimmed. He wore an extravagantly jewelled pin on his lapel.

'Herr Schneider, isn't it?' said Lady Hardcastle brightly. 'I believe we're fellow guests at Steep Holm View. I'm Lady Hardcastle. How do you do?'

The man's scowl didn't lessen, but politeness got the better of him and he couldn't stop himself from bowing and clicking the heels of his brightly polished boots.

'How do you do?' he said stiffly, then returned to trying to comprehend the incomprehensible puppet show.

Lady Hardcastle, it seemed, had decided that his ill temper should not go unrewarded. She winked at me as she tapped him on the shoulder.

'It's frightfully good fun, isn't it?' she said.

He turned back towards us, his face reddening. 'It is hard for me to find out how much fun it is, madam, because you keep interrupting.'

With a devilish glint in her eye, she persisted. 'We were just saying how much people seem to love it even though not one of us has the faintest idea what's going on. We think it has something to do with all the characters being hit with sticks.'

'I am beginning to think that someone should perhaps have hit you with a stick, madam,' said Herr Schneider. 'Perhaps it would have taught you some manners. Please be quiet.'

'Do you think it would have done any good? Nanny always said I was incorrigible, but she never struck me. I always loved her for that.'

'You really are a most infuriating woman. Please shut up.' His face had gone from red to purple.

'Yes, that was another word she used. Infuriating. Do you find me infuriating, Flo?'

'No, my lady,' I said. 'I always enjoy your company.'

'Oh, how sweet. You see, Herr Schneider, with a different approach you might enjoy my company, too.'

'I cannot bear your company a second longer,' he said. 'Good day.'

With that, he struggled free of the now slightly larger group of onlookers and strode fussily off down the promenade.

Lady Hardcastle was grinning broadly. 'What a charming fellow,' she said.

'I'll be honest, missus,' said a woman a few paces to our right. 'He might be a pig, but he did have a point. You'd be doin' us all a favour if you'd shut your trap.'

'Quite right, dear,' said Lady Hardcastle, still grinning. 'Come on, Flo, let's leave these nice ladies and gentlemen to their show.'

We set off once more on our stroll. As we cleared the entrance to the pier, a particularly strong gust caught the hat of a man walking a few yards in front of us and sent it soaring into the sky. We stepped aside to allow him to pass as he set off to recapture it.

As he drew level he said, 'How do you do?' and raised his hand to tip the now-airborne hat. With his hand halfway to his bare head he realized his error and attempted to turn the gesture into a cheery wave.

'You might be right,' said Lady Hardcastle. 'Perhaps we should seek the shelter of a nice tea room.'

'More tea?' I groaned. 'What about the museum?'

'And its collection of "fascinating archaeological specimens"? Yes, why not? They might have a tea room.'

We crossed the road and headed for the comparative calm of a side street where the buildings provided some protection from the wind.

'Do you know where this museum is?' she asked as we walked in the vague direction of the middle of town.

'Of course,' I said. 'It's on the Boulevard. Next to the hospital.'

'And where's the Boulevard?'

'In town,' I said. 'It's where the library and museum are.'

'One can go off people, you know.'

'Fear not,' I said, pulling a piece of folded paper from my pocket. 'I picked up a street map from reception.'

I unfolded the hand-drawn map and found that we were only a little way from the museum. We struck out along Regent Street, glad of the respite from the wind. Despite the absence of sunshine, the weather was comfortably mild once in the shelter of civilization, making the short walk rather a pleasant one.

We passed a telephone pole on to which a small poster advertising a concert had been pasted.

'I say, what fun,' said Lady Hardcastle. 'We should go.'

I looked more closely at the poster. 'Robinson's Ragtime Roisterers', it told me, would be playing at the Arundel Hotel on Friday, the eighth of July, 'for one night only'.

'I see no reason why not,' I said. 'They are, after all, London's "foremost exponents of intoxicating syncopated revelry". Advertising posters never lie.'

'Never,' she agreed. 'So that's one evening's entertainment sorted out. Well done, me.'

'And there's the library and museum,' I said, pointing to an impressive red-brick building a little way ahead. 'So that's this afternoon's entertainment sorted out. Well done, me.'

As promised, the museum housed a fine collection of archaeological finds, which it displayed well. Sadly, though, there are only so many flint arrowheads and other knapped stone tools one can look at before one feels that one has been shown all the possibilities that small rocks had to offer our Neolithic ancestors. It wasn't long before we had exhausted the entertainment potential of the museum.

There were no tea rooms nearby.

'I think we need to return to the Steep Holm View for afternoon tea,' said Lady Hardcastle. 'Especially if it's going to be free.'

As we strolled westwards towards our hotel, we mused on the case so far.

'I keep coming back to the "back later" business,' I said once we'd talked through the dismayingly few details we had. 'It sounds awfully like a break-in. As Eleanora tells it, someone visited Dr Goddard and scratched at the door for a little while. He got no reply because Goddard was in the salon with us, so he said he'd be back later. She was half asleep so she didn't question any of that, whereas I immediately had questions bubbling up everywhere. For starters: why scratch instead of knocking? Why did he say he would be back later if he got no reply?'

'It does sound fishy,' she said. 'It's a pity she didn't go and investigate – she could have told us who it was.'

'What if we assume that the visitor succeeded in his attempt to break in?'

'Then that would make "back later" a way to explain away the noise. People say that sort of thing to empty rooms all the time. I've done it myself. "Oh, you're not here, then? I shall have to come back later," I'll say as I wander off.'

'That makes sense,' I said. 'Scratch, scratch. "Heigh-ho, no one here, I'll have to come back later", and then slip inside the newly opened door.'

'Plausible enough,' she said. 'But who could it have been?'

'Herr Schneider was seen on the landing at around nine,' I said.

'The Austrian.'

'Yes,' I said. 'Messrs Martin and Kusnetsov were on the same floor, and Kusnetsov was seen going to the facilities at the end of the corridor at ten.'

'The Frenchman and the . . . Russian,' she said. 'Russian . . . Russian. Why does that make my memory pull at the hem of my skirt as though it knows something it wants to tell me?'

'Are Russians known for saying "back later" when they get no reply?' I asked.

'Not that I know of,' she said. 'Although if they were they'd say it in Russian. Oh!' She stopped so abruptly that a lady walking behind us bumped into her.

'Why don't you watch what you're doing?' said the lady huffily as she bustled past.

'I can't help feeling that the collision could have been more easily avoided if *she* had been watching what I was doing instead, but I don't want to argue. I've had a brainwave.'

'I'm all ears.'

'Well, now,' she said. 'My Russian is a little rusty—'

'I told you: you need to pat him dry with a towel and then thoroughly oil him before you put him away. It's no wonder he gets rusty.'

'It's such a faff, though – one has servants to take care of that. But shush, I'm being a genius. Say "back later" again.'

I did as I was asked.

'Now say it with a Russian accent.'

I frowned, but complied.

'What did that sound like?' she asked.

'It sounded like a Welsh woman saying "back later" in a Russian accent,' I said.

'It did. But it also sounded like "*proklyatye*". Or, rather, a Russian saying "*proklyatye*" might sound like "back later" to a sleepy American girl with no knowledge of Russian.'

'Oh, you clever old stick,' I said. 'Because "*proklyatye!*" means—'

'"Damn!"' she said. 'Now imagine a new situation: a Russian is trying to pick the lock on Dr Goddard's hotel room door. One of his tools breaks – Eleanora said she heard a snap – and he curses in Russian.'

'Eleanora dozes off to sleep and doesn't hear the Russian's successful attempt to open the door,' I said. 'So Kusnetsov stole the strongbox?'

'I have no idea, but it's a starting point, at least.'

'If he did, he might also know where Goddard is.'

'We need to get a move on before he vanishes.'

Afternoon tea was served in the hotel dining room promptly at four. The silently gliding waiter brought finger sandwiches, scones, and delicious miniature cakes and pastries to the tables where the hotel's overseas guests consumed them with an air of indulgent condescension. Those funny English and their quaint ways.

As it turned out, there were only two overseas visitors present when we arrived: Herr Schneider and the Japanese military man, Mr Takahashi. They occupied separate tables and were studiously ignoring each other. Herr Schneider glowered at us briefly, earning him a cheery wave from Lady Hardcastle, then returned his attention to his scones.

We chose a vacant table near the door and gave the waiter our request for a pot of Earl Grey and a quiet word with the hotel manager, Mr Hillier.

The tea and the first round of sandwiches arrived within minutes, but of the manager there was no sign.

'He was so eager for us to be involved this morning,' said Lady Hardcastle. 'I should have thought he'd be equally eager to hear our latest news.'

'To be fair to the poor chap, I imagine he has a large number of other things to be getting on with. Hotels don't run themselves.'

'I suppose not, but I'm itching to pass on the news now. We might not have found Dr Goddard, but we've a good idea that Kusnetsov has the strongbox. He ought to be champing at the bit for news like that.'

'Did I hear someone taking my name in vain?' asked a Russian-accented voice from the doorway.

'Ah, Mr Kusnetsov,' said Lady Hardcastle. 'We were, indeed, just talking about you. Would you care to join us for tea?'

'You have the advantage of me, Mrs . . . ?'

'I do beg your pardon,' she said. 'I am Lady Hardcastle and this is my friend and associate, Florence Armstrong.'

'How do you do?' he said. He sat in one of the vacant chairs at our table. He seemed glad of the rest – he had the windswept appearance of one who had been recently braving the seafront.

'We were just musing on the fact that there are so many visitors from overseas here. Dr Goddard pointed you out to us last night.'

'Ah, yes,' said Kusnetsov. 'I remember seeing you in the salon. I had hoped it was empty so that I could smoke a cigar without disturbing anyone. I know that some ladies do not approve of the smell of cigars.'

'You're very thoughtful, Mr Kusnetsov. Thank you. But we should have welcomed your company. It's always a pleasure to meet people from distant lands.'

'Now you are the one who is being thoughtful,' he said. 'But regretfully I had important matters to attend to.'

'At a quarter past ten at night?'

He frowned. 'Yes,' he said after the briefest of pauses. 'I have business interests in St Petersburg and I needed to . . . send cables.'

'I see. Well, we shall have to have a drink some other time. Although possibly without Dr Goddard. Have you heard about poor Dr Goddard? Terrible business. Simply terrible.'

'I heard only that he has not been seen. Has something happened to him?'

'His room has been ransacked and he has vanished,' she said. 'His strongbox has been stolen.'

'This is indeed terrible news,' said Kusnetsov.

'Do you know Dr Goddard?'

'Not well,' he said. 'We have exchanged greetings but I could not really say that I knew him.'

'I'm sure it's nothing. He seemed a bit of an eccentric fellow. He's probably gone out for a walk and forgotten the time. You know how scientists can get.'

'Eccentric,' he said with a smile. 'Yes, I like that word. He is an eccentric fellow.'

'He'll be back later, I'm sure,' she said. 'And what about you? Has your business been keeping you busy today?'

'It has, as a matter of fact. I am required in St Petersburg urgently so I have been making arrangements to travel.'

'Oh, so we shan't see you again, after all. What a shame.'

'It is a shame, indeed. Although I shall probably not be leaving until tomorrow. I am awaiting a telephone call from London to confirm my booking.'

As though he had been waiting for this cue, the waiter reappeared, bearing a three-tiered cake stand. He nodded to us as he put it down.

'Mr Kusnetsov,' he said. 'There is a telephone call for you at reception, if you would care to follow me.'

Kusnetsov rose and bowed. 'Thank you for your company, ladies, but I fear my business claims me. Perhaps we shall meet again this evening.'

He followed the waiter out into the corridor.

'When it's ten o'clock here . . .' I began.

'It's one in the morning in St Petersburg,' said Lady Hardcastle. 'Yes, I know. Sending cables, my eye. He wasn't being considerate about smoking alone, he was making sure Goddard was out of his room. We really need to speak to Hillier – master key or not, I want a third-party witness when we find that strongbox.'

'He's not going anywhere until tomorrow,' I said. 'We've plenty of time. Have one of these macarons – they're delicious.'

It wasn't long before Messrs Schneider and Takahashi left, and we found ourselves alone in the dining room. Soon after that, when the entertainment possibilities of a pot of Earl Grey had been completely exhausted, we chose to retire to the salon.

The salon's regular waiter appeared and offered us further refreshment but neither of us could fit anything else in. He left us to relax, having first pointed out the location of the electric bell should we change our minds.

'I don't know about you,' said Lady Hardcastle when he had gone, 'but I need to have a word with Mrs Jones. I'll be back presently.'

I took the opportunity to examine the bookshelf beside the fireplace. It had been thoughtfully stocked with a broad selection from worthy classics to popular novels. The latest editions of *The Times* and the *Weston Mercury* sat in an elegant brass newspaper stand to the other side of the fire. I was about to pick up a book intriguingly entitled *The Adventure of the Missing Scientist* when Lady Hardcastle returned.

'Looking for a book to read, eh?' she said. 'Is my company no longer good enough?'

'You were attending to certain matters,' I said, returning to my seat. 'So I was looking around. I don't cease to exist just because you're not here, you know.'

'It's funny, isn't it? We all do that, don't we? We all find it difficult to imagine that other people get on with their lives when we leave the room. The only Flo I know is the Flo that exists in my company. I have no knowledge of the other Flo, the independent Flo who goes about her business, examining bookshelves, buttoning her boots, picking lint from her dress. You have conversations with people, but I can't imagine them. She's a different woman, this other Flo.'

'I almost always tell you what I've been up to,' I said. 'It's usually at your bidding, after all.'

'You do, and it so often is,' she said. 'And yet I still think of those adventures as having happened to a different entity. The Flo telling her tales of derring-do seems to me to be a different woman to the Flo doing the daringness. I'm not alone in these ponderings – the question of existence and perception is centuries old.'

'I'm sure you're not,' I said. 'But I confess I've never pondered them myself.'

'I bet you will now,' she said with a grin.

'Every time,' I agreed. 'I shall think, "Has Lady Hardcastle ceased to exist now that I can't see her? And if she doesn't exist, then who keeps tearing her clothes? If she falls over a pile of her junk in the orangery and no one is there to hear her, does she make a sound?" You've added a metaphysical dimension to my day.'

'Then my living has not been in vain. Look out – here comes trouble.'

The salon waiter had arrived bearing a silver tray upon which sat a telegram envelope proclaiming itself to be 'On His Majesty's Service'.

'A telegram for you, my lady,' said the waiter. 'The boy didn't wait for a reply.'

Lady Hardcastle took the envelope. 'Thank you,' she said. 'I feel dreadfully rude – I've never asked you your name.'

'Ribble, my lady,' he said. 'Albert Ribble.'

'Then thank you, Ribble. You're most kind.' During this exchange she had reached into her purse for a few coins, which she passed to him with a smile.

'Thank you, my lady. Ring if you need anything further.'

'I shall,' she said.

He evaporated.

'I wonder who this can be from,' she said.

'There's one sure way to find out,' I replied.

'There is, but I enjoy the anticipation. And the speculation. An opened telegram is a mundane thing, but an unopened telegram represents an infinity of possibilities.'

'I'm inclined to think that it's from your brother,' I said. 'You sent him a wire earlier today – this is most likely his reply.'

'I thought you Celtic types were supposed to be more romantic than that. It's we English who are stodgy and pragmatic.'

'Very well, then. I think it's notification from the Royal Society that a unicorn has been discovered on the plains of Patagonia and that it has been named Emilia Hardcastliensis in your honour. You are being invited to ride it in next year's Grand National in the new king's colours. But it's from your brother. I'd bet on it.'

'A guinea?'

'If you want to lose your money, that's up to you,' I said. 'Why not make it a fiver?'

She opened the envelope.

'Will you take a cheque?' she said.

'Cash only,' I said. 'If I can't slap it down on the bar at the Dog and Duck and treat the whole place to drinks with it, it's no use to me. What does he say?'

'"What ho, sis," is what he says. The man's a respected civil servant writing from the Foreign Office. "What ho", indeed. I mean, really.'

'He says other things?'

'Oh my word, he certainly does. And none of them much more impressive than "What ho, sis". I am firmly instructed not to get involved in anything regarding the disappearance of Dr Goddard – he's an eccentric gentleman who has probably wandered off on his own, apparently. Nor am I to do anything about his strongbox. It is a matter of national security – I mean, really, a man who says "What ho, sis" goes on to bandy about the phrase "national security" as though anyone will take him seriously. Anyway, the whole thing is a matter of "national security" and will be taken care of by the proper authorities.'

'Does he give any details?' I asked.

'No, but he has given me a telephone number and strict instructions to call it at once – before speaking to anyone else – if anything further happens. Oh, and Lavinia sends her love. As though that will make me take any notice of him.'

'So you won't?'

'Won't what, dear?'

'Take any notice of him.'

'Good heavens, no,' she said. 'I was trusted with "matters of national security" while he was still making tea for the mandarins in Whitehall. We shall press on regardless. I've done my bit by telling him what we're up to. We shall just have to solve the mystery and hand him the solution on a silver platter. With brass knobs on. That he can put in his pipe and smoke. Insufferable little tick. He was like this when we were young, you know. Always trying to boss me about.'

In truth, I couldn't imagine anyone successfully managing to boss her about, but I decided not to say anything. Her dander was up.

Thankfully, Mr Hillier arrived before she could launch into another display of indignation.

'Ah, Lady Hardcastle,' he said. 'I got your message. I'm so terribly sorry I couldn't come to you sooner – we've had something of a palaver over a meat order and I've been trying to arrange for . . . Well, never mind all that. How may I help you?'

'We have reason to suspect that the Russian, Mr Kusnetsov, is responsible for the theft of Dr Goddard's strongbox. He may also be involved in the disappearance of the man himself, but we have no evidence for that. We should like to confront him, and we should like you to stand as witness – it's your hotel, after all.'

'Good heavens,' he said. 'Really? He seemed like such a pleasant fellow. I can hardly . . . Well, if you say so. Is he in his room?'

'We don't know, but that's a good place to start. Shall we?'

She stood, and I did the same.

'Yes, of course,' said Mr Hillier. 'Follow me.'

We followed him through reception and up the main staircase. From the mezzanine landing we could look down into the hall, where we saw Herr Schneider waiting at the reception desk.

'How do you find Herr Schneider?' asked Lady Hardcastle as we began to mount the stairs to the first floor.

'Professional discretion prevents me from passing judgement on hotel guests, Lady Hardcastle,' said Mr Hillier. 'I'm sure you understand.'

'One should have thought that the professional code of the hotel manager also extended to protecting guests from theft and abduction. And yet here we are, with Armstrong and me giving up our own holiday to dig you out of the results of that particular dereliction of duty—'

'Now look here,' he interrupted. 'I—'

'Yes, yes, I know,' she said before he could go on. 'You take your duties very seriously, no one could have predicted that someone would rob and kidnap Dr Goddard, your hotel is run to the highest standards, and you're terribly grateful for our assistance. We shall take all that as read. But let's also be clear on this: Armstrong and I are helping you out of nothing more – when one gets right down to it – than the goodness of our hearts. We can, and shall, withdraw that help at any time and hand the matter over to the police if you make things awkward for us out of a misguided sense of proprietorial pride. With that in mind, what do you make of Herr Schneider?'

'He's a rude, arrogant fop,' said Mr Hillier after the briefest of pauses. 'He is a condescending, demanding bully who treats my staff as though they are the dirt on the soles of his oh-so-shiny boots. And he's mean with tips.'

'There,' she said. 'That's better out than in, isn't it? Your opinion of him confirms my own first impressions. We encountered him on the promenade and he displayed all those characteristics. I freely allow that I might have deliberately goaded him into displaying the worst of himself, but curiosity got the better of me. It turned out that I didn't have to push him terribly far for him to behave like an absolute oaf.'

Mr Hillier was still sulking after his scolding and could only manage a surly nod in reply.

We were on our way up to the first floor now and we could hear conversation coming from above us. Two young women were talking.

''Ere,' said one. 'Your Sam works down at the golf course, don't 'e?'

'Trainin' to be a greenman, he is. He loves it,' said the other.

''Swhat I thought. Our ma reckons she's seen lights up the old fort down at Brean. Your Sam said anythin' about it?'

'Not to me. What sort of lights?'

'Oh, she reckons someone's campin' up there. Keeps goin' on about tramps. Reckons we's gonna be overrun with 'em if they moves in. "There'll be a city of tramps up that old fort on Brean Down," she says. "Then they'll be marchin' into town, thievin' and murderin'. You mark my words." So I said you might know what was goin' on up there.'

'Well, Sam a'n't said nothin'. I'll ask, mind. I don't like the sound of an army of tramps.'

The voices stopped as we reached the head of the stairs. Two chambermaids who had, I surmised, been seeing to our rooms pressed themselves against the wall to allow us to pass.

'Thank you, girls,' said Mr Hillier and carried on past. Lady Hardcastle, though, stopped.

'Good afternoon,' she said to the two young women. 'I'm Lady Hardcastle from room four. Or is it five? I can't for the life of me remember which is which. What's your room number, Flo, dear?'

'Five,' I said.

'There,' she said. 'I was right first time. Are you two the ones who are taking care of us?'

'We are, ma'am,' said the taller of the two. 'May and June, we are.'

Lady Hardcastle appeared momentarily puzzled.

'They's our names,' said the girl. 'We works so well together on account of how we's May and June. It was fated, like.'

'Oh, how delightful. It's a pleasure to meet you, May and June. Thank you for taking such good care of us. If we bump into April, we'll send her your way.'

We set off up the next flight of stairs to the second floor.

We passed the Wilsons' rooms and were finally heading towards the corridor at the rear of the hotel where Mr Kusnetsov was staying.

'This is his room,' said Mr Hillier as we reached it.

'Thank you,' said Lady Hardcastle. 'We called on him earlier, actually.'

She knocked smartly on the door.

There was no reply.

Mr Hillier put his hand in his pocket, presumably to retrieve his master key, but Lady Hardcastle was already turning the door handle.

The damage to the door frame revealed that the lock had been forced. The door swung open.

Chapter Six

Inside Kusnetsov's room was another scene of chaos. Drawers were emptied, furniture upended, with clothes, bed linen and toiletries scattered everywhere.

Mr Hillier made to enter the room, but Lady Hardcastle held him back.

'What do you make of it, Armstrong?' she said.

'It's been searched, but only after a struggle,' I said.

'Not merely a hurried search, then?' she asked.

'It was hurried, certainly – the level of chaos suggests haste. It was methodical, too – everything has been investigated. But the position of the furniture, the way it has fallen over, is more indicative of a fight.'

'I agree,' she said. 'In you go then, dear. Let's not mess things up too much by having us all traipsing about in there.'

I stepped into the room and looked about. There was little to see on this side of the bed that I hadn't already seen from the doorway. I crossed the room, stepping carefully between the randomly scattered piles of Mr Kusnetsov's possessions. I noticed an unlabelled bottle of what appeared to be his home-made Macassar oil.

On the other side of the bed, I found the owner of the hair oil.

'Kusnetsov is here, my lady,' I said.

I knelt to examine him. I could feel no pulse and there was a thin, red line around his neck.

'Dead,' I said. 'Garrotted by the look of it.' I took another look at the violent disorder of the room. 'He put up a fight, but his attacker got the better of him.'

I checked through his pockets. They were empty.

'Can you see the strongbox?' asked Lady Hardcastle.

I cast around again, looking under the bed and poking at the piles of clothing.

'Not immediately,' I said. 'It would take a more thorough search to be certain, but I'd say that if it ever had been here, it's almost certainly gone now. Someone was definitely looking for something and I can't believe they missed it.'

'This is horrifying!' said Mr Hillier. 'Shocking beyond words. There's nothing for it now. We have one man dead, and another missing. I must call the police, no matter what the owners say.'

'Are you still willing for us to be . . . how shall we say . . . "consultants" on this case?' asked Lady Hardcastle.

'Yes,' he said. 'Of course. But a man has been murdered! I have to tell the police. It's the law. My desire to protect the reputation of the hotel doesn't extend to actually breaking the law.'

'You recall that I insisted on sending a telegram as a condition of our involvement in the case?'

'I do. A confidential telegram, you said.'

'I did say that. The telegram was to my brother, a senior official at the Foreign Office. With Dr Goddard being employed by the government, and with so many foreign nationals staying at the hotel, I wanted to make sure that we weren't treading on any toes by being involved. My brother has given me a telephone number to call immediately should anything else happen that I think he should know about. I should say that this' – she indicated the chaos of Kusnetsov's bedroom – 'falls within the category of "Things He Should Know About". I suggest we make that telephone call before we contact the local police.'

Mr Hillier thought for a while. He seemed like the sort of man who was used to giving the orders, and I got the feeling that he was far from comfortable with the idea of having anyone else – much less a woman – take charge. Whatever sort of man he was, though, it was obvious that he was most certainly not a stupid one. I hoped that he could see the sense of Lady Hardcastle's suggestion and might possibly also see a glimmer of hope that the local police might not have to be involved at all if this unknown man from the Foreign Office could smooth things over. It made no difference to me one way or the other, but I was rather enjoying the investigation and I knew that if the rozzers became involved, our involvement would be over.

'That would be acceptable,' he said at length.

'Thank you, Mr Hillier,' said Lady Hardcastle. 'Would you be able to spare a vigorous young man to stand sentinel and ensure that no one gets into this room? Vincent Fear might do the job. He's a bright enough lad. He looks like a strong gust of wind might knock him over, but the wiry ones can be surprisingly handy in a punch-up. I'm sure he can look after himself.'

'He's a boxer, actually,' said Mr Hillier. 'I'll send him up. We can make the telephone call from my office.'

Downstairs in Mr Hillier's office, we were waiting for the operator to connect Lady Hardcastle's call. We had expected to wait some time for a trunk call to be connected but, unusually, the operator had asked her to hold the line, having implied that the connection would be made immediately.

Mr Hillier, meanwhile, was having second thoughts about the whole plan.

'Are you certain this is the right thing to do?' he said.

Lady Hardcastle had her back to him and said nothing, though she did roll her eyes at me.

'Lady Hardcastle's contact at the Foreign Office will be able to put your mind at rest, I'm sure,' I said. 'We have a certain amount of experience with matters like this.'

'With dead bodies in hotel rooms?' He seemed more than a little shocked.

'Dead bodies in all sorts of places,' I said. 'One or two of them were our fault. But we really do know how to handle things for the best.'

'Your fault?' His voice was rising in pitch – he definitely wasn't the 'calm in a crisis' sort.

'One or two of them,' I said. 'There was one time in Antwerp when—'

Lady Hardcastle held up her hand for silence.

'Yes, that's right,' she said, 'Featherstonhaugh, Harry Featherstonhaugh . . . The Foreign Office, yes . . . Yes, I do – it's twenty past six . . . Well, then, who *is* available to speak to me at this hour? . . . I see. And does he work with Mr Featherstonhaugh? . . . He's not really much use to me, then, now is he? . . . Yes, I'm sure he's a capital fellow, but unless he knows . . . Yes, I'll hold the line.' She put her hand over the mouthpiece. 'Why is it that duty officers are so often such utter dunderheads?' she said. '"Call this number," says Harry. "National security." "Utmost importance", and then the buffoon on the other end of the line—' She uncovered the telephone mouthpiece. 'Yes? . . . Is he, indeed? That's splendid, thank you.' She covered it again. 'He's found Harry. He's just connecting me.' And then uncovered it once more. 'Harry? It's Emily, dear . . . What? But the man *is* a buffoon . . . Well, you'll just have to apologize to him on my behalf. You told me to call you if anything happened . . . Well something has happened . . . A situation has developed . . . A situation, dear . . . With a Russian gentleman by the name of Sergei Kusnetsov . . . No, we've not lost him as well, we know exactly where he is – he's lying dead on the floor of his hotel room. Flo is certain he was garrotted . . . No, Goddard is still missing – we definitely suspect foul play now . . . As is the strongbox, yes – still no sign of that. What on earth is in it? . . . Well, it seems to be important. It's part of a game of pass-the-parcel and at least one man has died because of it . . . No, there's no sign of it. We were certain Kusnetsov had it, but he hasn't got it now . . . Don't take that tone with me. Looking after secret government strongboxes isn't my responsibility, as you pointed out yourself . . . You did tell us that, yes, but you didn't really expect us just to leave things alone . . . No . . . Righto . . . You'll send someone? . . . Verification? . . . Oh, I see. Most amusing. It was a mistake anyone would have made . . . Aunt Agatha and Grandmother, then . . . That's the intention, darling brother . . . Very well. Thank you, dear. Give our love to Lavinia.'

Mr Hillier was gesturing that he wished to speak to whoever was on the other end of the line.

'Oh, hold on, Harry, I've got Mr Valentine Hillier here, the hotel manager. He'd like to have a word.'

She handed the telephone earpiece to Mr Hillier, who began to seek reassurance that matters were in hand and that he was breaking no laws by not informing the local police and coroner.

'Harry's not pleased, then?' I said while we waited for Mr Hillier to finish.

'Harry's never pleased with me, you know that,' said Lady Hardcastle. 'He likes to play either the amiable buffoon or the bossy big brother whenever he's with me. Today he's a bossy big brother and he's terribly grumpy that I still seem to have a will of my own. But he's sending some chaps round to take care of the body later this evening – something about them coming from Bristol. I didn't know he had chaps in Bristol. He's taking care of informing coroners and what have you.'

By this time, Mr Hillier seemed to have had his doubts settled and his tone had become a good deal more bonhomous.

'Yes, indeed,' he said. 'We have a splendid links course here in Weston . . . I'm afraid I'm seldom asked, but I can certainly make enquiries to see if ladies can play . . . Yes, sir, of course. Thank you so much. Goodbye.'

He returned the earpiece to its hook.

'Your brother suggests that you might enjoy a round of golf, my lady,' he said. 'I can telephone the club in the morning if you should like me to.'

'Thank you, Mr Hillier, but there's no need. He told you I play?'

'He told me you play very well,' he said.

'Well, that was nice of him, at least. You know that he's just trying to keep me busy, don't you? He's not really interested in me enjoying my holiday – he wants to keep me away from his missing scientist.'

'And a dead Russian businessman,' said Mr Hillier forlornly. 'We don't usually have dead people staying at the hotel.'

'I imagine they'd be a good deal less trouble than living people,' she said. 'But we now have a fresh mystery. Or perhaps a fresh event in our existing mysteries. What say you, Armstrong?'

'I think our reasoning was sound,' I said. 'Kusnetsov was almost certainly the one who broke into Dr Goddard's room last night. It also seems more than likely that he stole the strongbox. Dr Goddard would have raised the alarm if his room had been ransacked while we were all out, but he might not have checked on the strongbox. It seems to follow that another party came along later last night and incapacitated Goddard before searching in vain for the now-missing strongbox. It had been easy enough for the maid to come across the box as she went about her business, so if it remained under the bed it would be just as obvious to the thief and there would be no need to turn the place upside down searching for it.'

'One of the maids knew of the box?' said Hillier.

'Yes,' I said. 'But she was very discreet. There's nothing to worry about there.'

'So far, so good,' said Lady Hardcastle. 'Kusnetsov was making arrangements for an urgent return to St Petersburg, presumably to carry his spoils back to his masters – I'd lay odds he's a government operative—'

'A spy?' said Hillier. 'Oh, my word.'

'A spy, yes,' said Lady Hardcastle. 'So he had what he wanted and there was no real reason to wreck the room and carry Dr Goddard off. It may have been a diversionary tactic, but it adds unnecessary complication to an otherwise straightforward operation.'

'Which means that someone else has Dr Goddard,' I said. 'Possibly the same person who killed Kusnetsov and took the strongbox from him.'

'Possibly,' she said slowly. 'Though by no means definitely. It could be a third person.'

'But you've just said you prefer not to add unnecessary complication,' I reminded her. 'Occam's Razor and all that: the explanation with the fewest assumptions is more likely to be correct.'

'It is,' she said. 'It is. It's just . . . it's all a bit . . . messy. I'm not at all sure I have a proper grasp on this one yet. It's still far too slippery. But there's nothing to be done until Harry's boys have picked up the corpse—'

'I say, would you mind using more decorous language,' interrupted Mr Hillier. 'We owe it to the poor fellow to treat his passing with some respect.'

I felt that he had owed it to the poor fellow to keep the hotel safe enough that he wouldn't have passed in the first place, but I kept my counsel.

'Of course,' said Lady Hardcastle. 'There's nothing to be done until Harry's men have collected Mr Kusnetsov's remains, so Armstrong and I will dine early while we wait. Please be kind enough to have someone inform us when the agents of the Crown turn up. We'll solve this one for you, Mr Hillier, and keep your hotel out of the newspapers.'

Without waiting for a response, she swept out of the office with me close behind her.

◆ ◆ ◆

It was a pity we didn't wait for Mr Hillier's response – he might have reminded us that dinner wasn't served for another half an hour. The dining room's glass-panelled doors were closed and we could see the dining room waiter busily setting the tables.

Lady Hardcastle looked crestfallen. 'We're early, aren't we?' she said.

She was talking to me, but glass-panelled doors offer little soundproofing. The waiter turned and smiled apologetically.

'Dinner is served from seven o'clock, my lady,' he said loudly and clearly. 'If you take a seat in the salon, my colleague will be happy to bring you an aperitif.'

She smiled and nodded. 'Thank you, we shall,' she said.

We took what had already become our usual seats and the waiter arrived with his customary promptness and stealth.

'A little something to wet your whistles and whet your appetites, ladies?'

'It's as though you read our minds,' said Lady Hardcastle.

'It's hardly a conjuring trick, my lady,' he said. 'More often than not, someone sitting in the salon is after a drink of some sort.'

'He's a card, isn't he?' she said to me. 'He must have trained at the same place as you. I'll be boring and have a gin and tonic, please.'

'And for me, please,' I said.

He vanished.

'I confess I've not taken Goddard's disappearance all that seriously up to now,' said Lady Hardcastle. 'He's a sweet man, but prone to a certain . . . absence. I genuinely had imagined him wandering the streets in his dressing gown trying to fathom out some abstruse problem, completely unaware of the passing of time or the consternation he might be causing. But now people are dying.'

'One person, certainly,' I said. 'And not of natural causes.'

'There's more than one malefactor at work here, isn't there? Occam's Razor be blowed.'

'I'm afraid I'm starting to think so. I agree with your earlier thought now – I make it a minimum of three.'

'One to take the strongbox,' she said. 'That'll be Kusnetsov. One to take Dr Goddard—'

'And stash him away somewhere,' I interrupted.

'True,' she said. 'That might take two. But we'll say it's one for now. Then there's one to steal the strongbox from Kusnetsov and garrotte him.'

'Actually, that might make it four – one to steal, one to kill.'

'Four? Where are all these people coming from?'

'If we're lucky, they'll all kill each other,' I said. 'The last one standing will have the strongbox and will lead us to Dr Goddard.'

'You suggested that as a method of detection once before. I'm not sure "last man standing" is an entirely ethical way of going about things. It would also be slightly more interesting to know who they all are before they kill each other.'

'I presume you're thinking along the same lines as I am,' I said. 'Everyone here is a spy.'

'Undoubtedly,' she said. 'It can't possibly be a coincidence that representatives of most of the world's more powerful nations just happen to be at the same hotel as a British scientist with a box full of secrets.'

'Most?' I said.

'Indeed,' she said. 'We're short at least one German.'

'Ah, of course,' I said. 'And an Italian.'

'It's still well beyond a coincidence, even without those two.'

Somehow our drinks had arrived, along with a plate of canapés.

'Did you . . . ?' I asked.

'Not a glimpse. I told you – waiters have magical powers.'

I looked up to see Mr Takahashi hovering in the doorway. I wondered how much he had overheard.

Lady Hardcastle beckoned him in. 'Mr Takahashi, isn't it?' she said genially. 'We haven't been introduced but if we can take a holiday then formality can take one, too. Would you care to join us?'

He bowed deeply. 'Good evening,' he said in almost unaccented English. 'I do not wish to intrude.'

'Nonsense,' she said. 'I am Emily Hardcastle, this is Florence Armstrong, and this chair is vacant. Have a drink with us.'

He came in and sat stiffly on the indicated chair.

'Have I heard correctly?' he asked. 'Have the staff been calling you "Lady" Hardcastle?'

'Yes, that's right,' she said. 'My late husband was Sir Roderick Hardcastle. You're familiar with the English honours system?'

'I studied at Oxford,' he said. 'I met many titled Englishmen and the "system", as you term it, is no less complex than in my own country.'

'Of course – our feudal pasts cast long shadows. You returned to Japan after your studies?'

'I did. I spent some years in the Imperial Army, and then put my logistical knowledge to work on my country's railway system. But in the end my skills proved to be more diplomatic than military. I have been serving at the Japanese embassy in London for nearly five years now. Have you visited the Japan–Britain Exhibition? It is proving very popular.'

'We just missed it,' she said. 'We were last in London in April. We saw the posters.'

'It is running until the end of October,' he said. 'You should visit. My department was heavily involved. Do you have family in London?'

'I do,' she said. 'I managed to escape, but my brother and his wife are still there.'

He frowned. 'Escape? You find it unpleasant there?'

'Heavens no,' she said. 'But I do find life in the countryside much more convivial. Away from the hurly-burly.'

I could see Mr Takahashi mulling the term 'hurly-burly' and thought it particularly mischievous of Lady Hardcastle to try to get a Japanese man to say it. He was a step ahead of her, though.

'It is a chaotic and busy place,' he said. 'Tokyo is much the same. I, too, prefer my family's estates in the hills. It is tranquil there.'

Lady Hardcastle and I sipped our drinks in silence for a few moments.

'Are you alarmed by the events in the hotel?' he asked.

'Events?' she said. 'Oh, the fuss with Dr Goddard's room. It's a trifle, I'm sure. Just a chambermaid making a fuss over nothing.'

He looked at her curiously. 'I hope it is nothing serious. I like Dr Goddard. A very interesting man. He is working on a new railway locomotive design, you know.'

'Is he, indeed?' said Lady Hardcastle.

The dining room waiter appeared at the door and announced that dinner would be served in ten minutes. We began gathering ourselves for the journey next door. Mr Takahashi never did manage to get his drink.

We hadn't made the five yards along the corridor to the dining room before we were waylaid by the porter.

'Beggin' your pardon, m'lady, Miss Armstrong,' he said. 'Mr Nightengale sends his compliments and asks if you would be good enough to come to reception. Two gentlemen have arrived and are asking for you and Mr Hillier. They say you'll know what it's about.'

'Two gentlemen?' said Lady Hardcastle. 'How splendid. Come along, Armstrong, we mustn't keep two gentlemen waiting.'

We followed the porter back to reception where there were, indeed, two grey-suited men waiting by the front desk. They wore near-identical grey Homburg hats, near-identical waxed moustaches, and carried near-identical black leather gloves in their hands. Matching Balliol College medallions hung from near-identical Albert chains on their waistcoats and I was sure that there would be matching gold hunters at the other ends of the chains, ticking in unison and telling precisely the same time. I wondered if there was a factory somewhere stamping out Special Branch officers.

I guessed from the slight distortion of their jackets beneath the shoulders that they were carrying pistols in some sort of concealed holster, and that the one nearer the door – with his gun in his right armpit – was left-handed.

Over the years, Lady Hardcastle and I had developed a complex language of phrases, signs, and signals to communicate our observations and intentions in situations where being overheard and understood might be disadvantageous.

I discreetly tapped the back of her hand and said, 'I forgot to mention that the butcher sent word that he can get us some lamb shoulder if you fancy it.'

'Thank you, dear,' she said. 'I was hoping he might have one left.'

She had already spotted the potential weapons, it seemed, and was well aware of the left-hander.

'Ah, Lady Hardcastle,' said Mr Nightengale. 'These are Messrs Perch and Tench. You're expecting them, I understand.'

'We are,' she said. She looked towards the left-handed man. 'Aunt Agatha says that storks are remarkable birds,' she said.

He looked uncomfortable. 'Must we?'

'If you don't want Armstrong to drop you where you stand and beat your colleague insensible with your gun, yes.'

He sighed. 'Grandmother says they only land in bushes.'

I suppressed a smile.

'Satisfied?' said the man's right-handed companion.

'Oh, you have no idea, dear,' said Lady Hardcastle, making no attempt to hide her own broad smile.

'It's as well to make certain that we are who we say we are,' said Right-Hander. 'You've been fooled before.'

'More than once,' she said. 'And I'm sure I shall be again. But for now I'm happy that you really are emissaries of my darling brother.'

Mr Hillier, meanwhile, had arrived.

'Ah, Mr Hillier,' said Lady Hardcastle. 'These two gentlemen are Stickleback and Minnow of . . . actually I was going to say "of the Foreign Office", but they look awfully like Special Branch to me. My brother has kindly sent them to collect the package from room seven.'

'Ah, yes,' said Mr Hillier. He frowned. 'Stickleback and Minnow?'

'Code names,' said Lady Hardcastle, tapping the side of her nose. 'It's all very hugger-mugger down at Special Branch.'

'Oh,' said Hillier. 'I see. Well, there's a goods lift at the rear of the hotel. Do you have a vehicle, Mr . . . er . . . Mr Stickleback?'

'No,' said Left-Hander. 'We thought it would be all right to carry the "package" to the railway station on a handcart. We can pretend he's drunk. Of course we have a vehicle.'

Mr Hillier was plainly not used to dealing with men like these. 'Then perhaps you would care to bring it to the trades-man's entrance – that way we can at least maintain some semblance of discretion.'

'Mr Bream will see to it,' said Right-Hander. 'Off you go, Bream.'

'I thought I was Tench,' said Left-Hander.

Right-Hander sighed. 'Just get' – he rolled his eyes and shook his head – 'just get . . . "Pike" to move the bloody wagon,' he said. 'And bring in the bag.'

Left-Hander stalked sullenly out through the front door.

Right-Hander regarded Lady Hardcastle appraisingly. 'Mr Featherstonhaugh assured us that you were experienced in these matters,' he said. 'Quite the agent in your day, as he told it.'

'We had our moments, didn't we, Armstrong?'

'One or two,' I said.

'You don't really look the part, either of you.'

'Appearances can be deceptive, dear,' she said. 'Which is convenient when one thinks of it. We'd not have got far with "Look at me, I'm a spy" embroidered on my hat ribbon and "Agent of the Crown" tattooed on Armstrong's forearm, now, would we?'

'I do have "*Cymru am byth*" tattooed on my thigh, though,' I said. 'Memento of a drunken night in Budapest.'

115

'He also warned us that you might not take things quite as seriously as they warrant,' he said.

'My big brother has always had the measure of me,' she said. 'But I tend to view it entirely round the other way – I rather think that everyone else takes things much more seriously than they warrant.'

'You may be right,' he said with a trace of a smile. 'Ah, here comes Gudgeon with his bag. All set, Gudgeon?'

'Yes . . . Trout,' said the returning Special Branch man.

'Coarse fish, Gudgeon, coarse fish. Keep up,' said Lady Hardcastle. 'Trout are game fish. You could have gone for Carp. Or Dace, perhaps.'

This earned her a glare, but no rebuke. As the junior man, Left-Hander was wary of overstepping the mark with Lady Hardcastle, whom he obviously knew to be the boss's sister.

'Would you care to accompany us?' asked Right-Hander. 'I'm sure Mr . . . ?'

'Hillier,' said the hotel manager.

'Quite so. I'm sure Mr Hillier would prefer to oversee things. One can't imagine it's a hotelier's dream to have strangers tramping about the place removing packages and scuffing the paintwork.'

'You're certainly not going to "tramp about" my hotel, no,' said Mr Hillier.

'Then, come. Lead the way, sir.'

Mr Hillier set off towards the stairs with the two Special Branch men close behind. Lady Hardcastle and I followed.

'By all means come along, too, Lady H,' said Right-Hander over his shoulder. 'The more the merrier. We can make a party of it.'

We waited in the corridor while the two Special Branch men went into Mr Kusnetsov's room. Left-Hander went over to the far side of the bed while his colleague examined the rest of the room with a calm efficiency that spoke of years of detective experience.

Several minutes passed and Left-Hander was still struggling on the far side of the bed. He looked up when Right-Hander coughed.

'What?' said the left-handed man testily.

'Haven't you got him wrapped up yet? To be honest, old chap, I thought you'd have made much more progress by now. What have you been doing?'

'Instead of swanking about like the big I am and trying to impress the ladies, *old chap*, you could come in and give me a bloody hand. They sent two of us for a reason, you know.'

'Very well,' said Right-Hander with a sigh. He had been leaning against the door frame since completing his search and now he lazily pushed himself upright, crossed the room and crouched down beside Kusnetsov's body.

'Have you been through his pockets?' he said.

'Of course I bloody well have. They're empty.'

Right-Hander turned back to the doorway. 'Have you been through his pockets?' he asked me.

'Of course she has,' said Lady Hardcastle with a smile. 'I thought we'd established that we're not amateurs.'

'And . . . ?' he asked.

'They were empty then, too,' I said. 'Whoever killed him isn't an amateur, either.'

We watched the two Special Branch men struggle to get Kusnetsov's body into the large canvas bag they'd brought with them.

'Perhaps if you opened up the bag completely and then dragged him out into the middle of the room,' suggested Lady Hardcastle, 'you might be able to roll him on to the canvas and then strap it up around him. You'll never get anywhere trying to stuff him into it like that.'

'You see, Tench?' said Right-Hander. 'You're so useless you're being out-thought by a woman.'

'I think you meant to say *mere* woman, dear,' said Lady Hardcastle. 'If you're going to bully the man, you ought to do a thorough job. Don't spare my feelings.'

This time it was Right-Hander who glared at her while Left-Hander smirked. Nevertheless, they took her advice and soon had the large Russian securely strapped into a canvas bag for easy transport. It was still obvious to anyone who cared to look closely that the heavyweight bag held a heavyweight corpse, but it was slightly more discreet than a coffin.

They picked up the bag by the leather handles at each end, with Left-Hander taking the heavier head and torso. He led the way past us and off in the direction of the goods lift.

'Cheerio then, ladies,' said Right-Hander as he passed. 'Mr Hillier.' He inclined his head slightly towards the hotel manager. 'We'll leave you to tidy up.'

And with that they were gone. It was time for a more thorough search of the room.

Chapter Seven

'What happens now?' asked Mr Hillier. 'Are we in the clear?'

'In the clear, Mr Hillier?' said Lady Hardcastle.

'Well, I mean to say, now that those government fellows have the body, are our legal obligations discharged? Do we just carry on as though nothing has happened?'

'You're free to carry on entirely as you please, Mr Hillier,' she said. 'For my part I feel obliged to find out what's happened to Dr Goddard – there's every chance that he needs help. If I can also find out who was responsible for strangling Mr Kusnetsov, I'll count my week well spent, especially if the same miscreant is responsible.'

'But surely Special Branch is taking care of all that now,' persisted Mr Hillier.

'I'm certain my brother meant well, but if those two foppish fools are the best he can muster, I rather think we oughtn't to let things go just yet.'

'I see,' he said. 'Well, I can't really stand in your way, but I do need to get this room tidied and cleaned. The longer it stays in this state, the greater the number of people who might see it, and the more rumours will spread.'

'If you'll allow Armstrong and me an hour for a thorough search we can make sure that no evidence has been overlooked and then you can make it appear as though nothing went on here.'

He looked doubtful. 'I'd really prefer to get the place squared away as soon as possible,' he said.

'And I'd really prefer to have the chance to spend a quiet week by the seaside,' said Lady Hardcastle. 'But one doesn't always get one's preferences. We'll be swift and thorough, then the room is all yours. A pleasing side effect of our search is that we'll tidy as we go, so we'll be saving your staff quite some time and effort.'

While he contemplated this latest news, I contemplated the fact that I would be the one doing the tidying, Lady Hardcastle being more inclined towards chaos and disorder than tidiness. His deliberations didn't delay us for long.

'Very well,' he said at length. 'Please use your master key to lock up after yourselves and let Nightengale know when you've finished.'

I smiled apologetically and indicated the damaged door frame. 'We'll pull the door to,' I said. 'It's the best we can do.'

He shook his head and walked off.

'Come, then, tiny servant,' said Lady Hardcastle. 'Pull on your deerstalker, grasp your magnifying lens firmly in your hand, and let us minutely examine the scene of the crime. We can do as we promised and tidy as we search.'

'If I fetch a duster I can give the place a once-over as well,' I said.

'Why not? We might be able to persuade Mr Hillier to slip you a few bob if you do a good job. You start at the wardrobe and I'll start with the bedside table. We should be able to meet somewhere south of the foot of the bed.'

I began with the clothes scattered about the floor. As much as it irked me to be tidying up on my holiday, by far the easiest way of proceeding was to carefully examine every item, then fold it and put it in a pile. The linings of his jackets had been neatly sliced open with an extremely sharp knife, or perhaps his own razor, as had the hems and waistbands of his trousers. If there ever had been anything concealed within, it was gone now. The original search had ignored the few coppers in one of the trouser pockets and a set of engraved silver shirt studs that had been wrapped up in a discarded shirt. The motive was not petty theft.

With the clothes neatly sorted and folded, I moved on to the toiletries. The toothbrush was perfectly ordinary. The toothpaste tube contained nothing but toothpaste – something I learned by squeezing it all out into the washbasin. There was nothing in the shaving soap nor concealed in the silver handle of the badger-hair shaving brush. In fact, there was nothing of interest to be seen in any of the toiletries until I came to the leather case that had once contained all the grooming paraphernalia I had just painstakingly examined. It was of a fine-grain leather and, once filled, would be held closed by two buckled straps. Outwardly it was a case like any other, with leather loops to hold the hairbrush, the silver soap tin, the razor, the bottles of mysterious unguents, and the assorted whatnots and thingummies associated with keeping a travelling gentleman looking spruce and dapper.

But there was something not quite right about it. I sat on the floor and held it in my lap. There was plenty of light from the big window and I stared at the case for some while, willing it to give up its secret. What had I seen to make me think there was something worth looking at here?

'You've stopped moving, dear,' said Lady Hardcastle from the bed. 'Have you found something? Or do sponge bags make you melancholy?'

'There's something odd about this one,' I said. 'I'm letting my mind wander over it until it reveals itself to me . . . Oh. Stitching.'

'Something odd about the stitching?'

'Oddish,' I said, examining more closely the area that had caught my eye. 'This part here is of a different thread. It almost matches, but not quite – it's the same colour more or less, but slightly finer.'

The mismatched section was about four inches long across the top edge of the case and formed the seam where the outer cover was sewn to the lining. That's what it was supposed to look like, anyway. Upon closer inspection, though, it became clear that the stitching was for appearances only. The cover and the liner were both neatly stitched, but not to each other.

I tested the opening but there was some resistance. I wasn't surprised – there was little point in going to the trouble of creating a secret opening in the case if it was going to gape open and give the game away. I picked up Kusnetsov's nail scissors from the floor where the burglar had dropped them and used them to pry the two sides apart. They weren't tacked or glued and I remained baffled as to what might be stopping me from getting inside.

I felt along the inside of the fake seam and found that there was a length of spring steel on either side, like the bones of a corset but narrower. This gave me an idea and I squeezed the two ends of the opening together. The steel bent and the mouth of the secret compartment gaped open.

Lady Hardcastle had stopped what she was doing and was looking on. 'You clever old stick,' she said. 'Anything inside?'

Still holding the mouth open, I rootled around inside with my fingers. There was no cash, there were no diamonds, but there was what felt like a small piece of silk. I pulled it out, expecting to be disappointed – it was probably just a torn piece of the lining of the secret pocket.

It was a folded silk square. I opened it and found it to be about the size of a gentleman's pocket handkerchief but of much finer, thinner silk. It was off-white and printed with tiny text and diagrams.

'You joked about a magnifying lens,' I said. 'But do you actually have one?'

'I never travel without one,' said Lady Hardcastle, leaning over my shoulder.

'Please may I borrow it?'

'I never travel without it, but I don't always carry it with me. It's in one of my bags in the room.'

I passed the silk to her. 'What do you make of this, then?'

She took it and examined it. 'It's covered in writing and dia-grams,' she said, and handed it back. 'But my eyesight is getting worse and worse so I can't say more than that. We need some sort of magnifying lens.'

'There's one in your room, apparently,' I said. 'Have you found anything?'

'Nothing of note,' she said. 'A copy of *Pride and Prejudice* in English, a bedside clock – the usual hotel room miscellany. Oh, and a little piece of glass. Green. A piece of a broken wine bottle, perhaps?'

She handed me the tiny, transparent green chip.

'Your eyesight is terrible,' I said. 'This is a gemstone. Or something that's supposed to look like one. It might be glass, but it's not a bit of broken bottle. Where was it?'

'Underneath the bedstead, behind one of the legs.'

'It could have been here for weeks,' I said. 'Even the best chambermaids can get a bit lackadaisical about sweeping round the backs of bed legs.'

'My thoughts exactly.' She looked around at the now-neat pile of clothes and travel items. 'Not much to show for a lost life, is it? One leaves so small a footprint.'

'A traveller does,' I said. 'If we were to pop our clogs now, the things in our rooms would leave quite a puzzle for people to solve. But they'd not tell even a tiny fraction of the story, would they?'

'You're getting very wise in your old age, Florence Armstrong. There's nothing else helpful here, is there?'

'Not as far as I can tell,' I said. 'I'd like a quick look behind the tallboy before we go, just in case. But I think we're done.'

'I'll give you a hand.'

Together we pulled the large chest of drawers away from the wall but found nothing other than a ball of dust. We agreed it was time to leave the room to Mr Hillier's chambermaids and to put Lady Hardcastle's magnifying lens to good use.

◆　◆　◆

Back in the room, Lady Hardcastle was rummaging through the top drawer of her own tallboy.

'Where did you put it?' she asked.

'The magnifying lens?' I said. 'I'm sorry, but I haven't seen it. I didn't pack it and I wasn't aware that you'd brought it with you.'

'I take it everywhere. The ladies in my family are blighted by the early onset of presbyopia. You knew that.'

'I did,' I said. 'But I thought it mostly involved forgetting where you put your lorgnettes. I didn't know you forgot where you put your magnifying lens, as well.'

'A lady has to maintain at least a little mystique. One doesn't mind growing older, but it's not without its inconveniences and some of them are arriving all too soon. I'm only forty-two, and here I am relying on the services of opticians and lens grinders just to read a newspaper.'

'You've been relying on the services of a lady's maid to get you up and dressed for years.'

'That's different. I've never been able to lace a corset – no one can do that – but I was once able to read unaided.'

'Ah, well,' I said. 'It comes to us all in the end.'

'Oh, I'm not grumbling,' she said. 'To tell the truth I'm rather looking forward to silver hair, wrinkles, and the opportunity to be unpardonably rude. We allow our elders much more leeway in that regard, don't you think? I shall cultivate an air of curmudgeonly cantankerousness and insult my way through society. You shall follow in my wake, apologizing. "I'm so sorry," you'll say. "She doesn't mean any offence, she's just getting on a bit – you know how they can be at that age." We'll have such larks.'

'So I don't get to be rude, too? I saw myself as one of those stern-faced old harridans making young housemaids' lives miserable for no readily discernible reason.'

'Oh no, dear, you're far too lovely for that. You'll be the kindly one. They'll be terrified of you because I'll spread rumours about you having once killed a man with a pen, but you'll be winsome and agreeable.'

'It was a mechanical pencil and he was trying to shoot you.'

'Nevertheless, they'll be adoring but wary. But none of this is helping me find the lens.'

'Is it in your handbag?'

'Why on earth would I have put it in there?'

'I'm never entirely certain why you do anything, I just thought it would be a good place to start. I packed all the other bags, but I seldom go near your handbag. You might have sneaked it into one of the other bags, but I'd have seen it when I unpacked.'

'Yes, but it's so large and cumbersome. Why the devil would I have put it . . . Oh, here it is.' It was in her handbag. 'Now then,' she said. 'Let's see what we can see.'

I handed her the square of silk and she spread it on the writing table where we could both get a good look at it. There was plenty of daylight coming through the window, and we were both able to make use of the lens – it really was quite a size.

The larger of the diagrams turned out to be a sketch map of Weston-super-Mare. There was a cross marking a spot a short way along the prom.

'A meeting place?' suggested Lady Hardcastle.

'Somewhere where messages might be left?' I said.

'It could just be an indication of the best place to get half a pint of cockles and see a Punch and Judy show. We're assuming it's a bit of spy gubbins, but it could just as easily be a tourist guide.'

'A confidential tourist guide that needs to be hidden in a secret compartment in a sponge bag?'

'It's a cutthroat industry. I heard that Thomas Cook once bludgeoned a member of staff insensible for revealing details of their camel-hire arrangements in Cairo to a competitor.'

I shook my head. 'No,' I said. 'No, you didn't.'

'Oh, here we go,' she said. 'These are instructions for secure communication, I think. And this section here' – she pointed to a block of Cyrillic text – 'is a description of Dr Goddard. Oh, and it mentions the "plans for the new weapon". I think we can rule out tourist information.'

'And we have more of an idea of what was in Dr Goddard's strongbox.'

'We do seem to, don't we. Except we already knew he was a radio engineer – Miss Wilson told us that. And that he designed railway locomotives – Takahashi mentioned that. And now here we are with Kusnetsov's masters convinced that he had something to do with weapons.'

'A radio-based weapon mounted on a train?' I said.

'Well, quite,' she said. 'No one seems to know for sure what our Dr Goddard was up to, and everyone seems to have a different idea of what he was carrying. There's more to this than meets the eye.'

'Would it do any good to ask Harry?'

She laughed. 'None whatsoever. He's made it quite plain that he doesn't want us to be involved in this – he's certainly not going to give us any further information. We'll just have to puzzle it out ourselves.'

'Do you think he's got men looking for Dr Goddard?'

'I'm certain of it. But that needn't prevent us from trying to track him down ourselves. I'm sure we just need a nugget of information, something that will give us a toehold, a starting point.'

'The strongbox is probably still here at the hotel,' I said. 'If we can get our hands on that, perhaps we can get closer to the truth of what Dr Goddard was up to. And if we know that, then perhaps we'll have a better idea of what happened to him.'

'As always, Flo, dear, you're quite right. And we won't find out anything further up here – let's get to where our double-dealing fellow guests are most likely to be congregating.'

'We can eat, too,' I said. 'I'm starving.'

◆ ◆ ◆

We arrived at the dining room to find our way politely but firmly blocked by the waiter.

'I'm most terribly sorry, Lady Hardcastle, Miss Armstrong,' he said. 'There was a slight mishap in the kitchens and service is delayed. We're asking guests to wait in the salon where complimentary cocktails are being served.'

'Oh, you poor things,' said Lady Hardcastle. 'We were invited to take our seats just before seven but we were called away. And here you are still trying to keep a roomful of guests amused more than an hour and a half later. We promise not to cause you too much more trouble.'

'Thank you, my lady,' he said with a grateful smile. 'Some are taking it better than others.'

'I can well imagine which ones are making a fuss. We'll do our best to quell the rebellion.'

She led the way to the salon, where the conversation was quiet and calm. It really didn't feel as though there were any impending rebellion to quell.

Lady Hardcastle leaned in close. 'I must say I imagined we'd be no more than a gin and tonic away from open revolt,' she whispered. 'But this all looks rather civilized.'

To the left of the double doors, Adelia Wilson and her niece were deep in conversation. To the right, Mr Takahashi and Herr Schneider were engaged in a heated discussion. I caught the word 'Manchuria' – perhaps the two men had found common cause in their mistrust of Russia and were discussing the recent Russo-Japanese war.

Jean Martin, the bear-like French engineer, sat alone. He was the only one of them we hadn't yet spoken to and Lady Hardcastle made a beeline for him.

'Good evening, Monsieur Martin,' she said. 'We've not been properly introduced but as I've already said to at least one other person, formality can take a few days' holiday. Lady Hardcastle.' She held out her gloved hand, which he enveloped in a meaty paw. 'And this is Miss Armstrong. May we join you?'

He had stood as we approached and now nodded his assent. He indicated the two empty chairs and resumed his own. The salon waiter appeared.

'Ah, there you are, Ribble,' said Lady Hardcastle. 'Gin and tonic for me, please.'

'Certainly, my lady. And for Miss Armstrong?'

'A glass of champagne, please,' I said.

'Oh, I say, what a splendid idea,' said Lady Hardcastle. 'Cancel my gin – I'll have what she's having. Would you care to join us, Monsieur Martin? Of course you would – what Frenchman wouldn't? Just bring a bottle, Ribble, dear.'

'I'm afraid I've only been instructed to serve complimentary cocktails, my lady,' said the waiter. 'I'm not certain the offer extends to champagne.'

'Tell Mr Hillier it's for me,' she said. 'I'm sure he'll stretch the point for us. We're old pals now.' She winked and the waiter disappeared.

'So, tell me, Monsieur Martin,' she said, 'how are you enjoying Weston-super-Mare?'

'It is very . . . English,' he said. 'Of course we have our seaside resorts in France, but I have never seen one like this. I find it . . . charming.'

'The English at play. You're from Nantes, I believe?'

'I am. How did you . . . ?'

'Oh, it's another thing we English love to do – we gossip. Dr Goddard told us on our first evening here. He gave us full details on all the runners and riders.'

'The runners and . . . ?'

'Riders,' she said. 'Horse-racing term. We use it to mean "all the people involved in a thing".'

'Ah, yes. Of course. Yes, I am from Nantes. Do you know it?'

'I'm not sure. Do we know it, Armstrong?'

'It's on the Loire,' I said. 'It's the one with the island in the middle of the river.'

'Of course it is. Weren't we there for . . . umm . . . something to do with—?'

I widened my eyes, warning her not to complete her thought. We had been there to try to find the identity of an Austro-Hungarian agent who had somehow managed to steal plans from one of the shipyards, but that wasn't the sort of thing we ought to be revealing in what we now knew to be a roomful of active agents. We would do better to maintain the fiction that she was just a batty upper-class Englishwoman on holiday with her pal.

'—the cathedral, yes,' I said.

'The cathedral,' she said. 'Of course. Beautiful, Gothic thing in the middle of town.'

This was vague enough to apply to any number of European cathedrals, but it happened that she was right. I nodded. 'Yes,' I said. 'St Peter and St Paul.'

'You have travelled much?' asked Martin.

'Hither, thither, and to some extent yon,' said Lady Hardcastle.

Martin frowned.

'Yes,' she said with a smile. 'Yes, we have. Less lately, but we've seen much of Europe, haven't we, Armstrong?'

'We have,' I said.

'Many cathedrals,' said Martin.

'Many,' said Lady Hardcastle. 'Do you travel much?'

'For my work,' he said. 'I am an engineer.'

'I'm afraid we already knew that,' she said. 'The gossip, you know. You work in Nantes, so perhaps you build ships?'

'I do. You know more about my city than you pretend, I think. We have some of France's more important shipyards.'

'I confess I guessed that one. Once Armstrong reminded me that it was on the Loire I just put two and two together.'

'You English have a . . . a fondness for shipbuilding, I think. Dr Goddard is very interested in our shipyards.'

'Have you heard from him at all?'

'He is missing, I understand,' said Martin. 'I have not seen him since he joined you at your table at dinner last night, but I have been out all day on an . . . excursion? An excursion, yes. To the Cheddar Gorge. The caves are very interesting. I hope nothing has happened to Dr Goddard. I enjoy his company.'

'You spent time with him?' I asked.

'As I said, he was interested in shipyards. It was his line of work, I think?' He inflected this as a question, seeking confirmation.

'I'm afraid I have no idea,' I said. 'We spoke about Offenbach and the hotel guests. We never found out what he did for a living.'

'Ah, Offenbach,' said Martin. 'Another of our great French composers. You saw *Orphée aux enfers*, then?'

'We did,' I said. 'A rather competent production for a seaside concert hall.'

'I missed it,' he said. 'A pity.'

At this moment, the waiter arrived with a bottle of champagne, three glasses, and an apologetic expression.

'Your champagne, my lady,' he said.

'You look distressed, Ribble,' said Lady Hardcastle. 'Have you come to tell me that the champagne will appear on my bill after all?'

'No, my lady,' he said. 'Nothing like that. Mr Hillier is most insistent that you should have anything you require. My disappointment has another source. I do like to see our guests getting along and making new friendships, but I'm sorry to say that I have to drag Mon-sewer Martin away from you. There is a telephone call for you at the reception desk, sir.'

'Ah, *merci*,' said Martin as he stood. 'You will forgive me, ladies? I must take my leave.'

'Go, Monsieur Martin, your caller awaits. It has been a pleasure to meet you.'

'And you, madame. Mademoiselle.' He bowed and left.

As the salon waiter expertly uncorked the bottle and poured the champagne, his dining room colleague appeared at the door.

'Ladies and gentlemen,' he announced. 'Chef apologizes for the long delay, but order has been restored to the kitchen. If you would care to take your seats in the dining room, dinner will be served very soon.'

'How splendid,' said Lady Hardcastle. 'Would you be an absolute poppet and bring the champagne through, please, Ribble?'

'Of course, my lady,' he said with a smile.

'Oh, and I've been meaning to ask: what's your colleague's name?'

'In the dining room?'

'Yes.'

'Kibble, my lady.'

Lady Hardcastle goggled. 'You're having me on,' she said.

'Would that I were, my lady, would that I were. Ribble and Kibble of the Steep Holm View. We should do a comedy turn at the hoteliers' Christmas Ball. A crosstalk act, perhaps. It would go down a storm.'

'How absolutely marvellous,' she said with a happy laugh. 'I say, Armstrong, you should—'

'Nothing rhymes with Hardcastle,' I said. 'And I'm not changing my name anyway. We've been through this before when you wanted me to be Florence Lawrence. It's never going to happen.'

'Spoilsport.'

By this time the other diners had already returned next door. We followed.

We found the Misses Wilson in the corridor, apparently waiting for us.

'Lady Hardcastle?' said Adelia.

'Yes, Miss Wilson? What can I do for you?'

'My niece and I were wondering if you'd care to join us at dinner. It would be good for Eleanora to meet some real Englishwomen. We've come all this way and so far we've met only men, and just one of them has been English.'

'We'd be delighted,' said Lady Hardcastle. 'Well I would, at least. Armstrong?'

'Of course,' I said. 'I'd love to.'

'Bully,' said Adelia. 'We can take one of the larger tables at the back of the room.'

She set off at pace and we had no option but to trail along in her wake.

Kibble was already pushing her chair in by the time we'd navigated past the other tables and he rushed to help the three of us to sit. Ribble, meanwhile, was still with us, now equipped with an ice bucket on an ornate stand into which he placed the open bottle.

'We have champagne,' said Lady Hardcastle. 'Do you indulge?'

'I'll say,' said Adelia. 'Thank you.'

'And for you, Eleanora?'

The younger Wilson looked to her aunt for confirmation before nodding. 'Yes, please,' she said quietly. 'I've never had champagne before.'

'Two more glasses, then, please, Ribble.' She turned towards Eleanora. 'You'll love it,' she said. 'And if you don't, at least you'll get a giggle when the bubbles tickle your nose.'

The dining room waiter, Kibble, meanwhile, was still fussing with napkins and menus.

'Are you allowed to tell us what happened in the kitchens, Kibble?' asked Lady Hardcastle.

'I'm not entirely sure as I should, my lady,' he said. 'But seeing as it's you . . .' He leaned in conspiratorially. 'Chef is a Welshman, see? Fiery tempers, the Welsh. Coal dust in the blood, my wife always says – makes 'em very combustible. Anyway, he comes into the kitchen to check that everything is ready for service, and he finds that all the bread he made this morning has gone missing. And a ham. And about a pound of best Cheddar. We gets it from a dairy in Cheddar its very self. So obviously he blows his top, doesn't he. Turns the air blue with his cursing, then threatens to do his kitchen hands to death with a cleaver. They calmed him down and convinced him they'd not taken it, but then he sets off again because what were they all doing while someone else was in there pinching it?'

'I say. What a palaver,' said Lady Hardcastle. 'Do they have any idea what might have happened?'

'None at all. The only time there was no one in there was about six o'clock so they reckons it must have been then.'

'No one in the kitchens an hour before service?' said Lady Hardcastle. 'Isn't that a little unusual?'

'Chef likes to take them to the plate room and give them his Agincourt speech before battle commences. He says it focuses their minds, or some such.'

'So he was responsible for there being no one guarding the goods,' she said.

'I suppose he was at that,' said Kibble. 'Didn't stop him blaming everyone else, though.'

'It seldom does,' she said. 'No rolls with our soup this evening, then.'

'No soup, neither – it was to be pea and ham.'

Lady Hardcastle laughed.

'I still don't understand how that caused such a delay,' said Adelia. 'It's just a few missing ingredients, and not very important ones, either. A good chef could work around that, I'm sure.'

'He can and he has, ma'am,' said Kibble. 'But once he came back and found things missing, he stormed out of the kitchen and locked himself in his room in a fury. It took them much more than an hour to persuade him to come out.'

Adelia Wilson harrumphed. 'You should fire him. What is it you say over here? Give him the sack?'

'We can't do that, ma'am,' he said. 'He's fiery, but he's brilliant. And he's back in his kitchen now, so all's well that ends well.'

'Unless one wants pea and ham soup with bread,' she said.

'And did you, ma'am?'

'No, I can't abide pea and ham soup.'

'Very good, ma'am. I just need to attend to one of the gentlemen and then I'll be back for your order.'

In due course, more champagne glasses arrived and our orders were taken.

But I couldn't settle. I put my hand under the table and tapped the word 'kitchen' in Morse code on Lady Hardcastle's leg. I stood to leave.

'Would you excuse me, ladies?' I said. 'There's something I need to attend to. Please start without me.'

Calmly and unhurriedly, I left the dining room and headed for the staff door at the end of the corridor.

I found my way down the stairs and past the noticeboard. Once again I heard the sounds and smelled the smells of a working kitchen, but this time I pressed on to pursue them to their source. One of the key things to remember about being where you probably shouldn't, is to act as though you have every right to be there. It happened that Mr Hillier had given us carte blanche to go wherever we wished, but experience had taught me that not everyone agrees with their bosses on the subject of outsiders roaming about the place. Most especially not cooks, who are known to be fiercely territorial.

I pushed open the kitchen door and strode in as if I owned the place. A pot washer ignored me – scullery maids and their ilk are usually too timid or too uninterested to bother with interlopers. A sous-chef looked up from his work, took in my appearance, and then returned to his labours without a second glance.

A squat man dressed in white and wearing an absurdly tall toque rounded a workbench and blocked my path. He was no more than three or four inches taller than me, but he was at least twice as wide. His face was red and sweaty, his expression unfriendly.

'No guests in the kitchen,' he said brusquely.

'I'm working on Mr Hillier's behalf,' I said just as brusquely. 'I shan't be in your way, but I do need to check one or two things.'

'Mr Hillier can go to blazes,' he said, and launched into a tirade of Welsh invective which expressed his opinion of Mr Hillier and his managerial policies in the most colourful terms. It was very impressive to watch.

I waited until the storm had blown itself out and responded calmly in the same language. 'To be perfectly honest with you, I might feel the same if I had to work for him, but that's by the by. I'll not be long and I'll keep well out of the way, but I really must insist on taking a look round. I might be able to learn something about recent events in the hotel if I examine the back door and your storerooms.'

He frowned as though baffled. I wondered if he was unused to people not taking any notice of his temper tantrums. Eventually he said in English, 'Just keep out of the way. And don't touch my food.'

'Thank you,' I said. I carried on towards what I presumed were the stores and the outside door.

Having stood firm against their tempestuous gaffer, I attracted slightly more attention from the junior staff as I made my way past their benches. It ranged from the cautiously furtive glance of a girl mopping a spill from the floor, to the open-mouthed goggling of another sous-chef, whose inattention to his work caused him to burn his hand on a pan handle. But none of them said anything and I reached the stores without further obstruction.

To tell the truth, I wasn't entirely sure what I was looking for, but I was confident that I'd know it when I found it. I started with the back doors.

The double doors to the courtyard at the back of the hotel were painted white on the inside and, I soon learned, a rich, dark blue on the outside. The left-hand door was bolted top and bottom, but the bolts were well maintained and obviously in constant use – it would be opened often to allow the delivery of bulky provisions. The right-hand door was unlocked and opened easily.

I had been hoping it would be locked and would show signs of having been forced, but that would make things too easy. Whoever stole the food could simply have wandered in, pinched the bread, ham, and cheese, and wandered out again. I turned back towards the kitchen. My view was blocked but as I rounded the corner by the first storeroom door, I could see the second sous-chef's back as he toiled away at the stove. It was possible for a food thief to get into the kitchens unnoticed, but anyone working at that end would be able to see him as soon as he got as far as the stores. No one had seen anything, but we did know that the kitchen was empty at about six o'clock.

I returned to the door and opened it again, this time stepping out into the yard. The area was almost sparklingly clean and the only clutter was a small pile of empty crates stacked against the wall. I returned my attention to the door.

There were no signs that it had been damaged by someone trying to break in. It didn't even bear the marks of having been kicked in irritation. The lock plate showed the usual scratches of clumsy attempts to insert the key and I was about to give up and take a look at the storerooms instead when I noticed an additional mark. A scratch on the inside edge of the keyhole had exposed shiny, untarnished brass. It was by no means conclusive, but it very much looked to me like the sort of mark that might be left by a picklock. Its freshness meant that it had been made very recently. Even if the food thief had been able simply to walk in the door, this could well be how the kidnapper got in to take Dr Goddard unseen from his room.

I cast my eye over the storerooms, but I could see nothing in there that might tell me anything useful. It was time to return to the dining room – I was starving hungry and I was keen to convey news of my discovery to Lady Hardcastle.

Chapter Eight

I found Lady Hardcastle and the Wilsons where I had left them, now deep in conversation.

'. . . but we only got as far as Edinburgh,' Lady Hardcastle was saying. 'We thought of taking a train into the Highlands, but there's so much to see and do in the capital that we never managed it. Ah, Flo, there you are. Is all well?'

'Tidy,' I said. I resumed my seat.

'Eleanora is a great admirer of Sir Walter Scott and would love to see the Highlands,' she said. 'They'd like recommendations for places to visit but I was explaining that we've never been further north than Edinburgh.'

As usual, she had put me in an awkward position. The truth was that we had once spent more than a week in northern Scotland trying to track down a German spy who was believed to have arrived in Inverness by boat from the North Sea. From Inverness we had visited Drumnadrochit on the shores of Loch Ness in response to news that a 'foreign-sounding gentleman' had been spotted nearby, and then headed east to Aviemore on another tip-off. We got as far as Aberdeen before the trail ran cold, but it was safe to say that we had well and truly visited the Highlands.

Among friends, or in the company of receptive strangers, my instinct would have been to tease her about her forgetfulness and make an oblique reference to our espionage exploits, but this wasn't at all the right audience for that. I had convinced myself that everyone in the hotel was a spy of some sort, and if the Wilsons didn't already know about our past I felt it was definitely to our advantage to keep it that way.

'It was a shame to be so close and not see the beauty of the landscape,' I said. 'But it's true – the delights of Edinburgh proved too much of a draw.'

'I shall see it one day,' said Eleanora. 'The craggy mountains, the wild heather. And the cattle with their adorable long coats. Were there men in kilts in Edinburgh?'

'Not as many as you'd hope,' said Lady Hardcastle. 'It's a rather more cosmopolitan city than a tourist might wish for. We saw some bandsmen from the castle walking along Prince's Street in ceremonial uniform one day, but that was our only encounter with kilts.'

'And the coos are terrifying,' I said.

'Coos?' said Eleanora.

'The Highland coos. Fearsome, shaggy beasts with horns that could skewer an armoured man.'

'You'll have to excuse Flo,' said Lady Hardcastle. 'She's not fond of cows.'

'I can't say that I am, either,' said Adelia.

'Oh,' I said. 'How so?'

'Well, now,' she said. 'I was engaged to be married to a man . . . oh, must be about twenty years ago now. He was kind and handsome, but Maryland wasn't big enough for him. He took a notion to move to Texas to raise cattle. Longhorns. I told him I wasn't going to be a rancher's wife, but he was set on it. He said, "Delia" – he always called me Delia. He said, "Delia, I'm going to Texas to raise cattle. You can come with me as my wife, or you can stay here. I know which I'd prefer, but it's up to you." I was raised in the East. We had money and influence. I wasn't going to dress in homespun and keep a rifle by the door in case of coyotes. So I stayed behind. Cattle have got a lot to answer for.'

'What became of him?' I asked.

'He's one of the richest men in Texas,' she said with a sigh.

'I had no idea cattle ranching was so profitable.'

'It can be, if you have land and herds big enough. And they say it took a man two days to ride from one side of his ranch to the other, so he definitely had the land. But that's not what made him rich. You've heard of the "Texas oil boom"? He discovered oil on his land in oh-three. But I've no regrets. Any man who could leave me for a cow – even a hundred cows – isn't worthy of my regret.'

'Hear hear,' said Lady Hardcastle. She raised her glass and she and Adelia clinked.

As is so often the way, we appeared to be on the verge of shutting the youngster out of the conversation, so I clumsily changed the subject to draw her back in.

'What else do you enjoy aside from the works of Sir Walter Scott?' I asked her.

'Oh, so many things,' she said. 'I love to paint. I love to shoot.'

'Do you, indeed?' I said. 'Lady Hardcastle is quite the markswoman.'

'Just target-shooting, mostly,' she said. 'The boys don't like to take girls hunting, and I'm not overly keen on tramping about in the backwoods anyway.'

'Can't say I blame you,' I said. 'What else?'

'Oh, few things give me as much pleasure as playing the piano.'

'A girl after your own heart,' I said to Lady Hardcastle.

'I'll say,' she said. 'There's a piano in the salon, you know. Would you play for us? I should love that.'

The younger woman looked down at her cutlery. 'I'm not good enough to play in front of people,' she mumbled.

'Pish and fiddlesticks,' said Lady Hardcastle. 'I'd wager none of these shambling oafs can play a note. We shall play a duet at the very next opportunity and astound them all.'

It didn't seem that Eleanora thought this was as generous an offer as Lady Hardcastle had intended, but she smiled politely. 'Do you play, Miss Armstrong?' she asked.

'Sadly no,' I said. 'I never had the opportunity to learn when I was young. Lady Hardcastle has been trying to teach me, but progress is slow. I do play an instrument from your own country, though.'

'Please tell me it's not the banjo,' said Adelia.

'I could,' I said, 'but it would be a lie.' I smiled.

'Heaven save us from the banjo,' she said.

'Aunt Adelia!' said Eleanora with an uncharacteristic sharpness. 'Don't be so rude. I love the banjo. Do you . . . ? Are you familiar with ragtime music, ma'am? I love it.'

'It happens that we know a couple of young ragtime musicians,' I said. 'We've played with them at the house.'

'Good lord,' said Adelia with a huge sigh.

I ignored her. 'There's a ragtime band playing in town at the end of the week. At the Arundel. Would you like to come with us?'

'I should like that very much,' she said. 'You don't mind, do you, Aunt Adelia?'

'As long as I don't have to hear any of that ungodly racket,' said Adelia, 'you can listen to it until your brains seep out through your ears.'

'That's settled, then,' said Lady Hardcastle with a smile. 'Richard's Ragtime Rollicks at the Aristotle on Friday.'

This time I knew she was doing it on purpose, so I felt more confident in wearily saying, 'Robinson's Ragtime Roisterers at the Arundel.'

'That's right. What did I say, dear?'

'Something else,' I said. 'As you very well know.'

'Well, whoever they are, it'll be a splendid evening. And look, here comes our first course.'

The food, as before, was absolutely delicious. And despite my misgivings about the Wilsons – Adelia Wilson, at any rate – they turned out to be rather pleasant company and we had a most convivial meal.

We parted company shortly after ten o'clock. The Wilsons had declined our invitation for a nightcap, saying that it was already past their bedtime. Lady Hardcastle was disappointed, but salvation was at hand in the form of Ribble, the salon waiter.

'Ah, Ribble,' she said. 'The very man. Would you be an absolute poppet and bring a couple of glasses of brandy to my room, please?'

'Certainly, my lady. I shall be just a few moments. Would you like anything else?'

'Some cheese and biscuits, perhaps? Our dining companions were eager to get away before I could summon the cheese board. A little fruit. And the rest of the brandy bottle?'

'I shall see what I can find,' he said.

'You're an angel,' she said.

We set off upstairs.

Back in our rooms we made ourselves comfortable while we waited for Ribble to arrive with the tray.

'That was rather more fun than I would have predicted,' said Lady Hardcastle as she fastened her robe.

'Getting dressed for bed?' I said.

'No, silly – dinner with the Wilsons.'

'It was. Adelia's a grumpy old bird, and she wears far too much perfume, but she's not so bad once she's got some champagne inside her.'

'Not so bad at all.' She regarded her discarded corset with animosity.

'Do you think I'd be shunned by polite society if I stopped wearing these wretched things and allowed my weary body to assume its natural shape in public? I'm sure a talented dressmaker could design something fashionable and flattering without my stomach and liver having to find new lodgings every time I went out.'

'But what would become of me?' I asked. 'What use would you have for me if you didn't need a competent pair of hands to lace you into your corsets? I'd be out on the street.'

She laughed. 'I'd not let you starve, dear,' she said. 'We could make a room for you in the garden shed. You'd be perfectly comfortable.'

A knock at the door heralded the arrival of Ribble and his Tray of Wonders. It contained everything Lady Hardcastle had asked for as well as a few extras.

'Chef sent up some of his petits fours with his compliments, my lady,' said Ribble as he placed the tray on the writing desk. 'So I added a pot of coffee. I hope you'll find everything to your liking.'

'I should say we shall,' said Lady Hardcastle happily. 'Thank you, Ribble.' She discreetly palmed him a few coins and sent him on his way.

'If you could do the honours, dear,' she said once he was gone, 'I'll get back to the old journal.'

At home, it was Lady Hardcastle's habit to make notes about a case on a large blackboard. It would be my job to set the cumbersome thing on its easel – usually in the dining room or drawing room – and she would fill it with sketches and notes until the mystery had been solved. She had learned this method of 'thinking aloud' while studying at Girton College and despite the scepticism of almost everyone who heard about it, it seemed to work. Away from home, though, she had to resort to keeping her notes in her journal.

'I know needs must when the devil butters the parsnips,' she said, holding up the octo-sized notebook. 'But I'm starting to find this a little restrictive. There's barely room for one thought to the page – I much prefer to be able to see the whole picture.'

'If you need to see the "picture",' I said, 'why not use a sketchbook?'

'I say, you are a marvel, aren't you? I was so caught up in the idea of making notes in a notebook, that I never thought of sketching ideas in a sketchbook. There'll be much more room to think there.'

While I continued to divvy up the treats on the tray, she retrieved one of her large sketchbooks from the wardrobe.

'It doesn't look as though I'll get much of a chance to do any drawing on this trip,' she said. 'But we can make good use of this, after all. Your packing shall not be in vain.'

'Always good to know,' I said. 'So where are we?'

'Let's start with the strongbox,' she said. 'I'm reasonably certain we can follow its path. It starts with Dr Goddard, obviously. Kusnetsov stole it from him.'

'And then person or persons unknown stole it from Kusnetsov.'

'Correct.' She spoke aloud as she wrote: 'Whereabouts of strongbox . . . currently . . . unknown.'

'But we suspect it's still here at the hotel.'

'Do we?' she said, still writing. 'I suppose we do. So one of the other guests has it. The Wilsons. Schneider. Takahashi. Martin. The simplest thing would be to search each of their rooms.'

'Risky,' I said. 'The odds are three-to-one against us starting with the correct room and word would get around. By the time we reached the box's latest possessor they could have spirited it away – we'd still never find it.'

'Agreed. We need to fathom it out before galumphing in. So we move on to other matters. Dr Goddard is missing and Sergei Kusnetsov is dead.'

'Different culprits,' I said.

'Why?'

'Honestly? Just a feeling,' I said. 'Let's say Dr Goddard died in the struggle. That would mean the killer went to a huge amount of trouble to remove the body and leave little to no evidence of what had happened. Why would he go to all that effort and then just leave Kusnetsov lying there? Whereas if Dr Goddard were taken alive, it was presumably to try to extract information about the contents of the strongbox, or perhaps to ransom him. Why then risk detection and the foiling of carefully laid plans by murdering Kusnetsov? It's all a bit flimsy, but it feels like the work of two different people.'

'Men?' she asked.

'No way to say for certain,' I said. 'The Wilsons could drug Dr Goddard and carry him between them. And there's no reason why a woman couldn't garrotte Kusnetsov. I could, certainly.'

'Hmm. All right, then. And we're sure the burglars are different people again?'

'Of course. Kusnetsov had the strongbox – what did he need Dr Goddard for?'

'To explain the contents of the strongbox?'

'But he'd have done a bunk, wouldn't he?' I said. 'If he had the box and the scientist, what would he need to hang about here for? He was still here and making preparations to leave just before he was killed. If he had Dr Goddard he'd be in some hidey-hole somewhere, torturing him for information.'

She was still making notes. 'Granted,' she said. 'And Kusnetsov's killer?'

'That's not so cut and dried. My instinct is still that the person who took the strongbox from Kusnetsov didn't turn the room upside down. It's a big box by all accounts – you wouldn't need to fine-tooth comb the room to find it. It would just be there. All big and box-like. But as to which of them killed Kusnetsov . . . I'm not certain. He could have disturbed either of them.'

'Wait,' she said, looking up from the sketchbook. 'If the box is so obvious, why turn the room over at all? The most cursory search would reveal its absence.'

'We still don't know what's in the box. If Thief Two thought that Kusnetsov had opened the box and removed its contents, the absence of the box itself need not be significant – the documents, or plans, or whatever is in there, could be concealed anywhere in the room. It wouldn't necessarily mean that there'd been a Thief One who had already removed the box.'

'I can't say I disagree with any of your reasoning so far,' she said. 'Let's move on to the contents of the box.'

'We've still no idea what it contains,' I said.

'But everyone else knew exactly what was in it,' she said. 'And each of them thought it was something different. That's more than a little significant.'

'Much more than a little,' I agreed. 'It smells of misdirection. Dr Goddard was definitely up to something there.'

'Telling each of them a different story, yes,' she mused. 'But to what end? What did he stand to gain from that?'

'Just a bit of mischief?'

'I'd never rule it out,' she said. 'Dangerous mischief, though. I might have thought he was a fantasist but for Harry's stern admonitions not to get involved and the swift arrival of Barbel and Chub of the Special Branch.'

'We're back to misdirection, then. He told each of them something different to keep them off the scent. Oh.'

'Oh?'

'Oh, indeed,' I said. 'He told each of them what they were most likely to want to hear. Mr Takahashi had worked on the Japanese railway system, and Dr Goddard told him that he was working on locomotive design. Mr Martin is something to do with shipbuilding in France, so Dr Goddard told him he had a new ship design.'

'Kusnetsov was told about his weaponry work by his masters in Moscow,' she said. 'So he had nothing to do with that.'

'True,' I agreed. 'And the Wilsons thought it was something to do with radio – I'm not sure why he would have thought that would impress them.'

'Radio impresses everyone. It's magical.'

'What if . . . ?' I began. 'What if he suspected that one or more of them was a spy and fed them the stories to flush them out?'

'How would that have helped? What would he have done about it?'

'Told Harry?' I suggested. 'He could have Grayling and Rudd swoop in and arrest anyone who showed too much interest in what he was doing.'

'Our fishy friends were suspiciously close at hand,' she agreed. 'They have the air of London men about them, and yet there they were in Weston to deal with Kusnetsov's corpse in no time at all.'

'Harry said something about them coming from Bristol, didn't he? I come back to the idea that we need to talk to your brother,' I said. 'He's just going to have to trust you.'

'He really is. But what about Goddard? We can't just leave him out there, wherever he is. What do we know?'

'From Eleanora's account it seems likely that Kusnetsov stole the strongbox while Dr Goddard was downstairs with us.'

'Right. And she said that was at about ten o'clock. Actually, we should have remembered this – it's another argument in favour of there being two different men. Kusnetsov picked the lock and took the box, someone else kicked the door in and took Goddard.'

I could see that she was drawing a timeline on a fresh page in the sketchbook.

'The only other event we can place with even vague accuracy is the presence of the fisherman in the alley at three in the morning,' I said.

'Do you think he could be our kidnapper?'

'There's not much against him other than his having piddled in the alley, but we can't rule him out. Oh no, wait. In all the distractions I completely forgot about my trip to the kitchens.'

'I had, too. What did you learn?'

'Nothing very much,' I said. 'I don't think there's anything in the theft of the food – I'd bet that food goes missing from hotel kitchens all the time. But I strongly suspect the lock was picked.'

'The outside door?'

'Yes – fresh scratches on the escutcheon. Someone broke in.'

'This afternoon?'

'No, the door was unlocked – probably always is during the day. But it would be locked overnight, obviously. I'd say it casts our fisherman's presence in a new light.'

'Hmm,' she said. 'I'll note it, but we need more before I'll start looking for fishermen to question. What next?'

'We met Kusnetsov in the salon not long after four o'clock this afternoon,' I said.

'And he was called away to the telephone,' she said. 'He'd not been in his room for a while – I remember him looking distinctly windswept, as though he'd been outdoors – so the box could have been stolen from him at any time this afternoon.'

'Yes,' I said. 'We left the dining room at five and went to the salon for an hour. By the time we left there at six he had long-since finished his call and returned to his room where we found him dead at, what, five past six?'

She finished making her notes and closed the sketchbook.

'We've at least seven hundred-weight of facts, a few stone of supposition, a pound of clues, but not an ounce of an idea what's going on,' she said. 'I think it's time to think of other things and let our subconscious minds work their wonders while we pay close attention to all this delicious scoff. I bitterly regret never having been to a boarding school, you know. Do you remember Lavinia and her pals reminiscing at Riddlethorpe? I should have loved to have raided the school kitchens for midnight feasts.'

'You'd not have been so keen on lumpy beds and cross country runs,' I said. 'You're the sort of girl who likes her comforts.'

'You're probably right. But I still might get up in the middle of the night and finish this lot off, just for the fun of it.'

'You're presuming we'll have left any,' I said. 'And on past performance, I really don't see that happening.'

I was right. As we talked, we worked our way through the sweet pastries, the coffee, the cheese, and the biscuits. We'd made a significant dent in the brandy, too, before we called it a night.

Chapter Nine

We rose late on Wednesday and once again entirely failed to make it down to breakfast in time to see any of the fabled kedgeree. As before, though, we managed to cobble together a perfectly satisfactory repast from what remained on the sideboard and left feeling uncomfortably full.

'We need to walk this off,' said Lady Hardcastle, patting her midriff. 'Or at least give it a chance to get past the corset.'

'This is becoming an obsession,' I said. 'Why don't you just take a stand and stop wearing it?'

'Because none of my clothes would fit. I'm trapped by a sinister cabal of dressmakers. It's a conspiracy.'

'A conspiracy?'

'Yes, it came to me this morning. The Dressmakers' Guild – I'm sure there is one, though I'm equally sure they'd deny it – is in cahoots with the International League of Corsetmakers to ensure that fashionable women can never be comfortable.'

'Why?' I asked. 'What do they hope to achieve?'

'World domination.'

'By dressing women in constrictive clothing.'

'Exactly that. Think how strong and agile you are when you're free of restrictive undergarments. You've burgled embassies and government buildings, foiled robberies and assassinations, solved crimes and baked delicious pies. Imagine if all of womankind were similarly unencumbered – we'd be an unstoppable force.'

'We'd be a good deal plumper after eating all those pies,' I said. 'And there'd be nothing to hold it all in.'

'I shall write a letter to *The Times*. They must be stopped.'

I laughed. 'Let's get you out in the fresh air before you have what I'm sure Adelia Wilson would describe as a "conniption". Your blood is up.'

'My dander, too. Our colonial cousins have all the good words.'

We were ready surprisingly quickly and stepped out into the watery sunshine. I had fully expected the wind to attempt once more to carry us off to Gloucester, but it was calm.

'This is more like it,' I said as we set off along the prom. 'If the sun would actually come out it would be almost as good as being in the South of France.'

'We should go back to Cannes one day,' she said. 'But without the gang of racketeers from Marseille chasing us.'

'I'd like that,' I said. 'Although I'd miss the Punch and Judy show and the whelk stall. Oh, and fish and chips.'

'They have *moules frites* instead.'

'I thought that was Belgium,' I said. 'But I take your point.' I looked out to sea. 'There's one thing I wouldn't miss about this place.'

'What's that, dear?'

'That vast expanse of mud masquerading as a beach. Has the tide actually been in since we've been here?'

'Four times,' she said with a laugh. 'I still have the tide table I got at reception yesterday.'

She rummaged in her bag and withdrew a folded piece of typewritten paper.

'Here we are,' she said. 'High tide was at thirteen minutes past five on Monday afternoon, fourteen minutes to six yesterday morning, twelve minutes past six yesterday evening and four minutes past six this morning. It'll be high again at seven minutes past seven this evening.'

I harrumphed. 'We've managed to miss all of them,' I said. 'When's the tide going to be in at a time when I might see it?'

'Well, you could see it this evening if we come out again before dinner. But if you want something more in the daytime'– she scanned the sheet – 'there are high tides at sixteen minutes past nine on Saturday morning and three minutes past ten on Sunday morning. There's still time to see the sea.'

We walked down past the Punch and Judy man, past a troupe of Pierrots trying to drum up business for their show on the end of the pier, and on to the Grand Atlantic Hotel, where we turned round and started to make our way back. The drop in the wind had prompted more holidaymakers out on to the seafront today and the atmosphere was decidedly jolly.

'How did your subconscious get on last night?' I asked.

'There was something about a Norwegian Elkhound called Margaritte who was running a theatrical company and wanted me to design the costumes for a canine production of a musical called *Piff! Paff! Pouf!*' she said. 'They've no thumbs, you see.

They can't hold a pencil. And then I had to sit an examination on organic chemistry for which I hadn't prepared. I was completely unclothed, but for some reason that didn't trouble me nearly as much as my inability to remember the melting and boiling points of any of the compounds. Or even their names. It was most disturbing.'

'I meant about the disappearance of Dr Goddard,' I said. 'But I'm sure Dr Freud would have a field day with your naked chemistry.'

'Oh yes, of course. I'm so sorry. Nothing yet. How about you?'

'No. I'm as baffled as ever.'

We were approaching the Punch and Judy man once more. He was between shows and the crowd had dispersed, all save for a tall man with his back to us, wearing a sailor's coat and heavy boots. He had his cap in his hand, which revealed a head of tousled blond hair. He appeared to be deep in conversation with the puppeteer. I pointed him out.

'Ah, yes,' she said. 'I told you there was no point in fussing about the fisherman. They're ten a penny round here.'

He was gone by the time we drew level with the red-and-white tent and we carried on without further incident. We were back at Steep Holm View in time for elevenses.

◆ ◆ ◆

Elevenses came and went without incident, as did lunch and tea. We amused ourselves with books and a few energetically aggressive card games, broken up by another stroll into town. I bought postcards for Edna and Miss Jones, and one for my twin sister, Gwenith, who lived in Woolwich with her husband, a staff sergeant in the Royal Artillery.

We changed for dinner and were at the dining room door at ten past seven. Everyone else was already seated – it seemed they all preferred to dine early. Ernst Schneider sat alone in one of the far corners of the room, with Takahashi Kaito in the other. Jean Martin sat with his back to them at a table nearer the centre, forming a sullen triangle of well-dressed solitude. Having met them all, I wondered why they didn't sit together – I thought they'd probably get along.

The Wilsons were at the table nearest to Martin. Adelia Wilson saw us at the door and beckoned us in.

'Good evening,' she said with a warmth I hadn't expected. 'We were hoping to bump into you two. We did so enjoy having dinner with you last evening and we were wondering if you would join us again.'

'How utterly charming of you to say so,' said Lady Hardcastle. 'We enjoyed ourselves, too, didn't we?'

'We did,' I said. 'Although you missed a treat by skipping out before the cheese board. They have a wonderful selection.'

'You stayed for the cheese after all, then?' said Adelia with a smile.

'We had it delivered to our rooms,' said Lady Hardcastle. 'We can be quite decadent when the mood strikes.'

'I don't doubt it. But sit yourselves down – we were just wondering whether to order champagne again.'

We sat and made ourselves comfortable. I was once again struck by the strength of Adelia's perfume, but I knew I would become accustomed to it as the evening wore on.

'Did you enjoy the champagne, then?' I asked Eleanora.

She looked up from her intense scrutiny of the menu. 'I did, thank you, ma'am,' she said.

'I think I'll take a leaf out of Lady Hardcastle's book and insist that while we're on holiday, formality can take a holiday, too. Please call me Flo – all my friends do.'

The younger Wilson smiled. 'Thank you, Flo,' she said. 'That would be an honour. My friends call me Ellie.'

'I'll still be calling you Eleanora, if you don't mind,' said Adelia.

'That's entirely appropriate,' I said. 'My mother and sister both call me Flossie. It's nice to have a name for family only.'

'Not Florence, then?'

'Only Lady Hardcastle calls me Florence now that my grandmother has gone, and only sometimes.'

'And yet you call her Lady Hardcastle,' she said.

I felt disinclined to try to explain this one but Lady Hardcastle came to my aid.

'It's something of a private joke between us,' she said. 'You know how we English are with our gentle mockery and not taking things seriously. It's a way of keeping my feet on the ground.'

'By reminding you of your title?'

'Exactly that. We're a complex folk. It's not even my title, truth be told. I'm only Lady Hardcastle because my late husband was Sir Roderick – it's a courtesy title, you see? I was plain old Mrs Hardcastle until he was knighted.'

'Oh,' said Eleanora, suddenly interested. 'Is that why you're not Lady Emily?'

'It is. That's reserved for ladies who are related to members of the peerage. And here's a fun thing: if the title had been mine – if I were Dame Emily – Roddy wouldn't have been given a courtesy title at all. I sometimes wonder if the inconsistencies are placed there as traps for the unwary. We can winkle out the spies and imposters in our midst by uncovering their ignorance of our peculiar naming conventions.'

'For my part,' said Adelia, 'I sometimes wonder if we threw out the baby with the bath water when we cast off the yoke of monarchist oppression. "Lady Adelia" has a ring to it, don't you think?'

'I can think of some titles for you,' muttered Eleanora under her breath.

'What's that?' said Adelia sharply. 'You really must stop mumbling. Especially when we have company.'

I winked at Eleanora, who returned to her close study of the menu with a little smile.

'Have you had a pleasant day?' asked Lady Hardcastle, suppressing a smile of her own.

'We have, thank you,' said Adelia. 'We took the train to Clevedon – a delightful little town. They have a pier there, too, you know.'

'So I understand,' said Lady Hardcastle.

'Not so grand as the pier here, but rather more pretty, I felt. There was a steamer there but we couldn't ascertain where it might take us.'

'It might have just taken you for a trip into the Bristol Channel and back,' I said. 'Or it might have been the ferry to Wales – that operates from there.'

'To Wales? Is there no train?'

'There is now,' I said. 'But the tunnel was only opened some twenty-odd years ago. Before that it was the ferry or the long ride to Gloucester to cross the Severn there.'

'It's like going to another country.'

'It is another country,' I said.

'Nonsense,' said Adelia. 'Now I know you're teasing the witless foreigner.'

'No, it's true,' said Lady Hardcastle. 'Flo is Welsh, and they're very proud of their nation's heritage. It might have been joined to England by political shenanigans since the thirteenth century—'

'Since it was invaded by the English in 1283 and then annexed in 1284,' I said.

'Not that they bear us a grudge and have the dates seared into their collective memories, or anything. But it's quite definitely another country.'

'Well, I never,' said Adelia. 'Perhaps we should get on that steamer and visit another foreign land on our trip.'

'You'll not be disappointed,' I said. 'It's beautiful.'

'I shall make enquiries of the hotel clerk,' said Adelia. 'And what about you two?'

'What about us, dear?' said Lady Hardcastle.

'How did you amuse yourselves today? Are you still looking into the . . . what was it you called it? The "goings-on" in the hotel?'

'We still are.'

'I have to say I'm most alarmed by the news that one of the hotel guests has been murdered. I know you Britishers pride yourselves on your sangfroid but no one seems to be taking this especially seriously. A stiff upper lip isn't going to protect me and my niece from murderers. We're no strangers to violence, it's true, but Eleanora is really quite frightened, and I can't say I blame her one bit. Will we be safe? Had he taken the strongbox?'

'How did you—?' began Lady Hardcastle.

'Oh, come now,' said Adelia. 'We've been through this – we're foreign but we're not stupid. You came to our rooms and asked about Dr Goddard, then you asked about his strongbox. It doesn't take the mind of a genius to figure out that both have gone missing.'

'You're right, of course. Yes, we believe Kusnetsov did have the strongbox.'

'Did have?'

'Yes, by the time we went to search his room and found him dead, the box – if it had ever been there – was long gone.'

'So the thief was robbed,' said Adelia. 'Got any ideas?'

'None at the moment,' I said. 'We had a couple of suspects in mind for the first robbery, but we were sure that Kusnetsov was the one whom Ellie heard scratching at the door. The words you heard were Russian, not English. His fingers slipped while he was picking the lock and he said "damn!" in Russian but it sounds like "back later" in English.'

Adelia had flinched at the mild oath, but said nothing.

'Oh my,' said Eleanora. 'How wonderfully clever of you.'

'Who was your other suspect?' asked Adelia.

'Herr Schneider,' I said. 'He'd been seen lurking about the corridor, but it turned out not to be him at all.'

'Did the robber kill Kusnetsov?'

'We've been trying to puzzle that out, but we don't think so,' said Lady Hardcastle.

'Are we safe?' asked Eleanora.

'From the killer?' I said. 'Of course you are. There's nothing to worry about.'

'Unless you have the strongbox,' said Lady Hardcastle with a wink.

'My Colt Vest Pocket pistol will see them off,' said Adelia.

'You use the Vest Pocket?' said Lady Hardcastle. 'I must say, I'm very fond of mine. Flo bought me a derringer to fit into a holster in a specially made hat, but it only holds two rounds and I've never found it to be terribly accurate.'

'I'm a woman travelling alone with my young niece, but what does a titled English lady want with a pistol?' asked Adelia.

'These are dangerous times, dear,' said Lady Hardcastle with a wink. 'A lady should always be able to look after herself, titled or not. Although I confess I've left them both at home – we're on holiday.'

'What about you . . . Flo? Are you armed?'

'I favour the swift biff on the conk if things cut up rough,' I said. 'But if weapons are required I'm more of a blade sort of a girl.'

'A biff on the what?' said Adelia. 'Ah, there you are, waiter. You've arrived just in time to spare my embarrassed confusion.'

Kibble had indeed arrived and took our dinner orders, to be accompanied this time by two bottles of champagne.

'I feel we ought to be matching the wine to each course like proper European snobs,' said Adelia. 'But when there's champagne on offer . . .'

'I couldn't agree more, dear,' said Lady Hardcastle.

The champagne had already arrived. Kibble poured. We drank a toast to happy vacations and jolly holidays. It was all set to be another pleasant dinner.

And so it was. Our new American friends were charming company, and even when the conversation flagged I was able to amuse myself by looking round the room at our fellow guests. There was the French giant, Jean Martin, hunched uncomfortably over his dinner like an adult forced to eat at the nursery table. The Japanese diplomat, Takahashi Kaito, sat ramrod straight and ate with a delicate precision, each movement graceful and efficient. And then there was the disagreeable Austrian fop, Ernst Schneider – he even managed to eat soup in a condescendingly supercilious way. And as for that ludicrous lapel pin. Honestly it was more like a brooch with its rubies and emeralds and . . .

'It was Schneider,' I blurted before I could stop myself.

Lady Hardcastle frowned. 'What was, dear?' she said.

'I'm so sorry, it just hit me. In Kusnetsov's room. That shard of glass you found. It's from Schneider's ridiculous pin. There's a green stone missing. He was one of the ones in the room. Either he has the box or he killed Kusnetsov.'

'I can't look without drawing attention to us,' she said. 'But I'll take your word for it. We'll have to play it canny or we'll blow the gaff. We need to get to his room before he knows we know, but this might be our chance to at least get the box back.' She paused for a moment, contemplating her next move as she ate another morsel of the delicious Dover sole she had chosen for her fish course. 'Would you mind awfully helping me, Miss Wilson?'

Both the Misses Wilson looked up.

'I'm so sorry, I meant you, Adelia,' she said.

'Happy to oblige,' said Adelia. 'What did you have in mind?'

'I thought if we left together, as though to visit Mrs Jones, it might look less like we were up to something. It would give me the chance to see if Mr Hillier is still about without attracting undue attention.'

'Visit Mrs Jones?' asked Adelia.

'Visit the ladies' room,' said Lady Hardcastle. '"Strain our taters", as the vulgarians have it. I rather like that one, though, I must say.'

'It happens that I do need to,' said Adelia. 'By all means, let's go.'

They went.

'And we sit here,' I said to Eleanora. 'We chatter away without making anything of it, because we'd not think it out of the ordinary for our companions to nip off to attend to a call of nature.'

'You have experience of this?' she asked.

'Of Lady Hardcastle getting up in the middle of dinner and going to the—'

'No, silly,' she said. 'Of cloak-and-dagger stuff, like in adventure stories.'

'Oh, I see,' I said. 'No, not really. But I've read enough adventure stories to know how it's done.'

'I'd love to have adventures,' she said, wistfully. 'My life seems planned out for me before it's even begun. Finish school, tour Europe with Aunt Adelia to "broaden my horizons", find a suitable husband, tend house, have babies. And it has to be the right sort of man – marrying for love is for lesser folk. He'll have to have serious political ambitions or be the heir to a substantial fortune to be considered as a prospective husband by my family. Preferably both.'

'I'm sure adventures are overrated,' I said. 'There's a lot to be said for a warm, comfortable home with enough to eat and someone to keep you company on the long winter evenings.'

'I'm sure you're right. But I'd still like my life to amount to more than a full belly and a seat by the fire.'

'What would you like to do?' I asked. 'If you didn't have to please anyone else, what would you choose to do with your life?'

She thought for a while. 'I'd still need to eat,' she said at length. 'And I'd still need somewhere warm and safe to live. So I guess I'd have to earn a living for myself. Maybe I could write. Maybe I could make my own adventures on the page – live a life of danger and excitement through the characters in a book.'

'Well, now,' I said. 'You didn't say you could write. That sounds like a wonderful ambition.'

'I don't like to say it out loud. People don't take it seriously. Painting and playing the piano – those are suitable pastimes for a young lady, they say. But writing fanciful stories? Folk just laugh.'

'Folk are idiots,' I said.

She laughed.

'You two seem to be having a jolly time without us,' said Lady Hardcastle.

'As I said yesterday: we don't stop existing just because you're not here.'

'Quite so. Is Adelia not back?'

'Not yet, no. What news of Mr Hillier?'

'He's not in his office, but the night porter has put the word out. He lives not far away with his wife and two sons so there's a chance he might be willing to pop back for us. I'd still like to have him as a witness.'

'It feels more proper,' I said. 'And he wants to get to the bottom of all this even more than we do. I'm sure he won't be long.'

She harrumphed.

A few minutes later, Adelia Wilson returned and we tried our best to resume casual conversation as our dinner continued.

Mr Hillier did not show himself before we finished, so the four of us retired to the salon. We were the only ones there – the gentlemen having all drifted off when their meals were done – so we reasoned that we wouldn't be at all difficult to find once the hotel manager returned to work.

Despite the seriousness of the coming task we were having such a pleasant time that we ordered a round of drinks to go with our coffee and petits fours. Eleanora declined the offer of cognac, saying that the champagne had been quite enough, but we other three were more than ready for our brandy. I was just about to tuck in to a particularly delicious-looking pastry when the porter arrived and bowed to Lady Hardcastle.

'Mr Hillier's compliments, my lady,' he said. 'He says he will meet you in reception at your convenience.'

'Thank you.' Lady Hardcastle rose from her seat. 'Come along, Flo, let's not keep him waiting. Excuse us, please, ladies, but duty calls. We'll be back this way if we can.'

We followed the porter back to reception and the waiting Mr Hillier.

◆ ◆ ◆

'I'm so sorry I wasn't here,' said Mr Hillier as we approached the reception desk. 'I do like to be at home to see the boys safely to bed.'

'Please don't worry, Mr Hillier – your devotion to your family does you credit. It is we who should be apologizing to you for dragging you away from your home at this late hour. Your day's work ought to be done by now.'

'This is an important matter,' he said. 'It needs to be settled as soon as possible.'

'Quite so,' she agreed. 'Quite so. We do have a slight problem, though. When I first came to look for you, all the hotel guests were safely in the dining room and I foresaw no difficulty in searching Herr Schneider's room in his absence. It would be an invasion of privacy, to be sure, but we could have worried about that afterwards. Now, though, they've scattered to the four winds. It could well be that Schneider is in his room and might object to a search. Are you prepared to back me if he gets uppity?'

'He'll most certainly get uppity,' said Mr Hillier.

'Yes, we know full well what he's like – we've met him. But will you stand firm?'

'I'm in charge of the hotel, and we reserve the right to enter guests' rooms at any time. I'll not take part in any violence, mind you.'

'Don't worry,' she said. 'Armstrong will take care of the violence – it's one of her many talents.'

I smiled and nodded reassuringly, but that seemed to make him even more uneasy.

'Come along, then,' said Lady Hardcastle. 'Let us tarry no more. I have a feeling we'll get the strongbox this time.'

We mounted the stairs to our floor and hastened to the end of the corridor. At the bathroom and lavatory we turned along another corridor, empty but for two plain doors, presumably store cupboards. At the rear of the hotel was another corridor. From our conversation with the night staff we knew that the two doors were to the rooms of Schneider and Takahashi.

Mr Hillier knocked smartly on the first of them.

There was no answer.

He knocked again.

He reached into his pocket for his master key, but I stayed his hand.

'Would you mind standing back, please, sir?' I said.

He didn't look delighted at the idea, but he nevertheless stood aside. I reached out for the door handle and turned it. With a gentle push, I established that the door was unlocked. I released the handle and pushed firmly on the door, opening it quickly inwards. I was braced in case anyone sprang out at us, but nothing happened.

The room faced east, away from the dim evening sun. The heavy curtains had been drawn, making the room gloomier still. I reached in and found the electric light switch. The lamp on the wall came to life immediately, illuminating an all-too-familiar scene.

The room was in disarray. It smelled rather pleasant, it has to be noted, but it looked an absolute mess.

This time, though, it was not the mess of a systematic search for hidden secrets, but the aftermath of a violent struggle. A fashionable standard lamp lay on its side, its glass shade smashed. Bottles and jars – of which Schneider possessed a surprising number – had been swept from the washstand on to the floor. Some of them had spilled their contents, leaving perfumed, oleaginous smears on the floor where the combatants had slipped during the fight.

I took a step into the room and looked around.

'Are you squeamish, Mr Hillier?' I said calmly.

'Am I what?' He leaned in and looked round.

'Squeamish, sir. Are you disturbed by the sight of blood?'

'The sight of—' He fainted. Dead away. There was a soft thud as his head hit the luxuriant carpet that ran down the centre of the corridor.

'That answers that, then,' I said.

Lady Hardcastle checked that he was breathing and laid him on his side before joining me.

'I say,' she said. 'That's rather a mess, isn't it?'

Ernst Schneider, still in his dinner suit, lay motionless in a pool of his own blood. There were at least two stab wounds to his chest, but his assailant had made sure to finish the job by slitting his throat. From the surprisingly small size of the pool and the absence of the tell-tale spray of blood that accompanies a severed artery, I guessed that the *coup de grâce* was an unnecessary flourish – he had already been well on the way to being dead of his wounds before then.

'What do you see?' she asked.

I took in the state of the room. 'A fight, obviously. And not a quick one – the extent of the damage to the room suggests that they were at it for a minute or more.'

'Evenly matched, then?'

'In skill, if not size,' I said. 'You see the face cream on the floor? A large foot and a smaller foot.' I bent to examine Schneider's shoes. 'A dapper little man with dainty little feet. So the larger shoe prints are those of his attacker.'

'Martin?'

'He's the right sort of size. And sailors do tend to opt for the knife in a close fight. Sharp ones – look at how clean that cut is.'

'Sailors?'

'He's a "marine engineer", but did you see the size of his hands? And the coarseness of the skin? He's spent time at sea.'

'Actually, yes – I agree,' she said. 'I don't suppose it's worth even looking under the bed for the strongbox.'

'I doubt it, but we'd look a right couple of chumps if we didn't bother and it turned out to be there all along.'

I knelt on the floor and looked under the bed. There were scratches on the polished floorboards but nothing there that might have caused them. Lady Hardcastle, meanwhile, had taken a look in – and on top of – the wardrobe.

'If it were ever here,' she said, 'it's gone now. Let's revive Hillier and get down to the telephone. I need to speak to Harry. Do you have any smelling salts?'

I frowned. 'Why on earth . . . ?'

'It's the sort of thing lady's maids carry. You're always so well prepared for every eventuality, I thought you might have some.'

'I don't,' I said. 'But I know a man who might. There are pills, potions, and patent nostrums of all sorts among the face creams and hair oils. I'll bet the late Herr Schneider has some.'

I was right, and a quick whiff brought Mr Hillier splutteringly to his senses. He sat up.

'Is he . . . ?'

'Dead? Yes,' said Lady Hardcastle. 'And if the strongbox were ever here, it's long gone now.'

'Who would . . . ?'

'We have an idea, but we need advice from my brother before we proceed. This is getting out of hand.'

'Your brother . . . ?'

'Harry Featherstonhaugh. Of the Foreign Office. You spoke to him yesterday.'

'Ah, yes. We should telephone him.'

'We should, indeed. Can you stand?'

'I think so.'

'Splendid. You lock the room with your master key and I'll make the call from your office.'

'I'll . . . er . . . I'll need to be with you,' he said. 'I lock the office door at night.'

She held up her own copy of the master key.

'I think we'll be all right,' she said, and we set off downstairs together.

◆ ◆ ◆

173

Once we were safely inside Mr Hillier's office with the door firmly shut, Lady Hardcastle began rummaging in her handbag for her address book.

'I ought to start committing people's telephone numbers to memory,' she muttered. 'It's not as though they're terribly complicated.'

'I thought you had his new office number on that telegram he sent you yesterday,' I said.

'I'm always impressed by my brother's dedication to his work,' she said, still rummaging, 'but I doubt that even he would still be in the office at' – she looked at her wristwatch – 'nine in the evening. I'm going to call him at home.'

'He'll be delighted by that, I'm sure.'

'It's his own fault. If he's going to "What ho, sis" me and then sternly instruct me not to get involved, he ought to expect telephone calls at nine o'clock on a Wednesday evening inform-ing him of dead foreign visitors and still-missing strongboxes. We're perfectly capable of handling all this on our own, but he insisted we leave it to him. Ah, here we are.'

She picked up the telephone earpiece and gave the number to the operator. There was nothing to do then but wait for her to call back when the trunk call was put through.

'Are we sticking with the idea of there being two burglars?' I asked.

'A thief and a killer?' she said. 'We can't rule it out, but it's less clear-cut this time. I'm definitely inclined towards the "two killers" hypothesis now, though. A garrotte and a knife seem like the weapons of different men.'

'Unless one killing was planned and the other improvised,' I said. 'What if Martin planned to kill Kusnetsov and was ready with his garrotte, but had to fight for his life against Schneider using the first thing he could think of: his trusty knife?'

'Except that Martin was out all day yesterday at Cheddar Gorge. He told us when we met him in the salon.'

'He did, indeed. He's unlikely to be lying – it's too easy an alibi to break. A decent spy could do better than that.'

'This isn't at all the holiday I'd hoped for,' she sighed. 'It's not even sunny. I mean to say—'

Her grumpy musings were interrupted by the ringing of the telephone.

'That was quick,' I said.

She picked up the earpiece and held it so that we could both hear. The difference in our heights meant that she had to sit on the edge of Mr Hillier's desk to try to get our heads at a more or less equal level.

'Hardcastle here,' she said.

'Connecting your trunk call with Mr Featherston-huff . . . Mr Feather—' The operator was interrupted by a voice in the background which we were unable to hear clearly but which seemed to be imparting vital information. 'Fanshaw?' she said with no small amount of incredulity. 'But it's spelt with feathers . . . Well I never. You live and learn. Please hold the line, caller.'

Lady Hardcastle rolled her eyes but said nothing.

'Is that you, Emily?' said a familiar female voice.

'Lavinia, darling,' said Lady Hardcastle. 'It is, indeed, I. In the flesh. Or lurking inexplicably in the electronic mysteries of telephonic whatnots, anyway. How are you?'

'Quite well, thank you. What a delightful surprise to hear from you. At least I hope so. Is everything all right? I thought you said you were holidaying in Weston-super-Mare.'

'We are, dear,' said Lady Hardcastle. 'Exactly as planned. There's nothing to worry about. I take it Harry hasn't said anything of current developments in the West Country.'

'I've not seen him this past week. He's away on important Foreign Office business.'

'He's abroad, then?' asked Lady Hardcastle.

'I've no idea. He had his valet pack him a bag, said, "Cheerio, Jake. I'll be back by the weekend", and then toddled off.'

Thanks to a chain of lavatorial schoolgirl logic that shortened Lady Lavinia's name to 'Lav', whence it became 'Jakes' and then 'Jake', few of her friends had called her anything but Jake since she had been a girl.

'Does he do that a lot?' asked Lady Hardcastle.

'It's a recent development since he was attached to the new department, but yes, he does now. He seems to be having great fun so I never mind. It's not as though I've not got plenty to do without him.'

'New department, eh?' said Lady Hardcastle. 'He's a dark horse. So you've no idea where he is?'

'None at all, dear. Is it frightfully urgent?'

'Yes,' said Lady Hardcastle. 'But then again, no. I have a number where he might be reached – I'll try that.'

'Right you are, dear,' said Lady Lavinia. 'Do be careful, won't you?'

'I'm renowned for my cautiousness, have no fear.'

'Hmm. That's not how Harry tells it, but you have darling Flo to look after you. Give her my love, won't you.'

'She's here,' said Lady Hardcastle.

'Hello, your ladyship,' I said. 'Don't worry – I won't let her come to any harm.'

'See that you don't,' said Lady Lavinia. 'Aunts are so important.'

'I say,' exclaimed Lady Hardcastle. 'Really? How wonderful. When?'

'January, the doctor says.' Even on the crackly telephone line I could hear the smile in her voice.

'Well, congratulations to you. You know I shall spoil it horribly, don't you?'

'We expect nothing less. Harry also anticipates you being a thoroughly bad influence on the infant Featherstonhaugh and I, for one, wholeheartedly approve.'

'I shall make it my mission to lead the little kipper astray,' said Lady Hardcastle. 'This really is very wonderful indeed. But I must tarry no longer. I have information for your errant husband and I really do need to try to track him down. Do look after yourself. Yourselves, I should say.'

'Of course, dear,' said Lady Lavinia. 'If I hear from Harry, I'll tell him you called.'

'Thank you. Goodnight.'

She put the earpiece back on its hook.

'Well I never,' she said, grinning. 'Aunt Emily, eh? Fancy that.'

'You'll make a marvellous aunt,' I said. 'But we need to get someone to see to our dead body before Mr Hillier has another fit of the vapours and calls the police. I really don't relish the thought of having to deal with the rozzers, even if the alternative means pretending to be polite to the Fish Brothers again.'

'Quite right, too. There's nothing for it but to try that other number.'

More rummaging followed, culminating in the retrieval of the crumpled telegram. She was about to pick up the earpiece again to order the trunk call, but as she reached out, the telephone rang. She gave me a puzzled look and answered it.

'Steep Holm View Hotel. Good evening.'

'Sis?' said another familiar voice, this time male.

'Harry, dear. I was just about to try to telephone you. We tried you at home but you're not.'

'Not what, old thing?'

'Not at home,' she said. 'Congratulations.'

'On not being at home?'

'On the baby,' she said, shaking her head. 'We spoke to Lavinia.'

'Oh, that. Thank you. Good thing I decided to check on you, then.'

'Quite the coincidence,' she said. 'We've good news. And bad news. But mostly bad news.'

'Go on,' he said.

'We tracked the strongbox from Kusnetsov's room to that of Ernst Schneider. An Austrian chap. He's . . . actually, I'm not sure what he is. He has a very common name, though. As does everyone else in the hotel, now I come to think about it. Commonplace, nondescript names. Of the sort designed to attract no attention. One might almost think they were *noms de guerre*. The sort of names spies might use while they were working abroad.'

Harry was not to be distracted by her musings. 'So where is it now, then, this strongbox I explicitly and unambiguously told you not to pursue?'

'That's the first part of the bad news,' she said. 'It has been stolen. Again.'

'I see. And the second part of the bad news?'

'Schneider is dead.'

'Not of natural causes, I presume.'

'Stabbed several times in the chest before having his throat cut,' she confirmed. 'Not a very tidy job, but effective.'

'Has Hillier called the police?'

'No. He's very much out of his depth, the poor lamb. Once he'd come round, we set him to work locking up. He seemed very much inclined to let us take charge.'

'Come round? Was he attacked?'

'No, dear, he fainted when he saw the blood on the floor.'

Harry laughed. 'One would have thought a hotel manager saw worse than that during the course of an average year. All right, I'll get some men to deal with it. We'll take care of the reporting.'

'Your fishy friends?' she asked.

'The very same. You irritated and impressed them in equal measure,' he said. 'But don't poke them too much. I've got them on a reasonably tight leash, but they can be inclined to bite if they're teased.'

'We can handle them,' I said. 'Don't worry about us.'

'Ah, Strongarm, good evening,' he said. 'I didn't realize you were there. I'm sure you can. But I might need them, so don't damage them, please.'

'Of course not, dear,' said Lady Hardcastle. 'But I'm still goggling at the idea of you keeping fish on a leash. Didn't they teach you anything about mixing your metaphors at that expensive school you went to?'

'Didn't that string of equally expensive governesses teach you anything about doing as you're told?' he replied. 'Now for the love of all things holy will you please – and I can't emphasize the importance of this enough – stop meddling.'

'Will you tell us what's going on?'

'There's nothing going on. Now stop meddling in it.'

'As you wish, dear,' she said. 'We shall retire to the salon for a reviving brandy while we await your Special Branch minions.'

'What makes you think they're from Special Branch? I never said anything about Special Branch.'

'It couldn't have been more obvious if they'd had it tattooed on their foreheads,' she said. 'I take it they'll clean up after themselves? I don't think Hillier's staff should have to mop up puddles of blood.'

'I'll send a specialist with them,' said Harry. 'Keep out of the way.'

'Righto, dear. We'll speak again soon, I have no doubt.'

'I'm sure we shall. Goodnight, sis.'

She returned the earpiece to its hook again.

'Come along, Flo. Let's go and see if the Wilsons are still in the salon – I could do with finishing off that brandy.'

We left Mr Hillier's room as we had found it and returned to the salon to await Harry's Fish Men.

Chapter Ten

It was already after half past nine and I fully expected the Misses Wilson to have retired to their beds. I was surprised and amused to find them still in the salon, giggling like schoolgirls over some shared joke. We sat down and joined them.

'How wonderful to see you again,' said Adelia. 'We weren't at all hopeful you'd make it back. Is all well? Did you find the mysterious strongbox?'

'We did not. And that's not the worst part – I'm afraid we found Herr Schneider dead.'

'I don't believe it!' said Adelia. 'In his room?'

'On the floor by the bed,' I said. 'Murdered.'

'Murdered?' said Eleanora. The cognac-induced flush that had suffused her cheeks when we arrived drained quickly away. 'Another man murdered?'

'I'm afraid so,' I said.

'You're afraid so?' Adelia exclaimed. 'Just like that? Like the duchess can't make it to dinner after all or the train is going to be a few minutes late? You're afraid so. Nothing to worry about. Just a minor hiccup.'

I shrugged apologetically.

'Are we safe?' asked Eleanora. 'Should we take precautions?'

'I'm sure we're all safe,' said Lady Hardcastle. 'The killer was almost certainly after the strongbox.'

'And he has it now?'

'The circumstances of the death suggest otherwise,' I said. 'But we need to make a proper search of the room to have a clearer idea.'

'When will you be doing that?' asked Adelia.

'As soon as the authorities have collected the body,' said Lady Hardcastle. 'They'll want to take a look at the room themselves before we go poking about.'

'The police are coming?'

'Something like that. How are you getting on with those brandies? Do you need top-ups?'

'But if the killer doesn't have the strongbox,' persisted Eleanora, 'how can you know we're safe? If he's still looking for it he could be trying all our rooms in turn. We could be next.'

'I understand what you mean,' said Lady Hardcastle. 'The only comfort I can offer is that so far the killer has waited until he's been certain where the box is before striking. It seems we're safe as long as we don't have the strongbox.'

'There you are, dear,' said Adelia. 'I have to agree with our English friends – we've nothing to worry about.'

Eleanora was not to be so easily fobbed off with glib reassurances. 'Do you even know who the killer might be?'

'We have an idea this time,' I said. 'But we can't be certain.'

'This time?' said Eleanora. 'This time? So it might have been someone else the other time? And what about Dr Goddard? Was he taken by a different person, too?'

'There you have us,' said Lady Hardcastle. 'We strongly suspect so, but again we have no proof so we can't be certain.'

'You're not certain of very much, it seems to me.'

'Eleanora Wilson!' said Adelia sharply. 'You mind your manners.'

'I really mean no rudeness,' said Eleanora with only the faintest hint of contrition, 'but you have to admit that horrible, frightening things are happening all around us and our only comfort is the word of two—'

'That's enough, Eleanora,' said Adelia. 'Really.'

'No, it's not enough, Aunt Adelia. I mean you no offence, ladies, but you tell us that awful things are happening and you reassure us that you know we're safe because . . . well, because of what, exactly? Why are *you* "investigating" all this? What qualifies you to take charge and tell Mr Hillier to call in "the authorities" instead of the police?'

Lady Hardcastle looked at me questioningly but I merely shrugged. I didn't mind telling Eleanora the truth, but I thought we were trying to keep it on the QT until we were certain who was who among the hotel's improbable mix of overseas visitors. If she had a better plan, I was happy to go along with it.

'Very well,' she said. 'Perhaps it is time to come clean, after all. Are you all right with that, Flo?'

'Whatever you think best,' I said. 'We could certainly do with an ally or two.'

'Thank you, dear. And if our two countries can be allies, what better place to find personal allies? So, then . . . how to begin? My late husband, Sir Roderick, was a diplomat – a rather talented one, as it happens – and I . . . well, I was a spy. There's no way to sugarcoat it, I'm afraid. While Roddy undertook the Crown's legitimate business abroad, I skulked in the shadows doing the things that all governments do, but none care to admit to. I'm sure you understand.' She looked pointedly at Adelia, who gave a small shrug, but said nothing. 'For the most part I simply needed to be in the right place at the right time with my elegantly bejewelled ears open – one of the few advantages of men thinking we're all simpletons is that they can be catastrophically indiscreet in the company of "mere" women. But sometimes I needed to employ more hugger-mugger tactics – sneaking about, breaking and entering, that sort of thing. For that I needed an assistant, an accomplice, and so I recruited my wonderful lady's maid, Miss Florence Armstrong.'

I smiled as the Wilsons both looked sharply towards me.

'We had many adventures together while Roddy helped to maintain our cover by being one of the most brilliant young diplomats the Foreign Office had ever employed. When he died, we carried on the good work, as it were. After a short break.'

'I'm so sorry,' said Eleanora. 'Does it distress you to talk about it? How did he die?'

'He was murdered in Shanghai by a German assassin called Günther Ehrlichmann. One of the most feared assassins of his day, as it happened. There were stories of him everywhere and only half of them could be true. He couldn't be killed, they said. It was almost as though he had supernatural powers – he would pop up in one place, murder someone, and then be seen thousands of miles away only days later. All stories, of course, to frighten their enemies. But they sent him after my Roddy. Shot him in the eye with a small calibre pistol. I proved the myth wrong when I killed Ehrlichmann, but then Flo and I had to flee across China.'

'Across China?' said Adelia with more than a little astonishment. 'Are you kidding me? From Shanghai? Why didn't you just get on a boat and skedaddle out of there?'

'The streets were full of Chinese rebels and the port was full of German agents. Our only escape lay to the west.'

'How did you survive?'

'On our wits, for the most part. We had Chinese clothes so we attracted little attention from a distance. We were adept at the dishonest arts so we were able to steal food when we couldn't afford to buy it. And then we chanced upon a guide. Flo tells it better.'

'I do? Oh. Umm. We were in Hunan Province and we met a monk. I'm reasonably sure you could tell them that just as well as I.'

'But the good bits are more about you. You tell it.'

'All right, then,' I said. 'We met a monk. He was trudging along on his own and we just sort of fell in with him. He was . . . I think "taciturn" best describes him, but as the weeks went by we learned a little about him. His name was Chen Ping Bo and he had left his monastic order to wander in the world. I was never able to find out if he left of his own accord or had been expelled, but he moved from town to town, village to village, working where he could. He agreed to be our guide and to take us all the way west and into Burma so that eventually we could find a ship to take us to Calcutta and a way of getting home.'

'That's not the part that everyone loves to hear, dear,' said Lady Hardcastle. 'Tell them the good bit.'

I sighed. 'We had been travelling steadily westward with our new guide for less than a week. He had insisted that we stopped skulking across the fields and travelled on the roads instead. Neither of us was particularly comfortable with the idea, but he insisted. He had a quiet, confident way about him and he made it seem as though it would be perfectly safe.'

'I'll bet it wasn't,' said Eleanora, her grumpy demeanour suddenly gone.

'As it turns out,' I said, 'it was and it wasn't. Shortly after dawn one day, we ate our meagre breakfast, broke camp, and set off towards the next village. Chen Ping Bo was in good spirits – he knew the village and was sure it would welcome us. We'd walked no more than a mile when we were set upon by three bandits.'

'Oh, my,' said Eleanora. 'It's like an adventure story, but in real life.'

I do like a good audience. 'One of them had leapt out at us from behind a tree,' I continued. 'He was brandishing a hefty stick, and when we turned to get away from him, his two comrades emerged from the ditch beside the road, each armed with their own rather nasty-looking sticks and barring our retreat. Chen sighed and put down his pack.'

'I knew he was going to be more than he seemed,' said Eleanora.

'Calmly and politely, Chen said a few words to the first man in a dialect I didn't recognize – we already spoke some Mandarin and Shanghainese from our time on the coast, but there are dozens of languages in China. The bandits laughed and jeered. Chen said a few more words and got the same reaction. Then in Mandarin, he quietly said, "Ladies, would you be so kind as to step to the side of the road." So we did – we had no better plan, after all. Chen bowed to the first bandit, who laughed again and said a few words in an unmistakably mocking tone. Chen just stood there, relaxed and smiling. The first bandit advanced on him, leering and swinging his stick menacingly, but still Chen did not move. The bandit aimed a blow near Chen's head, and seemed slightly disconcerted when Chen didn't flinch. Becoming increasingly angry, the bandit swung again, this time clearly intending to make contact – I feared that our newfound companion would be killed.'

Eleanora fanned her face with her fingers.

'The next thing I was properly aware of was the bandit lying on his back on the ground clutching his throat and gasping for breath, and Chen – now holding the stick – turning to face the other two men. There was a moment's pause before they dropped their own sticks and fled down the road in the direction we had just come. Chen helped their friend to his feet and bowed to him once more. The bandit, shaking slightly, bowed in return before he, too, fled in the same direction as his fellows. Slowly and deliberately, Chen picked up his pack and indicated that we should resume our journey. I asked him what we had just seen and he said, "What do you think you saw?" I told him I'd seen the man go to strike him with his stick, Chen took a step towards him, there was a flurry of hands, feet and elbows, too fast for me to make out, and then the man was lying on the ground, choking. And he just said, "Then that must have been what happened."'

'That was all?' asked Eleanora.

'That was all,' I said. 'In the short time we'd known him, we'd learned that Chen was the sort of fellow who really rather enjoyed not giving direct answers to direct questions.'

'The strong, mysterious type,' said Eleanora.

I smiled. 'I asked him if it was something I could learn to do. And he said, "You strike me as a very capable young woman. I am sure that with a lifetime's study, prayer, and meditation, you could become very skilled. Alas, the rules of my order are very strict and women are not permitted." I wasn't to be put off, so I asked if he could teach me to defend myself. I argued that they were dangerous times and that we wouldn't always be able to rely on him for protection.'

'What did he say?'

'He looked at me solemnly for a few moments, then said, "It is against all the rules of my order, but you make a good case. I shall teach you. And your mistress, too?"'

'You, too, Emily? Did he teach you, too?' Eleanora was quite caught up in the story.

'Me?' said Lady Hardcastle. 'That would be have been fun, wouldn't it? But I had to decline – I'm not cut out for the rough and tumble. And I wouldn't want to damage my hands.' She held up her elegant hands. 'I might never play the piano again.'

Eleanora laughed.

'Whereas I knew for a fact that she was no stranger to rough and tumble,' I said. 'She's also an expert markswoman with pistol and rifle. But I confess I was rather pleased that I should be the only one to learn Chen's mysterious arts so I said nothing. As the months passed and our journey took us further and further west towards Burma, Chen Ping Bo trained me in the basics of his own particular brand of hand-to-hand combat. As I learned not only the physical skills, but also a little of the philosophy that shaped them, I realized that he had been right: it would take a lifetime of diligent study to master them. Nevertheless, by the time we had slipped across the Burmese border and had eventually arrived at Mandalay, I was deemed more than capable of protecting myself and Lady Hardcastle. Chen even went so far as to suggest that if ever a monastic order were to admit women, I should apply at once to be their first student.'

'I'm sorry I doubted you,' said Eleanora. 'Can you kill a man with your bare hands?'

'Eleanora, really,' admonished Adelia. 'What sort of thing is that to ask a woman?'

'I'm sorry,' she said. 'What happened next? How did you get home? You had a long way to go.'

'Yes, we were still only in Burma,' said Lady Hardcastle. 'Down in the docks in Mandalay, we managed to find an old gentleman with a boat—'

She was interrupted by a discreet cough from the night porter.

'Excuse me, m'lady,' he said. 'There are two gentlemen in reception to see you.'

'That was quick,' said Lady Hardcastle. 'Very well. Would you be a dear and see to them, Flo? I'll stay here and regale our new chums with the tale of our heroic voyage down the Irrawaddy to Rangoon.' She handed me the master key.

'Of course, my lady,' I said. 'But bear in mind, ladies, that the python was only three feet long and the hole in the boat was easily fixed by stuffing it with leaves and tree sap. I've heard versions of the story where we fought a ten-foot snake and had to frantically bail out the boat with our cupped hands to keep us from drowning.'

'Spoilsport,' she said. 'Go and deal with the fish.'

I left the Wilsons to be entertained by a tale of tropical derring-do whose level of inventive exaggeration would have made Baron Munchausen blush, while I took care of more pro-saic matters like the removal of dead bodies and the searching of hotel rooms.

The two Special Branch men were waiting in reception. They had adopted exactly the same poses in exactly the same positions as when we first saw them. The only appreciable differences to the scene were a hefty hold-all, and the now-familiar canvas body carrier which lay on the floor at Left-Hander's feet.

The porter said, 'Mr Oryx and Mr Kudu for you, miss', and scuttled back to the elegantly appointed porter's chair by the front door.

'Good evening, gentlemen,' I said. 'We're ungulates of the African plains this evening, I see.'

'We like to ring the changes,' said Right-Hander. 'A moving target is harder to hit and all that.'

'But it's so difficult to keep track of,' I replied. 'Even you can't remember your names half the time. I shall call you Mr Righty and Mr Lefty – that's much easier.'

'And why . . . ?'

'I should have thought it was obvious,' I said. 'You're right-handed and your charming colleague is left-handed.'

'But how . . . ?' said Mr Lefty with evident surprise.

'Your guns,' I explained. 'You surely don't imagine passers-by don't notice that you're carrying shooters.'

He self-consciously tapped the poorly concealed weapon under his right armpit. 'Well, aren't you the tricky one. Is your mistress not joining us?'

'No, Mr Lefty,' I said. 'She's otherwise engaged. You'll have to make do with me.'

'What about Hillier?' asked Mr Righty.

'He's about somewhere. We'll keep him informed. But he'd definitely like you to clean up, please. Mr Featherstonhaugh said you'd be bringing an expert.'

Mr Lefty lifted the substantial hold-all from the floor. 'I've all the specialist equipment we need, thank you.'

'Then follow me,' I said.

I took them to Schneider's room and opened the door with the master key. I waited outside while they did what they needed to do.

They were not grand company. They talked to each other only when necessary and rebuffed all my own attempts at genial chit-chat. I began to wish I'd brought a book, but a pleasing consequence of their brusque efficiency was that they bagged the body, cleaned the floor, and conducted a professional – if brief – search of the room before I'd had time to become properly bored.

'We'll be on our way,' said Mr Righty.

'Thank you for your help,' I said. 'Do you have a card? We shall recommend you to our friends.'

'Why don't you—' began Mr Lefty, but his colleague cut him off before I could find out what he was going to suggest I do.

'That's enough,' said Mr Righty. 'We're all on the same side here.'

'Tell *her* that,' sneered Mr Lefty. 'Uppity little—'

'I said that's enough. Good evening, miss.' Encumbered as he was by the bagged corpse of Herr Schneider he was unable to tip his hat, but he nodded a farewell and together they carried their grim burden towards the goods lift.

I watched them disappear round the corner and then set about undertaking my own search of the room.

There really wasn't much to see that we hadn't seen when we first entered the room and found Schneider dead a couple of hours earlier. His astonishing collection of ointments, unguents, medicines, and potions would have put a decent-sized chemist's shop to shame, and most of it was spilled on the floor. If nothing else it gave the room the pleasant smell we'd noted earlier and went some way to softening the lingering tang of blood and the sharp whiff of the Jeyes Fluid Mr Lefty had used to clean it up. Specialist equipment, my eye. I could have done that.

Carefully avoiding the spilled toiletries, I knelt on the floor to have one last look under the bed, this time from the side nearest the door, where Schneider's body had been lying. As I brushed my face against the embroidered bedspread, I noticed a new smell. It was faint, but unmistakeable.

I knew who had the strongbox.

There was no time to lose – I had to abandon the idea of completing the search. I stood and brushed the dust from my skirt, took one last quick look around just in case, and hurried from the room. I locked the door and made my way to the staircase as quickly as I could.

I took the stairs two at a time – the new possessor of the box could be back at any moment. I proceeded as quickly as I dared along the corridor. Nothing draws attention more rapidly than the sight of someone running, but there was no one there and my haste went unnoticed. Nevertheless, I needed to get out of sight as quickly as I could.

I reached the door and panicked briefly when I couldn't find my master key. With an actual, unprofessional, giving-the-game-away sigh of relief I found that I'd put it in the other pocket of my jacket. I took it out and presented it to the lock, which submitted without further drama. I slipped inside.

There was that perfume smell again. Adelia Wilson must bathe in it. But I wasn't about to complain – at least she'd let me know where to find the strongbox.

The search didn't take long.

Under Adelia's bed was a large box. It was about a foot deep, a foot high, and eighteen inches wide. It appeared to be made of steel, with heavy reinforcement riveted along each edge and more at the corners. There were sturdy handles at either end. The lock looked elaborately sophisticated. Clearly, no one but the owner was supposed to get in either by stealth or brute force.

I dragged the strongbox out by one of the handles and finally learned why everyone had chosen to hide it under their beds – it weighed a ton. It would take altogether far too much effort to get it up on to the top of a wardrobe and I'd be wary of putting it inside – I'd not be confident that a shelf could support its weight.

Time was still against me, so I couldn't examine it further. Checking that I hadn't disarranged the room and that the bedspread was exactly as I'd found it, I grabbed the box by both handles and heaved it out to the corridor. I had to put it down to relock the door, then hefted it on to my shoulder to carry it back to our room.

It was a gamble. If I met anyone on the stairs, I was in trouble. Martin or Takahashi would definitely put up a fight – we were already sure that Martin had killed Schneider and it was quite possible that Takahashi had garrotted Kusnetsov. Adelia Wilson was less of a physical threat, but a confrontation would still be inconvenient. I was confident that I could handle any of them, but the jig would most definitely be up. And once news of any run-in on the stairs became public, the remaining players would quickly work out where the strongbox was and we'd have to fight everyone off.

Luck, though, was with me. I made it to my own room without seeing a soul. Ever one to follow fashion, I pushed the strongbox under my bed. I took a couple of hatboxes from Lady Hardcastle's wardrobe and pushed them under, too. The strongbox wasn't exactly hidden, but it should be sufficiently out of view to escape the notice of the chambermaid.

I brushed myself down again, straightened myself out, and set off back to the salon.

◆ ◆ ◆

'Here she is,' said Lady Hardcastle. 'Is all well? Did the Fish Brothers behave themselves?'

'They are the Antelope Boys this evening,' I said. 'But they took care of things.'

'Fish Brothers?' said Adelia. 'Antelope Boys?'

'Two Special Branch men sent by my brother,' said Lady Hardcastle. 'They seem to enjoy making themselves appear more glamorous and exciting by working under pseudonymous codenames. Yesterday they were European freshwater fish, this evening they appear to be even-toed ungulates from Africa. It's all larks and japes down at Special Branch.'

'Your brother?' said Adelia. She had a very concise inter-rogation technique.

'My brother is Harry Featherstonhaugh of the Foreign Office. He seems to have taken an interest in the goings-on here. I've no idea why, but we seldom talk about work.'

I could see that she was watching Adelia Wilson very closely as she revealed this unnecessarily indiscreet informa-tion. Her efforts were rewarded – Miss Wilson's eyes widened ever so slightly at the mention of the Foreign Office. Now Lady Hardcastle had also confirmed what I already knew:

Adelia Wilson was more than just a holidaying spinster from Maryland.

'Your family seems to be heavily involved in British politics,' said Adelia. 'Husband a diplomat, brother a civil servant, you a . . . spy.'

'Our father was something terribly grand at the Treasury, too,' said Lady Hardcastle. 'Mother was just Mother, mind you. Although who knows what great affairs of state were settled during her Wednesday-night bridge games?'

'I'm sure more than one international treaty has been brokered over a game of cards.'

'Well, quite,' said Lady Hardcastle. 'Flo, dear, you seem to be rather short of brandy. Shall we see if we can summon . . . Ah, Ribble, there you are. Another round of cognac, please. Is that all right for you, ladies?'

'Actually, it's rather late,' said Adelia. 'May we have some cocoa, please?'

'A splendid notion. Cocoa and cognac all round. And some more of those little biscuits you brought out earlier. Thank you, Ribble, you're a marvel.'

'It's my pleasure, my lady,' said Ribble and vanished as smoothly and silently as he had arrived.

'I've been terribly inconsiderate,' said Lady Hardcastle. 'We're keeping you up. I'm so sorry. Do please retire if you need to.'

'Don't you worry about us,' said Adelia. 'We're having a fine time, aren't we, Eleanora?'

'Mm-hmm,' mumbled the sleepy younger Wilson.

'Emily was telling us all about the man with the boat and the journey down the Irrawaddy,' continued Adelia enthusiastically.

'He was a nice old chap,' I said. 'Very friendly. Not a tooth in his head, but quite charming. He seemed pleased to get rid of the boat, although we weren't able to ask him about it.'

'I know,' she said. 'Imagine you two being able to speak so many languages and then finding yourselves somewhere where no one understands any of them.'

'It was a bit of a stumper,' I said.

'I tried to remember what we offered him for the boat,' said Lady Hardcastle. 'But that turned out to be a bit of a stumper, too.'

'A gold sovereign, an opal ring that had been a gift from your aunt—'

'I never liked that.'

'—and a silk blouse I'd bought in a market in Shanghai for next to nothing.'

'That was it,' she said. 'I think both sides did well out of that deal.'

'How far did she get?' I asked.

'You had arrived at Rangoon,' said Eleanora.

'There's not much more to tell from there,' said Lady Hardcastle. 'We made contact with the British officials, there was a flurry of cables, most of them expressing astonishment that we were still alive, and we secured berths on a ship bound for Calcutta.'

'The folks at home thought you were dead?' asked Eleanora.

'Understandably,' said Lady Hardcastle. 'We'd been gone for nearly two years. I think we only trekked a couple of thousand miles, all in all, but there were mountains, jungles, more chaps with sticks – you know the sort of thing. And we had to hunker down during the winter, of course, so it took a little longer than one might expect.'

'They must have been glad to see you.'

'One would have thought so, but it was all a bit of an anticlimax, to be honest. Much less fuss was made than we'd expected so we ended up staying in Calcutta for a couple more years before finally coming home.'

The cocoa arrived and was eagerly consumed – all the more eagerly when Lady Hardcastle encouraged them to fortify the chocolate drink with the brandy.

It wasn't long before we were all yawning and offering half-hearted variations on, 'Well, I suppose we'd better go up', but without actually moving. Eventually it was Adelia Wilson who took the lead, summoning her niece and wishing us goodnight.

We weren't far behind them.

◆ ◆ ◆

'How did it go?' asked Lady Hardcastle once we were safely behind the locked door of our 'suite'.

'Not as interesting as I'd hoped at first,' I said. 'I essayed a little light persiflage with Harry's thugs, but they were having none of it.'

'That's no fun. Too disciplined?'

'Or too dull-witted – it's hard to tell with hired muscle.'

'Did things brighten up at all?'

'I'll say. Once they'd gone, taking the late Ernst Schneider with them, I had another quick nosy round the room and I noticed a familiar smell.'

'Blood? Hair oil? Disinfectant?'

'All that and more,' I said. 'How did you know about the disinfectant?'

'How else would one clean up blood from a hotel room floor?'

'What do you know about cleaning anything from anywhere?'

'I read. I observe.'

'Hmm,' I said. 'Well, you're right. Their specialist crime scene expertise extended only as far as wandering in to the nearest hardware shop and buying some Jeyes Fluid. But none of those smells, however distinctive, was as significant as the faint whiff I got off the bedspread.'

'Adelia Wilson's perfume,' she said.

'You can be most infuriating sometimes.'

'I'm right, though, aren't I?'

'You are.'

'So do we think the Wilsons have the strongbox?'

'They do not.'

'Oh, that's a shame,' she said. 'I wonder who does.'

'We do.'

'Oh, well done, you. Where?'

'Where everyone else keeps it – under the bed.'

I led her through to my bedroom and hauled the box from its hiding place.

'Goodness me,' she exclaimed. 'That's not something one could overlook in a search, is it?'

'It's not something one can carry about particularly easily, either – it's exactly as heavy as it looks. It's a wonder none of us were seen lumbering about the place with it.'

She gave an exploratory tug at one of the handles. 'Adelia Wilson is stronger than she appears. I'm not certain I could carry it very far and she . . . what? Carried it to her room?'

'And put it under her bed, yes.'

'She must have sneaked up there while I was waiting for the night porter to contact Hillier. The slippery little weasel.'

'Do they have weasels in America?' I said.

'I believe they do, actually, yes. You were careful?'

'No trace of my presence was left. Not even the lingering ghost of my perfume.'

'You don't wear perfume.'

'And a good thing, too. It turns out that wearing perfume is a dead giveaway in our game.'

'So even if she should chance to check under the bed, she'll not be certain that we have the box.'

'I'd say we'd be odds-on favourites, though,' I said. 'I was gone for quite a while and our skulduggerous past is no longer a secret.'

'That was a wasted gambit as it turns out,' she said. 'I was trying to flush them out.'

'I know.'

'As it was, she didn't bat an eyelid until I mentioned Harry's name and by then you'd already twigged her game. Ah, well. No harm done, I suppose.'

'And it entertained Eleanora,' I said. 'She needed a distraction – she's quite frightened.'

'I believe she is, yes. It's really rather reckless of Adelia to bring her along on a mission. She's only, what, sixteen? Seventeen?'

'I was only eighteen when you recruited me,' I said.

'I suppose you were,' she said. 'But you were so much more worldly. And you were already a dab hand with a knife – I'd seen you doing the tricks your father taught you. I don't imagine little Miss Wilson would be much use in a skirmish but I knew you could hold your own, even before Chen taught you his arcane fighting arts.'

'There's more to her than meets the eye, I think, but I take your point.'

She resumed her examination of the strongbox. 'Have you tried the lock?'

'Not yet, no,' I said. 'It looks rather sophisticated, but I'm sure it will yield to my trusty picklocks.'

'I'm sure it will.'

It didn't.

After half an hour of fruitless fiddling, I finally chucked up the sponge.

'This, I'm afraid, is hopeless,' I said. 'I'm getting nowhere. We might manage more in daylight when I can actually see what I'm doing, but for now I'm going to have to admit temporary defeat.'

'Not to worry, dear,' said Lady Hardcastle. 'Let's sleep on it. Do you think it would be worth searching through Dr Goddard's things for a key? It's the sort of thing that might have been overlooked in previous searches.'

'We could give it a go,' I said. 'First thing in the morning. I don't suppose you brought one of your pistols?'

'I was just this very moment regretting my decision not to. What about you? Any knives in your luggage?'

'Sadly not,' I said.

'We'll just have to defend ourselves the medieval way.'

'Solemn prayers and a lucky amulet?'

'I was thinking more along the lines of building a castle,' she said. 'Or of barricading ourselves in, at any rate. Between the two of us we should be able to bar the doors with these tallboys. That should hinder any would-be attacker long enough for you to adopt a fighting stance and prepare to give him—'

'Or her.'

'—or her a biff on the conk.'

'It's as good a plan as any,' I said.

We moved the two hefty chests of drawers across the rooms to block both bedroom doors and settled down for the night in our new fortress.

Chapter Eleven

Despite the urgency I perceived in the need to find Dr Goddard's key and open the strongbox, Lady Hardcastle was her usual infuriating self.

'The contents of the box will be exactly the same after breakfast,' she said.

'But if anyone should chance to work out that we have the box, they'll have the perfect opportunity to relieve us of it while we're stuffing our faces,' I said. 'The contents will remain the same, but the box itself will be once more on its travels.'

'No one knows we've got it. Takahashi will think that either Martin or Adelia Wilson has it. Similarly, Martin will suspect Takahashi or Wilson.'

'But Miss Wilson knows that we're also part of the game now. And after her own little act of larceny last night, she'll pretty soon wonder why it took me so long to see to Tweedle-Dum and Tweedle-Dee when they took Schneider away.'

'She has no idea how long it took them — they left by the back door. As far as she knows, you came straight down once they'd gone. You worry too much. And if she nicks it from under your bed, we'll just send you up to her room to nick it back.'

I harrumphed.

'You see? You're hungry – you always get grumpy when you're hungry. A good breakfast will set you up for a day of key finding and box opening. Then we can have a session of Harry calling, opinion giving, and information demanding before embarking on some scientist finding.'

'On the whole, I'd rather be riding the donkeys.'

'Donkey riding can come later. For now, though, we need to do some breakfast eating as a matter of urgency.'

We arrived in the dining room at eight, a full hour earlier than our previous efforts.

'Clearly this is the time one has to arrive to have any hope of seeing the kedgeree,' said Lady Hardcastle as we surveyed the groaning sideboard. 'A full dish, look.'

'Completely full,' I said. 'No sign of its having been touched at all.' I looked around. 'In fact, there's no sign of any of these dishes having been touched. Nor of anyone having sat at any of the tables.'

'That can't be right,' she said. 'We've been here at just after nine for the past two mornings and the groaning board has long since stopped groaning and has heaved a sigh of relief that its burden has been mercifully lessened. Surely they don't swarm in here at half past, strip the place bare and disappear before we turn up.'

'It does seem particularly odd.'

The dining room waiter appeared with fresh coffee.

'Here's someone who'll know,' said Lady Hardcastle. 'Kibble, my dear chap, are we the first down to breakfast?'

'You are, my lady, yes,' he said. 'Which is odd, now you come to ask about it. Things change in a hotel week by week as guests come and go, but there's usually a steady . . . well, you can't call it a "steady stream" with this being such a small hotel, but there are comings and goings from before seven most mornings.'

'And this week's guests are early risers?'

'They are, my lady, yes. Or, at least, they have been so far.'

'Most peculiar,' she said. 'Still, more choice for us. Is that fresh coffee I smell?'

'Yes, my lady. Shall I pour you a cup? Which table would you prefer this morning?'

'That one there where we can see the door,' she said. 'Armstrong? A cup for you?'

'Yes, please,' I said. 'How long has this toast been here?'

'Quite a while, I'm afraid, miss,' said Kibble. 'I'll get you some fresh.'

I thanked him and followed Lady Hardcastle to her chosen table with my first helping.

'That's quite a plateful you have there, young Flo,' she said.

'The first of several,' I said. 'Or that's the plan, at least. There's something about seeing a generous selection of goodies at breakfast time that makes me want to scoff the lot.'

'I know that feeling. Perhaps I should be grateful for corsets after all.'

Kibble arrived with my toast.

'What time does Miss Wilson usually take breakfast?' I asked.

'Which one?' he said.

'Adelia.'

'She usually arrives at about half past seven.'

'And Eleanora?' said Lady Hardcastle.

'She comes down with her aunt at half past seven,' he said with the faintest hint of a smile.

'He went to the same training school as you and Ribble, Armstrong,' she said.

'Can I get you anything else?' he said.

'No, thank you. Everything is simply splendid.'

'Thank you, my lady. You know where the bell is if you need me.'

He vanished.

I tucked in to my breakfast.

'This kedgeree was worth waiting for,' I said. 'It's delicious.'

'I shall get some on my next trip. I say, what's that over there?'

By the time I realized I'd been had, there was a sausage missing from my plate.

'You've lost none of the old magic, then,' I said. 'Still the mistress of subterfuge and deception.'

'None of the old skills seem to be doing me much good lately. We still don't have the faintest idea what happened to Goddard and we've lost two foreign spies while we've been waiting for inspiration to strike.'

'To be fair, we do have the strongbox now. And the spies were never actually our responsibility.'

'I suppose not. I still can't work out why Harry's not doing more. "National security" is all well and good if all one is going to do is tap the side of one's nose and decline to reveal the location of one of His Majesty's frigates. But if one is going to spirit away the bodies of recently murdered foreign agents, I can't help but feel that nose tapping and "national security, old thing"-ing is somewhat inadequate. I expected this place to be knee-deep in armed men with false names by now.'

'Perhaps it is,' I said. 'Perhaps they're better at hiding than we suppose.'

'I'm going to demand answers the next time we speak to him,' she said. 'But for now, let us fortify ourselves for the day's toil with this hearty grub and talk of cheerier things.'

So we did. I wondered for a time if the plan had backfired when I found myself feeling too full to get up and search Goddard's room, but my curiosity won out over my post-breakfast lethargy, and I led the way up the stairs.

We let ourselves in to Dr Goddard's room. Myra the maid had done a good job of tidying up after the break-in and the whole place seemed to be in perfect order. It looked for all the world as though Dr Goddard had just gone out for the day.

'I'd say there's little need to scour the place,' I said. 'Myra did say she was one for looking under the bed and the room was thoroughly searched by whoever broke in. If there's a key here it'll be in a clothes pocket or in that valet case on the writing desk there.'

I indicated the shallow leather case.

'Hunter and chain,' she said, prodding through the scant contents of the tray. 'Cufflinks. Collar stud. A fiver and some change.'

'Nineteen shillings and fourpence?' I asked.

She counted the coins. 'Exactly that.'

'Then Myra is as refreshingly honest as she is conscientious and efficient in her work. That's what I counted when we first came in here.'

'No key, though.'

'Then Myra didn't find one. If she were going to nick anything she'd have taken the nineteen bob. Who takes a key and leaves almost a pound behind?'

'You are wise in the ways of the petty thief.'

'Common sense, my lady,' I said.

I opened the wardrobe and began going through the pockets of the suits that had been carefully rehung there since we had first searched the room. I found another penny, a button (curiously from a different jacket to the one I found it in), three farthings, and a used tram ticket.

'Nothing here,' I said. 'I'll try the shoes.'

'Wouldn't your pal Myra have found anything hidden in a shoe, even if the burglar had missed it?'

'Perhaps,' I said. 'But I'm better at this than they are.'

I checked inside the shoes where, of course, I found nothing. I felt around the uppers and the tongues for hidden pockets. I teased up the insoles, looking for anything concealed beneath. I tried the heels to see if the top plates were loose or hinged, in case they might reveal a secret compartment. Nothing.

I cast around the room, but now that it was tidy it was obvious that there were few places to conceal things. Few places that hadn't already been thoroughly examined, at least.

Lady Hardcastle, meanwhile, had been rifling through Dr Goddard's sponge bag and another small bag containing his clothes brushes and shoe polish.

'We remain keyless,' she said. 'We are bereft of keys. *Non habemus claves. Nous n'avons pas de clefs. Wir haben keine Schlü—*'

'Why would you go to Latin as your first choice?'

'I am a lady of culture and learning – it's what we do. I would have tried it in ancient Greek as well, but my Greek is as rusty as my Russian.'

'And it used to give you so much pleasure. But I'm stumped. We can have another go at picking the lock in the daylight, but I think we have to accept that we're stuck firmly on the outside of the strongbox for now.'

'I agree. We'll just have to tell Harry we have it without the pleasure of knowing what's in it. He's going to be insufferably priggish about not telling us, too. Heigh-ho. Come, then, diminutive one. We shall hie us to Hillier's lair and try to book an urgent trunk call to London.'

We locked the door behind us and made our way to the stairs.

We passed our own landing and were on the last flight of stairs leading down to reception when we met the porter on his way up. He stopped us.

'Beggin' your pardon, m'lady,' he said, bowing slightly, 'but Mr Hillier asks if you would be kind enough to speak to him. He's in his office.'

'Thank you,' she said. 'We'll go straight there.'

The porter bowed again and hurried away.

'That's handy,' she said as we continued our journey.

'What is?'

'That Hillier wants to see me. Us. It means he's in his office and we won't have to break in to use his telephone.'

'Is it breaking in if we have the key?'

'You know what I mean. I wonder what he wants.'

'He probably wants to know where all his guests are,' I said. 'We've not seen a soul all morning.'

'That's not encouraging at all.'

We arrived at Mr Hillier's office and she knocked on the door, then opened it without troubling to wait for a response.

'Good morning, Mr Hillier,' she said breezily. 'I understand you wanted to see us?'

He put down his pen and looked up. His face was grey and careworn. The news, I surmised, was not good.

'Lady Hardcastle. And Miss Armstrong. Thank you for coming. Things are . . . things are getting worse. Terrible. I don't know how much more we can take. I'm afraid I can no longer keep the police out of this.'

'There's been another death?'

'Two,' he said, his eyes widening. 'Two more. I've had to send Myra home. She's in an awful state.'

'Good lord,' she said. 'Who?'

'Monsieur Martin and Mr Takahashi.'

'In the same room?'

'No,' he said, as though that idea were even more shocking than the men's deaths. 'They were each in their own rooms.

Myra found the Frenchman first and came to me in a panic. I checked on him, locked the door, and told her to carry on – I knew Mr Featherstonhaugh would want me to speak to you before I . . . before I took any further action. I was about to call on you when Myra returned and said that she had discovered Mr Takahashi's body and . . . well, as I say, we had to send her home. I do wonder if she'll come back after all that, actually. I'm not sure I want to come back. I'm not used to so much . . .'

'Was there much?' I asked.

'Much what? Blood? No, I didn't mean that. Good lord.' The colour drained from his face. 'I meant so much death.'

'You're certain they're both dead, though?'

'I . . . well . . . I didn't examine them closely. I . . . look, you know what happens to me when I . . . you know. I'm not proud of it, but there we are. I looked in, saw the inert bodies, noted with great relief the absence of blood, and shut the door on it all. I need to call the police now, I really do. To the devil with the hotel's owners and their reputations – we need to alert the proper authorities.'

'I would counsel you against it for the moment, Mr Hillier,' said Lady Hardcastle. 'For all his blithe bonhomie and breezy badinage, my brother genuinely does represent "the proper authorities". And while I find the dear boy's lack of candour on the matter utterly exasperating, I believe he really does have things . . . I was going to say "under control" but that would be rather overstating it. "In hand", perhaps. There is something afoot here – oh, I say, I've got my hands and feet all jumbled up – something afoot of which we know little. I'm prepared to take Harry's word for it that involving the local rozzers would put spanners in works and cats among pigeons to a degree that may well, as he so irritatingly puts it, "compromise national security". Please allow us to examine both rooms and then leave it to me to contact my brother.'

The poor chap looked utterly defeated. 'I only want to do the right thing,' he said, staring at his leather-edged blotter. 'If you're certain that what you propose is the right thing, then I'll not stand in your way. I just wanted to run the finest small hotel in Somerset. "Bijou", they called it in the society pages. "Elegant". "Refined". "Exclusive". We have one of the finest chefs in the whole of the south of England. And our wine cellar . . . Well, you've sampled our wines. I wanted to welcome elegant and refined guests to my exclusive, bijou hotel. To show them . . .' He looked up again. 'I'm sorry. Please carry on. You'll need my telephone, I presume.'

'Thank you,' said Lady Hardcastle. She rummaged quickly in her handbag to find Harry's telegram and her own notebook. Picking up Mr Hillier's pen, she wrote down the exchange name and telephone number and tore out the page. 'Please book a trunk call to this number while we check the rooms. We've been lucky with quick connections so far, but knowing our luck this will be the one time we have to wait an hour for a line.'

He took the piece of paper and smiled wanly. 'As you wish, my lady,' he said.

We left him to his task and hurried off upstairs.

We began with Mr Takahashi's room. It was at the rear of our own floor, next to that of the late Herr Schneider. Lady Hardcastle unlocked the door with her master key and we stepped inside.

The room was in less disarray than I had anticipated. There was evidence of a search but it had been less vigorous than the others. It was obvious that few things had been moved about. From his manner and appearance, I judged Mr Takahashi to live a well-ordered life, but his personal effects were not as neatly arranged as I would have expected. The wardrobe was open and the bedspread lifted, as though someone had looked under the bed.

The main reason for the visit, it seemed to me, had been to eliminate Takahashi himself. I had thought we'd find him, like the others, on the floor, but he was lying serenely in his bed. He definitely appeared to be dead, and if I were as squeamish as Mr Hillier I would have taken the same quick look that he had, come to the same conclusion, and beaten the same hasty retreat. I, though, felt obliged to examine him more closely.

His head was turned away from us, facing the window. I could still see the side of his face, but nothing more. I rounded the bed.

'What's your diagnosis, Dr Armstrong?' said Lady Hardcastle.

'The skin is pale and . . . waxy looking,' I said. 'But there's no sign of discolouration.'

'That would fit with what we know,' she said. 'We saw him at dinner last night and he left the dining room at around eight. That's only just over twelve hours, and even in the comparative warmth of our mild summer that's not long enough for putrefaction to become unpleasantly evident.'

'And he was in bed asleep,' I said. 'In his rather natty silk pyjamas. So he wasn't killed promptly at eight.'

'Asleep?'

'He was lying down when he was . . . Oh.'

'Oh? When he was what?'

'When he was shot. In the eye. Small calibre.'

'Small and low-powered,' she said. 'There's no exit wound – the back of his head is unmarked. And you're right about lying down. At least there's no indication that he was sitting up in bed and reading or anything like that. Perhaps he didn't even wake.'

'Possibly not,' I said. 'There's no sign of a struggle. Then again, the killer might have tidied the bedclothes to make it look like he was just sleeping.'

'He—'

'Or she,' I interrupted.

'Or she, yes. He or she might have done exactly that. Do you think it could be Adelia?'

'She has a small calibre pistol,' I said. 'What if she woke up in the night and had some peculiar urge to check whether the strongbox was still under her bed? Perhaps she set off, Colt in hand, to get it back.'

'So she picked Takahashi's lock, checked under his bed, saw that he didn't have the box and thought, "Well, dash it, I've come all this way I might as well shoot him now I'm here"?'

'More like "darn it",' I said. 'But something along those lines, yes. We don't know what her brief was, after all. She might have been sent here to assassinate any and all foreign agents operating in the hotel.'

'Foes and allies alike?' she said. 'I'm not so sure. I can't rule her out, but it seems unlikely.'

'Who then? There's no one else left alive. If Martin died last night, too, that only leaves the Wilsons, the hotel staff and us. And you haven't got a gun.'

'You're forgetting our burglar,' she said.

'You think he came back? What for?'

'To kill Takahashi and Martin.'

'Hmm,' I said.

'Or Goddard,' she said slowly.

'Goddard faked his own kidnap and has been sneaking back to eliminate the "competition"?'

'Why not?' she mused.

'How did he happen to pick exactly the people who had his mystical box of wonders?' I said. 'If he were hiding somewhere, how would he be able to follow the trail to Kusnetsov and Schneider? We were here and it took us a while to fathom where it was.'

'A man on the inside? Or he's hiding in the hotel? The room next to mine is empty – the one directly below his.'

'I admire your efforts to explore every possibility,' I said. 'But no matter how unlikely I find the mysterious burglar idea, I can't help but think it's more likely than it being all down to Goddard.'

'You're probably right, dear. There's nothing more to be learned here, though. Shall we see what happened to Martin?'

We locked the door behind us and set off upstairs.

What happened to Martin, it turned out, was exactly the same thing. The bedclothes were slightly disarranged, hinting that Martin might have woken before his assailant had struck, but a similar small calibre bullet fired into the right eye had the same lethal effect as before. And, as before, there was no exit wound.

'Same gun, same MO,' I said.

'Hark at you and your fancy police jargon,' she said. 'But yes, I agree this is likely to be the same killer.'

'And different from the other two,' I said.

'A garrotting, a stabbing and two shootings . . . At first glance it does seem more likely that it's the work of different people . . . but . . .'

'But?'

'Well, Goddard is a clever fellow. And who knows what training he has? How many ways can you kill a man, for instance?'

'Me personally?' I said. 'Many more than three, certainly. So you think Goddard is an assassin as well as a scientist?'

'Or perhaps instead of being a scientist. We only have his word for it that he knows the first thing about science, or maritime engineering, or radios, or whatever else it was he claimed to be involved with.'

'His word and Harry's,' I said.

'Harry hasn't actually offered any confirmation of who or what Goddard is.'

'He did mention him being a scientist. "His" scientist if I remember correctly.'

'Those were my words, dear,' she said. 'Harry has never used the words "Goddard" and "scientist" in the same breath. Not within my hearing, anyway. This is most frustrating.'

'We could get a step closer by speaking to Adelia Wilson. We could – what's the phrase? – "eliminate her from our enquiries".'

'We could let her know what's happened and see how she reacts, yes. It's a starting point, I suppose. Well, perhaps not a start. There are a couple of things we need to do first.'

'Which are?'

'Well, obviously we need to speak to my infuriating brother as soon as the trunk call goes through. But first, we need to indulge me a little.'

'Sticky buns and a pot of coffee?' I said.

'Hardly – I'll be feeling the effects of breakfast well into the afternoon today. No, I'd like you to indulge one of my more recent fancies. Come with me and take a look in the empty room next door to ours.'

'If Goddard were in there, wouldn't the hotel staff have tumbled to it by now? It's quite hard to hide in a fully staffed hotel.'

'Just as a special favour,' she said. 'So I can reassure myself that we've explored every possibility before I start giving Harry what for.'

'Of course. Come on, let's do it now.'

We relocked the door and made our way back downstairs.

The empty room, to my overwhelming lack of surprise, turned out to be empty. It was furnished, as expected, to the same exquisitely elegant standard as the rest of the hotel, but it was entirely devoid of scientists. Nor was there any sign that a scientist had been present within recent memory. Nor an assassin. Nor, indeed, anyone.

'That's rather an anticlimax,' said Lady Hardcastle.

'I can't say I'm surprised,' I said. 'We'd have noticed someone bumping about in the next room.'

'Well, yes, but I do like to be thorough. You know my feelings on not looking like a couple of chumps. It's a shame, though.'

'What is?' I said.

'I'm just not sure about Goddard any more,' she said. 'I really had begun to think he could be kipping in here by night and slipping out to lurk unseen in the backstreets of Weston by day.'

'He could,' I said. 'But. I mean. Really? How would he get in and out without being seen?'

'Through the back door and up in the goods lift.'

'Hmm. But I'm as certain as I can be that no one's been here for a while.'

'I have to concur,' she said. 'But . . .'

'But?'

'Well, why, now we come to be talking about it, hasn't Harry made more of a fuss? He got himself all of a dither about the blessed strongbox, but one would have expected Tweedle-Dum and Tweedle-Dee to have been ordered to conduct the most energetically vigorous enquiries into the disappearance of a respected government scientist. So far, nothing. It's as if he doesn't care. Or as if he already knows. I shall be demanding some answers when next we speak.'

'Which shouldn't be too long now,' I said. 'Perhaps we should go back to Mr Hillier's office so that we don't miss the call.'

'Via the Wilsons.'

'The Wilsons aren't in any sense "on the way",' I said. 'But as you wish.'

We locked the door and went back upstairs.

◆ ◆ ◆

I stood to one side of the door while Lady Hardcastle rapped sharply on it. There was no reply. She knocked again. Still no answer.

'They're early risers, aren't they?' I said. 'Perhaps they've gone out.'

'Without having breakfast?'

'Maybe they wanted to try a genuine Olde Englishe café,' I suggested. 'They're on a cultural trip, after all.'

'Hmm. Gristly sausages and all the greasy fried bread you can eat. I'm sure they'd love it. It's worth asking at reception in case anyone saw them go out, I suppose.'

'Or perhaps Adelia really did shoot Mr Martin and Mr Takahashi. She might have waited till we were at breakfast, pinched the strongbox, gathered young Eleanora to her bosom and is even now on a train to Liverpool and a fast ship home.'

'Or they're lying dead in their beds,' she said.

'We have a master key – we can take a look.'

'It would be far less awkward if we enlisted a member of staff to do that, don't you think? If they were shot by the mystery assassin, there's nothing we can do to help and they're not going to get any more dead. If they're having a lie-in after our late night together, us bursting in with a "What ho, ladies. Anyone for a donkey ride?" is going to be a little tricky to explain. What would we say to justify just letting ourselves in like that?'

'How about, "We know that you're spies, and because all the other spies are dead we were worried about you"? That would do the trick.'

'Blunt but effective,' she said. 'Though I think we'll stick with my plan. I shall impose upon Hillier to send someone up.'

'As you wish,' I said. 'Can we just check under my bed before we go down, though, please? I want to make sure the box is still there.'

'Certainly we should. As you said before, we'd feel like proper chumps if we didn't check and it turned out to have been pinched.'

A quick check of our own rooms confirmed that we were still in possession of Dr Goddard's strongbox. Satisfied that at least that tiny part of the growing chaos was under our control, we decided to return to Mr Hillier's office. Harry needed to know what was going on, and we needed to get some answers in return.

Chapter Twelve

'Any sign of that line to London?' said Lady Hardcastle. She had once more breezed into Mr Hillier's office without waiting for a response to her knock. She was polite enough not to make herself comfortable on one of his visitors' chairs, but she looked at them pointedly enough that he hurriedly invited us to sit anyway.

'No, Lady Hardcastle, I'm afraid not,' he said. 'Was it . . . you know . . . was it what we expected? Upstairs, I mean.'

'Takahashi and Martin both dead,' she said. 'Yes. Shot.'

'Shot? But no one heard anything. I've asked.'

'Small calibre weapon. They're much quieter than people suppose. It might have been mistaken for a door slamming.'

'I see,' he said. 'At least there was less blood this time.'

'That'll be to do with where they were shot.'

'In bed?'

She laughed. 'In the eye,' she said. 'They would have died instantly – no opportunity to bleed.'

He blanched. 'I do wish you hadn't told me that.'

His lily-liveredness was becoming a bit wearing, but I didn't think it was entirely fair of Lady Hardcastle to tease him about it. I decided to change the subject.

'Did you manage to find a replacement for Myra?' I asked.

'For . . . ? Oh, yes. Well, sort of. Marian was still on duty from last night and she agreed to do a few more hours so I asked her to do a couple of rooms. She should have started by now. May and June have other rooms to attend to, but they've assured me they can cope with the extra workload. I'll set them to work on the rest as soon as the . . . ah . . . the bodies have been retrieved.'

'That's good,' I said. 'We were wondering if you wouldn't mind sending one of them – Marian, perhaps – to check on the Misses Wilson. They've probably gone out for the day, but we couldn't get a response when we knocked on their door and we thought . . .'

I trailed off as I realized that my attempt to change the subject had been a little misguided. Everything about the comings and goings of the hotel, it seemed, was likely to increase Mr Hillier's dismay and despair.

'That's where I suggested she start,' he said bleakly. 'I'm sure we'll be hearing the bad news any moment.'

'Oh, do pull yourself together, Hillier, there's a good chap,' said Lady Hardcastle. 'You're supposed to be a manager, you know. A leader. Things are unpleasant, but your staff are looking to you to take command, to set an example. You can't help passing out at the sight of blood – that's more commonplace than one might suppose – but you *can* help moping about as though the world has ended just because things got a bit nasty. Show a bit of backbone, man.'

'Now look here—' he blustered.

'That's the spirit,' she said. 'Exactly like that. That's what we're looking for.'

'I've been more than patient with you, Lady Hardcastle, but—'

A knock at the door interrupted what was undoubtedly going to be a most entertaining rant.

'What now?' he said loudly.

The door opened and the round face of Marian Higdon peered round. 'Beggin' your pardon, Mr Hillier,' she said. 'But could you come quick. It's Miss Wilson.'

'She's not—?' he began.

'She's alive, sir,' said Marian. 'Far as I can tell. But I can't wake her. I knocked and there was no answer so I went in and found her there. I apologized for bargin' in, but she didn't say nothin'. When I looked she was . . . you know . . . out cold.'

Mr Hillier appeared to be retreating into his hysterical torpor. Lady Hardcastle looked at me and rolled her eyes.

'Do you have a doctor that you can call for hotel emergencies, Mr Hillier?' she asked.

'A doctor?' he said distractedly. 'Yes. Dr Kenniston. Lancelot Kenniston. Nice old chap.'

'Perhaps you might call him,' she said. 'Or send someone to fetch him. Urgently. Marian – which Miss Wilson is it?'

'Miss Adelia,' she said.

'Where was Eleanora?'

'Weren't no sign of her niece, m'lady. Just Miss Adelia out cold in her bed.'

'Summon the doctor at once, Mr Hillier. Armstrong and I will go and do what we can.'

Without waiting for a reply, we followed Marian out of the room. I kept an ear out as we walked towards reception and was relieved to hear Mr Hillier placing the call to the doctor.

Marian unlocked the door to let us in to Adelia Wilson's room, but opted to wait in the corridor while Lady Hardcastle and I stepped inside. With the curtains still drawn, the room was oppressively gloomy and my first move was to open them. The sun was still hiding shyly behind grey curtains of its own, but even the wan light it provided was an improvement on the efforts of the electric bulb on the wall.

Adelia Wilson's breathing was shallow, but steady.

'Adelia, dear,' said Lady Hardcastle loudly. 'Can you hear me?'

There was no response.

Lady Hardcastle shook her.

Still no response.

'Your eyes are better than mine, dear,' she said to me. 'Take a look at her and see if you can see anything.'

'Am I looking for anything specific?' I asked.

'My guess is that she's been drugged. There's no sign of a box or bottle of pills, so she didn't take the drug herself. There's no cup or glass on the bedside table, so someone didn't slip something into her drink.'

'Unless they tidied up after themselves,' I said.

'Of course. But if you were going to put something in someone's drink, would you come back after they'd drunk it and climbed into bed so you could clear the glass away?'

'You make a good point,' I said. 'Although Eleanora might. Maybe she dosed her aunt so she could get away on some romantic adventure.'

'Let's not rule it out until you've inspected Adelia for pin pricks.'

'Ah,' I said. 'Of course. Give me a sec.' I gently turned Adelia's face away from me and examined her neck. 'You're on form today,' I said. 'There's a little red puncture mark there.'

'She was injected with something, then. While she slept. Probably Veronal – fast acting and reliable. She might be out for hours depending on the dose. At least he didn't overdo it.'

'So he wanted her unconscious while he . . . what? Searched the room?'

'Possibly,' she said. 'But why not just kill her? He wasn't bothered about killing the other two. Why did he want her alive?'

'Oh,' I said.

'There you go with your "oh"s again. What's on your mind?'

'One moment,' I said, and went through the connecting door to Eleanora's room.

Everyone's morning habits are different, but I'd yet to discover anyone who rose from their slumbers and threw all their bedclothes on to the floor. In my experience, most people simply lifted a corner and slithered out to greet the day. I returned to Adelia's room.

'Eleanora was taken,' I said.

'You're sure?'

'Not absolutely sure, no, but that's my best guess for now. Someone came in here and drugged Adelia – they might or might not have had a quick look under the bed for the strong-box. Then they went through to Eleanora's room and drugged her, too. Once they were certain she was under, they tore off the bedclothes so that they could pick her up and carry her off. She's a tiny thing – it would have been no effort at all.'

'This is a troubling development,' she said. 'Four dead, one unconscious and two missing. One of the two might be responsible for all the others, but the other is a young non-combatant. Harry is going to have to give us some answers now.'

'We'll get to the bottom of it,' I said. 'What can we do for Miss Wilson right now?'

'If it's Veronal, there's nothing we can do – we just have to wait for it to wear off. I'll be happier once this Dr Kenniston chap has had a look at her, but I fear we just have to let her sleep and hope for the best. She's a robust-looking sort – she should be fine.'

I looked out of the window while Lady Hardcastle sat on Adelia's bed.

'I'm not saying I'm inured to violent death,' she said, 'but it's easier to accept when the victim is aware that they're playing a dangerous, high-stakes game. I find it much harder to deal with when civilians are involved. Especially young ones.'

'I know what you mean,' I said. 'Although we don't know for sure that Eleanora's not a player in this particular game. And we don't know that anything has befallen her. We don't even know for certain that she's been taken.'

'You're right,' she said with a sigh. 'But the odds are against her, I fear. This has been a particularly brutal few days and I can't help but think that being a pretty young girl isn't going to be much protection if she stops being useful.'

'Useful?' I said.

'Why else take a hostage? The kidnapper is clearly after the strongbox. When he couldn't get it, he took Goddard – perhaps to try to get him simply to tell him what was in it. That's failed – perhaps Goddard is holding out, perhaps he died under torture – so he's come back for another go. He tried the remaining suspects but no one had it and he killed them. His last resort has been to take Eleanora Wilson. I predict we – or rather Adelia – will be hearing from him soon with a demand that Adelia find and hand over the box in exchange for her niece's safe return.'

'It's a very plausible scenario,' I said.

'Plausible, but not encouraging. Our only hope is that whoever it is has either concealed his identity well enough that releasing Eleanora and Goddard unharmed poses him no threat, or that he has no fear of the British and United States governments and any retribution they might mete out. If he hopes to get away clean, I fear we may not see them alive again.'

We were saved from further defeatist speculation by the arrival of the doctor. He accepted Lady Hardcastle's untrained diagnosis of involuntary Veronal intoxication with good grace and dismissed us from the room so that he could examine his new patient.

We returned to Mr Hillier's office.

We found him on the telephone. He beckoned Lady Hardcastle somewhat frantically towards the desk.

'Yes, Mr Featherstonhaugh,' he said. 'Yes, I appreciate that . . . Yes, yes I shall . . . But there are two this time . . . Yes, of course . . . Lady Hardcastle is here now. Would you care to—? Yes, I understand . . . Of course . . .' His beckoning became a little more urgent. 'I shouldn't dream of it . . .'

Lady Hardcastle held out her hand to take the telephone earpiece from him. He was more than glad to hand it over. She bent towards the mouthpiece.

'Harry,' she said, sharply. 'Harry, do shut up, there's a good boy . . . Well, who on earth do you imagine it is?'

Mr Hillier, meanwhile, had slid out from behind his desk and was heading towards the door.

'I'll just go and check that everything is all right in reception,' he whispered as he passed. 'Leave you to it.'

He closed the door behind him.

It was Lady Hardcastle's turn to beckon as I was summoned to listen to the call.

'. . . have to ask you a favour,' said Harry's crackly voice in the earpiece.

'Flo's listening in now,' said Lady Hardcastle.

'What ho, Strongarm,' he said. 'Did you hear that?'

'It sounded like you were going to ask Lady Hardcastle to do you a favour,' I said.

'That's right. Both of you, in fact. I've had to redeploy my chaps—'

'Your chaps?' said Lady Hardcastle. 'So the Fish Brothers are your chaps, then? Not Special Branch?'

'They are. And they're needed elsewhere for now, so I'll be sending a different couple of lads to pick up the bodies. These two aren't quite as . . . as specialized as – what do you call them? The Fish Brothers?'

'They were antelopes last night,' I said.

'Good lord,' he sighed. 'Well, they might be a couple of jokers, but they're damned good at what they do. Their replacements, on the other hand, are merely menials, so for heaven's sake just let them get the bodies and get out. You're not to play with them.'

'That's the favour?' said Lady Hardcastle.

'No, that's an earnest entreaty – please don't make my life more difficult than it already is. The favour is a little more in your usual line. I'd like you to have a jolly good hunt round the hotel for Goddard's strongbox.'

'The strongbox you told us in no uncertain terms to forget all about?' she said.

'That one, yes.'

'You want us to find it?'

'Yes, please.'

'Even though you told us not to?'

'Even though.'

'Got it,' she said.

'Good. So you'll have a look?'

'No, dear, I mean we've got it.'

There was a pause. If the line had been any clearer I like to imagine we might have heard Harry's brain whirring.

'You've got Goddard's strongbox?' he said.

'We have,' she said. 'Flo fetched it last night.'

'From . . . ?'

'From under Adelia Wilson's bed.'

'What was she doing under Adelia Wilson's bed?'

'Fetching the strongbox, dear. Do try to keep up.'

'Does Wilson know?'

'No, I don't think she knows very much at all. And that's something else we really do rather need to talk to you about.'

'Oh no,' he said. 'Not her as well?'

'She's not dead, but she has been drugged. And her niece is missing. I think it's high time you 'fessed up, as her compatriots have it. What exactly is going on here?'

'I'm not in a position to "'fess" at the moment, sis. Maybe later, but not yet.'

'A girl's life might very well be in danger, as might that of a British government "scientist". I'm going to assume that he's another one of your "chaps" and not a scientist at all, by the way, but that doesn't make his peril any less real.'

'You do focus on the most irrelevant things,' he said. 'Tell me exactly what's happened.'

Thoroughly but succinctly, Lady Hardcastle outlined our morning's discoveries, including the bullet wounds to the eyes of the two murder victims, the puncture mark on Adelia Wilson's neck, and the state of Eleanora's bed.

'At least Adelia's still alive,' he said when she had finished.

'Well, that's something, I suppose. We've made several more assumptions. We've assumed that Kusnetsov, Schneider, Martin, Takahashi and Wilson are all – for want of a less melodramatic word – spies for their respective governments.'

'Were,' he said.

'Indeed – the majority of them are very much in the past tense. We're assuming that you knew all about it.'

'I can neither confirm nor deny, sis. It's an ongoing operation.'

'But there is an operation,' she said. 'And you're running it?'

He said nothing.

'Do they know about us?' she said.

'About you and Flo? It's possible that they might know who you are – you're surprisingly famous in certain circles, you know. But none of them has communicated any suspicion of your involvement to their embassies or consulates. As far as I know, no one is aware that you've come off the sub's bench.'

'We were barely aware of it ourselves until recently,' she said. 'But it's your operation. What's our next move?'

'I agree with your assessment,' he said. 'There's another player and he has Goddard and the Wilson girl. He wants the strongbox so he's going to bargain for it. You need to sit tight and wait for him to contact Adelia Wilson.'

'Right you are.'

'Have you opened the strongbox, by the way?'

'No, we can't find the key and it's not proven susceptible to Flo's lock-picking charms.'

'Good. Don't try anything else. Are you armed?'

'We're on holiday, you idiot,' she said. 'Of course we're not armed.'

'See what you can scrounge up – you might need it.'

'Charming.'

'Look, sis, I'm sorry it's come to this, but actually I'm rather glad to have you there looking after things. Can't think of anyone I trust more. Just sit tight and don't take any unnecessary chances.'

'We'll be fine,' she said. 'Just get your removals men here as quickly as you can, before Hillier has another attack of the vapours.'

'He's not exactly a steely fellow, is he? Can we rely on him?'

'We can rely on him to keep this place running,' she said. 'Although with only three surviving guests it pretty much runs itself. I'll not be asking him to do anything dangerous, though, don't worry.'

'That's my girl. I'll get those men to you as quickly as I can. And telephone me as soon as you hear anything.'

'Cheerio, Harry,' she said, and replaced the earpiece on its hook.

'If I might make a suggestion,' I said.

'I would welcome all and any suggestions at this point,' she said. 'Especially from you.'

'Then let's go and search the latest victims' rooms. Perhaps these two were armed.'

'It's that or asking round the staff,' she said. 'I've not seen any likely former soldiers among them, but one never knows. Someone might have an old revolver at home. Or a shotgun.'

'I'm beginning to regret not packing your golf clubs,' I said. 'A mashie-niblick would make a fine substitute for a shillelagh.'

We left Mr Hillier's room and headed for the stairs for the umpteenth time that day.

I was beginning to tire of the routine of going through dead men's pockets. We had begun in Mr Takahashi's room and once again I was in the wardrobe searching his suits and shoes. At least this time – as with Dr Goddard's room – everything was neat and well-ordered, but it was still a bleak and dismaying task, especially with the room's occupant still lying dead in his bed.

Whether by convention and habit, or more likely a shared set of needs, we all seem to travel with the same things. A few changes of clothes, some maintenance equipment for those clothes and for ourselves, and a handful of the personal items we imagine we can't be without even for a few days – a favourite pen, a treasured book, a photograph of a loved one. A life miniaturized and made portable. Each man's room had been different in subtle ways, but the overall effect was strikingly similar. Similar, too, was the feeling of melancholy as I methodically searched through those travelling snapshots of their lives, knowing that those lives were over.

I forced my mind to turn away from its maudlin meanderings and on to more pressing matters.

'Do you think any of them did recognize us?' I said.

'I certainly didn't know any of them,' said Lady Hardcastle. 'Did you?'

'We've not come up against them in person. At least, I don't think so. But they might have observed us from some concealed spot at an embassy ball or on the backstreets of some foreign city.'

'True. Although I'm not bad at faces. I affect a little anomia from time to time, but mostly because it amuses me to have you irritatedly correct me when I get people's names wrong. But faces . . . that's another matter entirely. I never forget a face. And I'm as certain as I can be that I'd never seen any of our fellow residents before this week, even lurking in a ballroom or skulking in an alley.'

'What about Harry's claim that we're famous?'

'Ah, now there you have me. We did rather make a thing of hiding in plain sight, didn't we? That Lady Whatshername and her maid swanning about the place being sociable and charming while pinching secrets and foiling other people's best-laid plans. Sooner or later we were bound to be twigged, so I'm sure our names are on lists of undesirables pinned up on noticeboards in government offices around the world. On the other hand, the whole spying business is still a little ad hoc, isn't it? It's very much a game played by powerful gentlemen among themselves. It hasn't been properly industrialized yet, so perhaps those lists of undesirables don't exist. Perhaps I really am just a flighty middle-aged widow with a strange fascination for moving pictures, after all.'

'I'd still be happier if you were a flighty middle-aged widow with a gun in your handbag,' I said. 'And . . .' I pulled a heavy wooden case from the back of the wardrobe. 'I think I might have found you just the thing.'

I put the case on the end of the bed and opened it. Inside was an elegant but unfamiliar automatic pistol, two spare magazines, a box of ammunition, a cleaning rod, rags, and oil.

'I say,' said Lady Hardcastle. 'A Nambu. Well done.' She hefted the pistol. 'Heavy, mind you. What do you think, a couple of pounds?' She handed it to me.

'About that,' I said. 'Rather you than me.'

'Well, its bulk notwithstanding, it'll keep Jabberwocks and Bandersnatches at bay. It's not terribly powerful but it's accurate enough. A good find.'

I gave her the pistol and she set about checking it while I returned to my search of the bottom of the wardrobe. I pulled out a familiar small bag that I expected to contain clothes brushes and boot polish – I would happily have sworn that they were all getting their luggage from the same London shop. Sure enough there were all the usual whatnots and thingummies associated with vestimentary maintenance, but it was another little item that caught my attention.

'And here's something else,' I said.

I held up what looked like an ornamental cheese wire – a length of silk cord between two beautifully carved bone handles.

'Exhibit A,' I said. 'A garrotte, most likely the one used to kill Mr Kusnetsov.'

She carefully returned the gun to its case and took the new weapon.

'Elegant,' she said. 'Light and portable. Silent and effective. And mess-free. Do you remember that chap we found who'd been done in with a wire cheese-cutter? Blood everywhere. This cord would kill without breaking the skin.'

'Just so,' I said. 'And it would leave exactly the mark we found on his neck.'

'So Takahashi-san was an assassin as well as a diplomat and promoter of exhibitions.'

'It's not much help, but it does solve one of our many murders,' I said.

'Every step on the road to . . . somewhere or other . . . has its own . . . something. I'm sure there's bound to be some mystical saying about the importance of everything. But yes, we do at least have a reasonable suspect for the killing of Kusnetsov.

Harry will want to know, I'm sure. Whatever game he's playing he won't like loose ends.'

She put the garrotte with the gun and we both carried on looking through the room. We found nothing further and moved on to see what fresh information the late Mr Martin might have to offer us.

We followed the same depressingly familiar routine in Monsieur Martin's room, with Lady Hardcastle searching the bedside table and washstand, and me rummaging through the wardrobe while Martin himself lay unseeing behind us. There was nothing at all remarkable about his travelling paraphernalia except, perhaps, that his whatnots and thingummies had all been purchased in Paris rather than London.

I was beginning to grow a little despondent. I was considering chucking it in and suggesting we go for some lunch when I made a rather pleasing discovery.

'And look what we have here,' I said, holding up a knife in a leather sheath. 'I said Monsieur Martin was the sort of bloke who'd carry one of these.'

I drew the blade – about six inches long, not too broad, wickedly sharp and with a deadly point. The bone handle had been carved with a hatched pattern for better grip.

'This isn't a gentleman's pocket knife,' I said. 'This is for killing people. Nicely balanced, too – I'm sure it would throw well.'

'Any blood?'

I examined the blade but it had been wiped clean and oiled. There were a couple of specks of something up around the guard but without some sort of magical chemical test I couldn't tell whether they were blood. The sheath, too, showed signs of dark staining, which was more likely to be blood, but could have come from anyone at any time.

'Nothing definitive,' I said. 'I'd confidently say it's been used for damaging people, but not who or when. The blade's about the right size to have caused the wounds to Herr Schneider's chest, though, so I don't think I'm going out on too precarious a limb to suggest that Monsieur Martin was responsible.'

'I can't say I disagree, dear,' she said. 'If there's one thing to be said in favour of all this unpleasantness, at least they seem to be cleaning up after each other. They shan't be clogging the courts with lengthy trials.'

'Or making the newspapers huff and puff about the exploitation of diplomatic immunity when they get let off.'

'Or that, yes. Although I'm sure Harry and his pals would do their best to hush it all up.'

'Have you had any thoughts about what he's up to?' I said. 'Or who the mystery player might be?'

'Not really. It's clearly all been set up – all the Great Powers are represented as well as some of the new players.'

'Apart from Germany and Italy, I thought we'd said.'

'Apart from them. Although, actually, I'm not surprised about Italy. I bow to no woman in my admiration for the Italians – the people, the culture, the history, the landscape . . . the food – but I'd never expect to see them at the top table in any important meetings about world affairs. That Germany is missing, though . . . that's a puzzle.'

'There's an embarrassingly simple solution,' I said. 'Our missing player is German.'

'Embarrassingly simple and rather alarming, yes. They're really rather good at this sort of thing.' She stood and retrieved her sketchbook and pencil from the writing desk. 'I need to get all this clear in my head,' she said, and opened a fresh page.

'The strongbox starts with Dr Goddard,' she said. 'Kusnetsov steals it from him, and some unknown person kidnaps Goddard in frustration at having missed it.'

'That sounds reasonable,' I said.

'We work out that Kusnetsov has it and Schneider overhears us. Adelia did warn us that conversations in the dining room are only notionally private. Schneider takes the box. But Takahashi has also overheard us, and he kills Kusnetsov – probably a second-ary mission. You know the sort of thing: "Get the Englishman's box of secrets and kill the Russian while you're at it." They're still not pals, the Japanese and the Russians.'

'A war will do that,' I said.

'Quite,' she said. 'We tell Adelia Wilson that Schneider is the thief and she slips off to nab it while I'm trying to get Hillier. But Martin overhears and he also goes off to get it. But by the time he gets there, the box is gone and Schneider is back. There's a struggle and Schneider gets knifed. I'd not be surprised if that was part of his mission as well. There's no love lost between those two countries, either.'

'Then I work out where the box is, and I pinch it from Adelia Wilson.'

'Just so. Then our mystery man – probably a German – arrives in the night and goes hunting. I'm going to assume he just goes from room to room, looking for the box, killing as he goes. He ends up in the Wilsons' rooms and takes Eleanora as a hostage.'

'How did he know which rooms to go to?' I said. 'And how did he know where the box had ended up? Why kill the other two and not Adelia Wilson?'

'I've been wondering that myself,' she said. 'The only thing I can think is that he has someone on the inside. A maid, perhaps? Young Myra knew all about the box – perhaps she's been selling her knowledge.'

'Perhaps,' I said. 'She was hugely upset by the latest two murders. Perhaps she realized that it was her tittle-tattle that got them killed. Then again, it could be any of the others. I'm not sure it matters much now.'

'No,' she said. 'Now we need to find out who has Goddard and Eleanora, and what we can do to get them back.'

Further contemplation was halted by a knock at the door.

'Come,' called Lady Hardcastle.

The porter opened the door and poked his head round.

'Beggin' your pardon, m'lady,' he said. 'Mr Hillier sends his compliments and asks if you would join him most urgently in his office. He said to tell you that a message has arrived for Miss Wilson.'

'Thank you, Brine. Tell him we'll be there presently. We just have one or two things to finish here.'

'Right you are, m'lady,' he said. He shut the door and was gone.

'At least I have a knife now,' I said, holding up the weapon.

'A knife and a pistol,' she agreed, lifting the gun case from the bed. 'For all the use they may turn out to be. We'd better go and take a look at this message.'

We locked the door once more and went to find out what the kidnapper had to say.

Chapter Thirteen

We found Mr Hillier pacing about in his room. He had an envelope in his hand.

'Ah, there you are,' he said, holding out the note. 'This was delivered a short while ago. It's addressed to Miss Wilson. It's marked "urgent".'

'So we're given to understand,' said Lady Hardcastle. 'Do you mind if we take a look?'

'It's addressed to Miss Wilson,' he said.

'Indeed. But Miss Wilson is still unconscious and it's marked as being urgent. If it's from the kidnapper, this note probably details his demands. If we wish to get Eleanora back safely, we need to see it at once.'

'Eleanora Wilson?' he said. 'Kidnapped?'

She looked at him blankly.

'We didn't tell him, my lady,' I said. 'We told Harry, but no one else knows.'

She sighed. 'The reason for rendering Adelia Wilson insensible was so that her niece could be carried off.'

'And you think that this note' – he held it away from himself as though he had just discovered it to be poisonous – 'is from whoever took her?'

'Yes,' she said. 'May I?'

He passed it to her.

'Cheap stationery,' she said as she examined the flimsy brown envelope. 'Badly sharpened pencil, too – very messy lines. And there's something not quite English about the handwriting.'

She took a letter opener from Mr Hillier's desk and slit open the envelope. She read the note.

'It's as we predicted,' she said. 'It reads, "I have your niece. You have the strongbox. If you do not have it you will get it. You will place it in a sack and leave it behind the first bench on Knightstone Causeway at half to eight tonight. You will not remain. You will not contact the police. If you do you will not see the girl again. When I have the box I will release the girl unharmed. I will tell you where to find her." That seems clear enough.'

'And it confirms our earlier guess,' I said.

'Half to eight, yes,' she said. 'A very German way of saying half past seven. A German tourist in Weston-super-Mare. It's a pity he's not the only one who doesn't want us to contact the police – I can't imagine he'd be at all difficult to track down.'

'But you can't contact the police,' said Mr Hillier. 'He specifically says.'

'Don't worry,' she said. 'Even if my brother didn't wish us to leave things to him and his men, we'd not bother with the police. We have rather more experience of this sort of thing than any seaside policeman. What time is it?'

He drew his watch from his waistcoat pocket. 'Ten past one,' he said.

'Plenty of time between now and half past seven to finalize our plans, then,' she said. 'Do you fancy a spot of lunch, Armstrong?'

'Oddly, yes,' I said. 'After such a huge breakfast I wasn't sure I'd ever eat again, but I'm surprisingly peckish.'

'Lunch for two, then,' she said. 'We'll keep you apprised of our plans, Mr Hillier. Do please send word when Adelia Wilson regains consciousness – we must speak to her the moment she's up to it.'

'How can you eat at a time like this?' he said.

She gave him a puzzled frown.

'Things are coming together nicely,' she said. 'We'll have Eleanora safely clutched to her aunt's fulsome bosom before breakfast. And we'll surrender the German cove to Harry's slightly less tender embrace, too. Eating seems like a perfect part of the plan.'

'You have a plan, then?'

'You leave it to us, Mr Hillier,' she said. 'I presume the kitchen is open, despite the shortage of guests?'

'Naturally,' he said. 'I'll tell them to expect your order.'

'Thank you. And would you be good enough to place another trunk call to my brother, please? He'll want to know about this.'

We left and walked along the corridor to the dining room.

'So what's the plan?' I said as we settled at the table furthest from the dining room door.

'Heaven only knows,' she said. 'Hillier is starting to get on my poor nerves a tiny bit – I just wanted him to shut up and stop mithering. If he imagines we have everything firmly in hand, he might calm down a tad.'

'Poor little chap. He can't help it. He hasn't spent the past twenty years learning how to deal with spies and scoundrels like some people have. You should have a bit more patience with him.'

'I probably should, you're right. Ah, Kibble. You're just in time. What's for lunch?'

The waiter had arrived. I hoped he hadn't heard our conversation.

'Chef was unsure whether there would be anyone for lunch today, my lady,' he said. 'He hasn't prepared a menu but he says he will be happy to make anything you desire. As long as he has the necessary ingredients, of course.'

'Then why don't we leave it to him?' she said. 'We trust his skill – please ask him to make us whatever he wants. The man is a genius.'

'He'll be delighted to hear that, my lady,' he said. 'Shall I bring the wine list?'

'Not today, thank you. I think we'll need clear heads today. Just some water, please.'

He vanished.

'There's something we seem to have been going out of our way not to address,' I said.

'There is? What's that?'

'The two latest murders,' I said. 'And how they were committed.'

'Shot through the eye with a small calibre pistol, yes,' she said. 'I heard your "oh" when you saw Takahashi.'

'Are you all right?'

'It's never a pleasant thing to be reminded of. I can deal with most things, but I still have nightmares about Roddy's murder – I see him lying there. It's such an idiosyncratic way to kill someone. I confess it did give me a chill when you told me how Takahashi had died.'

'And our kidnapper is German, too. This must be very hard for you.'

'It's not the easiest case we've worked on these past two years,' she said. 'But I'll endure. At least we know Ehrlichmann is dead. And we have to press on – we have two lives to save. Even if one of them isn't at all our responsibility, I do feel rather protective of young Eleanora. And rather cross with her aunt for putting her in harm's way like that.'

'You put no stock in all the sightings we've been told about?' I said. 'Skins and Dunn seeing Ehrlichmann in London last year? Harry's warnings about him heading west from London in January?'

Our musician friends, Skins and Dunn, had visited us the previous autumn on their way to a performing engagement. As well as good company and music, they had brought news that a man calling himself Ehrlichmann had approached them in a club in London. He knew who they were and told them to give Lady Hardcastle his regards. Just after Christmas, Harry's men had spotted a man matching Ehrlichmann's description board-ing a train for Cornwall.

'I shot him, Flo. You were there. I shot him dead. Whoever everyone thinks they've seen, it wasn't Ehrlichmann. I know that's who the man Skins and Dunn met claimed to be, but it can't have been. One doesn't just get up and walk away from having half one's head blown off with a Webley service revolver.'

'I know,' I said. 'I know. I just wanted to make sure you were all right.'

'And I appreciate your concern. But we have more important matters to bother about. At the top of our list is how to trap this German rapscallion while he's picking up the strongbox.'

'Lie in wait? He'll be looking out for either Adelia Wilson or hired muscle. Who would ever suspect a dotty English lady and her maid?'

'You're in mufti,' she said. 'You'd have to be my pal. But he's unlikely to be stupid – he'll be looking out for lurkers, whoever they may be.'

'Very well. Let's look at it another way. How will he retrieve the box?'

'It's an odd spot, don't you think? It's handy for the main road, but I wouldn't care for the idea of being boxed in there if it were me. If Adelia ignored his warning and sought to nab him, a few sturdy chaps could block the way back to the road and trap him on the causeway with no way out but into the sea.'

'On to the mud,' I corrected her. 'There's no sea at Weston – it's a myth cooked up by the local council to attract visitors.'

'Even so,' she said. 'It's an exposed escape route – I shouldn't like to have to run across an open beach.'

'So he's relying on picking up the box and slipping away unseen, then. Oh. When does the show finish at the theatre?'

'About ten if it's anything like the other night.' She mulled it over for a moment. 'I think you might be on to something, you know. There'll be a crowd then. If he were to come out of the theatre – or appear to – he could stroll along the causeway, pick up the sack, and mingle with the other theatregoers as they make their way back into town. Even if anyone were watching they'd have a job catching him in a crowd like the one we were in on Monday. It's a narrow strip – everyone gets funnelled together.'

'Half past seven is a bit early, though,' I said. 'It's a bit of a risk to have the box lying there for over two and a half hours before he can get to it.'

'Do you think so? It's a safe enough spot. There's a load of old tat along that stretch of the causeway – bits of old rope, nets, even a lobster pot as I recall. An old sack won't draw much attention. And the sooner it's there, the longer he'd have to check that Adelia and any help she'd drafted in were out of his way. I like it.'

'Even if I'm right,' I said, 'it doesn't help us nab him, nor get Eleanora back.'

'It's a start, though. Something to build on.'

At that moment, both Kibble the waiter and Brine the porter arrived at our table. Kibble had food, Brine had a message.

'Beggin' your pardon, m'lady,' said Brine. 'But Mr Hillier says you wanted to know when Miss Wilson was awake.'

'We did, Brine, we did. Thank you,' she said.

Brine hurried away.

'And just as this rather delicious-looking dish has arrived, too. What a shame. Oh, but it's a salad. How wonderful. Please leave it there and we'll get back to it as soon as we can. If you wouldn't mind telling Chef to delay any hot courses, though, that would be wonderful.'

'Of course, my lady,' said Kibble.

We dropped our napkins on the table and hurried off to the Wilsons' rooms.

◆ ◆ ◆

Adelia Wilson was sitting up in bed, propped up by pillows and sipping a cup of tea. Dr Kenniston was packing arcane medical instruments into a large leather bag.

'She's quite well,' he said, as though Miss Wilson were not there. 'It was a heavy dose of Veronal, as I suspected, but there should be no lasting effects. She'll feel a bit woolly for a couple of hours but there's no harm done.'

'Thank you, doctor,' said Lady Hardcastle.

She gave me a nod and I held the door for him. He seemed momentarily indignant at being dismissed, but picked up his hat and bag and began to make his way out.

'Good day to you,' he said.

I closed the door behind him.

'You know, you Britishers have got terrible taste in food, clothes, and popular entertainment, but I'll go ten rounds against anyone who tries to tell me that a good old English cup of tea can't cure just about anything.' She held up her teacup as though toasting us and took another sip.

'It has remarkable restorative powers,' agreed Lady Hardcastle. 'Particularly when taken in company and accompanied by a biscuit or two.'

'You mean a cookie?'

'No, dear, I most definitely mean a biscuit. A nice chat over a cup of tea and a biscuit. Perhaps we should invest in a fleet of tea wagons to tour America bringing comfort and succour to all – it would put your nation's snake oil salesmen out of business in a twinkling.'

'I'll write you a cheque in the morning,' said Miss Wilson. She took another sip and smiled.

'It certainly seems to be having a most beneficial effect on you, I must say.'

'There's nothing wrong with me. I've suffered worse than a dose of Veronal in my time.'

'I rather thought you might have,' said Lady Hardcastle. 'The time for dissembling has long passed. I didn't quite expect our revelations of our former occupation to induce you to say, "Oh, what a coincidence, me too", but your reaction to news of my brother's occupation did confirm what we'd known for a little while.'

'And what was that?'

'You're an intelligence agent for the United States of America. A spy. Army or navy?'

'I'm from Annapolis, dear, take a wild guess.'

'Naval Intelligence, then. So we can talk honestly at last. Has anyone told you about Eleanora?'

Adelia sat up slightly straighter, slopping some of her tea into the saucer.

'Told me about her?' she said. 'That doctor feller said he thought she was out. He said you knew all about it.'

'He has a physician's facility for obfuscation – that charming bedside manner that allows them to tell the truth without alarming the patient.'

'And what is it about the truth that would alarm this patient?' said Adelia sharply.

'She has been taken.'

'Taken?'

'By whoever drugged you,' said Lady Hardcastle.

'But . . . why? They took the . . . Look, you're right, there's no point pretending any more. Whoever drugged me took Goddard's strongbox. I took it from Schneider's room last night. I put it under my bed and when I looked while Dr Whangdoodle—'

'Kenniston,' I said without thinking.

'Sure,' she said. 'I looked while Dr Kenniston was fussing with something in his bag. It's gone. If they've got the box and, I presume, your missing Dr Goddard and his key, what did they want with Eleanora?'

'You didn't have the strongbox when you retired last night,' I said. 'I'd already taken it. We have it.'

'You?' she said. 'You broke in to my room? How dare you!'

'I really don't think you're in a position to complain about break-ins, dear,' said Lady Hardcastle. 'Remember how you came by the box in the first place.'

Adelia glowered. 'But without your larceny I'd still have my niece.'

'I certainly can't deny that without our having retrieved our government's property it would currently be in the hands of an unknown but almost certainly unfriendly foreign power.

But while I understand the impulse to cast blame and accusations, you ought to remember, too, who chose to bring an inexperienced young girl on a mission. And, given that both the other spies ended up dead, if the kidnapper had found the box I wouldn't give good odds on either of you still being alive now.'

'It was supposed to be a simple one,' said Adelia. 'A few days in an English seaside town, an easy mark. Sweet talk him a bit, relieve him of the box, and head out of town on the next train to London. I was to hand over the box at the embassy at Victoria Street then we could continue Eleanora's European tour.'

'The best-laid plans,' said Lady Hardcastle. She took the note from her handbag and passed it to Adelia. 'The kidnapper sent this to you. We opened it in case there was something that had to be dealt with before you came to.'

Adelia read it quickly. 'Do you know who this guy is?' she said.

'Not yet, no,' said Lady Hardcastle. 'We're assuming from the nationalities represented here in your little espionage jamboree that he's German – that's one of the only nationalities not represented.'

'Doesn't narrow it down much,' said Adelia. 'They've got a lot of Germans in this town.'

'They have?' said Lady Hardcastle.

'Seems so to me. We even saw a German fisherman late on Tuesday afternoon, out on the promenade.'

'A German fisherman?' I said. 'How did you know he was German?'

'Tall, blond feller. We saw him chatting away to the Punch and Judy man. Asking him for food.'

'In German? The Punch and Judy man was English when we met him.'

'They were speaking English but the fisherman definitely had a German accent. Berlin, if I'm not mistaken.'

Lady Hardcastle regarded her shrewdly. 'This puts an entirely different complexion on things,' she said. 'We've considered the mysterious fisherman a number of times, but we've always ruled him out. Well, I have, at least. But if your knowledge of German regional accents makes you certain he's a Berliner, he's not likely to be a real fisherman, now is he? Berlin's not exactly famous for its long maritime tradition and its easy access to the sea. This will make nabbing him a great deal easier – we know who we're looking for now.'

'Nabbing him?' said Adelia. 'You're not risking Eleanora's life for the sake of your stupid strongbox. Let him have it and let me have her back.'

'I think this is one of those rare occasions when we might have our cake and eat it. Our priority will always be saving the life of the innocent girl whose safety you risked so recklessly, but if we can save our government's "stupid strongbox", too, then so much the better.'

'Now, look here—'

'No, I'm sorry, dear, but my days of looking here are most definitely behind me. You're a guest in our country intent on stealing state secrets. It shall be up to my brother and his Foreign Office colleagues what sanctions are imposed upon you for that little transgression, but in the meantime any looking here will be entirely on your part. In the absence of firm orders to the contrary, I'm taking charge of this matter. We shall apprehend this fisherman, retrieve the strongbox, and free your niece along with, I hope, Dr Goddard. Your primary role will be to shut up and do as you're told. Any more "now look here"-ing from you will not go well for you.'

Adelia simply glared at her.

'We'll leave you to get dressed,' said Lady Hardcastle. 'Please join us for lunch and we shall discuss our plans.'

I was growing weary of trudging up and down the stairs, but at least there was food waiting for me in the dining room.

To my intense irritation, we didn't make it as far as the dining room. As we passed the open door to Mr Hillier's office he called out to us.

'Lady Hardcastle? Miss Armstrong? I have Mr Featherstonhaugh on the telephone for you.'

As we entered the room he was already out from behind his desk and heading towards us. He pointed to the telephone on the desk.

'All yours,' he said. As he closed the door behind him he muttered, 'I'm not your blessed secretary, you know.'

'It's a good thing he isn't,' said Lady Hardcastle, picking up the telephone earpiece. 'I'd have sacked him ages ago if he were my secretary.'

We positioned ourselves once more so that we could both hear and speak to Harry.

'Sorry to bother you again, Harry, dear, but there have been developments,' said Lady Hardcastle.

'What ho, sis,' he said. 'Fire away.'

She sighed. 'What ho, indeed. We've had communication from the kidnapper. He's demanding we leave the strongbox on Knightstone Causeway this evening – it's a promontory near our hotel with a theatre at the end – anyway, we leave the box there for him and he'll tell us where to find the girl. He doesn't mention your man Goddard, but if he's not already dead I imagine we'll find him in the same place.'

'Excellent. Do that.'

'I beg your pardon?'

'Do that. Leave the box, collect the American girl – everyone's home in time for brandy and medals.'

'No, we'll not be doing that, dear,' she said.

'Oh, my darling sister, but you will. The box isn't worth a girl's life. Just give him what he wants and let me know where to pick her up.'

'We have an altogether better idea that will secure the box, the German and the girl.'

'I'm sure you do, but instead you're going to do as you're told.'

'When have I ever done as I'm told? I just need your two chaps – Fish and Chips, Campbell and Bannerman, Argyle and Sutherland – whatever they're calling themselves today. I need the two of them and their poorly concealed revolvers to be loitering on the causeway at ten o'clock when the theatre chucks out. They just have to wait until a tall, blond fisherman walks past with a sack over his shoulder and follow him. They'll track him to his lair and you get the box, the girl, and the German spy all in one neat package. We'll be on hand to look after young Miss

Wilson and to stand at longstop in case Kent and Lancashire aren't up to the task.'

'That all sounds splendid,' said Harry, 'but I see a fatal flaw. Perch and Tench are away on another assignment – as you ought to remember – and I can't get them to Weston until tomorrow morning at the earliest. You'll just have to— Wait a moment. Did you say you were dealing with a tall, blond German?'

'A Berliner disguised rather improbably as a fisherman, yes.'

'Berliner?'

'According to Adelia Wilson he has a Berlin accent.'

'Did he look at all familiar?'

'We've not seen him close to,' she said. 'But "tall and blond" is rather the German archetype, wouldn't you say? Or is it Dutch? I'm sure if we had seen him more clearly we might have thought, "Gosh, that fisherman looks rather Teutonic", but from a distance, I can't say I recognized him. Flo?'

'Well . . .' I said.

'If she mentions Günther Ehrlichmann in her next utterance I shall be beating her about the head and neck with this telephone earpiece,' said Lady Hardcastle. 'Ehrlichmann is dead and I don't care how many of your incompetent Special Branch chums think they've seen him.'

'Well . . .' said Harry.

'I despair of the pair of you,' she said. 'Meanwhile, though, we seem to have drifted away from the subject under discussion. We have the opportunity to kill three birds with one well-aimed stone and I think you're a dunderhead for not taking it.'

'And yet I remain firm. No trailing, no heroic rescues, just a simple handover of a metal box in return for a girl's life. I imagine your fisherman will make sure he's safely away before he sends word so we'll not know anything further until the morning. I'll have my men with you first thing tomorrow and we can complete our business.'

'I suppose so,' she said with a resigned sigh.

'That's my girl. Let me know if anything happens that might change things, otherwise, we'll stick to the plan.'

'Very well,' she said. 'Cheerio for now.'

'Cheerio, sis.'

The line went dead.

'Come on, minuscule one,' she said. 'We've got arrangements to make.'

'We'd better be rescuing Eleanora,' I said. 'I love your brother as if he were my own, but I don't think he's got this one right.'

'I love my brother as if he were a brother worth having, too, and he's an absolute dunderhead. A nincompoop of the first water. I can't imagine why he thinks our German pal won't just bump the girl off and slip away with the box. Who leaves loose ends like that? It would be very sloppy. We need to trail him and effect a rescue with or without Harry's help.'

'Just checking,' I said. 'But please may we have some lunch first?'

'Of course. Eat first, plan later. Let's see about those salads.'

We finally sat down to our salads, but we didn't start. We ordered an extra for our guest and decided it would be polite to wait for her before we tucked in.

Adelia arrived just as hers was being delivered.

'There are a couple of workmen in the lobby,' she said as she sat down. 'They seem to be upsetting people – they came in through the wrong door, apparently. Anything to do with you ladies?'

'I expect they're Harry's not-Special-Branch men,' said Lady Hardcastle. 'Would you be a poppet and go and see to them, please, Flo?'

I tried not to growl my displeasure at being denied my lunch yet again, but my stomach signalled my disappointment with a loud growl of its own.

The men in workman's overalls loitering in reception identified themselves as having been sent by 'Mr Feather-stone-huff'.

'Where are your bags?' I asked the older of the two, guessing him to be the leader.

'Bags, miss?' he said, somewhat vacantly.

'You're here about the . . . removals, yes?' I said. Mr Nightengale looked none too happy and I thought it best not to antagonize him further by talking openly about the corpses in his hotel rooms.

'Oh, yes, miss,' he said. 'I understand you now. We've a couple of coff— a couple of "boxes" on the wagon out the back.'

'I see,' I said. 'Mr Nightengale?'

The reception clerk looked up from whatever he had been reading on his desk.

'Miss Armstrong?'

'Would you mind if I asked Brine to show these men how to get their boxes to the goods lift? I'll meet them at the first floor so they can load the first . . . removal.'

'Certainly. Will they be returning?'

'I do hope not,' I said. 'Why?'

'Perhaps you could remind them to use the tradesmen's entrance if they do. The guests don't want to see workmen hanging around reception.'

I decided not to point out that almost all the hotel's guests were dead and that the survivors were the ones who had ordered the removal men in the first place. Instead, I said, 'Of course. Brine? Would you do the honours, please?'

Brine rose from the porter's chair by the door and led the two men away.

I, meanwhile, trudged my weary way back up the stairs. I had kept up the exercise regimen taught me by Chen Ping Bo and my work kept me active so I was usually untroubled by physical exertion. But this stair business was rapidly becoming a bit of a drag.

Nevertheless, I made it to Mr Takahashi's room without puffing and panting too much. I unlocked the door, but waited in the corridor until the men arrived with their porter's truck and large pine box. I stayed outside while they carried out their grim work, then left them to take the body out to their wagon, telling them that I'd meet them on the second floor.

As I reached the second floor landing, I heard the clatter of heavy rain being blown against the window. I looked out and noticed for the first time that the weather had well and truly closed in. The sky, which had been a gloomy grey all week, was now almost black. I could just see the promenade. It was empty of all but the hardiest holidaymakers and even they were hurrying towards the shelter of tea rooms and the pier. The many flags along the prom and on the pier were in danger of being ripped from their poles as the wind gathered strength. I hoped it would blow itself out before we had to go and stand on Knightstone Road waiting for a tall blond man who definitely wasn't Günther Ehrlichmann to pass by with a sack over his shoulder.

With the second body safely on its way out to Harry's men's waiting wagon I set off to have one more go at eating lunch.

'All done?' said Lady Hardcastle as I sat down.

'All tidied away, yes,' I said. 'I've let Mr Nightengale know he can clean the rooms. He wants to know what to do with everyone's personal effects, by the way. I suggested that since the rooms are paid for he might leave them there until their governments claim them, or until Harry tells him differently.'

'Splendid, thank you for taking care of things,' she said. 'Adelia and I ate as slowly as we could but I'm afraid we were both rather peckish and it's all sort of gone.'

'Not to worry,' I said. 'If you don't mind me eating while you chat, I'll be fine. Is there another course on its way?'

'Yes. Duck, apparently.'

'It's the perfect weather for it,' I said.

'Oh, that's a shame. It's going to be miserable this evening if it keeps up.'

'I thought there was a storm brewing,' said Adelia.

'Some homespun, folksy American wisdom?' said Lady Hardcastle. 'Pine cones in your room? A feeling in your knees?'

'No, I looked out the window before I came down.'

'That works, too. Do please eat, Flo.'

I tucked in.

'Did you clear everything with your brother?' asked Adelia.

'Irritatingly not,' said Lady Hardcastle. 'His local men are unavailable and he's under the mistaken impression that things will all work out splendidly if we just follow the kidnapper's instructions and collect Eleanora in the morning.'

'Mistaken? You disagree?'

'How long have you been in the hugger-muggery business? Have you ever known a situation like this end in anything but unpleasantness? We already know that bumping people off is part of his usual rules of engagement. If he wants to get away cleanly with his box of secrets, why would he lead us to his hiding place and the living witnesses within, even if he's already done a bunk? It doesn't make operational sense, as one of my mentors used to say.'

'You're not one for soft soap, are you?' said Adelia.

'Explaining it any other way would be a lie,' said Lady Hardcastle.

'Do you have a contingency plan?'

'I simply propose to follow the original plan, but without Harry's thugs to help us. Are you fit to join us?'

'I'll say. It'd take more than a Veronal hangover to keep Adelia Wilson down.'

'Splendid. Between the three of us we should be able to keep at least one eye on our faux fisherman. Do you have anything with more stopping power than your little pistol?'

'To paraphrase a lady I once had dinner with, I'm a middle-aged spinster on vacation,' said Adelia. 'You're lucky I've got my "little pistol".'

'No matter. I pinched a rather hefty handgun from our Japanese pal's room – we'll be fine.'

'What about you, Miss Armstrong? Did you find a knife?'

'Monsieur Martin had a rather splendid one, yes,' I said. 'I'll definitely be fine.'

I had just scooped up the last forkful of salad when Kibble arrived with a heavily laden tray.

'I'm so sorry, miss,' he said. 'Would you like me to come back in a moment?'

'Not at all,' I said. 'I've just finished.'

The duck was served and he disappeared with the empty plates.

'The plan, then,' said Lady Hardcastle, 'is a simple one. You will drop the box as instructed at half past seven. We'll take up position across the road and keep watch.'

'Straight away?' I said. 'Are we not going to wait for the show to finish at the theatre?'

'Too much of a risk, I think,' said Lady Hardcastle. 'I happen to believe you've got it just right – that's exactly how he's going to try to get away with it. But I don't want to risk Eleanora's safety on our best guess. We'll have to bundle up against the wind and the rain and find somewhere to huddle for a couple of hours.'

'I can't be seen,' said Adelia. 'He'll be looking out for me.'

'None of us can be seen, but we can keep you out of sight until the time comes,' I said. 'Oh.'

'I swear your "oh"s will be the death of me,' said Lady Hardcastle. 'What is it now?'

'If this storm keeps up, there won't be anyone taking a leisurely evening stroll, will there? I'd been counting on us blending in unnoticed among the late-night revellers and promenaders. Two pals – three pals now – out to catch the evening air. But everyone will be hurrying back to their digs, fighting for seats on the tram, trying to get in out of the rain. We might as well be carrying placards saying, "Don't mind us, we're just following that German bloke".'

'We'll cross that soggy bridge when we come to it,' said Lady Hardcastle. 'In the meantime, what say we make the most of having the chef's personal attention and complete our planning later. It's a very straightforward operation and there are only a few tiny details to iron out – let's enjoy a few moments of leisure before kick-off.'

It was a few moments of leisure over a quite delicious lunch, as it turned out. It was almost possible to forget how much was going to be at stake later that evening.

Chapter Fourteen

I had dragged the armchair from my room to Lady Hardcastle's and we were sitting together, looking out of the window at the storm. Common parlance has it that storms 'rage' and I've often thought that a tad melodramatic, but this one really did seem to be jolly cross. The rain was splattering against the windows and the view beyond was of a coastal tempest in full force.

We had prevailed upon Ribble from the salon to bring a pot of tea to the room and I was pouring as I contemplated the storm.

'It might be a bit grim out,' I said, 'and I'm not looking forward to standing in the rain for a couple of hours, but at least we don't have to venture out to sea.'

'That would be rather hellish, wouldn't it?' said Lady Hardcastle. 'I pride myself on being quite a good sailor, but I fear that in these conditions even I might get a chance to have another look at my lunch.'

'Not that sailing would be an option,' I said. 'It's not like there's any sea here.'

'I keep telling you – it comes in twice a day. There'll be waves crashing on the shore by eight o'clock this evening.'

'By when?'

'High tide is at two minutes to eight,' she said. 'At least it is according to that sheet I picked up the other day.'

Something had been niggling at me all afternoon.

'If you were trying to hide yourself in a seaside town full of day trippers and holidaymakers,' I said, 'what disguise would you adopt? How would you blend in?'

'I'd be one of those day trippers and holidaymakers,' she said. 'I'd wear my finest "walking along the prom" outfit and mingle with the crowds. No one would notice me.'

'You wouldn't, then, dress as a fisherman?'

'I've not got the figure for a fisherman's smock,' she said. 'But in any event it would only be a suitable disguise if . . . Oh.'

'You see? It's not just me who "oh"s, is it? You'd only need to be a fisherman if you didn't want you and your boat to attract any attention.'

'By George, you're right. A smartly dressed holidaymaker alone on a boat will draw stares and some amount of pointing. "What's that idiot doing in that boat?" people would say. But a fisherman on a boat? Heads would remain unturned, eyelids unbatted, gasts unflabbered. Our fake German fisherman is arriving by boat.'

'If it's him,' I said. 'He could be a real German fisherman.'

'He could,' she agreed. 'But he's not, is he? I mean. Really.'

'Well, no, I don't think so, actually, but you're the one who taught me not to jump to conclusions without empirical proof.'

'And proud I am that you listened to me. But if he's a real fisherman then I'm Fanny Fandango, Queen of the Fan Dance.'

'I, for one, would pay good money to see you if you were,' I said.

'Well, quite. But if he's arriving and leaving by boat, then he has to wait for high tide.'

'There's nothing to say that he hasn't been doing just that. You've said yourself that the tide comes in twice a day. He could do quick trips on one tide, but longer visits would take whatever it is – twelve or thirteen hours? He'd have to stay ashore which would be why we've seen him loitering about.'

She took out the tide times and smoothed the paper on her lap.

'Let's see,' she said. 'We saw the fisherman near the theatre—'

'Near the slipway on the causeway,' I said.

'Yes, that's true. We saw him there on Monday evening just after ten. Whatshisname the night duty chap—'

'Vincent Fear.'

'Even he. He saw the fisherman in the alley at three on Tuesday morning and Goddard disappeared sometime in the early hours. So he could have arrived on the thirteen minutes past five high tide in the afternoon and left on the fourteen minutes to five the following morning. Adelia and Eleanora spotted him on the prom late on Tuesday afternoon, and the food was stolen from the kitchen about that time, too. He could have come and gone on the twelve minutes past six high tide that evening – there'd be enough sea for him to come and go.'

'It all sounds plausible,' I said. 'We saw him yesterday morning, though.'

'He could have come back on the four minutes past six.'

'You make it sound like a train timetable.'

'It's not vastly different,' she said. 'We don't know what he did all day, but he didn't leave on the seven minutes past seven in the evening because he was still here last night to murder Takahashi and Martin, then drug and kidnap Eleanora. He'd have had to wait for the seven thirty-eight to get away in the morning, but a fisherman fussing with a boat on the causeway wouldn't attract much attention, even if he were heaving a suspiciously large sack aboard.'

'How did he get the message to Adelia if he'd already left?' I said.

'Good point. We'll have to ask about that, but paying an urchin a few pennies to deliver a message later in the morning when he was well away wouldn't be out of the question. Risky, but not stupidly so.'

'And now he's planning to come back on this evening's high tide, grab the box and sail away.'

'Leaving any watchers on the shore. He knew Adelia would take steps to have the place under surveillance no matter what he said, but he was banking on being able to grab the box and vanish before anyone could do anything about it.'

'Except that he can't now, can he?' I said.

'Not if this storm keeps up, no. I'm assuming he's in a little dinghy, or perhaps a small steam launch, aren't you? He'll never make it in this weather.'

'And so . . . ?'

'And so his best-laid plans seem to have gang agley, as the poet might have it.'

'Where does that leave us?'

'Well and truly kiboshed for the moment. We need to revisit our own plans.'

'We know he's coming by boat,' I said.

'We think he's coming by boat.'

'When I tried to pull you up on jumping to conclusions you proclaimed yourself Queen of the Fan Dance. Shush and let me finish.'

'Shushing now, dear. My apologies.'

'He's coming by boat,' I continued. 'And we know where he's coming to.'

'We think we know where he's coming to.'

'I shall slosh you in a minute. We think we know where he's coming to, but we've no idea where he's coming from. If we can fathom that out, we've got him without having to follow him at all.'

'Somewhere that can only be reached by sea? An island? One of the Holms? They're not too far away – you can see them from here. Or you could if the weather were better. Are there buildings on Steep Holm or Flat Holm?'

'I read that there's a fort on Steep Holm – it was in the same local book that told me about the other Palmerston Fort at Brean Down. But would you really hole-up on an island? It doesn't seem like the sort of place I'd choose. There's only one way in – by boat – so you'd see people coming, but there's also only one way out. I'm always happier with another exit.'

'The mainland, then. Somewhere secluded where he can hold prisoners without upsetting the neighbours. But somewhere that's easier to reach by sea than by land, especially if one wants to get to and from Weston.'

'The ruined fort at Brean Down, then?' I suggested. 'You can see it from the seafront, but it's a pig to get to by road from here. Do you remember? I said we'd have to go all the way to Bleadon to cross the Axe and then come back on ourselves. But by sea it's just a quick jaunt across the bay. As long as there's any sea in the bay.'

'Someone else has mentioned it,' she said. 'It wasn't just you suggesting we take a trip there . . . Someone else has been talking about the fort.'

I thought for a moment. 'Tramps,' I said.

'We've overheard tramps talking about it?'

'No, when we were on our way to Mr Kusnetsov's room and we met those two chambermaids . . . May and June – why does everyone here sound like they're a music hall act? We met May and June and interrupted them while they were wittering on about lights at the fort. One of them said her mother thought it was an army of tramps, massing for invasion.'

'You're quite right,' she said. 'It would be a splendid hideout. Secluded and isolated. One secure approach by land, but with an escape route to the sea. Even if the tide were out then sneaking off across the mud is an option. A rubbish option, but an option.'

'Do we think that's where he is, then?'

'It all fits, certainly.'

'And are we going to risk Eleanora's life on things that fit and conclusions we've jumped to?'

'Go down there, you mean?' she said. 'It's tempting, isn't it?'

'It's a bit of a disaster if we're wrong,' I said. 'I'd want to take the box with us rather than leave it at the drop – it would give us something to bargain with if the threat of shooting his knees doesn't do the trick.'

'Knees? I was just going to kill him.'

'That would get the job done, certainly. But if we go down there and we're wrong, we'll have failed to make the drop. That won't go well for Eleanora.'

'I've been thinking about that. You just said that you want something to bargain with – I'll wager he does, too. I'm not so sure Eleanora is in any danger until he gets the strongbox. Once he's got what he wants, I wouldn't give you better than four-to-one on finding her alive. But until then, he needs her.'

'We seem to be talking ourselves into it,' I said. 'Do you want to make certain that Adelia agrees before we go ahead? She ought to have a say.'

'She ought,' she said. 'Drink up and let's go and see her.'

'How confident are you that you're right?' said Adelia after Lady Hardcastle had explained our proposition.

'That's rather the beauty of it,' said Lady Hardcastle. 'All reason says that our German friend's only means of travel to Weston is by sea. If he had a motor car, he would already have used it, most especially if he had captives to transport. He might come by cart, but he'd have trouble persuading all but the hardiest of horses to venture out on a night like tonight. With the storm set to continue beyond high tide, he's not going to be able to make the journey. And that means that even if our guess is wide of the mark, he's not going to know that you've not made the drop – he won't be on Knightstone Causeway to see that the strongbox isn't there.'

'What if he came back already and is waiting somewhere?'

'He wouldn't have been able to return by boat. He travelled back to his lair on the high tide this morning and by the time he'd made Eleanora secure there'd be no way to return – the tide had turned. And the motor car and cart objections still stand.'

'Actually,' I said, 'now that we've explained it all again, I wonder if any of that matters – if we get cracking, we might be able to make it there and back before eight anyway. Even if we're wrong about the hiding place, or about our Berliner being stranded by the weather, it's just about possible to get back here in time to make the drop.'

Lady Hardcastle nodded appreciatively.

'So as far as you're concerned this venture is entirely free of risk?' said Adelia.

'To Eleanora, yes. As for us . . . It'll be two against one if we meet him, so the odds are in our favour, but I wouldn't count that as an absence of risk. We're used to it, though – don't worry about us.'

'Two? Three, surely. You don't expect me to wait here while you're attempting to rescue my niece, do you?'

'Ordinarily I'd be delighted to have you along,' said Lady Hardcastle. 'But it's a question of transport. We shall be haring down to Brean in our little motor car, and it's strictly a two-seater.'

'You can't find any other way of getting there? This is my problem to fix – I need to be there. Not to mention the practicalities of it. You only have a borrowed Japanese pistol and a French knife between you – I could double your firepower.'

'Undoubtedly true, but we've been in worse scrapes than this armed with far less and we're still here to make infuriatingly oblique references to them. We'll be fine. We work best as a pair.'

'I see. And if you rescue Eleanora, how will you bring her back? Lashed to the roof?'

Lady Hardcastle laughed. 'Don't worry, I've thought of that. We're hoping to find Dr Goddard safe and well so we'll need to bring him back as well, eventually. So I'll bring Eleanora straight back with me and Flo will wait with Goddard at one of the farms nearby. You don't mind, do you, dear?'

I smiled and shook my head. I might have known I'd be the one making small talk with a bewildered farmer in the middle of a storm.

'Splendid. I'll arrange for more commodious transport in the morning and we can pick them all up then.'

'What about the kidnapper?' said Adelia.

'I was imagining we'd overpower him and leave him there for a while. Presumably he has somewhere secure to keep his prisoners – he can take their place until the relief column gets there.'

'You seem to have it all in hand,' said Adelia. 'I can't say I fully understand why you're putting yourselves to so much trouble on my behalf, but it seems churlish to stand in your way. On the other hand, though . . .'

'Yes?'

'If this goes wrong and any harm befalls Eleanora, I'll shoot you both dead.'

'We'd expect nothing less, dear,' said Lady Hardcastle. 'But we have your blessing?'

'Piled high with reservations and a whole heap of doubt and worry, but yes, you have my blessing.'

'We'll not let you down,' I said.

We left her to make our preparations.

Back in our rooms I was marking the best route to Brean on our local map and measuring the distance using the edge of a piece of paper torn from Lady Hardcastle's notebook.

'What do you reckon, then, dear?' she asked. 'Ten miles?'

'More or less,' I said. 'I made it about nine and three quarters. Your mystic powers are strong this afternoon.'

'Lucky guess,' she said. 'Call it half an hour in the daylight. Three quarters of an hour in this weather, though?'

'There'll be no one out to get in the way, but I think the storm and the gloom will slow us down, yes.'

'It would be tight, but it's possible. You'd better drive, though, dear,' she said. 'You're better in the wet. I tend to get a bit over-exuberant – we don't want to waste time repeatedly hauling Phyllis out of hedges.'

'Upside down in a ditch would be a bit of a drag, too,' I said.

'That would be frightfully embarrassing. What do we know about this Brean Down place? It's that spit of land to the south, isn't it? We've seen it from the prom. It looks exposed.'

I already had the local guide book open to the appropriate page.

'It is, rather,' I said. 'There's a military track running along the north side below the ridge. If this sketch map is accurate it should give us decent cover until we're almost at the fort.'

I showed her the illustration and she nodded. She looked out of the window.

'Which direction would you say the wind is coming from?' she said. 'South west?'

'Or thereabouts,' I said. 'We should be on the lee side of the hill most of the way.'

'That's something. I still don't really fancy doing it in this, though.' She indicated her summer skirt and jacket. 'Fine for an afternoon stroll, but not really the togs for clambering across open hillsides.'

'We packed mackintoshes,' I said. 'But nothing that would withstand this sort of weather.'

'No, they definitely wouldn't be up to the job. We need something a bit more . . . trousery. Come with me.'

I followed her out into the corridor and round the corner to the bedrooms at the back of the building. She unlocked Takahashi's door and went in.

'Mr Takahashi wasn't much bigger than you,' she said. 'A shade taller, perhaps, but we can deal with that. More importantly, though, he was an Oxford man – he's bound to have something suitable for a walk in the country. Chaps who have been to England's oldest and second-best university know what's what.'

Following our search earlier that day, I was already well acquainted with the contents of Mr Takahashi's wardrobe. I knew just the thing.

'This tweed suit should do the trick,' I said, putting it on the bed. 'And these boots are a good deal more substantial than my own. They look about my size, too. Perhaps with these thick socks. And' – I drew a rather splendid gabardine raincoat from the back of the wardrobe – 'this should keep me nice and dry.'

'If you don't trip over the hem,' said Lady Hardcastle.

'I'll hitch it up and fasten it with a belt,' I said. 'It'll be fine. This will do.' I took a broad leather belt from one of the shelves.

'How about this lovely hat?' She plonked a flat cap on my head.

'Just the job. That's me set, then. What about you?'

'I think Kusnetsov was more my size,' she said. 'Perhaps a bit smaller across the chest, but we're not hoping to feature on the fashion pages – I'm sure we can make do.'

We dropped my improvised outfit on my bed and went upstairs to Mr Kusnetsov's room.

'Ah,' she said as she tried to shrug into one of his jackets. 'I may have misjudged his size a tad. And the lining's been sliced.'

She did look more than a little uncomfortable, and there was no hope whatsoever of buttoning it.

'I'm not sure these trousers are going to fit, either,' she said. 'He was a good deal slenderer than I remembered.'

'And they've been even more badly treated than the jacket,' I said, indicating the razor-slashed hems. 'Monsieur Martin might be a better bet.'

'But he was a mountain,' she protested.

'Well . . .' I said, and dodged out of the door before any retribution could be exacted.

We found her a more or less suitable outfit among Monsieur Martin's effects and returned to our rooms. Lady Hardcastle rang for another pot of tea and I spent three quarters of an hour making a few hurried alterations to both sets of attire. As expected, we definitely wouldn't feature on the fashion pages, but we wouldn't fall over or get tangled in overly baggy clothes, either.

By six o'clock we were ready to go.

Carrying the heavy strongbox between us in an oilskin sack we'd found in one of the store cupboards along the corridor, we struggled out of the hotel into the storm. We heard bewildered enquiries from Mr Nightengale and Brine but explanations would have to come later.

'Can I help you, my lady?' called Brine belatedly, when he worked out that it was us, and not two badly dressed men who had just bustled through reception with a suspiciously bulky burden.

Lady Hardcastle waved over her shoulder and offered a cheery, 'No, thank you, dear, we'll be fine.' We heaved the strongbox into the boot and then clambered into the passenger compartment, slamming the doors behind us.

The rain was hammering on the steel roof and I was once more glad that we no longer had the Rover. That little vehicle had been pretty and charming, and it had brought us unprecedented freedom, but it had been purchased on somewhat of an impulse. We had done no research into the practicalities of motor cars and had little idea what sort of things might be important to us other than that it should go when we wanted it to go and stop when we wanted it to stop. If it went in roughly the right direction in between times, that would be a bonus. The vehicle we had chosen did all those things, but no thought had been given to the fact that it had not been fitted with a folding roof to protect us from the elements. Wherever we had been, no matter how quickly and safely we had got there, we were out in the weather. This new arrangement, with glass all round and metal above, was much more satisfactory.

I hadn't had many opportunities to drive the new motor car since it had been delivered. We used to share driving duties in the Rover more or less equally, but once Phyllis arrived it had proven extremely difficult to prise Lady Hardcastle away from the wheel. I was rather excited as I shuffled in the seat to make myself comfortable and pressed the starter button. The engine wheezed and spluttered, but then caught with an impressive roar before settling to a subdued, but still oddly menacing burble.

'I always think of her as a tigress,' said Lady Hardcastle, who was still struggling to arrange her heavy, borrowed overcoat around her betrousered legs. 'She's purring now, but when you ask it of her, she'll let out a mighty roar and tear off up the street like she's hunting a water buffalo.'

'Very romantic,' I said. 'I'll settle for her not biting our legs off at this point. Are you ready yet?'

'Just a moment,' she said, still fidgeting. 'I can't quite get this . . . There we are. All done. Have you got your knife?'

'Strapped to my arm, as usual,' I said. 'Gun?'

'In my pocket,' she said. 'Spare magazines, too. Oh.'

'Again there are "oh"s. It's been a week of "oh"s. What is it now?'

'We've no lanterns.'

'An unnecessary encumbrance,' I said, putting Phyllis into gear and easing away from the kerb. 'They'll not help us much in this weather and they'll give away our position.'

'I suppose you're right.'

'Oh,' I said.

'What?'

'I can't see a blessed thing. Look.'

There was still enough daylight to see by, even with the thick cloud blocking the sun, but that would only have helped if we could actually see out through the rain battering the windscreen.

'I can help you there, tiny one,' she said. She reached forward and began to operate a handle. Outside, two arms – one on either side of the windscreen – swung from side to side, scraping away the rain with rubber blades.

'I'd been wondering what they were,' I said. 'I thought they might have had something to do with cleaning the windscreen, but I had no idea they'd be quite this useful. Are you happy to keep swishing?'

'I live to swish, dear. Let's go.'

I let Phyllis have her head and we steadily gained speed as we passed southwards along the promenade. The road, as I had predicted, was largely free of traffic. Pedestrians and horses alike had long since sensibly sought shelter, and the only thing we passed was an empty tram trundling in the opposite direction.

I turned left, then right, passing the golf course and heading towards Uphill. Phyllis's racing heritage inspired confidence in her abilities. We were really moving now and I was happy to urge her on.

The village of Uphill passed by in something of a blur and we were soon at the toll gate by Bleadon and Uphill railway station. The brakes squealed a little as I drew to a halt beside the gatehouse. An old man in a heavy ulster emerged from within, holding a lantern. He approached with infuriating slowness.

I waited until he was almost level with the motor car and unclipped the leather strap to lower the side window.

'Evenin', sir,' he said. 'Penny for the toll road, please.'

'My lady?' I said.

'What, dear?'

'Do you have a penny?'

'A penny?' she said. 'Why on earth would I have a penny?'

I looked out at the gatekeeper, who looked very much as though he wished he were back indoors with his pipe and a warm fire.

'Can we owe it to you?' I said.

'Owe it to me?' The thought seemed entirely new to him. 'Owe me for usin' the toll road? When would you pay me?'

'Some other time,' I said. 'We don't have any change and we really are in something of a hurry.'

'Everyone's in a hurry in this weather, lad,' he said.

'Give him this,' said Lady Hardcastle.

'Your card? You're carrying calling cards but no money?'

'One never knows whom one might meet. I say, gatekeeper?'

He leaned down to look inside the motor car. His eyes nearly bulged out of his head.

'Would you be an absolute love and let us through?' she said. 'There's my card. We're staying at the Steep Holm View Hotel. I'll send someone over with the penny first thing tomorrow, I promise.'

I handed him the card. He inspected it closely and then looked back at the two of us.

'You goin' to a masquerade?' he said. Then he chuckled. 'Or maybe you be goin' burglin'?'

'A little of both, if I'm honest,' she said. 'And perhaps a little fisticuffs. One never knows these days.'

This appeared to tickle him greatly. A combination of his amusement and his obvious desire to get out of the rain made up his mind.

'You'd better be gettin' goin',' he said. 'Don't want to be late for your party. You bring me the penny when you can.' He chuckled again. 'Or perhaps some of your swag. I'll take a share of that.'

'Thank you, dear,' said Lady Hardcastle to his retreating back.

The gate swung open and we roared through.

On into Bleadon, then south across the River Axe on the road to Lympsham. We were quite a way past Brean, but now that we were on the other side of the river we'd soon be able to double back on ourselves to head for the promontory and its abandoned fort.

There was no respite from the rain, which was hitting the windscreen as though thrown by angry villagers with buckets. Lady Hardcastle was tiring and periodically had to swap arms to keep cranking the windscreen wiping device.

'I'm reasonably sure,' she said as she shifted in her seat to get a better grip on the handle, 'that we could rig up some sort of electric motor to do this for us. I'll speak to Fishy.'

A right turn at the end of the road took us towards Lympsham. The roads were narrowing and becoming a good deal more winding. In better weather I should have been terrified of running into someone, but there was no danger of that this evening. I pressed on, increasing our speed.

'Left here,' said Lady Hardcastle suddenly. 'The sign says left for Brean.'

I braked hard and hauled the heavy wheel to the left. The Rover might have toppled over at that speed – if it could have managed to reach that speed – but Phyllis took it in her stride. We crossed the railway line again and sped on past welcoming farmhouses back towards the coast.

'Right here,' said Lady Hardcastle, but I'd seen the signpost myself and was already slowing for the turn.

In a few more minutes we could see the cottages of the tiny village of Brean.

'Straight through the village,' said Lady Hardcastle. 'And then on up the road until you can't go any further. We'll park as close as we can to the end of the footpath, then it's Shanks's pony the rest of the way.'

The road carried on past one more farm, but it wasn't long before it became no more than a muddy track.

'We can't get much further in Phyllis,' said Lady Hardcastle. 'The map says there are more farm buildings down there – it might even be another farm – but the footpath to the fort starts here somewhere.'

I pulled to a stop and switched off the engine. The storm had been playing second fiddle to Phyllis's raucous roar, but with her engine muted, the storm was free to take the solo. It was a virtuoso performance, and we had to raise our own voices to be heard.

'Ready?' said Lady Hardcastle.

'As ready as I'll ever be,' I said.

'Then let's go and rescue Eleanora.'

We clambered out of the car into the gale, heaved the strongbox out of the boot, and set off towards the hill.

Chapter Fifteen

'You know how I keep saying we should get away from home more often? See the country? Explore?'

'You never stop,' panted Lady Hardcastle.

'Do feel free to ignore me next time, won't you.'

We had found the footpath. It led inland for a way, following the contours of the headland, but it soon doubled back and began to take us westwards towards our goal. The track climbed steeply, leaving the shore far below, and leaving us breathless. I was trying to decide whether the day's seemingly endless stair climbing had hardened us for the current trial or simply worn us out.

'Ten years ago we'd have thought nothing of this,' said Lady Hardcastle.

'Ten years ago,' I said, 'we were trying to find our way across the Lincang mountains.'

'Exactly. And we thought nothing of it.'

'We weren't carrying a strongbox then,' I said.

'It doesn't make things easier, I agree.'

'My estimate of being able to get to the fort and back by eight was wildly optimistic,' I said. 'We need to hope they really are here or things could go badly wrong.'

'It'll be fine,' she said. 'Come on, best foot forward.'

The good news was that at least one of my earlier guesses had proven correct. With the wind coming from the southwest, the ridge of the promontory did indeed provide some shelter for the track running along its northern edge. The rain was still battering us, and the turbulent gusts that found their way down the slope still threatened to take my borrowed cap, but we were spared the relentless shoving of the belligerent wind.

'If the weather were a little calmer,' said Lady Hardcastle, 'we could probably see our hotel from here.'

'If the weather were a little calmer,' I said, wiping the rain from my eyes, 'I could probably see you from here.'

We trudged on for at least twenty minutes.

With the wind muted a little by the hill, I could just about hear the sea in the distance. It wasn't happy. By the time it arrived at the shore it would be in a terrible mood.

'No one's going to be going anywhere by boat tonight,' I said.

'Probably not,' she said. 'Can we stop for a moment? We might have to have a scrap at the other end and I'm already puffed.'

We put the box down and huddled in the shelter of some sort of bush or large shrub. I was sure Lady Hardcastle could tell me its common name and full taxonomic classification if I were to ask. But I decided not to distract her from the mission.

Instead, I said, 'Do we have a plan?'

'I had a look at the sketches in your guidebook,' she said. 'There are a couple of intact buildings – or nearly intact, at any rate. But there are a couple of buildings where a hardy man might hole up if he didn't mind a draught. A resourceful man might make himself a cosy little lair. I propose we do nothing more elaborate than leave the strongbox here, then approach as stealthily as we can and search them one by one. Our chambermaid friends were talking about lights, and there might be smoke from a fire, too – even if he doesn't want the warmth he might want to cook.'

'Finding the right building shouldn't be a problem,' I said. 'Then what?'

'Get in, point the gun, make threatening noises – the usual.'

'Seems straightforward enough.'

'You stay behind me, alert for attacks to the rear.'

'As it were,' I said.

I could sense her weary sigh, even though it was masked by the sound of the storm.

'I'll do the pointing and threatening, and we should be back at the hotel in time for supper.'

'Come on, then, my lady,' I said, heaving her to her feet. 'Onwards to glory.'

I pushed the box under the bush and made sure it was properly protected by its oilskin cover.

We weren't too far from our destination when we had stopped, and only a few minutes passed before the high ground to our left dropped away. To our immediate right was a sheer drop to a flat area – too large to be called a ledge, too small for a plateau. Straight ahead, we caught our first glimpse of what remained of the low, grey structures of the Victorian fort. As Lady Hardcastle had predicted, there was light flickering through the gaps in the boarded-up windows of the rightmost building.

We stopped again, and Lady Hardcastle pointed.

'Those are the officers' quarters, according to your guidebook,' she said. 'It doesn't look nearly so damaged as I'd imagined. I expected much more by way of devastation.'

'It's not encouraging,' I said.

'Why not?'

'If it's not too badly damaged on the outside, it'll be relatively unscathed on the inside. Plenty of places to hide.'

'We have surprise on our side for now, though,' she said.

'For now.'

We began to move closer. I was desperate to hug the hillside, to remain as invisible as possible against the rough terrain, but as we moved on we became more and more exposed. Eventually there was no more landscape to protect us and there was nothing for it but to cross the forty or fifty yards of open ground that led to a small bridge and a large open gateway in the gap between the two main buildings. Our approach would be unheard – the wind was now full in our faces and would carry the sound of our approach back to shore – but anyone who happened to glance out through a gap in the boarded windows would surely see us.

'Slow and stealthy?' I said. 'Or quick and dangerously obvious?'

Her answer was to begin to sprint towards the narrow bridge.

'Run like the clappers it is, then,' I said to myself, and set off after her.

My borrowed boots offered excellent protection from the elements but were absolute beasts to run in. I clumped and stumbled my way across the grass apron and skidded to a halt beside Lady Hardcastle. She was looking down into the steep gully that ran between the apron and the fort.

'Quite a drop,' she said. 'Careful on this makeshift bridge. One at a time, I think.'

She crossed quickly and I tried not to look down as I made my own way carefully across the planks. We edged through the wide passageway between the two buildings. There was a doorway to our right but it was firmly locked and appeared to be an unused side entrance to the officers' quarters.

Lady Hardcastle, pistol in hand, edged to the end of the passageway and looked cautiously round the corner. She signalled that it was safe to proceed.

Across a courtyard was the partially demolished gunpowder store. The entrance and the store itself had been below ground level, and the above-ground section was a shattered ruin. To our left, a large, roofless building. To our right, the officers' quarters. The door was tight shut, but light shone through cracks in the boarded windows on this side, too. This was the place.

We approached the door and took up our usual positions on either side, with Lady Hardcastle nearest the hinges. As the one most likely to be holding the gun, it was her customary role to open the door and enter swiftly while I followed, keeping my eyes open for surprises. She held up three fingers . . . two . . . one . . .

She opened the door and stepped in.

We entered what might once have been the main living room. There was a table against the wall. One of its legs was missing and it was propped up on a pile of stones salvaged from the yard outside. There was a chair, similarly battle-damaged, but this time patched up with limbs taken from its fallen comrades. Frankenstein's Chair.

An oil lantern on the table was the only source of light, and the large mound of cheese and stale bread beside it seemed to be the only source of food. There were scraps of wood in the fireplace but no fire, and a lumpy palliasse on the floor but no bed. It was hardly the Steep Holm View Hotel, but it was, at least, sheltered from the storm, the only evidence of which was a fierce draught whistling through the boards in the window frame.

There were two internal doors, both closed. One appeared to lead to another room at the front of the building, the other would most likely open to a room at the back.

I could hear voices in the room towards the back – a man and a young woman. That was encouraging. I signalled to Lady Hardcastle and we stole across the stone floor, our boots scrunching on the fine layer of grit.

Lady Hardcastle stood braced, her pistol raised, while I tried the door. It was locked. The conversation on the other side of it stopped abruptly. So much for surprise.

I turned sideways-on to the door and, standing on one leg, leaned back. I kicked at the door near the lock with all the strength I could muster and it burst inwards. I hopped out of the way and Lady Hardcastle rushed inside.

'Good evening,' she said, cheerily. 'How lovely to see you both again. Are you keeping well?'

There was a moment's silence before I heard Dr Goddard's voice say, 'Lady Hardcastle? What on earth . . . ?'

'She's come to rescue us,' said Eleanora. 'I knew you would. My aunt told me all about you after dinner – she knows more about you than she let on, you know. You're quite famous in her world and she really rather admires you, though she'd never say so. I just knew you'd come and save us.'

I turned at the sound of the other door opening.

'Close the door, my lady,' I said. 'We've got company.'

I reached for the knife concealed up my sleeve, but the new arrival shook his head. Ordinarily I might not have taken orders from sinister fishermen, but this one was armed with a particularly ugly-looking pistol. And now that he had come into the light he was also sickeningly familiar.

'What's the news, dear?' called Lady Hardcastle from behind the shattered door.

I kept my eyes on the gun. 'Armed fisherman,' I said. 'Automatic pistol. Ten shots.'

He put a finger to his lips but this time I ignored him.

'Ah,' she said. 'German?'

'German pistol, yes. There's something else you probably ought to know,' I said.

'Always happy for information, dear.'

'It's Günther Ehrlichmann.'

There was no cheerful reply.

The man laughed. 'Did I hear Dr Goddard correctly,' he said. 'Is that really Lady Hardcastle in the back room? Emily Hardcastle, wife of the late Sir Roderick Hardcastle, diplomat, spy . . . and corpse?'

'That's something I thought you and Sir Roderick had in common,' I said. 'I saw her blow your head off.'

'You did,' he said with an infuriatingly patronizing smile. 'But then, of course, you did not.'

'But you are Günther Ehrlichmann?'

'I am,' he said, still with the same annoying smile. 'But then again, I am not.'

I sighed theatrically. 'I'm not in the mood for this,' I said with a weary nonchalance I didn't feel.

'Nor am I,' he said. 'Slowly and carefully remove whatever weapon you have concealed in your sleeve and drop it on the floor.'

I complied.

'Lady Hardcastle?' he called.

There was no answer.

'Your companion is correct – I do have a pistol trained on . . . I thought "him" at first but now I see it is a "her". You will place your own weapon on the floor and open the door. You will kick the weapon towards me and you will approach with your hands up.'

'I'm not entirely sure I'm inclined to comply with your wishes,' she said.

'Then I shall shoot your friend in the head. I am not negotiating with you, I am instructing you. Your compliance is not optional.'

'Your English is terribly good,' I said.

'Neither is your silence optional,' he said to me.

The door opened and the Japanese pistol skittered across the flagstone floor. Lady Hardcastle came out of the back room with her hands raised.

'There,' he said. 'That is better. Now we can all have a nice little chat. I would offer you tea, but as you can see' – he gestured around the room with his free hand – 'my situation is not quite as . . . as luxurious, yes, it is the same word . . . not quite as luxurious as you are used to.'

'We're quite all right, thank you,' said Lady Hardcastle. 'We had one before we came out.'

He rolled his eyes. 'I always forget how you English find it impossible to take things seriously. No matter. You will both lie face-down on the floor with your hands behind your backs, please.'

Deftly, he secured our wrists with stout cord. Once we were restrained to his satisfaction, he hauled us upright.

'You will find it easier to be leaning against the wall, I think,' he said.

We shuffled into position and made ourselves as comfortable as we could.

'Are they all right?' I said.

'They seem hale and hearty,' said Lady Hardcastle. 'A little bedraggled and a good deal more tied up than I imagine they'd prefer, but no obvious signs of harm.'

'I do not remember inviting you to speak,' said the man who wasn't Ehrlichmann.

'And yet here we are, chattering away like a couple of old fishwives,' said Lady Hardcastle.

'I think you forget who has the gun,' he said.

'And I think you're forgetting that you haven't already shot us,' she said. 'If you intended us harm, you would have killed us by now.'

He lazily cuffed her across the face with his gun hand.

'Hurt,' he said, 'harm. It is easy to mix up the words in German, too. Do not make me hurt you again. I do not enjoy it.'

'I find that very hard to believe,' I said. I was treated to the same nonchalant, back-handed, pistol-holding slap. The blow nearly knocked me sideways. The pain was just on the southern border of bearable and I wondered momentarily whether he might have shattered my cheekbone. It eased quickly, retreating to a throbbing ache and I relaxed a little – I was hurt, not harmed. More importantly, we had his full attention.

'You are correct,' he said. 'Impudent and stupid, but correct. I enjoy it very much. Why are you here?'

'We came to rescue Miss Wilson and Dr Goddard,' said Lady Hardcastle. 'I should have thought that was obvious.'

'How is that going?' he said.

'Not as well as one might have hoped, I must say.'

'It seems not. But why you? Why is England's famous spy getting in my way? I thought you had retired.'

'We were staying at the hotel,' she said. 'It seemed like the proper thing to do.'

'You?' he said. 'You were at the hotel? But I was told there were no English people at the hotel. No matter.'

'Told?' she said. 'Who told you?'

'I said it was no matter. I cultivated a source of information. That is all you need to know. Have you spoken to the American, then? Did she send you?'

'We have spoken to her, but we came of our own accord. As I said, it seemed like the proper thing to do.'

'And so you know what I said to her? In my note.'

'We do. How did you get the note to her, by the way? You were long gone by the time it arrived.'

'A . . . *bengel* . . . *gassenjunge* . . .'

'Urchin?' suggested Lady Hardcastle.

'Like the sea creature? Urchin? Really?' he said.

'I believe so,' she said.

'I do not like it. I gave the boy two shillings to deliver the note at one o'clock. I knew I would be safely out of sight long before then.'

Lady Hardcastle turned to me. 'What did I tell you, dear?' she said. 'I knew it would be something like that. I even used the word "urchin". I guessed a few pennies, though, not two bob. The price of messenger boys has gone up.'

'You overpaid him,' I said to our captor. 'He'd have done it for tuppence. And he was about half an hour early.'

He ignored me. 'You know, then, that in return for everyone's safe . . . return, I require the strongbox. Dr Goddard's precious strongbox.'

'We know that, yes,' said Lady Hardcastle. 'We brought it with us.'

He gestured around the room. 'And yet I do not see it.'

'We didn't bring it all the way here, you chump,' she said.

He struck her again. 'Then where?' he said.

She spat blood. 'Under a bush on the path, just before the open ground.'

He fetched more cord and bound our ankles.

'You will sit exactly where you are. If you have moved before I return I shall shoot you through the kneecaps.'

He disappeared back through the door where I had first seen him, and emerged moments later in his pea jacket and cap. He left, slamming the front door behind him.

◆　◆　◆

Obviously we moved about a bit – there were things we needed to do, and sitting against the wall like good girls wasn't going to get them done.

'Are you OK in there?' called Eleanora after a while.

'Fine, dear, thank you,' said Lady Hardcastle. 'Just having a bit of a fidget. While the cat's away and all that.'

'Why were you goading him?' said Dr Goddard. 'He's a dangerous man, you know. Very dangerous. Not safe at all.'

'We just felt . . .' said Lady Hardcastle, puffing a little as she shuffled back towards her original spot, '. . . that it was impor-tant . . . to keep his attention . . .'

'Are you really going to give him the strongbox?' asked Eleanora.

'That's certainly the plan,' I said. 'He demanded that your aunt hand it over this evening. We thought that since he couldn't get there by boat, we might help him out.'

'Or help you out, more to the point,' said Lady Hardcastle. 'Has he been treating you well?'

'I'm so hungry I could eat an actual horse, but we have water.'

'That's very reassuring,' I said. 'It means he needs you alive and well.'

'That's what I thought. But you can't give him the box, you simply can't.'

'We already have, dear,' said Lady Hardcastle. 'It really is where we said it is.'

'But that means I'm responsible for letting important British secrets fall into enemy hands,' said Eleanor. 'You can't allow it.'

I decided not to tell her – if she didn't already know – that it had been her aunt's intention to make sure that the secrets fell into the Americans' hands. Instead, I said, 'Please don't fret. We'll work something out. But how about you, Dr Goddard? How have you been treated?'

'He roughed me up a bit at first, but I gave him my key and he's left me alone since. Can't quite work out why he's not killed me, to be honest. Not that I'm ungrateful, mind you. Not ungrateful at all. Just a little puzzled.'

'I'm sorry, dear, I have to ask,' said Lady Hardcastle. 'Curiosity will be the death of me one day, I'm probably part cat – but do you work for my brother?'

'Who's your brother?' he said.

'Harry Featherstonhaugh of the Foreign Office.'

Silence fell.

'Dr Goddard?' she said.

'Well, I'll be blowed,' he said. His voice had changed slightly. 'You're Harry's sister? Really?'

'All my life, dear. He can be a bit of a chump, but he's all I've got.'

'Well, I never. So you're the one who disappeared in China for two years.'

'The very same,' she said. 'He speaks of me?'

'Some days he speaks of nothing else. Well, I'll be blowed. He's embarrassingly proud of you. Holds you up as a model of excellence and all that. I'm dashed pleased to meet you.'

'It's entirely mutual, I'm sure,' she said. 'I wish he'd tell me how proud he is. He treats me like an absolute duffer most of the time.'

'Brothers and sisters, old girl. Brothers and sisters. I take it you've got a plan?'

'We're working on it,' she said.

I heard the sound of boots on the gravel outside.

'Cave,' I said. 'He's back.'

I rechecked that we were roughly as he had left us and we all fell silent.

The door opened and he came in with the oilskin sack slung over his back. He dropped it on the floor and settled into the rickety chair.

'It is heavy,' he said. 'I admire you for carrying it all that way.'

'Thank you,' said Lady Hardcastle. 'Well, then, now that you've got what you want, shall we be on our way? We don't want to hold you up.'

'No,' he said, 'there is no rush. I am not due to leave for another' – he took an expensive-looking watch from his pocket and inspected it – 'twelve hours. We have time to become acquainted. I have longed to meet the famous Lady Hardcastle.'

'And yet, if it weren't entirely impossible, I'd swear we'd already met,' she said. 'You're the spitting image of—'

'Of my brother Karl, yes. I am disappointed that you have not already worked it out. We were twins.'

'The man who murdered my husband wasn't called Karl, he was Günther Ehrlichmann,' she said.

'Yes, we were Günther Ehrlichmann, it is true.'

It wasn't like Lady Hardcastle to be this obtuse.

'Günther Ehrlichmann didn't exist,' I said. 'He was a fiction made up by the Imperial German authorities. The reason he could appear to be flitting around the world like some sort of ghost was that he was two men. Twins.'

'Your friend has it, Lady Hardcastle,' he said. 'It was a brilliant stratagem. We were a formidable team, Karl and I. He was the improviser, I was the planner. Tactics and strategy. He did most of the work in the field, I took care of mundane practical matters like hotels and transport. Of course, we used our appearance to give each other an alibi – Karl would kill while I would make sure I was seen on the other side of town. But as the stories of our mysterious powers began to spread, we became bolder. We encouraged those stories, we helped to embellish them. They thought Ehrlichmann was a phantom, a demon. How could he do what he did? How could he be in two places at once? Such fear.'

'So who are you?' said Lady Hardcastle.

'I am Jakob Gerber, from Berlin. And you killed my brother, Karl.'

'Bloody hell,' said Dr Goddard in the other room.

'What happened to you?' I asked.

'I spent nearly ten years in a Chinese prison, thanks to you,' said Gerber.

'To us?' I said. 'Your brother murdered Sir Roderick and the consequences were our fault?'

'Of course. Had it not been for you, I should not have been hunting for Karl. I should not have been taken by the Chinese army. They were very pleased with themselves. They had captured the famous Günther Ehrlichmann. They were not going to let him go.'

'Didn't your people try to get you out?' I said.

'My country disavowed me,' he said. 'Ehrlichmann was dead and they had no use for me. I was abandoned. Left to rot. I found out later that they were reluctant to reveal their deception in case they wanted to use it again. It had worked well, you see. There was nothing to be gained by letting the world know the secret, especially if they could find another pair of twins with our special talents.'

'But the Chinese released you?'

'Released is not perhaps the right word. They grew bored of me. They did not tire of torturing and beating me every day. Of screaming at me. Of convincing me that I was less than human. But I was not the great prize they hoped I would be. And they could not let me go for fear of reprisals. After a few years I was moved to a prison in the hills. The guards still had their fun with me, but they paid less and less attention to me in between times. Eventually, I was able simply to walk out.'

'Walk out?'

'Well, of course, one or two guards had to be bribed, one or two more had to be killed, and one very special one had to suffer great pain, but that is the essence of it, yes.'

'Who are you working for now, then, if not Germany?' asked Lady Hardcastle.

'For the highest bidder,' he said. 'I have become . . . a state-less mercenary.'

'And who is this highest bidder?' she persisted. 'Who has paid you?'

'As yet, no one. I undertook this mission on my own initiative. When I have the secrets in the Herr Doktor's strongbox I shall put them up for auction. Whoever wants them the most will, I think, pay the most.'

'How did you find out about the box in the first place?' I said. 'If you don't have a government behind you? How did you even know where to look?'

'I take my new job seriously,' he said. 'I have many sources of information. But you knew that, surely. How else would I have been able to locate your musician friends to send you a message last year?'

'You read about them in the newspaper, according to the boys,' I said. 'Then traipsed round London looking in every club you could find.'

'One can find out a lot by reading newspapers,' he said.

'It's not exactly skilled spy work, though, is it? Any fool can read a newspaper and go out to listen to a band.'

'And it is hardly skilled "spy work" to have your exploits repeatedly reported in the newspapers,' he said. 'One would have thought that . . . that an-on-ym-ity' – it was as though he were double-checking the translation as he went along – 'that anonymity, yes, it is almost the same word again. It would be a key . . . a key requirement of your work. Hah. Yes, a key requirement. You sneer at me but you were the ones who forgot how to do your own jobs.'

Lady Hardcastle sighed. 'We've retired,' she said. 'We live a quiet life in the country.'

'And yet here you are,' he said. 'A thorn in my side once more. Wrecking my plans once more. Trying to kill me once more. But you have saved me a job, of course, by your meddling. Once I had my payment I had one last task to perform before I retired myself.'

'Don't tell me,' said Lady Hardcastle, 'let me guess. You were going to travel to Littleton Cotterell and kill me?'

'But of course. You are the loose end, the unfinished business.'

'I'm back to my original thought, though, dear – if you were going to kill me you would have done it already.'

'On the contrary,' he said. 'What use is revenge if the subject does not know why their life must end?'

'He has a point, my lady,' I said. 'I've said the same thing to you myself more than once. I think we just need to resign ourselves to the fact that you're going to be shot soon.'

'Well, when you put it like that, dear, I suppose you're right. It's such a shame that it has to be this way, though. If I were going to be murdered I'd have picked a much more impressive murderer. And a much more glamorous location. Going out at the hands of a talentless former-assassin's insane brother in a derelict shed isn't at all what I had in mind.'

'You will be shutting up now, I think,' he said. 'And I will be examining my prize before ending your arrogant prattle forever.'

Kneeling on the floor in front of the strongbox, he reached into his pocket and produced an intricately cut key.

Chapter Sixteen

'You're going to be disappointed,' I said.

'I think not,' he said. 'I have the strongbox. I have the key. It is your government who will be disappointed when the secrets of their new chemical process are sold to a foreign power.'

'Have it your way,' I said.

The lock made a pleasingly complex mechanical sound as he turned the key. There was a loud clunk as the bolts withdrew. Slowly, he lifted the lid and looked inside. His face fell.

'She told you,' said Lady Hardcastle. 'You wouldn't listen, but she did tell you.'

'It is empty,' he said. He grabbed his gun and pointed it at her. 'What have you done with them? What have you done with the plans?'

'There were no plans, you chump,' said Lady Hardcastle. 'I'm sure I've already pointed out your chumpiness, but you wouldn't listen to that, either. I thought I might have been being a bit rude, but you really are the most dunderheaded imbecile I've ever encountered.'

He jumped to his feet and sprang into the other room, waving the pistol. 'Where are the plans, Herr Doktor?'

'They're quite right, dear boy. There are no plans.'

'But you have the strongbox. You work at the government laboratory. There are plans for a new chemical plant.'

'Two out of three, old chap, only two out of three.'

'I thought it was something about a radio,' said Eleanora. 'You told Aunt Adelia you worked on radio transmission equipment.'

I was busy so I left it to Lady Hardcastle to say, 'He told Kusnetsov it was a weapon. Takahashi thought it was a locomotive design, and Martin was sure it was a new ship. What did you tell Schneider? We never did find out what he thought.'

'High-powered optics,' said Goddard. 'I say, you're every bit as good as Harry says, you know. Well done, you.'

'One does one's best,' she said. 'You've been had, Herr Gerber. Conned. Tricked. Fooled. They all were. There was never a secret anything. You've all been killing each other for an empty box. It's a rather splendid box, mind you – I'm sure you could get a few bob for it. Flo couldn't get in and she's an absolute mivvy with a set of picklocks.'

Gerber let out a roar of rage. There was a sudden gunshot, horribly loud in the confined space of the small stone room.

'Is everyone all right?' called Lady Hardcastle.

'Yes,' said Dr Goddard. 'The table might never walk again now that he's shot it in the leg, but we're fine.'

'No!' roared Gerber as he raced back into the main room, still waving the pistol.

My outstretched arm caught him in the throat. In his shock he loosed off another round before collapsing to the floor, clutching his neck. The shot went harmlessly into the door frame, but it did serve to remind me that relieving him of the gun should be my priority.

He was more intent on his struggle to breathe than on holding on to the one advantage he currently had, and when I grabbed his hand I was able to twist the gun free with surprising ease. I struck the side of his head with the butt of the pistol grip and he fell like a proverbial sack of spuds.

I used my knife to free Lady Hardcastle and went through to the other room. Dr Goddard and Eleanora were both bound hand and foot, and were lying on opposite sides of the small room. Dr Goddard's face was badly bruised but, thankfully, Eleanora appeared untouched. I cut the cords and helped them both to sit up.

'If you stretch like this,' I said, demonstrating, 'and like this, the feeling will come back and you'll be able to move. Do you think you can walk a mile?'

'It might be a struggle at first,' said Dr Goddard, 'but we'll loosen up, I'm sure.'

'I'll be OK,' said Eleanora. 'How did you . . . ?'

'It's all to do with Gerber being a bit of a chump,' I said. 'Lady Hardcastle was quite right.'

'I don't understand.'

'Did you hear him disarm us?' I said. 'I dropped my knife on the floor, Lady Hardcastle dropped her gun.'

'Yes, I thought it was all over.'

'It would have been if the chump had picked them up,' said Lady Hardcastle, who had now joined us. 'He just left them lying where we dropped them.'

'Ohh,' said Dr Goddard. 'Which is why you kept needling him. Keep his mind on sparring with you instead of picking up the weapons.'

'It cost me a couple of smacks in the chops,' said Lady Hardcastle. 'But it was worth it.' She gingerly felt her jaw. 'No permanent damage done. The bruises will look a bit of a sight in the morning, though.'

'It was also why we gave up the strongbox so eagerly,' I said. 'To be honest, I thought we'd underplayed that one – we should probably have been a bit more reluctant. But he was so sure of himself that he never questioned it. Off he trotted and we retrieved the gun and the knife. Then I cut myself free. I seem to have been doing a lot of that lately, by the way – I'm thinking of asking for a rise.'

'And you shall have it, dear. You're worth every penny and more.'

'Thank you. All that remained was to keep him talking while the feeling returned to my wrists and then . . . well, you saw what happened then.'

'Hah!' said Dr Goddard. 'Harry's stories don't do you justice. I take it you've secured Gerber?'

'No need,' said Lady Hardcastle. 'I found the last of his Veronal and a syringe so I've dosed him with that. There wasn't much left, but we only need him to be out for a while until we can get Harry's chaps to come out and fetch him.'

'You should . . .' Eleanora was starting to shake a little. 'You should have killed him.'

'It certainly crossed my mind,' said Lady Hardcastle. 'But I'm keen for this particular Gerber to face justice. He should be lying peacefully there on the floor when the relief column gets here. He'll have a nasty bump on the head – well done, Flo – but he'll be fit to face trial.'

It was becoming obvious – to me at least – that Eleanora was clinging to hope and reason by the tips of her fingers. We needed to get her out of there and to somewhere safe and warm as quickly as we could.

'Good,' I said with a cheeriness that sounded forced even to me. 'Well, if everyone's fit, shall we get back to civilization? There are a couple of farms close to the other end of the headland. We should be able to shelter there while we work out how to summon help.'

'And you can tell us what my brother has been up to, Dr Goddard,' said Lady Hardcastle. 'I presume this has all been his doing.'

'Bound by the Official Secrets Act, I'm afraid, old girl,' said Dr Goddard. 'No can do.'

Lady Hardcastle harrumphed. 'I'll not press you, then,' she said. 'But Harry can bally well tell me what's been going on, Official Secrets Act be blowed.'

Dr Goddard laughed. 'Come on, then,' he said. 'Are you all right, Miss Wilson? Can I help you?'

'I'll be fine,' she said in a voice that belied her confident words. 'Let's just get out of here.'

I double-checked that Gerber was unconscious and breathing freely, then handed his pistol to Dr Goddard.

'I presume you know how to use one of these,' I said.

'Point the sticky-out bit at the bad fellow and pull on the curvy little lever underneath?' he said.

'That's the essence of it,' I said.

With an easy familiarity that I had, in truth, fully expected, he checked the magazine, clicked on the safety catch and put the gun in his pocket.

Eleanora was in her nightdress so I gave her my boots and raincoat.

'Oh, but what about you?' she said. 'And what about Dr Goddard?'

'I'll take Gerber's,' I said.

'And I'll be absolutely fine,' said Dr Goddard, indicating his suit. 'A well-made dinner suit can cope with anything. This one's seen better days, and it might need replacing by the time the night is done, but I'll be protected well enough. And I'm sure Harry can stand me a new one.'

The peacoat was absurdly large and I had to stuff the boots with some rags I tore from Gerber's shirt, but they were better than nothing.

I took the lantern from the table and passed it to Lady Hardcastle. Then we left the ruined officer's quarters and stepped out into the storm.

◆ ◆ ◆

The wind was at our backs as we crossed the apron of open ground and headed for the shelter of the hill. The light had well and truly gone, now, but this time we had the lantern to guide us.

Having been trussed up on a stone floor for almost three days, Dr Goddard was clearly weakened. He moved stiffly and stopped more than once to try to rub some life into his legs. Eleanora had only been held captive since the morning, but even she was finding it more difficult than she had expected.

'Time was when I'd have given everything I owned, and pledged everything I would ever own just for the chance of five minutes of adventure,' she said. 'But if this is what it does to you, I'm not sure I'll ever think that again.'

'Adventure certainly has its drawbacks,' I said. 'But it has its pleasures, too. You'll look back on all this with a lot more fondness and enthusiasm than you feel now, I promise.'

'Maybe,' she said. 'Do you mind if I ask you a personal question?'

'Of course not. I promise not to take offence at whatever you ask, as long as you don't take offence if I choose not to answer once I've heard the question.'

'You and Lady Hardcastle are . . . what do you call it? Pals? She talks about you as though you work together, like colleagues, but you call her Lady Hardcastle. And you're her servant, she said – her lady's maid.'

'That's right.'

'But you're still buddies? How does that work? I thought you Britishers were all tied up by your "class".'

'The best of buddies. Do you really think we could have been through everything we described to you last night and let an accident of birth build a wall between us? It's deeply ingrained, all the class rubbish, but there comes a time on a lonely track in the middle of China when the absurdity of it just sort of washes over you like a wave. It all seems to make sense when you're right in the middle of it, but when you're miles away from it all with only a mysterious monk for company, it begins to look a bit silly. Just think: if my father had been Sir Joseph Armstrong from Mayfair, or hers had been Perilous Percy Fanshaw, the famous tightrope walker, no one would have thought anything of us being pals. As it is, we play the game and mostly obey the rules. And that means that without thinking, I always call her "my lady" and refer to her as "Lady Hardcastle". It saves other people's embarrassment.'

'But you're still a servant.'

'I still am. I enjoy it. It keeps me busy and I like looking after her.'

'Wait. Did you say "tightrope walker"? Was your pop a tightrope walker?'

'Knife-thrower, actually,' I said.

'You're teasing me now,' she said.

'Honour bright,' I said. 'The Great Coltello, he was. He could cut the corner off a playing card from ten yards away.'

'Did he teach you?'

'Of course. I could take the other corner off. But I'd have to be eight yards away – I'm only little.'

She laughed. 'I'd like to see that.'

'We'll get them to put a board up in the salon when we get back to the hotel – I'll show off for you then.'

Lady Hardcastle had been leading the way with Dr Goddard. They slowed so that we could catch them up.

'What are you two muttering about back there?' she said.

'You, mostly,' I said.

'All good, I hope.'

'Why would you imagine that? I can't lie to the poor girl.'

'I suppose you're right,' she said. 'Heigh-ho. Another acquaintance's illusions shattered by your wretched honesty. You and your chapel ways.'

'Is there much further to go?' asked Dr Goddard. 'I'm pooped.'

'Not far,' I said. 'And it's more or less downhill for the rest of the way. But we can take a break if you need to. My lady?'

'Certainly we can,' she said. 'No point in wearing ourselves out now the difficult bit is done.'

We stopped beside a spindly tree. It offered little actual protection from the wind and rain, but we huddled closer to it nonetheless. I felt sure Lady Hardcastle would be able to explain it as some sort of primal instinct, and I was about to give her the opportunity to do just that when my thoughts were interrupted by the sound of a gunshot. It was muffled by the sound of the storm, but it was unmistakeable, and the explosion of splinters from the tree trunk left no room for further doubt.

'Everybody down,' I said. 'Now. And cover the lantern.'

'Where away?' said Lady Hardcastle. She was looking round for the source of the shot.

'Upslope,' I said. 'A little behind us to judge from the damage to the tree.'

Another shot. A spray of mud from where the bullet hit the ground.

'Sounds like a rifle,' said Lady Hardcastle. 'We should have searched the place a bit better before we rabbited.'

'We weren't to know he was going to come round so quickly,' I said.

'I was slightly worried about the dose,' she said. 'When the idea came to me I was concerned that I might give him too much and kill him accidentally, but when I found the bottle, my worries went the other way. Still I'd have put good money on his being out for another hour at least. He might be mad as a sack of gibbons but he has the constitution of an ox.'

A bang. Another spray of debris from the tree.

'He's not a frightfully good shot, is he?' said Dr Goddard.

'I imagine he's still a little groggy,' said Lady Hardcastle. 'And he's not allowing for the wind. Or, if he is, he's not worked out how turbulent it can be at the bottom of a slope. Do you know—'

'Really, my lady?' I said. 'Now? A lecture on fluid dynamics in the middle of a gunfight?'

'There's never a wrong time to learn new things,' she said. 'But you make a good point. I think he might be slightly unsighted, too. We're in a bit of a dip here. Which means he must be—'

Yet another bang.

'Yes,' she said. 'The flash came from over there.' She pointed to a spot halfway up the hill, but much further along than I had guessed.

'Do we stay or move?' I said. 'Could you hit him from here with that?' I indicated the Japanese pistol which was now in her hand.

'I could give him a nasty scare,' she said. 'But I'm even more hampered by the weather than he. I'd be shooting upwind.'

'We could give you covering fire if you fancied trying to get round behind him,' said Dr Goddard.

'As long as you stopped shooting before I got there,' I said. 'But no. Now I come to think about it properly, anyone who stood up would present too good a target. He's bound to make a lucky shot sooner or later if he has something definite to shoot at.'

'I know what I'd do if I were him,' said Lady Hardcastle.

'What's that?' said Dr Goddard.

'I'd pin us down with a few wild shots, and then when I was sure we'd hunkered down somewhere, I'd—'

She was cut short by a maniacal scream and a rush of wild movement from about twenty yards up the slope.

'Yes,' said Lady Hardcastle, jumping to her feet. 'I'd do exactly that.' She loosed off a couple of shots as the rest of us stood and spread out. 'Yours, I think, Flo, dear.'

He was already upon us but, as we'd already learned, his skills were more strategic than tactical. Mix in the after effects of a dose of Veronal, and the anger and disappointment caused by having all his plans come to nought, and he was never going to make the best decisions in a fight. He had overrun it badly and was skidding out of control as he drew level with us and tried to stop.

I set my own balance and braced to grab the rifle as he passed. He was holding it in both hands and as I took hold of it, I twisted my body to give him an extra impetus that sent him stumbling off the other side of the path and crashing into the undergrowth.

I threw the rifle to Eleanor, who caught it easily. She checked it and levelled it at the spot where Gerber had disappeared.

By the light of the now uncovered lantern, I saw a bedraggled figure emerge from the low bushes. Barefoot, and with his shirt in tatters where we had torn rags from it for my boots, he looked like a shipwrecked sailor. The rain was streaming down his face and his expression was not a jolly one. It wasn't even a sane one. He looked wildly about, his eyes darting between us.

There were three guns pointing at him now, with me the only one of us unarmed. I could see him briefly consider me as the easy target. It seemed he remembered how easily I had knocked him down twice already, though, and thought better of it.

Then again, he wasn't the tactical brains behind Günther Ehrlichmann.

He charged me. Of course he did.

With so little of him protected from the rain by intact clothing, it was slightly akin to trying to get a hold on a greased eel, but I did manage to take a firm grasp of his wrist. I twisted and pulled and he began to topple over once more. I usually try to bring a little subtlety and grace to these sort of encounters, but to be honest he was really starting to get on my nerves. I would usually rule it out as being just gratuitously nasty, but under the circumstances I truly felt he deserved it – I stamped on one of his bare feet with my borrowed boot. His howl of pain was cut short as I completed the throw and he landed face-first on a tuft of wiry grass.

'He gets full marks for persistence,' said Lady Hardcastle. 'I'll give him that, at least.'

'I say we just shoot him and let Harry sort it out,' said Dr Goddard.

'It would be less tiresome,' agreed Lady Hardcastle. 'But I meant what I said – I want at least one Gerber to face the consequences of their actions. I'd really be rather pleased if the Imperial German government were made to own up to Roddy's murder, too. I'm not one to bear a grudge, but . . .'

There was a groan from the floor and Gerber began to try to push himself up. He managed to get up, but he couldn't work out how to stand without putting weight on his shattered foot. He just knelt there, growling. He must have caught his forehead on a rock as he fell because there was a trickle of blood running down his face now, mingling with the rain.

'I'm really so very sorry,' I said, 'but I'm sick of this.'

I struck him at one of the points Chen Ping Bo had described as having an entirely negative effect on a man's ability to remain conscious. He collapsed once more.

'What are we going to do with him?' asked Eleanora.

'I say leave the blighter where he is,' said Dr Goddard. 'Pick him up in the morning. He's not going anywhere on that foot.'

'He could die of exposure if we leave him out in this storm,' said Lady Hardcastle.

'Don't look to me for sympathy,' he said. 'I was the one who suggested we shoot him.'

I sighed. 'Help me drag him to the shelter of this bush,' I said. 'We can cover him with my – with his – coat. That should protect him until Harry's men get here.'

We got him out of the rain as best we could, and wrapped him in the coat. Once again we checked that he was breathing all right, and set off to find a farm and a cup of tea.

◆ ◆ ◆

We followed the track all the way to where we had left the motor car. The rain still splashing on it made its dark green paint sparkle in the lantern light.

'Is that your motor?' asked Dr Goddard.

'It is,' said Lady Hardcastle proudly.

He looked more closely. 'Only two seats,' he said. 'How were you planning to get us all home?'

'We were going to do it in shifts. We just need to get everyone settled first.'

'Ah. Righto. I've never seen anything like it, though. Well, I have – I saw it parked outside the hotel. But I'd never seen anything like it until then. I had no idea it was yours. How did you come by such a machine? It looks like something in an illustration from a Jules Verne story.'

'A friend of Harry's – a friend of mine, now – designs them. He owns a racing team. Lord Riddlethorpe.'

'Well, I'll be blowed. Riddlethorpe Racing, eh? I've heard of them, of course. Seen his motor cars at Brooklands. He's building them for the general public now, then?'

'He's planning to,' she said. 'This is by way of a prototype. We're testing it for him.'

'Are you? Are you indeed? I wouldn't mind having a go myself when this is all over. What does she do?'

Eleanora hadn't said a word for the past ten minutes. Even in the dim lantern light I could see that her face was pale as she stared absently into the middle distance. I was concerned that the shock of the events of the past twenty-four hours had finally caught up with her. We had to get her somewhere warm and safe.

'I'm so sorry to interrupt,' I said. 'But I can't help feeling that we're standing in the pouring rain, being battered by a howling gale, and we seem to be discussing motor cars. Might I respectfully suggest that we'd be better off seeking shelter in one of the nearby farm cottages and admiring Phyllis in the morning?'

'Phyllis?' said Dr Goddard.

'The motor car is called Phyllis,' I said.

'Lord Riddlethorpe called his new racing car Phyllis?'

'Lady Hardcastle called her new racing car Phyllis,' I said. 'I hate to be presumptuous, but I really do think we'd benefit from getting out of the storm as quickly as possible. Perhaps we could discuss the naming of new vehicles over a nice cup of tea.'

'Quite right,' he said. 'Many apologies. Which way?'

'There's a farmhouse about five hundred yards down this track,' I said, pointing in the direction we had originally been heading in the motor car. 'And there's another about half a mile down there, back towards the main road. I propose the nearer one because . . . well, because it's nearer, obviously. But also because if anyone comes looking for us, they'll see Phyllis and know we're nearby. They'll look at the closest farm first. Probably.'

'Makes perfect sense to me,' he said.

'And to me,' said Lady Hardcastle. 'Come along.'

Eleanora gave up the rifle without comment when I held out my hands for it. Holding it in one hand, I put my other arm around her shoulders and helped her along the muddied track. She didn't react, and her plodding gait reinforced the impression I had gained from her pallor and empty expression – this was a girl on the verge of collapse.

It was almost eleven o'clock and the farmhouse was in total darkness – they're early-to-bed-early-to-rise types out in the country.

Lady Hardcastle hammered on the door with the side of her fist.

'Hello!' she shouted. I'd forgotten what an extremely loud voice she had.

She hammered again.

An upstairs window to our right opened and a man's head emerged.

'Do you know what bloody time it is?' he said.

With an exaggerated fussiness she raised her left wrist and pulled back her sleeve. She looked at her watch.

'It's just coming up to five minutes to eleven,' she said.

'It's good you's got a watch,' he said. 'Means you'll know when it's mornin'. You can come back then.'

'We're caught in the storm,' said Lady Hardcastle. 'We have a motor car but it won't carry all of us. We need somewhere to shelter until we can get help.'

From inside the room, a woman's voice said, 'What is it, Ronnie? What are you doin'?'

The man turned round. 'Got four people out here wantin' to come in out of the rain.'

'In this weather? What are you standin' there arguin' for? Go down and let 'em in. I'll get the kettle on.'

The window closed.

Moments later, the door was unbolted and opened by a short, round man in a patched nightshirt. His face and hair were wet from the few moments he had spent hanging out of the window. He was clutching a candle in an enamel holder and it was immediately extinguished by the wind.

'The missus says you better come in,' he said, picking off the wax that had blown on to his nightshirt.

We trooped in through the door and were joined almost immediately by a similarly small, round woman in a patched nightdress. She had a woollen shawl around her shoulders.

'Come through to the kitchen, my dears,' she said. 'The stove should still be hot. We can get you dried out a bit.'

We dripped our way through the parlour to the kitchen beyond, where we dropped gratefully into the sturdy wooden chairs arrayed around an equally sturdy table. The farmer's wife lit more lamps and fussed about, taking our coats and hanging them by the cast-iron range to dry.

She said nothing about the rifle leaning against my leg, nor the pistols that Lady Hardcastle and Dr Goddard clonked on the table. Dr Goddard's dinner suit earned a second glance, but still no comment.

'I'm so sorry for the imposition,' said Lady Hardcastle. 'We had no idea what else to do.'

'Don't you be worryin' about that,' said the farmer's wife. 'Can't have strangers out on a night like this when we've got a warm house you can wait in. Ron? Fetch some wood for the stove.'

Ron obediently plodded out the back door.

'But where are my manners? I'm Emily, Lady Hardcastle. This is Dr Percival Goddard, and these are Miss Eleanora Wilson and Miss Florence Armstrong.'

'Pleased to meet you, m'lady, I'm sure,' said the farmer's wife. 'I'm Ena Primrose and this old lump is my husband, Ron.'

Mr Primrose had returned with an armful of chopped wood which he began to feed to the stove.

'Don't mind my askin',' said Mrs Primrose, 'but what are you doin' out on a night like this? You been up the fort?'

'We have, as a matter of fact. We . . . ah . . . well, we had one or two things to attend to there.'

'Someone livin' up there, is they? We seen lights. We seen a little boat, too. Steam. Putt-putt-putt it goes, out across the bay to Weston. I says to Ron, I says, "We should get one o' they boats. Make it easier to get to town." Takes us a couple of hours in our cart, it does. Didn't I say that, Ron?'

'Ar,' said Mr Primrose. 'You did.'

'Well I shouldn't think there'd be much objection to you having that one,' said Dr Goddard. 'The current owner won't be needing it.'

'Goin' away, is he?' said Mrs Primrose.

'For a long, long time if I have anything to do with it,' said Lady Hardcastle.

'You hear that, Ron? You fancy a little steamboat?'

'What would I want with a steamboat?' said Mr Primrose. 'Be more trouble than it's worth.'

'We could get to Weston in half an hour.'

'We don't never go to Weston.'

'That's 'cause it takes us all mornin' to get there.'

'You 'ave it if you want it, then,' he said. 'I don't want no steamboat.'

'Suit yourself,' she said. ''Ere, is the little one all right?'

Eleanora was leaning on me and had begun to sob.

'She's had a shock,' I said. 'Quite a few, in fact. You'll be all right, though, won't you.'

I hugged her and she sniffed.

'Nice cup of tea'll sort her out,' said Mrs Primrose. 'Kettle's boilin', look.'

Over the sound of the boiling kettle, I thought I could also hear the sound of a motor car engine.

Moments later there was a knock at the door.

Mr Primrose muttered something about people not knowing what time it was and set off to answer it. Lady Hardcastle and Dr Goddard both reached for their guns.

I said, 'Just a moment, Mr Primrose. Would you mind if I got that?'

'For you, is it? More of your pals out in the storm? Or is someone after you?'

Mrs Primrose looked alarmed at this.

'I don't know,' I said. 'But let's just be on the safe side, shall we?'

I passed Eleanora into Lady Hardcastle's care and stood up.

'What's a little thing like you goin' to do if it's unsavouries?' said Mrs Primrose.

'You'd be surprised,' said Dr Goddard. 'I'll be behind you, Miss Armstrong.'

'Thank you,' I said.

I crept to the door as silently as my boots would allow. I was about to let out a loudly confident, 'Who is it?' but events overtook me.

There was another knock at the door, and a familiar voice called, 'Are you in there, sis?'

I grabbed the latch and pulled open the door.

'Strongarm,' said Harry genially. 'Don't just stand there, old sport, let me in. I'm getting soaked out here.'

I stood aside and he hurried in.

'Good evening, Mr Feather-stone-huff,' I said. 'What brings you all the way out here?'

'Oh, you know,' he said. 'I thought you and my errant sister might have ignored me and got yourselves into trouble.' He peered round me and through the kitchen door. 'Looks like I'm right.' He caught sight of my battered face. 'I say, you've been in the wars.'

'All in a day's work,' I said. 'Come through.'

Mrs Primrose was fetching another cup and saucer from her dresser.

'Another friend of yours caught in the storm?' she said.

'In a manner of speaking,' I said. 'Mr and Mrs Primrose, this is Harry Featherstonhaugh, Lady Hardcastle's brother. Mr Featherstonhaugh, these are Mr and Mrs Primrose of Brean Down Farm.'

They all how-do-you-do'd, Mr Primrose with markedly less enthusiasm than his wife.

'I'm sorry we a'n't got no more chairs in here,' said Mrs Primrose. 'It's gettin' a bit cosy, i'n't it?'

'That's quite all right, Mrs P – I've been sitting down for a while. It's quite a long old drive to get out here. Just glad to have found everyone. Are you all right, old man?'

'Never better,' said Dr Goddard.

'I doubt that,' said Harry. 'What about you, sis? You look a bit banged about, too.'

'There was some minor unpleasantness,' said Lady Hardcastle, touching her face. 'But I'll live. I've had worse.'

'At least no one shot you this time, eh?' he said. 'And this must be Eleanora Wilson. How are you, young lady?'

Eleanora looked up at him but said nothing.

'She's had quite a time of it,' said Lady Hardcastle. 'I'd like to get her back to her aunt as soon as we can.'

'We can take care of that in just a jiffy,' said Harry. 'What happened to Ehr— to the German chap?'

'It's all right,' said Lady Hardcastle. 'You can say his name. You knew he was here, didn't you?'

'I strongly suspected it,' he said.

'Did you know it wasn't his real name? Or how he managed to come back from the dead?'

'Not until very recently. I had a little chat with a chap from the German embassy.'

'They've admitted it?'

'It wasn't that sort of chat. This was more of a . . . well . . . you know. You've been in similar situations, sis. A disenchanted junior clerk . . . copies of certain documents . . . The long and the short of it is that we know all about Gerber but the Germans have no idea that we know.'

'And how did you find us?' I asked.

'Adelia Wilson,' he said. 'I stopped off at the hotel.'

'You got there awfully quickly,' said Lady Hardcastle.

'Time for explanations later. As soon as my men get here we can get Goddard and Miss Wilson back to town and checked over by a doctor.'

'Your men?' I said. 'Not Harris and Tweed?'

He laughed. 'No, they really are on other business. It's the other two chaps you met earlier. I dropped them off at Middle Farm and told them to meet me up here if you weren't there.'

'You made them walk in this weather?'

'Do them good,' he said. 'Idle beggars.'

Throughout all this, Mr and Mrs Primrose had been looking on with growing disbelief. Mrs Primrose managed to gather herself together enough to pour the tea.

'Thank you, Mrs P,' said Harry. 'It goes without saying that everything you just heard is strictly confidential, of course.'

'I i'n't certain I understood a word of it,' she said.

'That's the spirit. Knew I could rely on you. Patriotic and trustworthy, the pair of you. I can tell these things, you know. But I allowed myself to get distracted. What happened to . . . to Gerber?'

'He's lying unconscious under a bush on the track leading to the fort,' I said. 'Your men might need to carry him. He's hurt his foot.'

'Hurt it?' he said.

'I might have stamped on it a bit. In the heat of the moment.'

He laughed again. 'No less than he deserves. I'll send the boys out to him. They can mind him while we get everyone else to safety – I'll come back for them later.'

As we finished our tea, there was a knock at the door. It was Harry's men, looking as muddy and sodden as we must have looked ourselves. Harry gave them instructions to go out and retrieve Gerber. They weren't overjoyed at the prospect of having to spend another couple of hours in the rain, waiting to be picked up, but they obeyed nevertheless.

Harry rejoined us in the kitchen and pulled two five-pound notes from his wallet and pressed them into Mr Primrose's hand.

'For your trouble,' he said. 'And don't forget: mum's the word, eh?' He tapped the side of his nose.

'It weren't no trouble, sir,' said Mr Primrose, whose demeanour had brightened considerably in the presence of the unexpected windfall.

'Just you take good care of that girl,' said Mrs Primrose. 'She needs a hot bath and bed.'

'Right you are, Mrs P,' said Harry.

We gave the Primroses our heartfelt thanks and, once outside, we all stuffed ourselves into Harry's motor car. It looked blue in the light from the farmhouse doorway.

'I'll drop you at your motor, and we'll all get home as quickly as we can,' said Harry. 'Who's going with whom?'

'I want to stay with Flo,' said Eleanora.

'And I want a word or two with you,' said Lady Hardcastle.

'That's easy, then,' said Harry. 'Strongarm can take Eleanora in your terrifying beast and we'll all have a jolly family chinwag in here.'

He dropped Eleanora and me beside Phyllis and waited until we were safely inside with the engine running before setting off.

The rain was finally easing, and the drive back to Weston was a good deal less fraught than the drive to Brean. Eleanora slept and I had to ask for help to get her up to her room when we eventually arrived back at the Steep Holm View.

Chapter Seventeen

We were just about to go downstairs to see if someone would be prepared to make us a late breakfast, when there was a knock at the door.

'Are you decent?'

It was Harry.

'Come in, brother dearest,' said Lady Hardcastle. 'The door's unlocked.'

He poked his head around. 'That's not safe in a place like this, you know,' he said. 'People have been murdered in this very hotel.'

'While that is perfectly true,' she said, 'it's my understanding that almost everyone is dead now anyway. There's no one left to do any killing.'

'Logical as always. I say, Strongarm, you look a state. The bruise has come out nicely.'

'Thank you,' I said. 'It's astonishing how much damage a Broomhandle Mauser can do, even when the chap doesn't actually fire it.'

'I suppose we're lucky he didn't shoot you with it instead,' he said. 'But still. Anyway, are you girls coming down to breakfast? I've persuaded Hillier to sort us all out with something.'

'Just on our way, dear,' said Lady Hardcastle.

She had been looking in the glass above the washstand, fussing with some make-up, and turned to face him for the first time.

'Good lord,' he said. 'He made an even worse job of you, didn't he, old girl?'

'I used to wonder why you'd remained single for so long,' she said. 'Do you tell Lavinia she looks "a state"?'

'Jake doesn't tend to get smacked in the chops with the wrong end of a pistol so it never comes up. Can you eat?'

'Try and stop me,' she said. 'Are you with us, Flo?'

'Ready and willing,' I said.

We set off for the dining room.

Adelia and Eleanora Wilson were already seated and eating. The colour had returned to Eleanora's cheeks and she looked a great deal less haunted. She even smiled when she saw us.

'Good morning, ladies,' said Lady Hardcastle as we sat down. 'Is Dr Goddard not with us?'

'Oh, I forgot to mention Goddard, sorry. He's on his way,' said Harry. 'I called on him before I came to get you.'

'Good morning, Emily,' said Adelia. 'Flo. I can never repay you, but I'll never forget what you did for Eleanora. If you ever need anything. Anything at all. You only have to ask.'

'Think nothing of it, dear,' said Lady Hardcastle. 'All in a day's work. Or it used to be, anyway. How are you feeling this morning, Ellie?'

'Much better, thank you,' said Eleanora. 'The same goes for me, too, you know. You saved my life.' She inspected our bruises. 'I'm so sorry you came to such harm.'

'Nonsense,' said Lady Hardcastle. 'We've had worse. You should put it all behind you now. All's well that ends well. You'll soon come to see it as much ado about nothing.'

'Or a midsummer night's dream,' said Eleanora.

'That's the spirit. Although, actually—'

'Let it go, my lady,' I said. 'She indulged your little bit of whimsy – there's no need for a lecture on the date of the summer solstice.'

'As you like it,' she said.

Eleanora laughed. 'At least the tempest didn't turn it into a comedy of errors.'

'Cymbeline!' said Harry.

We all looked at him.

'Just wanted to join in,' he said.

'I despair of you, Harry, I really do,' said Lady Hardcastle. 'Now, then, what's for breakfast?'

'They'll make you whatever you want this morning,' said Adelia.

'And how shall I make my preferences kno— Ah, Kibble, the very man.'

'Good morning, my lady,' said the waiter. 'Shall I bring you some breakfast?'

'That would be splendid, yes,' she said. 'I should like a massive plate heaped high with everything Chef thinks suitable for a hearty breakfast. I've not eaten since lunchtime yesterday and I'm absolutely famished.'

'I'm sure Chef will be delighted to oblige, my lady. And for you, miss?'

'I'll have the same,' I said. 'And coffee, please. Lots of coffee.'

'We'll keep it simple,' said Harry. 'I'll join them and we can all be dyspeptic together.'

'Right you are, boss,' said Kibble. 'I shall see if there's any milk of magnesia in the medicine cabinet should you require it later.'

He disappeared.

Adelia took a sip of coffee and took her napkin from her lap.

'I've a suspicion that you folks need to talk about a few things,' she said. 'Things that can't be said in front of the likes of me.'

'Thank you, Miss Wilson,' said Harry. 'Although I would like a word with you before you go.'

'And I with you,' she said. 'The folks back home aren't going to be pleased with the way things worked out here. They might be too embarrassed to complain to you, but they'll sure as heck complain to me and I want my story good and straight before I have to face the music.'

'Will you be about later?'

'We're not leaving until Monday,' she said. 'To London, and then the boat train to Paris, via the embassy at Victoria Street.'

'Are you free this evening?' I said. 'We're still planning to see Robinson's Ragtime Roisterers at the Arundel, I believe. Would you care to join us?'

'While it will mean forgoing the pleasures of your charming company,' said Adelia, 'I'm afraid I'd rather spend the evening gnawing my own foot off than listen to any of that dreadful music. I'm sorry.'

'Oh, Aunt. Don't be such an old stick-in-the-mud. Come with us. You'll have a fine time. It'll make you feel young again,' coaxed Eleanora.

'I feel young now, you cheeky pup. Darn it, I am young.' She paused a moment, then sighed. 'Very well,' she said, 'I'll come.'

'Splendid,' said Lady Hardcastle. 'Perhaps we should dine at the Arundel – make an evening of it.'

'We'll call for you at eight, then. It'll be fun,' said Eleanora.

Adelia raised an eyebrow. 'Come along, then, Eleanora,' she said. 'Let's leave the Britishers to their plotting.'

Harry stood as the Misses Wilson rose and left the room.

Dr Goddard joined us moments later, but we waited until after Kibble had brought our breakfasts before addressing the serious business of the morning. The plates, as promised, were loaded with enough food to keep us going for several days, and we all fell on them ravenously.

'I've seen much of the world,' said Lady Hardcastle between mouthfuls. 'And there is little we English can teach anyone about the mystical culinary arts, but no one, not one single nation, can match us for our ability to create the most wonderful breakfasts.'

'Hear, hear,' said Harry. 'Although I did have some delicious Viennese pastries in Copenhagen.'

'Not in Vienna, then?' said Dr Goddard.

'Definitely Copenhagen. *Wienerbrød*, the Danes call it.'

'I'll take your word for it, old boy. It can hardly be as satisfying as this, though, what?'

'Have you eaten anything at all since Monday, Dr Goddard?' I said.

'Some bread and cheese,' he said. 'Nothing else.'

'It was bread and cheese from the kitchens here,' I said. 'Some ham went missing, too.'

'I never saw the ham, just some Cheddar and some increasingly stale bread.'

'Which leads us nicely to the first, and most important, item on this morning's agenda,' said Lady Hardcastle. 'What the blistering blue blazes has been going on here?'

'Ah,' said Harry. 'Well, now. There's a thing. It . . . ah . . . it all went a bit skew-whiff, I'm afraid.'

'Didn't it just?' she said. 'Here's what I've surmised so far – perhaps you can correct me if I take a wrong turn at any point. You no longer work in your old job at the Foreign Office – Lavinia told us that. You've been attached to some new section – the Department of Hugger-Mugger or some such, I'll warrant.'

'The Secret Service Bureau, it's called,' said Harry.

'Is it, now? Well, well. So they're finally taking intelligence collection seriously.'

'There are dark clouds on the horizon,' he said. 'Think of us as meteorologists keeping an eye on the gathering storm.'

'If I must,' she said. 'So, there you are in the lonely offices of the Secret Service Bureau in some basement in Whitehall, and you say to yourselves, "If we're starting to poke about in everyone else's business, it's not a great leap to presume that they're also starting to poke about in ours. But how on earth do we catch the blighters at it?" You sit around for a couple of days, drinking tea and making paper darts, and then one of you – I'm presuming it was you, actually – says, "I say, you chaps, I've just thought of an absolutely spiffing wheeze."'

'I don't talk like that, sis.'

'You absolutely do, dear. "A spiffing wheeze," you say. "Why don't we flush them out? We can get old Percy Goddard from the Ministry of Whatnots to play the dotty science-wallah and send him to a hotel somewhere. We'll let slip that he's carrying a strongbox jam-packed with the tastiest secrets and we'll see who comes darting out from under the rocks to pinch it." How am I doing?'

'Distressingly well, so far,' said Harry.

'You let the French know he's got plans for a ship. The Japanese somehow "just so happen" to come by the idea that it's a locomotive. The Americans find out he has plans for a radio. The Russians are convinced it's a new weapon. And the Austrians, we now know, think it's some breakthrough in high-powered optics. Each a shiny lure, tailor-made to attract a very specific fish. Goddard's travel plans are leaked – not too openly, though, you needed to keep it subtle or no one would bite – and everyone converges on the Steep Holm View Hotel in sunny Weston-super-Mare.'

'Friends and foes alike,' I said.

'There are still rules,' said Harry. 'Even one's best international pals should be discouraged from behaving dishonourably. Lessons have to be learned.'

'I see,' said Lady Hardcastle.

'She's got your number, old boy,' said Dr Goddard.

'Everything's clear to this point, at least,' said Lady Hardcastle. 'But this is where my understanding falters. What on earth were you hoping would come of it? You got everyone here, but what were you going to do about it?'

'The idea,' said Harry, 'was that once we'd got them all in the one place, we'd wait for them to break cover. We thought we knew who we were dealing with, but if one is going to round up foreign operatives and hand them back to their owners with a note saying "We know what you're up to, now pack it in", then one has to be certain of one's facts. As soon as we had the proof we needed, we'd swoop.'

'We?' she said.

'I wasn't nearly so far away as I made out. I was holed-up in Clevedon, just up the coast a bit. Close enough to keep an eye on things but far enough away so as not to keep bumping in to people.'

'So it *was* you I saw coming out of the hotel when we first arrived.'

'I nearly had kittens. I heard that infernal machine of Fishy's roaring up the road and I thought I'd been tumbled. I just kept my head down and got away as fast as my little blue motor car would carry me.'

'And then it all went wrong when Gerber showed up?' she said.

'As wrong as wrong could be,' he said.

'I take it he wasn't invited.'

'Not at all. Even if he were still working for the Germans he'd not have been on the guest list. We know who all their men are, you see. We've been keeping an eye on them for some time. It was all the others we needed to flush out. But Gerber is what the medieval chaps used to call a "free lance". And his arrival rather messed things up.'

'He had his own idea of what was in the box,' I said. 'He thought it had to do with a chemical plant. Where did he get that idea?'

'Yes,' said Harry. 'That was something of a wild card. We cast that one out to see if we could sweep up anyone we'd missed.'

'And you'd definitely missed him,' said Lady Hardcastle.

'With almost disastrous consequences,' said Harry. 'Once Gerber nabbed Goddard, all hell broke loose.'

'You could have stopped it at any time,' she said. 'You knew who they all were. Even without your proof you could have marked their cards and told them to sling their hooks.'

'Well . . . you see . . . the decision was taken at Permanent Secretary level to—'

'To let them all take care of each other,' she said.

'In a nutshell.'

'That's unpleasantly callous,' she said. 'And they'll just be replaced. Then you'll have no idea who the spies are.'

'They'd have been replaced anyway. The idea was to give everyone the message loud and clear that we were on to their games and that they weren't welcome to play them on our pitch. They'd all be a bit more circumspect.'

'And now?'

'There'll be some huffing and puffing, but they all know they got caught with their fingers in the till.'

'So you just allowed them to carry on killing each other because, what, it taught everyone a valuable lesson?'

'More or less, sis, yes.'

'Charming. What about us?'

'What about you? I did tell you to keep your noses out, after all. But I knew you could take care of yourselves if things got lively. As it turned out, you were as helpful as always.'

'And if we'd not been here, how would you have known what was going on?'

'Ribble and Kibble,' he said.

'We should have guessed from the names,' I said. 'Your men do love their silly names.'

'Does that mean May and June are yours, too?' asked Lady Hardcastle.

'May and June?' said Harry.

'Two chambermaids here at the hotel.'

He laughed. 'Really? How wonderful. No, they're nothing to do with us. Ribble and Kibble are local boys, ex-detectives from up your way – Bristol. We got them on the payroll just before we set all this up. Strict instructions not to interfere – which they obeyed, unlike some – but they kept me informed.'

'What about Hillier?'

'He has no idea,' he said. 'He was just pleased to get two temporary waiters at short notice. The permanent ones both won a fortnight's holiday to Scotland in a newspaper competition.'

'What a fortunate coincidence.'

'Serendipity, you might say.'

'Is that how you were able to telephone us so quickly that time?' I said.

'What time?' said Harry.

'We telephoned you at home and spoke to Lady Lavinia, then you rang us almost at once. Had Kibble or Ribble already alerted you?'

'Ah, no,' he said. 'A little more prosaic than that. I had a chap at the exchange listening to your calls. It's not just walls that have ears these days – anyone might be listening to your telephone conversations, too.'

'When did you find out Gerber was here?' she said.

'Yesterday. I had Steak and Kidney out looking into a couple of sightings nearby – that's why they weren't available. We already had the Ehrlichmann file – it was just a matter of dotting the Ts and crossing our eyes. We had no idea where he was, though, that was all you.'

'But you suspected his involvement? You suspected he was the kidnapper?'

'Actually, no. It didn't even cross my mind until yesterday. None of us had any idea where Goddard and the Wilson girl were.'

'Thank goodness for us, then,' she said wryly.

'Yes,' said Dr Goddard. 'Thank goodness for you both.'

She inclined her head in acknowledgement. 'And where is Gerber being held now?' she asked.

Harry was suddenly silent. He looked her in the eye, but said nothing.

'You haven't bally well lost him?' she said. 'Oh, Harry, you absolute fool. What happened?'

'The boys found the spot where you'd beaten him up – the ground was churned up there. They could see where you put him, too, but he'd gone. They searched as best they could, but it was a dark night and he must have got past them. I've got Gammon and Spinach out there now that they're available, but I don't hold out much hope.'

'He had a broken foot,' I said. 'He can't have got far.'

'Far enough,' he said. 'He's in a bit of a state so he'll be spotted eventually. We'll get him.'

'You'd better,' said Lady Hardcastle. 'He was definitely the less practical of the Gerber brothers, but he's still a danger.'

'We will,' he said. 'We will.'

'And what of you, Dr Goddard? You're not quite the timid little swot we met on Monday. Are you actually a scientist?'

'Engineer, actually, old girl. Engineer. The medicine thing was just something I made up the other day. Rather proud of that bit of improvisation, actually. But I did study at King's. Can't tell you what I'm working on – leads to all sorts of trouble, loose talk like that.'

'Percy spent some time in the army,' said Harry. 'And he's done some work for us before. We've been pals for a while. I knew he could look after himself.'

'Turns out I'm not much good at fighting Veronal, though,' said Dr Goddard. 'Or brandy. I was pleased to see the box gone when I got back to the room but after all that brandy I flaked out on the bed in my clothes. Woke up in that blessed fort. Not at all what I had in mind when I signed on.'

'What's going to happen now?' asked Lady Hardcastle. 'Are all your loose ends tied up?'

'More or less. It's just a case of writing the report now. And capturing Gerber, of course.'

'Of course.'

'Next time you get involved in a feud with someone, though, sis, can you make their name easier to spell? To maintain secrecy I have to type the reports myself, and I'm jiggered if I can type Günther – I don't know how to make an umlaut.'

'I gather you need to break some *eier*,' said Lady Hardcastle.

'Some what?' he said.

'Some eggs,' I said with a sigh. 'It's German. You can't make an umlaut without breaking some *eier*. Didn't they teach you anything at your expensive school?'

'You've been spending altogether too much time with my little sister, Strongarm. She's a bad influence on you.'

'What are your plans for the rest of the day?' said Lady Hardcastle.

'We're packing up and going home,' said Harry. 'There's nothing left to do here. I'm leaving the boys to hunt for Gerber and I'll draft in some more Special Branch officers later today.'

'Well,' she said, 'in spite of your appalling awfulness, it's always a joy to see you. Do give our love to your poor wife, won't you. And take extra care of her now that she's carrying my niece or nephew.'

'I say, old boy,' said Dr Goddard. 'Congratulations. You kept that quiet.'

'It's not been the sort of thing I could casually drop in to the conversations we've been having lately,' said Harry. 'But thank you. We're very excited.'

Talk moved on to babies and nurseries and other jolly matters. By the time we'd finished our enormous breakfasts we were sated and considerably more relaxed.

We said goodbye to them and got ourselves ready for a walk on the prom.

◆ ◆ ◆

The sun had finally come out, and with it the holidaymakers. Sadly there was still no sign of the sea, it having ventured towards shore at about eight that morning, but by now I was beginning to think that actually seeing it would be something of an anticlimax. The promenade was packed with day trippers, even on Friday, and there was an almost carnival-like air about the place. The clothes were lighter, the hats jollier, and the ice cream and whelks more eagerly consumed (though not, I should note, together – that would be a bold choice for even the most gastronomically adventurous traveller).

We paid to walk along the pier and enjoyed a Pierrot show in the theatre. On our way back to shore, my attention was caught by a commotion on the promenade.

'Is that the Punch and Judy man?' I said.

Lady Hardcastle looked in the direction I had indicated.

'I do believe it is,' she said. 'He's being bundled into that wagon by . . . oh, it's Fife and Drum, look. What busy little chaps they are. I suppose he must be a foreign agent, too. There's a lot of it about.'

'More and more each day, if the newspapers are to be believed,' I said.

'Actually, if Harry is to be believed they might be right, what with his distant rumblings and all that.'

'Still, that's one more off the streets.'

'Not the important one, though, dear. I felt sure we'd seen the last of Gerber. I don't like the idea of his being at large.'

'He'll have skulked off somewhere to lick his wounds. I don't think he'll trouble us again.'

'He's not at all well, though. Mentally, I mean. Ten years in a Chinese gaol have taken their toll and his grip on reality seems awfully tenuous. There's no telling what his troubled mind might cause him to do.'

'Harry and his men will take care of it,' I said.

'I'm sure they will. Is there anything else we need to do while the weather is fine?'

'Donkeys,' I said without hesitation. 'I demand a ride on a donkey.'

'You've ridden some of the finest horses in Europe,' she said.

'And highly trained circus ponies in my youth. And yet I can still think of nothing more gloriously giddy than plodding along the sand on the back of a donkey on a sunny summer's day. Preferably a donkey called Diego Hernandez. One of his forelegs should be a slightly different colour from the other, and he should be prone to bouts of melancholy as he contemplates the shortness of summer and the fragility of happiness.'

'Will he be partial to apples?'

'Baked into pies. And he'll drink beer, but only on Sundays.'

'We'll have to see what we can manage.'

'I'll settle for a Dobbin or a Doris, if I'm honest.'

To my delight, we actually found an adorable beast who rejoiced in the name of Lady Persephone McGuiggan and who seemed more than happy to take me for a gentle stroll across the beach. Lady Hardcastle joined me on Sir Algernon Fitzwarren and we posed on our mighty steeds for a seaside photographer who told us that our picture would be ready for collection at his shop in town in the morning.

By the time we had eaten yet another toffee apple and explored the mechanical wonders of the penny arcade, it was time to return to the hotel to dandify ourselves for our evening out.

◆ ◆ ◆

To my astonishment, everyone was ready at eight o'clock sharp. Lady Hardcastle did not have to be bullied or cajoled, and Eleanora Wilson all but erupted from the room when I knocked on the door.

'I take it you're ready, then?' I said.

'She's been standing by the door for ten minutes waiting for you to come,' said Adelia as we set off towards the stairs. 'We're simple folk. We don't get out much.'

'Is there much to do in Annapolis?' asked Lady Hardcastle.

'I've no idea,' said Adelia. 'I don't get out much.'

'It's going to be a hoot,' I said to Eleanora. 'We had Mr Nightengale book us a table near the band.'

'Saints preserve us,' said Adelia.

We found the hotel a couple of streets back from the promenade. It was already thronging with diners. We were shown to our table which was, as promised, right next to the low dais where the band's instruments were set up. The waiter took our orders and bustled off.

'Those drums look very familiar,' I said.

'Are drums not just drums?' said Adelia.

'One might ordinarily have thought so,' said Lady Hardcastle, 'but I do know what Flo means. Perhaps it's just that all ragtime drummers these days have the same instruments.'

'No,' I said. 'I definitely recognize that bass drum – it has a nick on the . . . on the . . . well, on the round hoopy bit on the front. It's exactly like Skins' drum except that he usually has his up on a stand. And he has the other drum higher, too. It looks like this chap is going to sit down, but they definitely look like Skins' drums.'

'We'll soon find out,' said Lady Hardcastle. 'They seem to be coming on.'

Sure enough, the band were slowly making their way to their seats. They were chatting among themselves, sharing a laugh and taking a last sip of a hastily concealed glass of beer before settling to play. The drummer, perched on a low stool, was our old pal Ivor 'Skins' Maloney. I cast about and there, at the back with his double bass, was his mate, Bartholomew 'Barty' Dunn.

Eleanora leaned close. 'Do you know that fellow on the drums?' she said. 'He's a looker, isn't he?'

'Is he? I suppose he's not bad if you like them thin. That's Skins – he's one of the musicians we were talking about the other night. I had no idea they'd be here.'

'Could you introduce me? Would he mind, do you think?' she said.

'He'd be thrilled,' I said.

The band struck up the first tune just as our drinks and first courses arrived. Adelia grimaced. I presumed it was the music, but it might have been the whitebait.

At the break, Skins put down his sticks and grabbed Dunn before coming over to our table.

'Evenin' ladies,' he said. 'This is a turn up. What the bleedin' 'ell are you doin' here?'

Adelia looked stricken.

'Sorry, lady,' said Skins. 'Ivor Maloney, how do you do?' He held out his hand, which Adelia tentatively shook. 'But you can call me Skins, everyone does.'

'Good evening, Skins, dear,' said Lady Hardcastle. 'We're on our holidays. And these are our newest pals Adelia Wilson and her niece Eleanora Wilson of Annapolis in Maryland, on the Chesapeake Bay.'

'Yanks, eh? Pleased to meet you, I'm sure,' he said. 'Say hello, Barty.'

'Hello, Barty,' said Dunn. He held out his hand, too. 'Barty Dunn, bassist.'

Skins looked at our faces. 'What's happened to your mush? You been scrappin'?'

'Long story,' I said. 'But the short version is, yes. Yes we have.'

He frowned.

'Won't you sit down?' said Eleanora, who hadn't taken her eyes off Skins since he'd come on stage.

'Love to,' said Skins, 'but the management don't like the musicians fraternizing with the patrons. Lacks class, they reckon. A drink after, maybe?'

'I'd like that,' she said.

'Talk to you later, Lady H. Flo.' He gave me a warm wink and the 'greatest rhythm section in London' disappeared through a side door to join their colleagues.

'He seems lovely,' said Eleanora.

'You barely exchanged a dozen words with him,' scoffed Adelia.

Eleanora paused for a few moments. 'Two dozen,' she said. 'Twenty-five, in fact.'

Adelia tutted and rolled her eyes.

'He's a charming chap,' I said. 'A bit rough round the edges, but with a heart of gold. It's his mate you have to watch out for.'

'A womanizer?' said Adelia.

'A different girl at every show,' I said.

'You steer clear of musicians,' said Adelia. 'Can't be trusted.'

Eleanora paid us no attention whatsoever. Throughout the rest of her meal and the second half of the band's performance, she said barely a word and kept Skins under strict surveillance from the moment he emerged from the back room.

As soon as the band had played their final number and had basked in the enthusiastic appreciation of the assembled throng, she excused herself from the table and went over to talk to the drummer.

'Well!' said Adelia.

'Oh, leave her,' said Lady Hardcastle. 'You're only young once. Wouldn't you like to have that feeling again?'

Adelia was not to be drawn. 'How old is he?'

'Do you know, I'm not at all sure. What do you think, Flo?'

'I always thought he was a youngster,' I said. 'Twenty, perhaps? He's all brash swagger and confidence, but there's something boyish about him. He's got a young face.'

'I thought he was older, but you might be right,' said Lady Hardcastle. 'He had a bit of a pash for Flo at one point but that seems to have gone off the boil.'

'So he's a philanderer as well,' said Adelia.

'Far from it,' I said. 'He has been nothing but gentlemanly and sweet. And when I didn't reciprocate, he backed off immediately. She has nothing to worry about.'

Adelia huffed. 'I don't know what I'm making a fuss about, anyway,' she said. 'We'll be on that boat train before he's had a chance to ruin her reputation.'

I laughed and shook my head. I was about to offer a few more words in defence of my friend Skins when there was a loud scream behind us. Chairs scraped and cutlery clattered. Men yelled. Another woman screamed.

'What the . . .' said Adelia. She looked around. 'Where's Eleanora?'

'Skins is taking her out into the side room with the band,' I said as I stood up and rounded the table. 'Looks like there's trouble.'

I motioned for Lady Hardcastle and Adelia to join me – putting a solid lump of wood between us and the trouble seemed like a good idea.

As the diners near the main door scattered, we were finally able to see the cause of the commotion. Standing in the doorway, still barefoot and with his shirt in tatters under his muddy peacoat, was Jakob Gerber. His hair was matted to his head with dried blood. His eyes swivelled about the room. He saw me and screamed – an unintelligible rasping bellow of German oaths and inchoate rage. He began lumbering towards us, limping on his ruined foot. A burly young man stepped forward to stop him, but Gerber drew a large fisherman's knife from his belt and the young man backed away.

'Hardcastle!' roared Gerber.

'Oh, for heaven's sake,' said Lady Hardcastle. 'What is it now? We're trying to have a quiet dinner here.'

He bellowed again and lurched forward a few more steps. Another man made to rush him but Lady Hardcastle stopped him. 'No,' she said loudly. 'Leave him. He's after me.'

The man looked confused, but her tone brooked no dissent and he, too, backed away.

By this time, Gerber had almost reached us, with only the table blocking his path. He looked baffled. How was he going to get to us? Even in his befuddled state he must have realized that trying to rush around the table would just result in something resembling a music hall skit where we'd all keep running round and round. And with his injured foot, running wasn't really on the cards anyway.

'Is this the guy?' said Adelia.

'Which guy?' said Lady Hardcastle.

'The guy who took Eleanora.'

'Oh, yes, this is the guy. Why?'

'I just wanted to be sure.'

As Gerber made a decision and grabbed an unoccupied chair, presumably to enable him to climb on to the table and approach us from above, a pistol popped. In the crowded room it was much quieter than I might have expected, but it was unmistakably a pistol. Gerber crumpled, shot in the eye. Yet another woman screamed.

I turned to see Adelia slipping a Colt Vest Pocket pistol into her evening bag.

'We'd better get out of here before they work out what just happened,' she said. 'You think that other door will take us outside eventually?'

We followed her out into the side room before anyone had a chance to think of stopping us. The band members were still milling anxiously about and we dragged an angrily disappointed Eleanora away from Skins and propelled her towards the outer door as we passed through.

'What's going on?' she said.

'We'll tell you later,' I said. 'Skins? Lovely to see you again. We'll be at the Steep Holm View for a couple of days, then at home – you've got the telephone number.'

'Yeah, but—'

'Quickly, dear,' said Lady Hardcastle, tugging at my arm. 'We really ought to be on our way out the door now.'

He handed me a card as Lady Hardcastle ushered us out.

'What's going on?' repeated Eleanora. 'What was all that commotion? Where are we going? When can I see Skins again?'

'Gerber was in the hotel,' I said, passing her Skins' card.

She stopped in her tracks. 'In there? Him?'

I took her arm. 'It's been dealt with,' I said. 'There's really nothing to worry about, but we need to be somewhere that isn't here.'

'Dealt with?'

'We can discuss this later,' said Adelia. 'For now, though, Miss Armstrong is right – we need to be somewhere far away as quickly as we can.'

'But why? What's going on?'

We ignored her and merged with the late-evening strollers, out enjoying the summer air. Even though it was past midnight, the sudden change in the weather had brought a few people out, and it was perfect for us. As a small crowd began to throng about the entrance to the Arundel, we were able to slip away unnoticed. Two policemen, blowing whistles, ran past us and by the time they reached the hotel, we were already out of sight round the corner and on our way to our own hotel.

We tried to persuade Adelia to join us for a calming drink before retiring, but she was insistent that they had to go straight to their rooms. We left them to it. In truth, I was still feeling the effects of the previous night's shenanigans and I was rather keen on the idea of sleeping, too.

◆ ◆ ◆

It was still dark a couple of hours later when I was awakened by someone hammering on my bedroom door. I wasn't conscious enough to do anything about it before the hammering resumed, this time on Lady Hardcastle's door. I struggled out of bed and went through to her room, where she was still groggily trying to surface from a deep sleep.

'See who it is, would you, dear,' she said. 'Tell them to come back in the morning.'

I unlocked and opened the door to find Harry's Special Branch men standing in the corridor.

'Where is she?' said Mr Lefty.

'Where is who?' I said. I was still more than a little sleep-fogged.

'You know bloody well who,' he said. 'Where is she?'

This cleared the fog a little. 'I don't know who, or I wouldn't have asked. Lady Hardcastle is over there. Is that who you mean?'

'Of course it bloody isn't. Get out of my way.'

I stood my ground.

He reached out to shove me in the chest. I shifted my balance, grabbed his wrist and pulled him. As he stumbled, I struck his cheek with my open hand and completed the business of flipping him on to his back. He landed with an 'Oof!' and lay there for a moment, winded.

Mr Righty had remained in the corridor.

'I do apologize for my colleague,' he said. 'He can be a bit excitable. I tell him time and again it'll get him into trouble, but he never listens. We're looking for the American spy, Adelia Wilson.'

'She's in her room,' I said.

'That's the thing, you see – she's not. Nor is her charming young niece. Their luggage is all there. At least we presume it's all of their luggage – one can never tell with ladies, you seem to travel with so much. But of the ladies themselves there is no sign. After last evening's excitement, we thought they might be with you. May I?' He gestured towards the room.

'Be my guest,' I said. 'But they're not here.'

Mr Lefty attempted to push himself off the floor but I kicked him down.

'Not you,' I said. 'You can stay there. You're not invited.'

Mr Righty conducted a quick but thorough search, checking inside wardrobes, under beds and behind curtains. He returned to the door.

'I'm so sorry to have troubled you,' he said. 'If you see them, do please tell them we'd like a word.'

'We'll tell Mr Featherstonhaugh,' I said.

'You do that. Come on, then.' He reached down to help Mr Lefty to his feet. 'Ups-a-daisy. Say goodnight to the nice ladies.'

They left and I locked the door behind them.

'She'll be safely tucked away in the American embassy before they've worked out what's happened,' said Lady Hardcastle.

'It's what we'd do in her position,' I said. 'The police were involved in this one so there's not much chance of hushing it up. They'll be on the next boat home. Poor Ellie. I rather think she wanted to see Europe.'

'Can't be helped,' she said. She consulted the travel clock beside her bed. 'Good lord, it's still only two in the morning. Will you be able to get back to sleep?'

'I'm going to give it a blimmin' good go,' I said.

It actually didn't take much effort and I slept the sleep of the just until nine o'clock the next morning.

Chapter Eighteen

On Sunday morning we made a last trip to the prom, where I was treated to my first proper view of the sea. Having spent so long complaining about its absence I decided I really ought to enjoy it properly. Leaving Lady Hardcastle holding my hastily removed boots and stockings, I hoisted my skirts and went for a paddle. The sea was achingly cold, but I managed to endure it for a few minutes before running back to retrieve my boots from my amused employer.

We left the Steep Holm View Hotel that afternoon. Mr Hillier was more than usually deferential. Not only did he waive the bill for our week's stay in its entirety as he had previously promised he would, but he also presented Lady Hardcastle with a cheque for an eye-popping sum.

'You've saved the hotel from a terrible scandal,' he said. 'The owners are most grateful.'

'I really couldn't accept,' said Lady Hardcastle. 'It was all in a day's work. And we did rather fail to prevent the deaths of four men.'

'While saving two other lives,' he said. 'Obviously, neither I nor the owners are privy to the full details of what went on here, but Mr Featherstonhaugh insisted that I sign very official documents swearing me to the strictest secrecy. I can only presume that the events of the past week have some special significance to national security and we at Steep Holm View are only too proud to play our part in keeping Britain safe.'

'Then I accept your generous offer,' she said. 'But I must insist that you share this among the many staff who tried so hard to make our stay a pleasant one.'

She handed him a sealed envelope.

'Thank you, my lady,' he said. 'But not Ribble and Kibble. I'm still rather annoyed by their subterfuge.'

'Even Ribble and Kibble. For rozzers they made exceptionally fine waiters. They went above and beyond their duties as observers for my brother and ersatz dining room attendants for you. Please include them.'

'As you wish,' he said. 'Is there anything else we can do for you?'

'I think not,' she said. 'Has Brine loaded everything into the motor car?'

'He has, my lady.'

'Then we shall be on our way. Thank you for a most interesting week.'

And we were gone.

The drive home in the sunshine was glorious, though I did begin to miss the open air motoring we had previously enjoyed in the Rover 6.

'Is Lord Riddlethorpe still working on the designs for the motor car?' I said. 'Or is this it?'

'I think it's a work in progress,' said Lady Hardcastle. 'If I'm honest, I don't think it will ever sell. It looks too outlandish. Why do you ask?'

'I was just thinking how wonderful it would be to be driving along here with the wind in our hair.'

'So you favour the removable roof after all? I thought you were thrilled with the enclosed cabin.'

'I am – I can't begin to imagine what the drive to Brean would have been like in that storm with no roof. But I wonder if it might be fun sometimes not to have one.'

'I'll add it to my report,' she said. 'Oh, I say, look at those sheep.'

I dutifully looked at the sheep. They were just sheep, but there was something comforting about the bucolic normality of a field of sheep and I entirely understood her need to point them out. The unpleasantness was over, there were sheep in the field, and all was finally well again.

It wasn't long before we were passing over Brunel's suspension bridge and leaving Somerset behind us. We threaded our way through the streets of Bristol drawing stares of admiration, astonishment, and annoyance in more or less equal proportions.

The journey to Gloucester was quiet – it was Sunday afternoon, after all – and we had soon turned on to the road to Littleton Cotterell. There was a cricket match in progress on the green and I fear we might have been recorded by the scorer as 'motor car stopped play' when both teams stopped what they were doing to watch us drive past. Lady Hardcastle gave a wave as we burbled up the lane to the house.

Edna and Miss Jones had been told to expect us 'some time on Sunday' but not to worry about waiting for us. We were delighted to find the shutters open, food in the larder, and fresh flowers in the vases.

It's lovely to go away, but it's even more wonderful to come home.

We were sitting down to lunch on Monday when the doorbell rang. Lady Hardcastle had been explaining an idea she'd had for a new shutter release mechanism for her animation camera.

'I mean, really,' she said. 'Who pays a call at lunchtime? Don't these people realize I like to hold forth at lunchtime?'

'It's a mystery,' I said. 'I'd better answer it, though.'

It was Harry.

'Good afternoon, Mr Feather-stone-huff,' I said. 'Please come in.'

'What ho, Strongarm. Lovely place you have here. Is Emily in?'

'She is,' I said. 'We're eating, but I'm sure she'll be delighted to see you. Would you like me to get Miss Jones to make you something?'

'Oh, I say, rather. I'm famished.'

I pointed the way to the dining room and popped in to the kitchen to ask Miss Jones if she wouldn't mind putting another plate together for Harry.

I rejoined them to find Lady Hardcastle still trying to describe her camera gadget.

'. . . and then, you see, I could shoot a frame without moving away from the table.'

'Your ingenuity knows no bounds,' said Harry.

'One tries. Here's Flo. Harry has news, dear.'

I sat down.

'I do, indeed,' he said. 'I thought you'd like to know what has transpired since last we spoke.'

'We know the Wilsons did a moonlight flit,' I said.

'And we know that your men Darby and Joan came blundering into my room shortly thereafter,' said Lady Hardcastle.

'Yes, my apologies for that. I've had words. There won't be a counter-complaint from Brownlow, by the way – he doesn't want to admit he was knocked on his backside by a woman.'

'Brownlow?' I said.

'Oops,' said Harry. 'The senior chap is Perlman, for what it's worth.'

'If he's not admitting it, how do you know what happened?' I said.

'Oh, he's not said anything, but Perlman thought it was hilarious – I couldn't shut him up. But there were further developments. I had to interrupt a few chaps at prayer yesterday morning, and drag a few more out of bed, but we tracked the Wilsons down at the American embassy.'

'At least they're safe,' I said. 'But how did they get there at that time of night?'

'Stowed away on a mail train is our guess. She's quite the girl, our Adelia.'

'I get the feeling she plays the priggish spinster the same way I play the dizzy social butterfly,' said Lady Hardcastle. 'You want to keep an eye on her.'

'Oh, we shall,' he said. 'And the Americans will be keeping an eye on you, old girl. My source at their embassy has heard your praises being sung in high places. Adelia Wilson, it seems, has been very complimentary.'

'How lovely,' she said. 'Have you heard anything of anyone else?'

'Not a dickie bird. I know it was Sunday, but London's embassies and consulates have been unusually silent, even for the Sabbath. I've had ears out all over town, but our friends have been quiet and our enemies quieter still. All but Imperial Germany, that is – their staff have been in a fearful flap. The names Ehrlichmann, Gerber and Hardcastle have been flying about, I'm told.'

'I should think so, too,' said Lady Hardcastle. 'What a shambles. They gave up on Gerber, then completely lost track of him. Your chaps did a better job of keeping an eye on him. Did they know what was going on at all?'

'Hard to tell,' said Harry. 'It's more difficult to find out what's going on with our German friends at Carlton Terrace, but a fuller picture will emerge in due course, I'm sure.'

'Will any action be taken against Adelia for shooting Gerber?' I asked.

'We're making sure it doesn't,' said Harry. 'The boys of Somerset Constabulary are investigating but, peculiarly, they have no witnesses.'

'None?' said Lady Hardcastle. 'But dozens of people saw what happened.'

'And yet when he went down, all eyes were on him. No one saw the gun, nor who fired it. The police wanted to speak to you two – almost everyone there was aware that he was coming for you.'

'I told them so myself,' she said. 'I had to stop some foolish young man from playing the hero.'

'Indeed, which is why they're interested in what you might have to say. Nevertheless, we told them to push off. Politely, of course, but quite firmly. We smoothed things over with the management of the Arundel, as well. I'm sure the chief constable will huff and puff, but he'll be politely and firmly told to push off, too. Not by me, mind you – I'll pass that happy task upwards.'

'So that's it, then,' I said.

'Well,' he said. 'Almost.'

'What else can there possibly be?' said Lady Hardcastle. 'I think we tidied up your mess rather neatly. Surely no loose ends remain.'

'There are no loose ends,' he said. 'But . . . well . . . now . . . you see . . .'

'Spit it out, dear.'

'The thing is, old girl, your efforts have not gone unnoticed, nor unappreciated. Indeed, that was rather the point of making certain you were at Steep Holm View in the first place.'

'I wondered when you were going to own up to that one,' she said.

'Own up . . . ? You knew I'd sent you?'

'Well, of course, dear. You're a clever enough chap, but you can be a little transparent sometimes. You want to watch that if you're moving into our world, by the way. But you surely didn't expect us to believe it a coincidence that all that was going on at exactly the hotel where we were staying at exactly the time we were staying there? I know we rather thrive on the improbable, but that was a good deal more unlikely than we're used to, I'm afraid.'

He appeared thoroughly crestfallen.

'Oh, don't look so glum,' she said. 'You can still dazzle us with the details. How, for instance, did you manage to arrange for us to be there? The hotel was recommended by Gertie Farley-Stroud.'

'Who do you think recommended it to her?' he said, brightening slightly. 'You'd already told Jake you were think-ing of going to Weston so I arranged the whole fixture around your plans. I needed someone reliable on the inside. Ribble and Kibble were there just in case, but you were to be my eyes and ears. I couldn't think how to get you to the Steep Holm View, but as soon as you asked old Gertie, I saw my chance. I had Jake telephone her about some charity matter and drop it into the conversation. I had other ideas, obviously, but that one worked.'

'And how did you know I'd spoken to Gertie?'

'The same way I knew when you were trying to call me from the hotel – we were listening in.'

'You were listening in?' There was a note of admiration in her voice. 'I say, well done.'

'We're spies, old girl. It's what we do.'

'And your telegram?' she said. 'You told me not to interfere – what if that had backfired?'

'I've known you all your life, dear heart,' he said. 'There's no surer way to get you to do something than to tell you not to.'

She harrumphed.

'There's something that's been puzzling me for a while,' I said. 'How did Gerber know what was going on at the hotel? Did he have someone on the inside?'

'I'm so sorry,' said Harry. 'I should have said. The Punch and Judy man had been working for the Italian government for years. Family connections in Rome. Gerber knew and was using him as a source of information. A few of them were, as it turned out.'

'The Russians knew about him,' I said. 'Kusnetsov had the location of his show marked on his little silk map.'

'Yes. So he, in turn, was bribing one of the maids. We pinched him but we couldn't actually charge him with anything – he'd not revealed any state secrets or anything, and being a weasel still isn't a crime. So we gave him the fright of his life and promised we'd be keeping an eye on him. We made sure word reached the Italian embassy, too.'

'I've always thought there was something sinister about Punch and Judy men,' I said.

'What about the maid?' asked Lady Hardcastle. 'Which one was it?'

'Myra,' he said. 'We just left her. She wasn't doing anything hotel maids haven't been doing for centuries, after all. But never mind that. It's not just our colonial cousins at Victoria Street who have been singing your praises, you know. There have been one or two appreciative choruses from highly placed people in

Whitehall, too. For both of you. And . . . you see . . . they've asked me to ask you—'

'No,' she said, firmly. 'Absolutely not. I made a decision two years ago to put being sloshed in the face with pistol butts and chased by knife-wielding maniacs behind me. Recent events have served only to convince me that my decision to retire was sound. I'm only forty-two, dear. I hope to have many years of village life and eccentric pottering ahead of me, and I'm rather of the opinion that those hopes would be dashed if I were to imperil my life by returning to government service.'

'I understand that,' he said. 'But the Bureau is very different to what you're used to. We have a budget now. A small one, admittedly, but we are at least funded. You would have proper support. Your country needs you.'

'You should put that on a recruitment poster. But it's not true – my country can do very well without me.'

'At least think about it,' he said. 'I mentioned storm clouds before – these really are dark and perilous times. I'll be asking again.'

'As Flo often says, dear, I shan't be at all offended if you continue to ask, but you must promise not to be offended when I continue to say no.'

'What about you, Flo? Don't you want to return to active service? The excitement, the drama. Doing vital work for your country. You must miss it.'

He almost never called me Flo.

'No, Harry,' I said. 'I don't.'

'Surely you can see how important it is. We need you both.'

'I agree with Lady Hardcastle. I've been captured, tied up, beaten, and shot at far more times than I care to count, and the most recent examples were on Thursday night. I was even the target of an attempted assault by one of your own men – men with whom we'd be expected to work. I've done my bit for king and country.'

He sighed. 'Very well. I'll say no more today.'

Miss Jones arrived with his lunch and we returned to eating. Lady Hardcastle directed the conversation once more to the preparations for the arrival for the infant Featherstonhaugh, a subject upon which Harry was woefully ignorant.

'I've been a bit distracted,' he said. 'You know, work and so on. Jake has it all well in hand, though. Nannies are being interviewed. Plans have been approved by the landlord to convert a couple of rooms into a nursery. Builders and decorators have been engaged. I'm sure it will all be splendid.'

'I'm sure it will,' said Lady Hardcastle. 'But you should take more interest. Father was always busy, but he always found time for us.'

'You're right,' he said. 'As always. You can be most infuriating.'

He left soon after lunch with strict instructions to give our love to Lady Lavinia and to pass on all family news without delay. We knew he'd forget before he'd even cranked his motor car to life, but Lady Hardcastle would be calling Lady Lavinia regularly anyway.

We spent the rest of the day going about our usual business. Lady Hardcastle made a mess in the orangery and I finished the unpacking.

◆　◆　◆

Saturday 16 July 1910 was the day of the Littleton Cotterell Village Fête. Lady Hardcastle had been co-opted on to the organizing committee in February and had almost had to beg for special permission to spend a week in Weston so close to the big day. But since she was primarily responsible for the painting competition, her coordinating efforts were required only in the week before the event.

I spent much of that week helping to erect stalls and directing an army of village children as they prepared the decorations. Banners and bunting were retrieved from the village hall's attic and labourers from all the local farms were given time off to help put them up.

I ruffled some feathers by offering advice on a more appealing layout for the attractions.

'But it's already been agreed,' said Miss Grove, the vicar's usually equable housekeeper. She was waving a piece of paper at me, bearing a pencil sketch of the plan. 'The vicar won't be pleased with this. You should have brought these ideas to the committee.'

'As you wish,' I said. 'I'm just trying to help.'

Lady Farley-Stroud, the head of the committee, had overheard.

'What's all this, Miriam?' she said. 'What's going on here?'

'Miss Armstrong suggested some changes to the layout of the stalls, my lady,' said Miss Grove. 'I was explaining that it was all agreed months ago. It can't be changed now.'

'What are these suggestions of yours, Armstrong?' said Lady Farley-Stroud.

I explained about getting a better flow of visitors to the less popular stalls by moving a few things and changing the pathway that ran between them.

'It would reduce congestion at the coconut shy,' I said, pointing to the sketch. 'And it would direct people past Mrs Spratt's bric-a-brac stand as they made their way to the competitions in the marquee. You can't move the marquee, but you can easily move this stand, this one, and this one.'

'I say,' said Lady Farley-Stroud. 'You're right. She's right, you know, Miriam. Always trust the word of an expert.'

'Expert?' said Miss Grove.

'Born and raised in a circus, this one,' said Lady Farley-Stroud. 'Knows a thing or two about separating unsuspecting folk from their money. I'd do as she says, if I were you. It's all in a good cause.'

Miss Grove harrumphed and went off to get things changed.

Finally, the day of the fête arrived and we made our way down to the village green in plenty of time. Lady Hardcastle checked that her volunteers were properly cataloguing the villagers' artwork as it arrived, and made certain that they properly understood how to display everything.

I sought out my friend Daisy.

'What ho, Dais,' I said.

'"What ho", is it, now?' she said. 'What happened to all your Welsh mumbo-jumbo? You been palling around with the la-de-dahs again?'

'I'm always palling around with the la-de-dahs, Dais, you know me. What are you up to today?'

'I don't know whether I'm comin', goin', or been today,' she said. 'Our ma is runnin' her junk stall.'

'Bric-a-brac,' I corrected her.

'Callin' other people's cast-off old junk "bric-a-brac" don't make it special,' she said. 'Our da's doin' the tombola. And Old Joe is in charge of the beer tent. The pub's only over there, mind – I don't know why he has to lug barrels out here when he could just open up the pub. Anyway, they all wants me to help 'em. I i'n't goin' to get a moment to meself.'

'You poor old soul,' I said.

'What are you doin', then?'

'Today? Nothing. I'll help Lady Hardcastle with the art competition later, but the day's my own.'

'How the other 'alf lives,' she said. 'I'd better be goin'. Joe will need glasses bringin' out. See you later?'

'I'll drag you away on urgent business and we can have a go at that new hoop-la thing.'

She waved as she hurried off to the beer tent.

By mid-afternoon, the green was thronged. Everyone was dressed in their finery, and spirits were high. People had travelled from the nearby farms and neighbouring villages on carts and wagons to enjoy an afternoon of games and sunshine.

I was standing by the coconut shy, admiring the success of my revisions to the layout of the stalls, when Lady Hardcastle emerged from the marquee. She looked around for a moment before spotting me, then strode over.

'How stands the empire?' she said.

'Everyone seems to be having a fine time,' I said.

'It seems very well organized this year. I like the new arrangement.'

I smiled. 'How's the art competition?'

'I'm rather astonished, to tell you the truth,' she said. 'I expected a few insipid watercolours and a couple of charcoal sketches of the family cat, but the good folk of Littleton Cotterell have rather more talent than I anticipated. Judging will not be easy.'

'When are the prizes being awarded?'

'Not until six – after the races. We've plenty of time for a wander round if you'd like.'

I won a coconut – throwing a ball is slightly easier than throwing a knife. Lady Hardcastle won a jar of humbugs on the tombola.

Then we came to a stall manned by Sir Hector Farley-Stroud, husband of the committee chairwoman, and Lady Hardcastle's good friend.

'Afternoon, Emily,' he said genially. 'How are the daubs and scribbles?'

'Better than expected, thank you, Hector,' she said.

'And good afternoon to you, Miss Armstrong,' he said. 'The memsahib has been singin' your praises all over the village. Loves the way you arranged the stalls. Absolutely loves it. I should prepare yourself for a call-up to the committee next year, what?'

Lady Hardcastle offered me a quizzical frown, but I just smiled again.

At first glance, Sir Hector's stall was one of the least inspiring. He was behind a trestle table, draped with a Union flag. Sitting in the middle was a large, ornately carved wooden box, bound with heavy cast iron bands. I checked the banner above the stall but it bore nothing but a neatly painted question mark.

'What's going on here, then, Hector?' said Lady Hardcastle.

'I'm glad you asked, m'dear,' he said. 'What you see before you, is the treasure of the Raja of the Seven Plains. In ancient India, d'you see, the raja directed his court alchemists to discover a treasure worthy of the king of the most magnificent palace in all of India. They laboured in secret for many years. Men died. Alchemical laboratories and workshops burned to the ground. But eventually, the head alchemist – a man whose name has been lost by time, but who should be celebrated by all humanity – was able to present the raja with this mystical box.' He reverentially tapped the wooden box in front of him. 'It contains the most precious treasure known to mankind.'

'How exciting,' said Lady Hardcastle. 'But what is it?'

'That, my dear,' said Sir Hector, 'is what you have to fathom. For just tuppence – two measly pennies – you may make a guess as to the contents of the box. If your guess is correct, your name will be placed in this brass bowl.' He indicated a large bowl carved with Indian designs. 'At six o'clock this evening, a descendent of the raja himself . . .' He lowered his voice. 'Actually, it's Jagruti Bland, the vicar's wife, but keep it mum – got to create the right atmosphere, what?' He returned to his rehearsed speech. 'A descendent of the raja himself will draw a name from the bowl and the winner will receive this magnificent magnum of champagne, kindly donated by the Littleton Cotterell Rugby Club.'

'Are we allowed to touch the box?' I asked.

'You may touch it, you may lift it, but you may not open it,' he said.

I picked it up. It was heavy, but that told me nothing – it looked heavy. I shook it, but it gave forth no sound. I handed it to Lady Hardcastle, who inspected it carefully.

'Ah,' she said, 'there's an inscription.' She opened her lorgnette and looked closer. 'It's in Hindi,' she said. 'That's handy.'

She spoke Hindi. We both did.

She laughed. 'Ah, no it's not. I see. That's very clever.'

She handed the box back to me and I looked at the inscription. They were Hindi letters, but the words were English. Or, at least, some of them were. It read: 'Mix four parts Azote with one part Dephlogisticated Ether.'

'A recipe?' I said. 'Or, perhaps, an alchemical formula. Is this an instruction for how to make the alchemists' treasure?'

'It's certainly a very valuable substance,' said Lady Hardcastle. 'Oh, Hector, you are a rascal.'

'I'm afraid you've both lost me,' I said.

'Well, it's—'

'Don't say it out loud,' said Sir Hector. 'Don't want to give it away. The fun's in the guessin', what?'

'Right you are, dear,' she said.

She picked up a pencil, wrote her guess and her name, and handed the small slip of paper to Sir Hector with her two pennies. He made a great show of looking at the paper without revealing its contents, nodded, and then placed it in the brass bowl.

'Well done, m'dear,' he said. 'I might have known you'd get it. Good luck in the draw. And how about you, young Armstrong? Will you have a go?'

'I'm afraid I'm completely stumped,' I said. 'And the last time I had to guess what was in a mysterious box I was very disappointed.'

Sir Hector just smiled.

Having no better idea, I wrote, 'A pygmy elephant wearing a bow tie' on one of the slips of paper and handed it over with my tuppence.

We walked away from the stall.

'So what was in it?' I asked.

'It helps if one knows a little of the history of chemistry and alchemy,' said Lady Hardcastle. 'Azote is the old name for nitrogen. While dephlogisticated air – or "ether" in this case to make it seem more mysterious – was Joseph Priestley's original name for oxygen. Four parts nitrogen to one part oxygen is air.' She waved her arm about her to indicate the air surrounding us.

'So the box is empty,' I said with a disappointed sigh.

'There's a lot of it about,' she said. 'Let's invest in a couple of glasses of beer, then we can watch the egg and spoon race before you come and help me judge the art competition.'

Author's Note

Quite obviously, Lady Hardcastle's motor car – designed by her friend Lord Riddlethorpe – is at least a decade ahead of its time. The use of a completely enclosed compartment for the driver wasn't commonplace until the 1920s and Fishy's design is actually more reminiscent of sports cars from the 1930s. But he's an imaginative and inventive person, so there's no real reason why he might not have come up with this futuristic design on his own. In truth, I'd begun to feel sorry for Emily and Flo as they struggled around in their exposed Rover 6 (a real car from the 1900s) and I thought they deserved a little comfort. For the same reason, I gave them an electric starter motor before such devices were commonplace. The rest of the mechanical parts are reasonable for the time, though, and the whole thing suits Lady Hardcastle's general air of non-conformity.

There is no Steep Holm View hotel in Weston-super-Mare, though the tiny islands of Steep Holm and Flat Holm in the Bristol Channel are visible from the shore so it's not an outlandish name. The Grand Atlantic is real, and is still there, as are the Grand Pier and the Knightstone Causeway. The theatre at the end of the causeway, 'the Pavilion', was opened in 1902 and was an important and popular venue until it was eclipsed by the Winter Gardens Pavilion built further along the promenade in 1927. The building still stands but it's no longer a theatre – there's a nice tea rooms there, though.

From 1901, the Weston Museum and Library was housed in a purpose-built building, designed by Weston-based architect Hans Price, on the Boulevard in Weston-super-Mare. In 1975, the museum moved to the old Gas Company building on Burlington Street and is well worth a visit if you're ever in the area. The library has also moved, and the old Hans Price library building has been sold. At time of writing it is owned by property developers who plan to turn it into flats.

The English summer of 1910 was, indeed, mild but often a bit grey. The Met Office has published its archive of weather reports online and it's possible for writers of historical fiction to find out what the conditions were like on any given day. The problem with this, of course, is that sometimes one needs a storm where there was none and so historical fact has to be ditched in favour of a more dramatic fiction. There was no storm on Thursday 7 July 1910. There were moderate to light north-westerly to northerly breezes. The day started cloudy, but brightened later with temperatures in Weston around 57°F (14°C-ish). Not great for a summer's day, but not quite the violent storm I needed.

That said, no matter what the weather conditions, Weston-super-Mare always seems to be unnaturally windy whenever I go there, so other references to blowiness are based on experience rather than weather reports. Confirmation bias has almost certainly played a part, but I remain convinced that it's a very windy place.

Similarly the absence of the sea. I mentioned the tidal range in the Bristol Channel in *The Burning Issue of the Day*, pointing out that it's the third highest in the world (many sources still say second highest, but it's a matter of contention and I favour English understatement, so third it is). This does genuinely mean that it's possible to visit Weston-super-Mare several times and never actually see the sea, which retreats more than a mile across the mud at low tide.

The tide times used in the story aren't genuine tide times for July 1910. For story purposes I needed the high and low tides to fall at certain parts of my characters' days, so the sequence is taken from the real sequence of tides at Weston beginning on 10 July 2018. Tidal prediction was a well-developed science by 1910 but I wasn't able to find out if tide times were published for the seaside town of Weston to the level of accuracy quoted in the sheet handed out by the Steep Holm View Hotel. I shall explain it away as an attempt by the hotel to lend legitimacy to the tables by quoting times to the exact minute, even though the prediction was, in fact, almost certainly a good deal more vague.

The route to Brean Down via Lympsham no longer passes through Bleadon – the modern road skirts the village to the south. There's no longer a toll gate in Bleadon (though there is a road called Toll Road), nor did the railway station survive the Beeching cuts of the 1960s.

The fort at Brean Down in Somerset was built between 1864 and 1871. Lord Palmerston was tasked by Queen Victoria with defending Britain against the strengthening French navy and ordered a series of fortifications around the coast which became known as Palmerston Forts. Brean Down was manned by the Royal Artillery and served to defend the Bristol Channel against an attack that never came. In 1897, Marconi set a distance record for radio transmission by sending a signal 8.7 miles across the channel to Lavernock Point in Wales. In 1900 part of the fort was destroyed by an explosion in the gunpowder store and the site was decommissioned and abandoned.

It fell into private hands. Accounts vary, with some saying it was a café by 1905, others confidently stating that it remained unused until it was turned into a 'ladies' tea room' in 1913. For the purposes of the story, I chose to believe the latter and the condition of the buildings has been imagined to fit my needs. There's no access to the inside of the officers' quarters now, so the layout has also been imagined.

The sea around Brean Down – when it deigns to come that close – can be a bit on the lively side. Attempts to build a deep water harbour while the fort was being built were abandoned when a storm destroyed the foundations of the pier. Nevertheless, it was important for the story for Gerber to be able to cross the bay at high tide with cumbersome cargoes and so I 'created' a makeshift jetty at the tip of the peninsula where his steam launch could be safely docked. There's certainly a comparatively sheltered inlet to the south side of the fort where such a thing might be possible and I strongly suspect from the layout of the fort that supplies could well have been unloaded there.

The site is now owned by the National Trust and is free to visit (although there is a parking charge for non-members). The fort and its WW2 additions are still mostly ruins with no effort having been made to reconstruct them. Brean isn't fantastically easy to get to and, once there, there's still quite a trek ahead of you. The top of the peninsula is over 300 ft above the sea and the fort is a shade over a mile from the top of the 200-odd steps that take you up the first part of those 300 ft from the car park. It's a tad less arduous – and usually a little better sheltered – if you take Emily and Flo's route along the military pathway to the north of the peninsula, but that does rob you of the spectacular views from the highest point which you reach by taking the track that runs along the ridge. The fish finger sandwiches in the National Trust café next to the car park are highly recommended.

In previous books, Skins has played the drums but I've never described his set-up. This is at least partly because percussionists at the turn of the twentieth century didn't have very exciting drums and I thought it would get in the way. At that time, percussionists mostly played a single instrument, as they would in a traditional orchestra, but there was a growing tendency – both for reasons of space and to avoid hiring more musicians – for percussionists to play more than one drum, often at the same time. These would most commonly be the orchestral snare drum and bass drum, which they would play with sticks while standing up. Bass drum pedals were around at the turn of the century, but it wasn't until William F. Ludwig in the USA invented an improved, sprung design in 1909 that the pedal became properly useful. The Ludwig brothers began selling it in 1910. In this book, for the first time, Skins has access to one of these pedals (I pictured him buying it from a visiting American musician in London) and is now sitting down to play.

The Secret Service Bureau was founded in 1909. It was a joint effort by the Admiralty and the War Office to coordinate British intelligence and counter-intelligence efforts, both at home and overseas, and it took a most particular interest in the activities of Imperial Germany. In reality it was staffed by just two men, a senior naval officer called Mansfield Smith-Cumming and an army officer by the name of Vernon Kell – I added Harry and his ad hoc staff of Special Branch officers. By 1914, the real Bureau still comprised just fourteen men, but it expanded massively during World War I. By 1920 it had split into two sections. First was the Secret Intelligence Service (SIS) headed by Smith-Cumming and responsible for overseas intelligence. Smith-Cumming, incidentally, usually dropped the Smith and would sign letters and memoranda as 'C'. Over time this became the codename for all heads of the SIS (or MI6 as it became known during WWII). Kell headed the domestic counter-espionage service that later became known as MI5.

About the Author

T E Kinsey grew up in London and read history at Bristol University. He worked for a number of years as a magazine features writer before falling into the glamorous world of the Internet, where he edited content for a very famous entertainment website for quite a few

Photo © 2018 Clifton Photographic Company

years more. After helping to raise three children, learning to scuba dive and to play the drums and the mandolin (though never, disappointingly, all at the same time), he decided the time was right to get back to writing. *Death Beside the Seaside* is the sixth novel in a series of mysteries starring Lady Hardcastle. There is also a short story, 'Christmas at The Grange'. His website is at tekinsey. uk and you can follow him on Twitter – @tekinsey – as well as on Facebook: www.facebook.com/tekinsey.